Also by Boris Todrin

Poetry
First Furrow
The Room By The River
5 Days
7 Men
At The Gates

Novels
Out of These Roots
Paradise Walk
The Plundered Heart

APHRODITE
and the Old Dude

BORIS TODRIN

IMAGES
PUBLISHING

Published in 1994 by
Images Publishing (Malvern) Ltd,
Upton-upon Severn.

British Library Cataloguing in Publication Data

A catalogue record for this book is available
from the British Library

ISBN 1 897817 26 6

Designed and Produced by Images Publishing (Malvern) Ltd.
Printed and Bound by Bookcraft Ltd, Midsomer Norton, Bath, Avon.

Perhaps the sexual life is the great test. If we can survive it with charity to those we love and with affection to those we have betrayed, we needn't worry so much about the good and the bad in us. But jealously, distrust, cruelty, revenge, recrimination . . . then we fail. The wrong is in that failure even if we are the victims and not the executioners. Virtue is no excuse.

Graham Greene
The Comedians

To my daughter Edwina

Summer the waves owned her
and the boys who rode them
filled her with surf.

Sea eyed she smiled
her body foam
humming with sun
through the basking season.

But when the gulls took back their autumn beaches
she came to me.
And through the winter night
I kissed a sea shell
and held the seas in my arms.

Fall
Winter

Prelude

The digital clock glowed 8:31 when Vera picked up the phone on the third ring. "Hi Mother," Dulcie said. "How are you?"

"I'm well, dear, and you and the children?"

"They're good."

You mean they are well, Vera thought. Why must you use such sloppy locutions? I taught you better than that. Both good and well are adjectives, but good refers to behaviour and well refers to health which is what we are taking about.

"Oh, sometimes they drive me up the wall, but I guess that's what being a mother is all about."

"It seems we only get to see them on holidays. I miss them," Vera said.

"Well you would live way out in the sticks." Dulcie laughed to soften the charge.

"Your father won't live in the city; much less the suburbs."

"Yes I know, Mother, I know. How is Dad? I'd like to talk to him."

"I don't know."

"Isn't he there?"

"He's here, but he went upstairs right after dinner. He usually does lately. I think he went to bed. He's probably asleep."

"Asleep at this hour? It's early. Is he all right?"

He's been working hard. Traveling. So many trips."

"And drinking."

"Well, yes."

"Wake him up, Mother, I've got to talk to him."

"I don't think I should do that. He needs his rest."

She heard Dulcie say "damn." She wished she wouldn't use such language. After all her upbringing. A pause, then, "I've got to talk to him, Mother."

"Why don't you call him tomorrow?"

"We're going to New York for the weekend tomorrow. Bob's parents are coming down from Rochester. We're leaving early. Bob wants to beat the traffic. And we have to get the kids ready. You know what that'll be like."

"Can't I give him a message?"

"Mother, please wake him up, it's important."

Important. Something's wrong. Why won't she tell *me*?

"Mother?"

"All right, Dulcie, but I don't know if he'll come to the phone. He

10

never does when he's like this. He had quite a bit to drink."

"You just tell him I said it's important. He'll come to the phone."

"Hold on then, I'll go up and see."

Important. She's probably overspent again and needs money so Bob won't find out. A bauble, clothing most probably. Something expensive she'll wear once and forget or maybe not wear at all. Like the clothing she'd bring back from college, boxes and boxes. A corduroy suit still wrapped in its tissue paper, never worn. Shoes. That lamb's wool sweater from England. "But Dulcie, why do you need more clothes when you have so many new things?" "Oh Mother, that stuff isn't in this season." That stuff. Beautiful things. Dollars down the drain. And Jud never backing me up, putting his foot down. Secrets, those two.

Someone was cheating him out of the booze blackout he'd bought and paid for, his package of Lethe, shaking him out of the black hole he'd staked out as his, the only place he could go.

"Wake up, Jud"

No, no. He kept his eyes closed to hold in the darkness, the net of sleep, to keep himself in it, to keep himself from knowing what he knew. What he didn't want to know. That it was over. Over, over, over. Finis, the end, curtains. That's all folks. Now the dark had been broken.

"Why are you waking me?"

"It's Dulcie, Jud, she's on the phone. She wants to talk to you." Sleep was running away and he after it. "Tell her to go away. I don't want to talk to her. I don't want to talk to anybody. Tell her I'm sleeping."

"She says it's important, Jud." He unpasted an eye. Important.

"I didn't want to disturb you. I told her you're sleeping. That you need your rest. I asked her to give me the message. She told me to wake you."

The message. It had to be she. Now it was as if he knew all that week it would come. Or did he? She had done it before, called Dulcie to get a message to him. But Vera . . .

"Tell her I'll call her tomorrow."

"She wants to speak to you now, Jud. They're going away tomorrow. New York, for the weekend; they're meeting Bob's parents."

He raised up on an elbow. The room throbbed, dipped in a rolling sea. "No, don't," he said as Vera reached for the light switch. "No light, please." He had paid for his dark. Profanity of light. A blasphemy against the sacred and religious dark, the dark country of the bed.

"If you're going to speak to her, Jud, then do it now, she's been on the line quite a while; a toll call."

"All right, yes, I'll speak to her."

Vera held out his robe. "Thank you," he said, shuffling his feet for his slippers. "You can't find things in the dark," Vera said. "No light," he said. "Here, sit down," Vera said. He sat on the edge of the bed, a

11

patient in an escape-proof institution. She put the slippers on his feet. Helped him into his robe. Conjugal kindness. For better or till death do us. "Thank you," he said. Vera stood there. He put his hand on the bedstand phone. She stood there still. He nodded. "Thank you." She shook her head. "I better go down and finish the dishes," she said and went out of the room. He picked up the receiver.

"Daddy, can you talk?"
    "Yes."
    "Where's Vera?"
    "Downstairs."
    "You sure? She can't listen in?"
    "She can, but she won't." Honest Vera. Truth above all. Even when it hurt. Truth the scalpel. Truth the light. Lying the mortal and ultimate sin. Deception equals betrayal. She wouldn't listen in. Not Vera.
    "Daddy, Billie called me half-hour ago. She was sobbing. She's shattered. She wants you back. She went out every night this week and says it was no good." Went out, I know what that means. "She loves you, Daddy, she says she can't live without you. She says better the three nights a week than nothing at all, than not seeing you. She can't stand it without you."
    "Take it easy," he said in a whisper, sensing a something. But never, not Vera. The phone flowered with Billie. The whole year of Billie. The year that had thirteen months. A phoneful of Billie. The big cat. The lioness. Her face leafed by yellow light in the carnal noon of the park under the heart-leafed lindens. In the everywhere snow. Her lamplight hair on the pillow. Her seawave body. Her tendril hands. Her petal fingers. Her blooming mound. The thermal springs of her mouth. "I love her so," he blurted.
    "I think you're both crazy," Dulcie said. "I told her so. You love each other. I know she loves you. One week without you and she's smashed, a wreck. You should have heard her." Yes, but the others. "She couldn't stop crying. I think you two ought to stop the nonsense and get married."
    "I wouldn't marry her if I could marry her tomorrow." His hand fisted.
    "Why not?"
    "Because I don't trust her. She threw me away once before." Last Maytime's agony. "Kept me on hold while she *tested* our love with others. She had to find out, she said, if she really loved me. I never had to find out, not from the first. Then when I caught her out and cut it she said that the others meant nothing to her. Well, they meant something to *me*. Ah, but, now she knew, really knew we were special and wanted me back."
    "Look, Daddy, we all have our hangups."
    That shadow of something again. He said "Hush," and listened.

12

The room was an ear. The whole house. But not Vera. Never.

"Hangups. Sleeping around."

"It might have been different if you had married her. She said she thought that you would."

"Dulcie, I told her I *wanted* to but not if the price was murder. Not if the price is another person's life. And that's what it would be. You can't throw thirty years out the window, not when it's another person's thirty years we're talking about. At least I can't. Just get up and say, I'm in love, I want out. See you around? Toodle-oo?"

"Oh come on now Daddy, let's stop kidding each other. We know what most of those thirty years have been like. What's Vera given you? All those rules and regulations."

"It was her way of putting some order in a disorderly world. A moral act."

"Thirty years of unhappiness, of pure misery."

No, daughter, it wasn't like that in the beginning, not in its springtime. What do you know about *our* moon-filled road in time's other country? A yellow ribbon tied, yes, to the fall of her young hair. Before love's arthritis set in.

"You were never right for each other, Daddy, you know it. As for Vera and me, well you know about that. She was never what I thought a mother should be. Not in my book. So you can't say you hung on for my sake. You should have gotten out a long time ago. Even before Billie."

"It may be too late. Billie's younger than you, my daughter."

"So what? You don't come on old. You're an attractive man. An accomplished man. You're interesting, fun. Lots of women, young women would think so. You've got something, Daddy, a lot of young guys don't have. Remember, Denise, my sorority sister? She said I could go for him."

Again the ear on a stick. "We've been talking too long," he said.

"Yes, I've got to go too. We're going away for the weekend. I guess Vera told you. Billie wants you to call. She made me promise to tell you. And I'll tell you what I'd do if I were you. I'd move in with Billie, or get a new place with her. Try living together. She wants to come home to you every evening. She wants the whole thing. I don't blame her. I'd take what I want and I'd take it now." They're so much alike, Billie and Dulcie, the same generation. Take what you want and the hell with who pays. "You'll call her now, won't you, the first chance you get?"

"I'll call her."

"I'll be talking to you Daddy."

"Yes, daughter, have a good trip."

"I love you Dads. Take care."

"I love you too, Dulcie."

He made it to the window seat. Lights in the valley, there used to be so few, a handful in the hills when they came here.

She wants me back. He sat on the doorstep of the world again basking in the summer of her sunny flesh, her sheness. Outside in the valley the first December night, trees budding stars. To come again to the shore of her ocean eyes, sunbathe in each other's arms. Her voice, grave children singing. And the shadows, the others. The walked-on moon. The heaven and hell of her. She'll kill you Judson, she almost did and maybe has already . . . Dead on the streets of his dream . . . She wants me back.

Now the lies would begin again. All this week he'd had only one thing to be grateful for. Somehow Vera hadn't found out, had been spared. At least that. Now again the giddy and terrible tightrope he'd teetered on day and night for so many months. Every minute vulnerable to discovery, to ambush by time with the odds going up every second. It was only waiting to happen and someday it would. Caught on the barbed wire of his lies. Like this. Vera would call the office while he was away from his desk and be answered by the receptionist. And Vera would ask whether Mr Bell had returned yet from Washington. And the receptionist would say Mr Bell wasn't in Washington, that he'd been in the office all day. And Vera would say, feeling the years start to crack and now hearing herself as if she were listening in to somebody else's party line conversation, Vera would say, "But Mr Bell left for Washington yesterday morning directly from home and said he'd be back in the office sometime this afternoon and I just called to have him pick up some things at the supermarket on the way home." And the receptionist would say, "Mr Bell was in the office all day yesterday, too," and maybe his plans had changed and was there a message? And Vera would say, "I see. Thank you. No message. It isn't important."

That's how it would happen some day but it hadn't. Because she believed me. Unto the pure all things are pure. Just once a close call. But she had been spared her portion of pain. Let that be mine. When I told her last week that the trips were over she was happy for *me*. "Now you'll come back to yourself, Jud. You haven't been well, you look like a ghost. Now you'll be home all the time I'll be able to take care of you. And maybe we'll get to know each other again."

Thirty miles to the east in her shuttered room she was waiting for his call. It was enough to live on through the weekend between them. It was cold by the window. He hitched his white terry robe closer around him, retied the sash. He listened for sounds downstairs. There were none, the house was thick with quiet. He went down the stairs, through the dining room and stopped at the kitchen. Vera was standing motionless at the sink staring ahead in a trance.

"Vera?"

She stood there unmoving.

She turned her head slow motion toward him, seeing not him but something, a film projected inside her, a smile that was not a smile on

14

her lips. A web in which something was caught.

"Revelations," she said.

He knew but he asked her, "What revelations?"

"Your conversation with Dulcie. I overheard it. I didn't intend to, believe me. But when I came down I picked up the receiver and was about to replace it when I heard Dulcie say – I heard her clearly, she was speaking quite loudly – I heard Dulcie say 'she was sobbing, she's shattered.' I couldn't imagine who, who would be sobbing and shattered that Dulcie should tell you. One of the children? So I listened."

He waited, offering himself up to rage, to tears, to the torrents of hate, to blows even. Only the smile that was not a smile and her eyes somewhere else. Then she said, "Aren't you going to call her? Poor girl, she must be in a terrible state."

She bloomed in the door of his office. Her ironed yellow hair buttering her black wet-look jacket. A suddenness of thighs issuing from the merest of black wet-look miniskirts to black wet-look boots. Someone coming alive out of a billboard into the street.

That's a lot more elevating, Judson, than interviewing some denimed genius in a fright wig and old army jacket. They were hiring by length of sideburn these days even here at old Fairleigh. You expected the art department to look like a rodeo. Now copywriters were coming to work as if typewriters were broncos.

"Have a seat, Miss Miller," he said. She did and the miniskirt nearly became a belt. The billboard smile she came in with hadn't moved.

She produced a cigarette lighter. He reached for it, snapped it to flame, lit her.

"Tell me about it," he said. "Your hopes, your dreams. I don't go by the book." He picked up the interview form, began folding it into an aeroplane. "You know, what are your hobbies, blood type, your favourite ads? Why you want to be a copywriter. Why you want to be a copywriter at Farleigh. Do you have a relative here? And if so what's his right name? Would you write an ad in front of a client? – No, you'd never do *that*. Do you get along with people? If not then what do you get along with?" She reduced her smile to a smile. "Are you willing to travel? Occasionally? Often? Not at all? Would you relocate? Oh yes, and social security number. Let's not start with that." He tossed the aeroplane up in the air. It sailed, stalled, dipped fell in a corner. She sat there smoking looking professional.

"I want to come to Fairleigh," she said evenly, "because Fairleigh is number one in Philadelphia and I think I'm ready for that. I know I'm ready for that." She put her hand on the portfolio propped against her chair. "OK, it's your show." he said.

She opened it on his desk. "Would you want this now or later?" she said, offering her résumé.

"Later."

Her portfolio was a mixed bag. Some of the ads just walked, a few of them skipped. You never knew, looking at somebody's work, just where the client, a supervisor, the lawyers snuffed out a good line, an idea. But there were a few goodies and that's what you looked for.

For a restaurant-bar, Upstairs with Sinatra, featuring Frankie's recordings –

He sings for your supper.

For a tufted, child-proof rug –
>
> The rug they can't pull out from under you.

For a bank –
>
> It's more than your money with us.
>
> 5½% more. Compounded daily.

For a hygienic mouth spray –
>
> 1 oz. of prevention. 95¢

For a gas water heater –
>
> Now you'll always be in hot water.

For a new oven –
>
> Home on the range.

For the city's tourist bureau –
>
> Summer is a good time in Philadelphia.

"Some nice things here," Judson said. She accepted it, a cat being stroked. "But I would have changed one thing. On your bank headline, I'd have changed 'compounded daily' to 'day after day'. More colloquial that way like the rest of your line. Has an additive feel, building up, growing."

She bent her head slightly. "I don't know. The bank wanted 'compounded'. Kind of heavy, but you know, like a bank. Sounds reliable, moneywise."

"Have you done any broadcast?"

"I did bring my reel but there isn't much on it. Some radio and just two TV spots. I want to do more. That's where it's at. Fact last year I took a scriptwriting course in New York."

He dialled the projection room. It was free. "Let's go down to the theater," he said.

Alone in the dark empty theater she seemed to displace the dark. It was strange, as if they were the play they had come see.

"Those spots on the reel, it was all on low budget, real cheapies," she said.

"I see what you mean," Judson said when the lights in the theater went on.

He was reading her résumé back in his office. Twenty-three. Two years of college, Temple at night, working by day. One year as a secretary to an architect, Gilbert Kerr. Then secretary and junior writer in a small agency, Hirsh/Meyers. And for the past three years copywriter at J.G. Manson. A pretty good record for twenty-three. Three and a half years of professional writing, college at night. It was something.

"Is Louie Bocca still creative director at Manson?" Judson said. "He used to work here." Wisecracking Louie, feinting and fending you off with a quip. Never engaging. Conversation impossible. Tap dancing away. Doffing a fictive straw hat. Man, watch my soft shoe routine. The perpetual end man, Mr Bones. Barber pole shirts. Tight ratty face.

Ferret of gossip and ace rumour monger. Knew who was fired before the firee. Who was shacked up with whom. Hey listen, can you keep a secret? Have you heard about? . . . Vitamin popper. Underarm sniffer. Living with Mama Mia in Camden. A once-over-lightly writer, a one liner specialist with one string to his bow. Well, if it isn't young Judson.

"Yes, Lou is my boss. He told me he worked here. He mentioned you, the fun times you had."

Fun times? With Louie?

She lit her fifth cigarette, her smile filled a silence, she said, "Lou told me that you were a published author with quite a few books, poetry, novels."

Poetry, novels . . . Another country, that. He drew his breath in, nodded and let it out. "Yes," he said, "yes." Then he said, "Do you do any other writing, Miss Miller? Short stories, poems?"

"Poems," she said. "I started some stories but after a point they just kind of sit there. I can't seem to end them. But poetry, yes, I write all the time."

"Have you brought any with you?"

"No, but I could bring them in if you'd care to see them. I'd like to know what you think, someone who's published."

"Yes I would like to see them."

"I'd appreciate that."

"The reason I asked – there used to be a tradition here about writing. When I came" – Lord the girl sitting there was three – "there were glass enclosed bookshelves all around the copy lobby, displaying the published work of people in the department. A few novels, mostly stories, poems, magazine pieces – even some record albums – songs, classic banjo. One man wrote children's books, one a year; he had twelve in the case. There were a couple of mystery novels, a travel book. Owen Pilgrim, the copy chief then, believed good writers make good copywriters."

"Do you believe that?"

"I think, at least, it shows how someone can handle words."

She nodded in the gold waterfall of her hair.

"It didn't always work out. Some writers couldn't – or wouldn't – channel their talents into ads. But it worked often enough to make Fairleigh a special place. The first thing Mr Pilgrim showed visiting clients, or prospective clients, was the work in the bookcases; then he showed them the ads. What he was saying is that there was no other copy department like this. He was right about that. It was an attitude about writing and writers."

"Your books were in the case?"

"Front and center."

"Fabulous."

"That's when copy was king."

"And now?"

"Well, I guess copy is queen."

18

She rolled the word around in her eyes. Does he mean *that?*

"What happened to the bookcases?"

"They were torn out a week after Mr Pilgrim retired, and the walls repanelled. The red carpet went, too."

"The red carpet."

"That is another story . . .

"Now, as for a job, the best thing I could do for you is arrange for two other people to see you, creative directors here. That way there'll be three opinions, you know – 'all in favour, say aye.' One alone wouldn't swing it with the head of department. Tad Houlighan – he does the hiring."

"That would be great."

"I'll set it up with Dan Cooley, our office manager. He's the one you checked in with. And when you come in next time you can drop your poetry off."

Again a debut of thighs. Walking her to the elevator, eyes rolled, heads turned on cue.

"Thank you so much for you time, Mr Bell, and your interest."

"Not at all. It's part of my job and I think you deserve a chance. I start my vacation next week, so good luck and I hope you make it. You'll be hearing from Cooley."

The doors packaged her.

2

It was a good month, October. He'd picked it for colour to ride through the fox hunted hills. Red maple and splashes of sumac and yellowing oak, the spears of evergreen pines. These dearly beloved and human hills rolling to meadow and pasture and creek. Ponds like pieces of sky and split rail fences, deer in the wilder places and pageants of pheasants. Crows clattering in the corn stubble. Crossbow of geese arrowing south clocked by the turning year. One month bought by eleven. After twenty years. October, a loaf of freshly baked bread.

It was something still to be able to slip from the house bed warm naked in the early fog bound morning, fog is my hill's dream, the grass heavy with dew, colder than air, chilling his toes, sprint the sixty feet to the pool, a blue cup in his green private hill, and dive into the slap of crisp fall water breaking the surface mist into swirls. The first cold shock shrinking him small shriven of sleep, his first lap into the redball sun burning the woods, the sorrow of mourning doves, then the turn and kick propelling him back stroking now in a good steady crawl past the well fed fountain splashing into the pool and back again cutting the water of his own small blue lake, an Adam alone. His body knew he would make thirty laps this morning. He was breathing right in rhythm with his smoothly socketed shoulders and strongly dipping hand cupped arms. Washing away the office year in the auroras of morning. A whole calendar page being himself again what was left of him. The farm his again and he like the trees on it because the time was his.

His bigboned black dog came bounding tongue lolling out of the woods, leaped the rain made creek and walked around the pool as he swam, tail saying good morning, eyes amber lovely and sat watching him and sniffing the season sorting the signals the change in the air. I guess the rabbit got away again old Blitz, black prince, big hombre.

The sun higher was breaking the fog into clouds, bringing the summer back.

Black dog this time we will get back to our book. We will unthaw it and let the people out.

On the last eastern lap his undipping eye saw the barn fired by the tree tangled sun, saw Vera coming through the pasture gate, the cats capering at her feet but staying close to the barn because of the enemy dog, and saw her stop, smiling to watch him swim. Then the last western lap toward the gray black shuttered house, the great bride and groom oaks planted before it by the first farmer here a hundred and thirty years ago. And he was out shedding water and towelling down in the light of the tree top sun. "Are we riding?" she said. "We're riding," he said.

The horses were crosstied in the shed, Jud grooming Roman, his chestnut, and Vera, Casey, her dun. Roman surged against the ropes with each stroke of the currycomb and brush. "Easy does it," Jud said, stroking his neck and coming round to his head lightly blew into the horse's nostrils, smelling his hay sweet breath, Roman pricking his ears, snuffling.

As Jud continued to curry him Roman lifted a hind leg in protest and Jud whacked him on the haunch with the brush and growled at him to stop.

"You would have a Thoroughbred," Vera said. "Just look at Casey, he stands like a lamb. He lets me do anything."

"Vanity," Jud said, "and aesthetics. There's nothing more elegant than a Thoroughbred. The old saw is true, the outside of a horse is good for the inside of a man."

He hefted the saddle and pad and snugged them back from the withers, tightened the girth leaving one notch to pull to when he was mounted, slipped the bridle over his horse's head, Roman opening his mouth and taking the bit.

"You're a gentleman, Roman," Jud said, "when you want to be. He is very good for a horse that's ridden only on weekends and a Thoroughbred at that. And you saw how he gave me his feet to pick out."

"I've learned to grain him just right," Vera said, "considering how lightly he's used." She was having trouble tightening Casey's girth around his big barrel.

"Let me help you," Jud said.

"No, I must do it myself. It's the arthritis. I've got to live with it."

Seeing her stiff knotted fingers tugging the billet straps told him again what he knew, that this place, this little farm world couldn't be without her. That so much life depended on her, the red life of cats, dog and horses, the green life of plants and young fruit trees and shrubs, mucking out stalls and the moil of the house.

So he said again, "Please let me help you." With an angry shake of her head she said "No, you do your horse and I do mine," angry more at the ice in her crabbed fingers than at him for noticing it but not telling him that.

He led Casey out to the maple block, held his head while she mounted then led Roman out, slipped his foot in the stirrup and swung into the saddle, settling in, thigh against leather, the feel of the horse like no other feeling, like love.

Roman balked at the edge of the woods, bobbed his head, moved to turn back, but Jud knowing he would – the pleasure of having a horse, knowing his ways – kept him between legs and hands and heeled him into the forest.

21

"Good boy," he patted his neck, "I know you'd rather be nibbling grass in the pasture than going with me for a ride, but you'll get to like it once we've had us a run."

They picked their way through the narrow rocky trail, ducking under low limbs, Sidestepping thorny vines, a crashed tree. Behind him Vera said, "We'll have to come back on foot and clear the trails."

"It was so nice when Mr Lloyd's man kept them open. But we'll do it. I'll take my axe and my saw and you'll take the pruners and Blitz will come too and we'll work in the woods. " He was rich, he had a month of woods.

The woods enclosed them, leaf thick, cool, puddles of sun in the open places. The trees stepped by them; they passed the dark spring in the hollow, did the Lenape drink here or Washington's men in straggling retreat from the Brandywine to their death's-head winter in Valley Forge? The horses snorted, it sounded like pleasure; they came to the three-trunked oak where the trail divided.

"Up or down?" he asked.

"Wherever you say," she said.

"Up then, to open country." It was more of an expedition, the horizons further. "let's make it to Pikeland Churches."

The horses swung their necks downward, their bodies bending to the easier trail, the shorter ride. They let them think they had had their way, let them move down a step, then kept them turning in their momentum, using their strength and up the steep gorge. "Up gentlemen, up." Up the rain washed away gully strewn with stones they climbed, easing forward off the horses' backs, the woods dropping sharply down at their sides and rising to meet them ahead. And then they were up at the top of the hill that they called a mountain, the ridge that ran out to the west from Valley Forge. It was loamier here and they trotted until they came to Indian Springs Road.

The country opened before them, the country morning that is another country. Cope's farm lay open on either side of the road creamy with Jerseys. They took the old wagon road through his woods, his bright fields of winter wheat, on through Pimm's small perfect orchard, the trees proud with apples and peaches and pears. He was about to pluck apples for them and the horses when he saw the papery yellow jacket hive hanging hidden in the leaves like a dark lantern and swung Roman back to the path. "Watch it," he called to Vera, "it's loaded with bees. Keep moving or we'll be all over the country." Then on single file through Pimm's craggy woods and there it was, Wellwood, the great Mallory place. The fieldstone manor house in its gardens, the stone house for the help, the opulent barns, the willows trailing their hair in the pond.

Side by side they went into a juicy trot along the long split rail fence all of them knowing they'd turn at the corner and go into a canter, the horses knowing and they and straight up the hill in a run. They let them out at the turn, go gentlemen, go, and they and the

22

horses were one, one in motion and life and the good springy earth, surging up along the running tree line, the slope easy and gentle, giving the horses their heads, letting the hill be their reins holding their strength. Their hooves beat out the galloping drum roll, like no other beat, Roman ahead but Casey almost right with him in his quick Quarter horse sprint as they came to the top of the hill. They blew through cupped fired nostrils snorted and tried to get at the grass. "That was great," Vera said, rosy and breathing the windy morning. "It makes it worth while," Jud said, "all the work that you do, the stables, the grooming, the tack, don't think I forget. "I don't forget either, the work that you do," she said, "what it means for you to do it." She looked young and trim in her riding gear, the black velvet hunt cap, the tweed hacking coat, the breeches, the black leather boots. What had happened to them? Where had it gone, their beginnings? The night of the yellow ribbon found on a country road.

The uplands rolled out from the top of the hill, Wellwood's high point. Tilled fields and the hills painted in smoky colours. The light so clear and hard it almost rang. This land my woman.

"Everything's yours from the back of a horse," he said.

Off to the west hills away the two everyday Sabbath steeples of Pikeland Churches shone in the sun. They were getting to running country. Crossing the brambled firebreak they saw the season's first deer. They stood statue still downwind, the horses' ears forward seeing the whitetail too. Then another came out of a thicket, also a doe. Then a young buck his head slowly sifting the breeze. Then a curious yearling and another. And as if they were told by a voice their heads turned to the riders. For a moment all were one life. Then a doe faded into the thicket and the other, then the yearlings. The buck looked at them still, turned and was gone.

Judson held up his hand. "Five," he said.

"Five," Vera answered, "the most we've seen at one time."

"That was a gift," Judson said.

On Merlin Road they clip-clopped across the wood planked bridge, time's old sweet sound, over Pigeon Creek, a blessing of clear pebbled water flowing, onto Biddle's place and cantering country, a chain of tree framed fields linked by little roads in little woods.

They hand galloped twice around the first long field, blood galloping, theirs, the horses', into cloud shadows and out, the wind in their ears, the earth running away. Slowed then into a trot, sitting it into a walk and stopped to rest all of them breathing hard. Judson you should have been born rich, working in morning country, riding the afternoons.

Roman's red gold skin rippled, his ears went forward, Casey's head went up just as they heard the horn halloo. In the arched shade of the woods, the huntsman in his scarlet coat.

Jud said, "It's the Pickering. Of course, today is a hunting day."

23

A handful of riders fanned out around the huntsman and scanned the field.

"Looks like they've lost the hounds," Jud said, "along with the fox." Roman was throwing this head and beginning to prance. "He thinks he's part of the hunt or back on the track."

The huntsman sounded his horn to no answering cry and trotted around the edge of the field, the five riders behind him spruce in their crisp white stocks against black melton coats, breeches canary or fawn, each on a sleek muscled horse, and into the dusk of the woods.

"That was out of an English print," Jud said. "Riding out here you're in two kinds of time, then and now. "The Pickering does itself proud, they really turn themselves out."

Another field and the twin churches stood up on their hill in the sun, the land all around in good heart.

Turning his horse to the west again he heard Vera say, "Aren't we going home?"

"It's such an incredible weather. I could ride all day."

"There'll be more days, Jud, like this, your vacation's just starting."

There were endings now in the air. The hills still blazed. The light was a bell.

"Every day is its own. Just a little bit longer?"

"We've been out two hours already. It'll take about that to get back. You can ride on if you want, but I'm going home."

"No, I don't want to ride alone." Wasn't he riding alone?

"I have things to do and you too. There's the mowing and lunch . . ." Practical Vera, impractical Jud. Did their clocks ever tell the same time? "OK," he said, "which way?"

"Let's not go back the same way, let's take a shorter route."

"Then we'll leave it up to the horses, they'll take us the shortest way home."

They slackened reins, the horses bending their bodies, turning as one.

Vera laughed. "I'll never get over it, how they know their way back. We must be ten miles from home."

Downhill through Indian Springs and its heathery places. Around the leaf painted lake. Through the sandy telephone swath, splashing across the stream, the horses bending to drink, on to Wilkins farm and the old Stayman apple tree leaning over the road, bees slow and drunk on the windfall. He stood in the stirrups and plucked four ruby apples down, giving the other three theirs, the horses chomping, and bit into his the juice spurting out in a foamy cider.

In the last homeward mile of woods they had come from they stayed at a walk to cool out the horses, feet dangling out of the irons, full of the burning hills they had ridden, the living waters, the light. The last good mile home of a good ride.

Vera riding behind, Jud in his old hacking coat weathered gray, once heather blue, the sweat skirts parted over the cantle. The coat he wouldn't give up, not Jud, that she'd mended and sewn, the rained on, sun faded, snowed on coat he had ridden in collar up through that blizzard that caught them, he laughing, drunk on the storm. How could he give that old friend up? Not Jud. And just look at his hunt cap, that moth-eaten thing, faded gray too, banged by tree limbs, it had saved his head too many times for him to give *that* up. She'd have to hide them or give them away and his worn breeches and boots so he'd have to get new. Or sell them down at the thrift shop. They were only things. Like that ugly old Morris chair he'd had at college. No telling who you'd run into while riding, like the Pickering Hunt today. And he was the one always said one should be well gotten up, it showed respect for the horse.

Jud flipped Roman's auburn mane to the right, the horse flowing under him in an easy head nodding amble, the reins on this neck. His first day's vacation and only half spent, the whole tenth great month of the year before him. He had slipped his collar, he was out of their reach, back to himself . . . *His mind assigned to trivia. Gentlemen, please return my mind to its rightful owner. I work among my murderers. We ask about each other's lives through closing elevator doors* . . . I will get back to that too, the unfinished book in the closet, it's been a long time. He was in a sanctuary called October.

And there was the black dog coming to greet them and romp them home. At the edge of the woods his place, the five buildings a village in sun, the barn, the house, the tack room with belfry and tilted bell as if being rung, the spring house the Quaker meetinghouse shed for tractor and car. His more than home, his town, his country. Population, seven. Blitz, Roman and Casey, the barn cats Dewy and Muskie, he and she.

They unsaddled the horses, rubbed them down, unsnapped the tie ropes. They stood there released blinking as if they didn't believe it then took a few steps down the pasture heads to the grass. They began weaving around like dogs about to lie down. Then finding the right spot of ground they knelt on their forelegs, turned over and rolled, their iron shod hooves in the air. Vera laughed. "I always get a kick out of that, big creatures like that rolling around like dogs."

He swam again for the clean live feeling of water after the ride, the streams and ponds he had passed and wanted to lie in, and sat with a glass of sherry on the back terrace, smoking his pipe, Blitz at his feet.

Vera said, "Isn't it somewhat early to start drinking?"

"I'm not starting drinking. This is only a glass of sherry. It's just the right touch after a ride and this weather. I was really considering cognac, but it's not cold enough. Cognac's the thing after a winter ride when you have a fire to go with it. Why don't you have one with me? Please, I'll be glad to get it."

"You know I don't drink and certainly not before lunch which I have to get ready."

"Oh come on, relax, it can wait. Let me get you a drink."

"That sherry you're drinking, it's not the sweet kind? It looks so pale, like gin."

"This? No, it's a manzanilla. It's too dry for you. But we've a fine oloroso, medium sweet, you'll like it."

She looked at his glass, at him, at her watch.

"Thanks, but no thanks. It's one-twenty-five. Already lunch will be too close to dinner."

"Then we'll have dinner later. Look, I'm on vacation."

"But that means I'll be in the kitchen all hours. I want to have my evening too."

"All right, but you're making a solitary drinker of me. Sets a bad example for the dog."

"You're making a fool of me," she said and went into the house.

The dog lay there, his man-sized head on his paws, listening to their lives. "Blitzer, man's best friend," Blitzer thumped his tail, "if you could only drink we'd elope. I'm not really such a bad fellow. I can cook pretty well. Just a few simple things. I'm neat around the house. I don't sleep in my socks. My pay check's regular. Haven't missed a day's work in two years. I don't snore. I passed my last physical with flying molars. I have all my teeth but three, see –" he clicked them – "I defy you to tell the false from the real. No questions asked when you stay out late and I expect the same consideration from you. I'll keep you in bones and you'll keep me from being a solitary drinker. Of course I can always drink in front of a mirror. What do you say?"

A cock pheasant double-squawked in the pasture. Blitz got up on his fist-sized paws, arced his tail, cocked his ears.

"Leave the peasants alone," he said. "They have a right to make love. Doesn't everyone? And now I'll pour me my first drink, we'll call this one my second," he held up his empty goblet. "So when she asks me is this your *second* drink? I can truthfully say no, it's my first. I was hoping she'd say drink was bad for the liver, then I would have said, liver and let liver."

The woods were shutting up shop for the winter: downfall of no longer breathing leaves.

The great oak lay in the woods, a fallen giant, its upended roots torn from the shallow hill a fist clumped with rock and earth. Its crash had taken a beech tree with it, her smooth woman curving limbs in tangled embrace with the oak's. He unslung his bow saw from his shoulder. Could be two cords of wood in that oak. Blitz sitting at the foot of a neighbour shagbark aimed his quivering wet nose at a squirrel praying in its upper branches. "You're a canine comedian, Blitzer, you can't get up there and that squirrel isn't about to come down." He worked from the top limbs down, his muscles feeling the snarl of the saw teeth biting into the still green wood, cutting the smaller logs first. He lugged them out in his canvas carrier, five, then four, then three at a time, as the logs grew larger nearer the trunk. Heavy as coal, burns like coal.

In the final dusk of his free breathing time, when all that was left was the oak's torso he apologised to it. "It wasn't I brought you down, but now that you are you may as well go out in fire, and I thank you for it." He power sawed it into boles (better a two-man saw than this damned machine, but no other hands to work with him) and split them with steel wedges and a ten-pound sledge. *In the parenthesis of evening/I split the windfall oak and ice-felled beech/For a final orchestration of green/In a last flowering of fire.*

He looked into the dark mind of the woods. A glim there? A girl with long gold hair riding a white horse?

A light bloomed in the house, a signal. He whistled for Blitz. A squirrel chuckled. A surfsound of leaves and the dog came to him like a piece of the night with eyes. "Let's go home, man dog."

Thirty-one days had October.

Irreversible
The weekend moves to Monday and the death
By memorandum:
Drowning in a paper sea
Epics of inanity
Dissolve the I
Into we.

Tomorrow the office.
I wonder if she got the job.

3

The Paoli Local gave up its terminal squeal, grunted into its berth at Suburban Station, disgorging suburban yeomanry.

Up there in the sky, atop City Hall like a wedding cake groom, Billy Penn staring with eroding stone eyes over the ungreening of his Greene Countrie Towne. The once man high city he had come to shouldered aside by robot cement and dead glass. *Mayflower and Mafia unite to put the country into a concrete casket.*

Walking/jogging the thirteen long blocks to Washington Square and the Fairleigh Castle, as the old chairman called it. A shaft of Indiana limestone thirteen stories high. A skyscraper by Philadelphia courtesy. The fountain still spurting in the park in the square, catercorner to Independence Square and the cracked bell. And the two-story high bronze doors of the Castle.

"It looks like a bank," a young prospective client once said, "not an ad agency."

"Exactly," the old chairman answered. "We protect our clients' money."

He opened the polished cathedral door.

Good morning, America.

She was there waiting for him when he walked into his office. He knew it was she, but it was like running into someone you had met in costume at a masquerade now in everyday clothes, someone grown up you had known as a child, a sameness somehow redefined.

It was the clothes.

She sat there as primly as she could in a long swirl of soft wool skirt woven of earthen colours. The spillage of gold hair fell halfway down her tailored creamy blouse. She held a binder in her lap.

"I got the job," she said, "thanks to you."

She shone like a lighthouse. "I've been here two weeks."

"You must have impressed the others," he said, waving her gratitude away.

"I guess so, but Houlighan said it was your recommendation that really swung it, that you hardly ever recommended anybody."

She held out the binder. "My poems – you said you'd read them." He nodded.

At the door she turned. "I looked for your books in the library, even the main branch and in all the bookstores." She shook her head, her eyebrows arched in surprise.

"They're out of print, have been for years."

He pulled the bottom drawer of his desk, took out a book and offered it. "My number two novel." *The House That Was Called September* it said on the cover, by Judson Bell.

"Oh wow, that's neat."

"What is?"

"You've got to be putting me on."

"No, really I'm not, but you haven't read the book yet."

"The title – it's like *now*." She must think I'm a hundred years old. "It's a good title," he said.

"And these reviews," skimming the quotes on the back of the dust jacket, "fabulous." She looked at him, a child on a Christmas morning.

"Oh yes, it was a *succés d'estime*, public pats on the head, published abroad in eight countries. Camus reviewed it in France. And it brought me a letter from Faulkner which I read every day for a month."

"Terrific," she said, and then "I've got a pile of stuff to do. Army – the women's end."

"I supervise that."

"I know, Tad told me. Well, see you," she said.

He watched her processional down the hall, a walking Statue of Liberty, and turned to his paper piled desk.

"My in box runneth over," he said aloud to himself.

"First day back and you're talking to yourself already. Welcome home, Squire, missed ya," Pat Mooney said sliding in. "Why don't you just heave the whole thing? It's all a crock anyway. No one will ever know the difference. Life will go on."

He put the lap load of paper back on the desk.

"Hi, Sport. As a matter of record there was an account man here some years ago who came back from vacation, contemplated his overloaded in box for a minute, shook his head and dumped it into his waste basket. He's president of a big New York agency now where he fired a guy for doing the very same thing."

Mooney laughed, easing his lankiness into a chair, stretching his long jeaned legs, wiggling his Adidas, smiling through aviator glasses, thumbs in his bronze Wells Fargo buckle.

I salvaged you, kid, from the production department, that day you delivered proofs and showed me your songs, words and music, which you played on your guitar that night I took you home to the farm, and sang through your Wyatt Earp hair in the rutting caterwaul of the asphalt cowboy. There were banshees in Nashville making a helluva lot more money on stuff no better than yours. You wanted to be a copywriter.

And like all the others you tried to be fast with the stand-up comic's one-liner. Everybody seems to be a member of Actor's Equity these days, wisecracking on a perpetual talk show. TV, the reel world, that's where you all want to be, cobbling effects – sound, music, camera angles – gift-wrapping an empty box. Except for Mr Bernbach and company. But when it came to Mr Gutenberg's invention you had to be able to *write*. To get from headline to payoff with words. I worked with your copy until it was ready for Tad, sprung you, our own young home-grown talent, and brought you up from production knowing Tad had been there himself. "It's getting to be a regular farm club," he said. And besides, he could get you on the cheap.

"Well Sport, what's up?"

"The usual thing, Doc," Pat quacked – his Bugs Bunny routine.

"My ever horny young protégé."

"Yep, lots of ass and a little grass . . ."

"Keeps you at the head of the class."

"Not bad, not bad for someone who leads such a sheltered life." Then, "Wait till you see the new girl on the block," Pat stretched a smile showing teeth, dreams in his voice. "Very nice. Very, *very* nice. Billie Miller, she's in our group."

"I take it, ah, you've been seeing Miss Miller?"

"You are a card, Doc." Again the Bugs Bunny quack. "To see Miss Miller is to fuck Miss Miller. End of the first week she was here."

"A week? What took you so long?"

"Man, you've got to show class. Drop into her office. Kid. Take her to lunch. Laughs."

"That's class?"

"Squire, today that's class. Anyhow, I took her out for drinks after work on Friday. You know, the Welcome Aboard bit – all that jive." His rubber band smile again. "Made sure to have my trusty geetar with me." A nod and a wink. "Never fails, always works like gangbusters. So after a couple of hours popping shooters at Watson's, we mosey down to her place. Pass a joint. I strum my old sad songs – you get the scenario. I saved "You Left Me Though So Much Was Left For You," for last. Always brings down the house and their pants. You wouldn't believe those groupies in Cowtown. Last weekend two fifteen-year olds had a fight about who would unzip me right there in the parking lot."

"Who won?"

Pat showed even teeth, rubbed his belly. "Ah did . . .

"Anyhow Billie turned on, said I ought to be in show biz."

"You are, Sport, you are."

"We fell into bed. Nice, very *very* nice jollies. It sure beats shopping the meet markets."

"Come again."

"You really should watch your language, Squire. You know, the singles bar scene."

"I must have been looking the other way," Jud said, "when the sexual revolution passed by."

"So the man finally came down from his mountain," Tad Houlighan said, coming in with his running walk. "Welcome back, Ace. How are the horsies? Good vacation? Come by when you've cleaned up your desk. Lots of stuff cooking." And was out the door, pedalling down the hall.

Feisty. The first thing anyone said about him. How true, a cliché in action. Onetime Villanova jock, second-third stringer in track, swimming, baseball, and clerk-typist in the peacetime Marines. Tad, *semper fidelis* to Tad.

. . . There was that first summons to Tad's office after he had been made head of creative. "Please stop by as soon as you can." One by one they had been called in and some had come out to pick up their hats and vanish. A new ball game.

> Was there something left unsaid?
> Did we smile when spoken to?
> Is the new man being groomed
> To take the place of you-know-who?

Small Tad, almost sunk behind the large raised desk, sitting tight as if in the blocks, tensed for the shot that would propel him down the track.

"I've been reviewing all the accounts in the house. The worst one," he shook his head, always matted damp as if he were still running in his chair, "is the College Aid Fund. It stinks. We've been doing the same dumb thing for ten years."

CAF, yes, one of those public service campaigns agencies take on without charge to show they have heart. Like Smokey the Bear, the Heart Foundation, Cancer Institute, campaigns against crime, drugs, littering. "Stamp out Mental Health," an agency wag had once written.

"Yes, I know," Jud said. "Opening shot on a corporation executive, zooming in to his lethal smile that would freeze a bird out of its tree. The old corporate highwayman shoots his cuffs, leans forward, his eyes hanging onto the Teleprompter. He then drones this canned spiel about colleges needing money so they can train more people to go to work for corporations like his, because corporations like his is what Ahmurica is all about. Meanwhile on campus the college kiddies are majoring in plastic explosives and joining the Weathermen. I believe the current spokesman is none other than the board chairman of U.S. Steel. Final freeze frame: the Lamp of Learning."

"Yeah, that's it, terrific," Tad said. "So it's a freebie, but it could be a showcase for us. Wide exposure. Look at Smokey the bear, everybody knows old Smokey. A household word. The top public service spot."

"On Top of Old Smoky," Jud said. "Sorry about that."

"Har. Lookit Ace, I'm turning the account over to you. He pointed a finger. "I want you to write it. *You* – not anyone in your group."

Finger – "the TV," finger – "the radio," finger – "the print. It needs a good stiff goose. A twist. Something different. Something that'll give them a hard on. Go out and get drunk, and – write me a poem."

I don't write for you, Tadpole. I work for the agency.

"Hey, I like that." Tad taps his head. "Now that's an *i*dea. I kid you not. I'll pay for the bottle. Just turn in a voucher. Just put it down, let's see, to writing materials. Har. And be sure to put the ad number down after it."

A poem, now. Well, what a surprise, coming from you, Tad. I didn't think you knew.

"You're on," Jud said. "It's a deal. I'll take you up on the bottle, so long as you make it Boodles. But I won't drink it until I've finished the piece. I've never believed that gammon about writers writing while drunk. Not even Hart Crane."

"Who? Who?" asked Tad, the ex-Villanova English major. "What agency is he with?"

"Hart Crane, an American poet. They said he wrote best while drunk and listening to records on his Victrola. He was also supposed to have thrown type-writers out of the window.

"I haven't read a book since I got out of college," Tad said with edgy pride.

A poem. Yes – a *ballad*. For guitar. A ballad the young might rise to as well as the heavy givers. He'd do the words (somewhere already a rhythm, a stir) – and the music? It would have to be someone who rode today's sound. Bacharach? Simon/Garfunkel? Probably out of sight. Couldn't afford them on a freebie budget . . . Yes, that song writing kid in production, Pat Mooney. A natural. It would be an inside job, a one hundred percent Fairleigh production.

He looked at Tad as if more than an assignment had been settled. His place here. Twenty years in the pits didn't count anymore, could work against you. He'd wondered how things would work out between them when Tad became head. He had twenty-two years on Tad, just old enough to be his father and, *pace* Oedipus, Tad had always said that what Fairleigh needed was a young creative department. Swingers. Not the old Philadelphia Main Line types, the sometime courtly gentlemen of family with social register names from Chestnut Hill and the past Arcadias of Bryn Mawr, old Merion Station, Strafford and Devon, lunching at clubs they had been born to: The Philadelphia Club, Merion Cricket Club, The Racquet Club, The Union League.

Good Philadelphia form had ordained their options. They could be stockbrokers or corporation (never criminal) lawyers, or run the old name department stores and banks. Physicians were borderline although there was a tradition of gentlemen doctors. But working in an advertising agency was unquestionably bad form, *infra dignitatem*. Except for Old Fairleigh as they fondly called it, as if it were an Ivy League college, the Harvard of agencies, venerable and Philadelphia and correctly on Washington Square. "The reason I'm here," their old joke went, "is because my parents could afford to send me."

It was acceptably old, the oldest, and once the best, agency in the country, founded by tithing Baptists whose one diversion from the religion of work was teaching Sunday School. For the first eighty years of its life it was a place for Protestants only of Anglo Saxon descent, except for an occasional German in the print shop or bookkeeping department.

But that was old Fairleigh. The gentlemen had been retiring, one by silvery one, back to the old manse, since he had come twenty years ago. There were a few left, but there was a terminal air about them, their luggage already packed, as if they were waving from the rear platform of a departing train, taking their Welsh and English and Scots names with them to be replaced by Italians from South Philadelphia, Irish and even a Jew – from *New York*.

This was becoming a new Fairleigh. It would have to if it were to survive. He knew that. They had been slipping. Houlighan was new Fairleigh. And Houlighan's crowd of young guerrillas, Jud knew they saw him as one of the Old Guard. This calling him Ace business. Patronising recognition by the young of his feats, saying: we know all about your scores – your three CLIOS, your four ANDYS, the gold medal for radio, at the Hollywood Broadcast Festival, the silver for a corporate film at the New York International, the *Sat Review* awards, the seven best-read ads in history and still used as texts at the Harvard Business School. Saying, yes, you're a pro, already a Fairleigh legend – but an *old* pro. But mostly, you are not *us*.

Still, he had not come out of this meeting unfrocked. He would still celebrate advertising. And while agency blood baths were SOP elsewhere, Tad had not yet turned the world completely upside down. He had survived. He would show them. He wasn't about to cash in his leggings. Maybe jocks were through at an early age. A writer could hit a home run, bases loaded, at eighty.

"Give me a showcase, Ace," Tad said.

4

The ballad was almost all there before he sat down to type. It marched. To a different drum. It was not written for the board chairman of U.S. Steel. Jud put his stop watch to it. Allowing time for the music and supers it would run a snug sixty seconds. By speeding tempo and cutting a little it would easily make a takeout thirty. The track would be right on for radio. And in print, just the look of the ballad would pull the eye to the page. He could already hear the music. He hoped Mooney would.

For the next two nights he took Mooney home with him to the farm to get away from the phones. Besides, Pat still worked days in production. Before she went up to bed Vera fixed them a pot of coffee and a jug of fruit juice, her special mix, apricot, pineapple, orange, "for energy," she said. "Your brain needs blood sugar. But try not to stay up too late, tomorrow's another working day . . . I really don't understand why this couldn't be done at the office."

"Hm," Pat said.

"Hm," Jud said, and when he heard their bedroom door shut, "It's nothing personal, Pat."

"Maybe we should have gone to my place."

"No, no, you just don't understand Miz Vera. She loves having you here, believe me or I wouldn't have asked you. It's just that she believes in an orderly clockwork world, everything in its place, things done at a given time. She takes it as a personal insult when the world doesn't cooperate. And she simply must say what she thinks. It's a kind of chronic affliction. But she means no offence. The office for work and the home for . . . ah well, forget it, let's get back to the ballad."

Big Blitz lay by the empty fireplace between them, and when Pat strummed into a minor key lifting his voice to a wail, his great head lifted too and he bayed, his basso rising to a treble yowl aimed at an unseen moon.

"He digs," Pat laughed.

"You've obviously moved him deeply, Mooney. An excellent omen. Now if we can get the client to react the same way, we have us a winner. But you better keep it down, fella," Jud patted the dog, "or Miz Vera will call out the constabulary."

They worked for a while in the night's camaraderie but the words and the music were leading their separate lives; they were not yet together.

"Look, Pat . . . your melody's fine and it runs, but in places, like here, it's running away from the words. You're getting chord happy, they keep going off by themselves. You're not an art director. What you have is in your head, not your fingers. This is like Braille for the blind. Don't just tap the words, *listen* to them. Put yourself back on campus, man, when you were playing a gig for your friends and a couple of beers."

"Joints."

. . . "You're a true believer trying to *tell* them something . . . Dig?"

"Si, si, maestro, I deeg."

"Okay, let's take it from the top."

It still wasn't there.

They shuttled back and forth for while, then, "I think I've got it," Pat said, marking the copy. "You cut a word here, and two there, and I'll bring baby home."

"You're a regular Johnny Cash and carry," Jud said. He cut where he had to, or filled.

"Do it," Jud said.

And Pat's guitar took a fever and the words and the music were married at 4:25 am.

5

"You owe me a bottle, Sire," Jud said coming into Tad's office.

"What? What?" Tad said.

"CAF – the new campaign."

"Does it pop or does it poop?"

Jud handed him the manuscript hot from the typing pool. "Neither one, Sire, it merely sings."

VIDEO	AUDIO
YOUNG GUITARIST ON STOOL IN LIMBO AGAINST EARTH-COLOURED HUES: OCHRES, BURNT ORANGE. CAMERA MOVES TO MCU, HOLDS.	MUSIC/GUITAR/VOCAL: Listen: our country has a chance, just one, but it has it: If they learn one thing at college, just one: That behind every different face is a different dream, and unless we live with difference it will turn to scream. That behind the beads or the button-down is a person. Help to open a closed-down mind, Help to let some daylight shine, Help by giving America time – to listen . . .
SUPERS: OPEN MINDS, GIVE TO A COLLEGE.	(V.O.) Listen: Tuition pays only one-third of a college education. Somebody's got to pay the other two-thirds. Open minds. Give to a college. MUSIC

(CAF SYMBOL)
(ADVERTISING COUNCIL
SYMBOL)
COLLEGE AID FUND

ADVERTISING CONTRIBUTED
FOR THE PUBLIC GOOD.

CAF – TV – 60 second

Reading the copy, nodding, gritting his teeth in suppressed approval, Tad picked up a pencil and about to write on the script put it down, looked up with his snarl of a smile, saying, "Hell, what's a Houlighan doing editing Judson Bell copy?"

He lit a cigarette. "It's tough, Ace," he said. "right on. Has balls." Tough, the Tadpole's highest accolade. "But what about music, is there money for that in the budget? We can't afford a whole lot of bread on this."

"You sound like a client, Tad. You know, make me look like five mil for five hundred thou."

"Okay, but I can hear management screaming, you know how they feel about freebies."

"No, there's no money for music except stock, but it's already written, an original score, and it didn't cost us a dime. Pat Mooney . . ."

" . . . That skinny kid from production? He's been bugging me for a job in copy department. I didn't know he wrote music. Even so, you've got to be kidding."

"He's written some very nice things – country, western – professional stuff, Tad. Plays the Cowtown rodeo on weekends. The kid has real talent. He did a great job with the ballad. Oh, by the way, I've been giving him sample copy assignments so he'd have something to show. I think he's about ready for a junior slot here. But, you'll judge for yourself, of course."

Tad's phone rang. "In a minute," he said.

"As for budgets, I'm your original low budget man. I'll probably bring it in under. I've blocked it all out. The production has got to stay simple, not only for cost but effect. No fancy dissolves, no electronic boloney, no special sets. Just a roll of seamless behind the singer. Some lights and gels to create the feeling of earth, land, vistas. And that's it. Less is more. The thirties takeout of the sixties. You just transfer the tracks for radio. The print ads are all black and white, no illustrations, just the ballad set in some real tasty type . . . So, we're not out-of-pocket except for studio time and talent."

"Why not Mooney, if he's as great as you say?"

"I thought of it, Tad. It would have completed the package – an all Fairleigh production down to the talent. Great for the kid and for us. But – not on the air. Pat looks like a bandit who's just blown the dean's office. He'd turn off the heavy givers. One look and the client would lose his water and call out the National Guard."

"You're somethin' else again, Ace," Tad said. "Go do the commercial."

"A challenge and an opportunity, Sire," Jud said.

6

They were driving to the studio in Primos in Tad's big black Mercedes so he could review the production tapes, Jud up front and global Ottavio Baffa, his art director, spreading slowly across the back seat.

"Is it great or does it stink?" Tad said.

"Neither," said Jud.

"There's no in-between."

"It's *good*, Tad, air worthy, better than that, but not great."

"How come? It's a great script. You're the creative director. A VP. You were there."

"Okay, I was there. Fourteen bloody hours, from eight in the morning till midnight. By the time I got anything near what I wanted, the talent had almost passed out – his fingers were stiff – the cameraman couldn't see straight, the sound engineer was in cardiac arrest. Right, Ottavio?"

"Fuckin A right."

"We had to run overtime."

"Beautiful," Tad said. "At sixty-five bucks an hour."

"We're still under budget. Look, Tad, I'm not passing the buck, but you know our system, the commercial producer runs the technical show."

"That fuckin Nazi," Ottavio said from the back.

"Who? Who?" said Tad.

"Bill Heintz, who else? I – any Fairleigh CD – can't even talk to the cameraman or the talent or the grips or the sound man once the shooting is on. I've got to go through the producer. Most you can work with, but you know the Red Baron. You tell him you want music up or music under, or a spot over there, or a take from another angle and he looks at you with his SS blue eyes – 'Right, right' he says, 'no sweat, you've got it.' And then he does his own drill."

"Achtung, achtung," Ottavio barked from the back. "Alles kaput if you shcrewballen katzenjammers monkeyshine mit die worken."

"Fourteen hours," Tad said, "what the hell were you doing? Beating your meat?"

"I could have done it in two – three at the outside if Heintz hadn't been there. I told him at pre-production and at rehearsal – we should have taped the *rehearsal* – this spot has got to be simple, it's a ballad not a Hollywood musical . . ."

"Yah, yah, I diggen, meinherr wordenshplitzen gruppenfuehrer. Shoven it uppen your assen," Ottavio crowed from the back.

"But, oh no, the Red Baron, he's got to 'contribute' his *technische hochschule* know-how. So he lays on the zooms and the opticals . . . Would you believe a star-burst on the guitar? . . . I told him no way. He says what's the sweat, this isn't film, it's tape. You get to see what you shoot while you're shooting. So why not play around. We *might* just get a *sensational* effect that would *make* the commercial . . . Take after take after take."

"Try it, you'll like it," Ottavio said from the back.

"You should have kicked his ass out of there," Tad said.

"Yeah, or made a citizen's arrest."

"You've got to have balls, Judson," Tad said.

They sat in the Anise Bar & Grille across the studio parking lot after the viewing. "Beefeater marts – all around," Tad said to the waitress. She had a slack pretty face and blinding dentures. Ottavio shoved his blubber back in his chair, his arms up like stop signs.

"Momento, momento. A glass of red wine for me."

"Domestic or imported, sir?"

"I don't care if it's Manischewitz . . . I don't know how you guys can drink those torpedoes. Me, I'm too young to die."

"Damn the torpedoes," Jud said, filling his pipe. "Full esteem ahead."

"Let's order something to eat," Ottavio said.

The waitress returned with the drinks, the marts in two healthy sized glasses, a bonus shaker half full on the side, the wine in a large ruby goblet. She had great long ago legs.

"Madonna mia," Ottavio said, "those aren't glasses, they're buckets."

"Our Studio Special," the waitress said. The name on her tag was Lonetta. "You gentlemen making a movie?" She nodded across the parking lot. "Lots of silver screen folks come to the studio. You know, for interior shots. Last week Charlton Heston," she sighed. "He sat at this very table. He's such a real person. And last month Lee Remick, a regular doll. I was even an extra once, in *Armpit Amour,* a waitress, ha, whadaya know. Got forty dollars. Very low budget. Sorta dirty, I guess. I was the only one wearing clothes at the end. I went to New York for opening night. Could hardly find the theater – phew, I can still remember the smell. What a hole. I was the only one in the audience. It closed the next day . . . What is your picture gonna be called?"

"*The Decline of the West,*" Jud said.

"John Wayne was here once, but that was to make a commercial . . . You must be a director."

"Yes," Judson said. "I'm Oswald Spengler."

"Oh . . . then you must have been Garbo's director – and *friend.*"

"A long time ago . . . Yes, yes . . . She had cold feet, quite large, you know, and chewed garlic to discourage her leading men from passionate kisses. Johnny Gilbert was always complaining to me. And

Freddie March . . ."

"Well, well . . . Will you gentlemen be having dinner."

Ottavio picked up the menu.

"We'll have another round, whenever you're ready," Tad said.

"I second the motion," Jud said. "Make 'em doubles."

"At last, a two-fisted drinker," Tad said.

"Jesus, Mary and Joseph," Ottavio said, covering his glass with his hand, "Listen guys, let's order something to eat. It's bad to drink on an empty stomach."

"Your stomach can't possibly be empty," Tad said. "You can live off your fat for a year."

Ottavio began stuffing his mouth with a fistful of pretzels. Looking around he said, "You know, for a nice place like this it has a dumb name. What kind of a cockamamie name is Anise?"

"What would you call it – Palumbo's?" Jud said.

"*Piglia á cula,*" he made the crooked elbow and finger gesture. "Up yours."

"Actually, Ottavio, I think of it privately, when I think of it at all as the Anus of Primos."

"Yeah, the ass end of the world," Ottavio laughed. "Why would anybody put a studio here? Primos . . . another cockamamie name."

"Primos, Ottavio," Jud said, starting his second drink, "is forever enshrined in one of the world's most hallowed songs."

Ottavio waited for the punch line.

"O Primos Me," Jud said.

"Har," Tad barked.

The waitress set down the new clinking round, the marts and the shaker.

"My girlfriend was asking," she said to Jud, nodding to a waitress across the room, "what were some of your other pictures?"

"Well, now, let's see. I've made so many. Oh yes, there was *Mind Over Mattress*. It was Groucho's greatest. Opposite Sarah Bernhardt – her last picture. You remember? That scene where she lost her wooden leg. Her last take. She died on the set. It was in all the papers."

Lonetta thumbed through some fan magazine in her head. "Hmn, I don't think I caught that one."

"And there was my first Academy Award Winner – *Anatomy and Cleopatra*. W.C. Fields and Eleanora Duse. The first talkie. Of course, her voice was dubbed."

Lonetta nodded gamely.

"The chariot race," Jud said.

Lonetta's dentures shone. "Yeah, the chariot race. Now I remember. A great picture."

"You're nuts," Ottavio said.

Tad was doodling on the napkin.

Jud swirled the ice in his glass, took a drink. a shy private smile. "But the one, I suppose, I would like to be most remembered for was

41

Panties Inferno. Shirley Temple and Harold Lloyd. Boris Karloff had a cameo role. We shot the whole thing on location in Dayton."

"Hey guys," Ottavio said, gripping the menu, "they have some great food here. Lobster Fra Diavolo, New York Strip Steak with Hash Browns, Snapper Soup, Oysters Rocke . . ."

"There are eaters and there are drinkers," Tad said. "And people who work together should drink together. And the family that drinks together says together. Understand?" Then to waitress, "Do us again."

"More wine for my friend," Jud said.

"A bowl of potato chips," Ottavio said, "or peanuts, while we are waiting."

"Here's to great ads," Tad said, raising his glass.

"Great ads," Ottavio said, cupping his still half full goblet . . . "Say, next time let's shoot in New York."

Tad's eyes narrowed. "What's New York got that we haven't got?"

"The Big A, that's where it's at."

"Give my regards to Broadway," Jud said.

"The big bullshit. Where it's at is right here." Tad tapped his chest. "Me. I'll take on anyone from New York. Fact, I have a dream." His snarling smile came on. "You know what? I'd like to get Mary Wells, Bill Bernbach, Dave Ogilvy and me in the Villanova field house. Just the four of us, see. Paper, pencils, typewriters . . ."

"At twenty paces," Jud said.

". . . The doors would be locked. We'd each get the same assignment – an ad, a campaign – in a sealed envelope. A time would be set. At the bell we'd open the envelopes and – vroom. Who do you think would win, huh? Who? You're looking at him, the greatest copywriter in the world." He stubbed out his cigarette. "That's who."

"I can write you under the table anytime," Jud said pleasantly. He felt a stinging kick on his shin under the table. Ottavio rolled his eyes, shook his head.

"I'll match you, Ace," Tad said, "ad for ad. Get out your proofs." He rose from his chair. "Right now I got to take a leak."

"What the fuck did you have to say that for?" Ottavio said watching Tad stilt walk his way to the gents.

"Because, as Miss Vera would say, it's the truth." Smiling.

"You crazy bastard, you've just been kissed on the mouth by the capo of capos."

7

Walking out into the lemony bright November noon over Washington Square, "Where would you like to have lunch?" Jud said.

"Makes no difference to me," Billie said.

"It's a great day for walking."

"Then let's walk."

He headed her north by west, a tug guiding a liner . . .

She walks, it seems, without putting her feet to the pavement, looking ahead, flowing along some path of her own, as if – he feels – for her this going to lunch with him is a kind of assignment, part of the day's work. You don't say no to your boss. Shouldn't there be conversation? *Kid, laugh. Man, you've got to show some class.* Sparkle, Judson. But he also feels she doesn't require instant palaver. Just add words and serve. So they walk, she in her sphere of silence, a halo of mist that moves along with her in space, outside his orbit. Link up, Judson, before she disappears.

"I love autumn," he said, feeling stupid, what a brilliant remark, Judson, suddenly out in the world away from the office, walking along with a girl whose world it suddenly was, with a woman, a primal nudeness even through clothes. When was the last time? With Vera, of course, years ago to hear Richter at the Academy; the Wyeth show at the Museum. I Musici. No one since Vera. Morning car to Paoli Station – train to the city – walk to the office – turnaround evening walk to Penn Center – train to Paoli – car to the farm.

"I love summer best," she said, "the beaches, the sun, the sea. I love the sea. I get excited the minute I smell it, even before I've seen it, you know, when I drive there. It turns me on. I have a thing about it. Sometimes I feel I was born in the sea, that it loves me. That it's my . . . isn't that freaky?"

"No, not at all. They say we all came from the sea."

"I know what you mean, evolution. This is something else."

"Any place special you go to?"

"Long Beach Island, mostly near Barnegat Light."

"Nomad is an island."

She smiled as if she was supposed to.

"Sorry about that," he said. "A compulsion. Writer's tic."

She's back in her mist, so he says, "Do you dig puns?"

"You don't have to say that," she says. And he knows what she means, but must ask, "Say what?"

"Dig," she answers. "It isn't you."

He wants to kiss her, then.

"Well," he says (now inside her mist), "there was this prince a long time ago whose best friend was a count. They were raised together from boyhood. And when the prince became king he made the count his chief councillor. But there were factions at court who resented the powerful count, who was incorruptible and served his friend, the king, with devotion. So they caballed" – he looked at her – "plotted against him, told the king lies. At first the king would not listen to them knowing the count was true. But, little by little, they began to convince the king that the count was plotting to take over the throne himself, accused him of treason. Now *that* touched a royal nerve. It was all false evidence, of course; but the king, who had been a good sleeper, wasn't doing too well lately. That word kept him awake, poking behind the curtains. So he had no choice but to confront the count with it. The count, of course, laughed it off. Ha, ha. Who? Me? But the jealous nobles insisted on a trial, which, being rigged, found the count guilty. The sentence was death by beheading. But the king, who was not a bad sort, just rattled by lack of sleep, spared his old friend the trimmings, like hanging drawing and quartering. Nasty stuff, that. And he really didn't want the count, his boyhood companion, to die.

"So the king begged the count to confess, saying that if he would, for the sake of their old friendship, he would spare the count's life and change the sentence to exile abroad where he could live pretty well on welfare. At least his friend's life would be spared. But the count said, No, he couldn't confess to something he hadn't done. Beside, the motto on his family's coat of arms was, *Never confess*. This saddened the king, but he needed his sleep; so he set the date for execution.

"The night before, the king secretly visited the count in his dungeon cell and begged him again to confess, but he still said he was innocent. 'You'll never get ahead that way,' the king said."

He looked at her.

"The king asked him again the next day as the count was led to the block. His answer was still, No.

"With great sadness the king nodded to the executioner. But as the axe was falling, the count looked up at the king and cried – 'I confess.' But it was too late."

He paused. She waited, getting a smile ready.

"The moral of the story is: Don't hatchet your counts before they chicken."

Her smile was not made from a mix.

"I know one about a maharajah," he said, "and an Indian chief who struck oil." Some other time.

Streets flowing outside them as if they were riding by in a car. Skid row wrecks of old buildings being torn down, the crane shovel lunching on smashed toilets and bathtubs and still smoking plaster and lath. The Trocadero Burlesque postered with boobies. Tattoo parlours tincting nostalgia and hepatitis. Peek-a-boo dildo emporiums – Pre-Xmas Vibrator Specials. Graffiti all over the place. *Vox* spray can *populus*, aerosol declarations of independence, the handwriting on the wall . . . ALL POLITICIANS IS A WHORE . . . PRAY ALWAYS . . . HIT THE JETS . . . GOD MADE CLAP . . . SANTA SUCKS . . . READ BIBLE . . . Rustoleum ghetto scribes. Cool Earl and Chewy, Moon Dog and Cornbread, Bad News Jimmie, Klepto Kidd, Sweet Dice, Comet 1, Top Cat, Flip 1 and Switch. My name is writ in spray paint . . .

Winos guttering in smegma hallways. One tallow man, his back against a building, legs surrendered to tatters outstretched on the leprous pavement, saluting them with his bagged bottle, singing in a phlegm-cracking Dublin tenor – "I don't want to set the world on fire. I just want to start a flame in your heart." Jud takes out a bill, puts it into his palm, closes his fingers over it. "Don't spend it on anything but liquor, Sir."

"Why did you say that?" Billie said.

"Because he would anyhow. This way it's not a handout, just buying someone a drink. He didn't ask for it. Also, there but for the grace . . ."

She looked at him as if he had spoken a language she had never studied but suddenly knew. Waking in a foreign country without being foreign there.

Chinatown, my Chinatown.

The Chinese waiter with the Ash Wednesday smudges for eyebrows put down their steamed striped bass with black bean sauce. She poured the tea. He spooned the white gobbets of meat under the gills, offering them.

"You mean you *eat* that?"

"A delicacy," he said, "the concubine's portion, reserved by mandarins for their favourite."

"Oh, wow. It is good. Sweet, tender. When I'm at the shore I eat lots of sea food, there's nothing like it fresh, caught the same day, with some nice chilled white wine." Her face thinking, her eyes oceanic. "I think I'll tool down next weekend, walk on the beach." He could see her running along the sand at the sea's rim, wind grabbing her hair. *Girl face peering through blonde waterfall, the garden of a weekend in your eyes.* With whom? With whom? Pat Mooney? World enough and time, it was all hers. He felt left out.

She opened her fortune cooky, laughed.

"What does it say?"

"'Love and fortune come to him who waits.' Oh great, the catch is," she said, "how long? What does yours say?"

"'Tomorrow is another day.'"

"Let me see your hand," she said, taking his hand in hers, turning his palm up.

"You don't believe in that mumbo jumbo, do you?"

"Absolutely. The stars, ESP, biorhythm. My horoscope's almost never wrong, just a little bit off sometimes. What is your sign?" She studied his palm. "I'm pretty good at this."

"Taurus, the professional bull thrower."

"I'm Aries," she said. "Earth and fire. Hold still." She drew his hand closer into the cowl of her hair. "See this line? it's your lifeline. Wow, you're going to live a long time. See where it starts, way back here on the Mount of Jupiter," her finger tracing his palm, "goes across Lower Mars clear around to the back of your hand. And this is your heartline. Well, Mr Bell, you sure started young. That first love lasted a long time. A great love, that line is real deep, like a cut. Uhuh, you've had two, two big loves in your life."

"One," he said.

"Two, the lines never lie, like a map, where you've been and where you're going. Seriously, your life is all there in your hand."

"Right now I'd say it's in yours."

She put down his hand.

Walking back, a block from the office, he said, "Let's take one turn around the square before we go in."

In the park, trying not to sound like an Independence Day tour, he said, "We're walking on thousands of unknown soldiers of the Revolution, buried right here under our feet in mass graves. Yellow fever mostly, and wounds, prisoners of war. I watched them dig up the bones of one, under that tree, to put in the tomb over there. An ancestor of mine fought at the Battle of Kings Mountain, which wasn't anywhere near here."

At the fountain she said, "There's a rock on the other side of the Art Museum, in the park, hidden by trees. I like to go there when I want to be alone and read. It's my own special place. I went there yesterday to finish your book."

He waits for a word from those who come after: The non-sons. The non-daughters.

"It's heavy," she said.

"Heavy, you mean dull."

"No, heavy good, not heavy bad, you know – deep. I'd like to read the others."

"On your own special rock?"

She stopped walking, turned her gold coin face on him. "What's a man like you doing here? You should be writing books."

"I began one some time ago. I work on it on and off, when I can."

"Why haven't you finished it?

"Yes, why haven't I? It's been a long time between drinks."

"Tell me?"

"I lack a vital ingredient."

She put her arm through his. He looked up at the Castle, its thirteen stories of windows. "It's a free country," she said.

"Free from what?"

"From what was."

At the great friezed bronze doors of the Castle, "Have you read my poems?" she said.

"I've read them:

> You say I want too much.
> How too much
> Is too much
> With your tabasco tongue
> In my forever mouth?"

"You've read them. Will you tell me about them some time?"

"Of course, but this is hardly the place or time."

"I said some time . . . Some place."

He found himself saying, "This evening, how about dinner tonight?"

"Tonight?" Her head tilted, tongue arching her lip. "Tonight? Mmn . . . Sure, why not? . . . And, oh, thanks for lunch . . . and the concubine's portion, Mr Mandarin."

8

"I'll be working late tonight, Vera," he said to the phone.

"How late? an hour?"

"Most probably more."

"How much more? If I know I can hold dinner."

"I really can't say. It's the Army account. It's up for grabs again; we've got to come up with a new campaign."

"What's wrong with the present campaign? You said it was good, that they like it."

"It *is* good, but once a year the Pentagon holds a review, calls in other agencies. It's the law, government regulation. Don't you remember last year? I stayed in town two-three nights."

"I guess I forgot . . . Poor man, be sure to have dinner."

"I'll probably pop out to Nick's for a sandwich, or have it sent in."

"A sandwich, and I had such a good dinner for you . . . Jud, try not to be too late, I'll wait up."

"Don't do that, dear, it looks like a long one tonight."

"Ah well, I'll have Blitz for company."

Drifting up Walnut on the going home tide, Billie said, "I'd like to freshen up before dinner. Let's stop at my place, have a drink" . . . Then, "You live on a farm in the country, horses, you ride."

"Unicorn Farm."

"That's some kind of horse, isn't it?"

"A mythical horse with a horn, a horse that exists only in dreams. I dreamed of that place for years, knew it was somewhere waiting. Must have looked at fifty or more before I found it. The minute I saw it I knew that was it. My place, my horses on it. But more than a place, a time, not just past time – how can I put it? not merely nostalgia, that too – but like time in a Wyeth painting, always still there. When I go home at night I'm coming home to more than a house, I'm coming home to my country and time."

"Wasn't there a poem about a man who dreamed of the past, wanted to be a knight or something? And sighed and sighed?"

"Miniver Cheevy who 'thought and thought and thought and thought about it.' Edwin Arlington Robinson."

"We had it in high school."

"How did you know where I live?"

"I have my spies.

"One month at Fairleigh . . ."

"Pat Mooney told me. I like him. He has his head together. A very straight guy, with it." . . . *Kid. Take her to lunch. Laughs. To see Miss Miller* . . . This isn't for me . . . *And I had such a good dinner for you* . . . *Ah well, I'll have Blitz* for *company* . . . I'll take her to dinner and head for the hill.

"Here's where I live," she said, stopping at an old brownstone house on a street that was like bad news you couldn't break gently. Her apartment in the rear, once a parlour, dark panelled walls. Plump plaster mouldings, cherubs, bunches of grapes around the high ceiling. Shuttered bay windows over an alley. Really one room, a long cave. Bathroom, kitchenette partitioned by bookshelves. A queen-sized bed on the floor. A bricked up marble fireplace and mantel. "I wish that thing worked," she said. "I love a fire." He had laid a fire at the farm, maybe Vera would light it, it would be burning when he came home, Blitz telling him: where the helluvya been? A walnut armoire. A large scarred oak desk, a guitar leaning against it. Fat foothigh candles, red, black. Stereo, records. And off to the side, a café table, a Tiffany lamp hanging over it from a long chain, and two café chairs. Posters: Paris along the Seine upriver from Notre Dame on the wall by the table. A tourist bureau bullfighter, olé. Andy Warhol's monster coke bottle. A swiped highway sign: soft shoulder ahead . . . So this is the way they live . . . She turned the lamp on. "I got most of this stuff from the Salvation Army or Goodwill," she said. "If you look you can find some neat things. Now that I'm making some bucks, I've thought of moving, but I still owe on my car, and this place is convenient." She lit the candles. "And the rent is real cheap, a hundred and forty a month. You can't beat that for center city."

She opened the armoire, took some things out. At the door of the bathroom she said, "I'll be out in a mo. Why don't you make us some drinks? There's Scotch in the cupboard under the sink and some vodka, I think, maybe a smidgen of gin. You'll have to use a screwdriver to get the ice cubes out," she laughed, "or an axe. That fridge is older than God." She closed the bathroom door, opened it, poked her head out. "You can put on some music – I've got Carmen McRae on, she's the greatest – or whatever you like. There's opera, all kinds of stuff."

He hacked the ice cubes out of a small glacier, fixed two Scotches, set them down on the café table, sat down under the spangled light, lit his pipe. He heard the shower splash on. A book by the lamp, Neruda's poems. Well, better than Kahlil Gibran. The phone rang, a long time, sixteen nagging rings. He looked at his watch, 6:11. She's sure taking her time. He took another swig. Chug-a-lug.

He got up drink in hand, the rain in the bathroom still on, folded a shutter back on the barred bay window, looked out on the alley – a tree, garbage cans, a brick wall – a shadow moving, someone with a sack. The Philadelphia night already thick with hazard. She's taking a chance living alone out here on the fringe. On her desk a notebook, Things I Only Say to Myself typed on the label. He opened it, a diary,

49

and closed it. He took another drink, down to ice water. He fixed a fresh one. Chug-a-lug. The table enclosed in its cone of light, an indoor outdoor café in its own spot of time. Once, long ago he had sat at the Dome, the Deux Magots in the afterglow of the afterglow . . . A girl on the Madeleine.

She came out of the bathroom dewy in a long high collared robe, her hair up in a towel turban. He heard the Great Gate of Kiev. "It won't take long to dry," she said. "I wash it twice a day to keep it straight. Ah, just what I need." She picked up her drink.

"There was a phone call, but I didn't think I should answer it."

"Doesn't matter," she said, "they'll call again. They always do." She sat down at the table, the robe clinging like skin. "Isn't this neat? My corner of Paris."

"I was thinking that while you were in there."

"Then you've been?" He nodded.

"I never have, never been anywhere. What was it like?"

"Like it will never be again."

"Someday," she said, cat sipping her drink.

Running feet in alley. A scuffle. Garbage can bangs. Shouts. "I'll get you man."

She shrugged.

"Aren't you afraid living alone out here, coming home late, someone as, as noticeable as you?"

"It gets pretty creepy. Phone calls at night, heavy breathers, door bells at three in the morning. Once in a while somebody moving out there, trying to open the window – it's pretty well barred. Last week the black guy in the parking lot asked me if I wanted a husband, did I need anything fixed, haha."

"What did you do?"

"What can you do? Big joke. Laugh it off – what else? You get used to it." She looked in her glass, swirling the ice with a finger. "No, that's not true. I've never gotten used to that crap. I'm afraid a lot of the time . . . Well, cheers, you only live once . . . My mop should be dry in a few minutes. Say, how about one more drink, this is nice, then I'll dress and we'll go out to dinner – unless you're in a big hurry?"

"No hurry."

"You must have a train to catch."

"Don't worry about my train."

"The last one's at 12:50"

His eyebrows went up. "It usually is, a 44-minute local, makes every stop, gets in to Paoli at 1:34."

"I know. I called the station."

Rising he took her glass and his and went into the kitchenette.

Coming back with the drinks, "Tell me something," he said. Chug-a-lug. "I think I know the answer but I'd like you to tell me. That day of the interview why did you wear that locker room matador's outfit?"

"Louie Bocca's idea," she laughed. "I thought, wow, not at conservative Fairleigh. He said, 'You'll be a walking ad, Babe, shock 'em, get their attention.'"

"Zen is now." Jud said.

"Louie told me, 'They're turning old Fairleigh around. Five years ago, no way, but now Houlighan will love it, he'll cream.' He said, 'You have nothing to lose. Look at Frankie Pigano.'"

"Yes, the South Philly Flash. I know all about Frankie," Jud said, pacing. "He barged into Fairleigh from the pushcarts of Catherine Street. A streetwise dese, dems and dose guy." Chug-a-lug. "Fresh from the College of Art. Not a bad painter, matter of fact, in the giant post card genre with a whisker of Dali. Louie was right, five years before – never. We were twenty light years behind New York. You know, the Jewish copywriter, the Italian art director. He came at the right moment, an idea whose time was overdue. His stuff was good, not great – a first-rate second-rate talent – but he had a freebooter's knack for packaging other people's ideas, putting his name on the package and shoving it down their throats."

"That's the name of the game," she said.

Chug-a-lug. "Let me freshen my drink – you?"

"Lots of ice," she said.

"Okay . . . I remember the day he reported for work, you wouldn't believe it – pizza face under a porkpie hat, funeral director's suit and baby lizard shoes. I thought he was running numbers for the Mob. And his tie – chug-a-lug – "could put the Palermo sunset to shame. A graffia Mafia soldier, an Al Capone who would one day bash us all over the head with a baseball bat." Pacing. "His first Creative Review Board – I was there – he begins to holler, bangs the table. This, in the sanctified board room of old social register Fairleigh – Chippendale chairs, hunt breakfast Sheraton sideboards. Persian carpets. 'Duh marketing on dis stinks,' he says. 'You're tying duh hands of creative. Dis is duh way we should go.' And he whips out his layouts. He happened to be right on that one. I've been through the decimal deaths of market research . . . Well, as they say, stunned silence. The old silver-haired remittance men just stood there like waxwork dummies. The real world had invaded the board room. They could smell the garlic winds of change. Then one of them found his voice – it was Curtis G. Dingman, IV, puffing his Royal Jamaica – 'Harrumph, gentlemen, I believe, kaff, kaff, we have a creative genius in our midst. I for one go along with his thinking.' Then the others hopped aboard the barrel organ as fast as they could." Chug-a-lug. Pacing. "The saga of Frankie Pig had begun. Three years later he was running New York creative. Another five years and he'll have the whole ball of wax."

Chug-a-

She was looking at him, the towel slipping from her hand to the floor, lamp lit hair spilling all over, her face cloudy, her mouth an O.

51

"Fuck me," she said.

He floated over fell into summer her mouth swallowing him in a rain of gold hair coming up a bloomy continent in his arms bathing him in warm fountains sunflesh hills breasting him into ague she unsucked her mouth from his

stepped away.

Her robe flowed around her feet.

She rolled the bedspread back like a wave of the sea and with one tidal motion hand under nape flung back her wheatfield of hair threshing the pillow. There is a haystack brimming with brine honey, her head writhing, eyes closed, finding too the nipples of her earth, her fingers leaving her hands to travel him, her palm water to his root . . . her thermal mouth flinging back come into me please as if answering a knock at the door he she go slow please don't go away O Jud I love your cock in me floating in air somewhere between bed and ceiling he she flying flying

He raised up on an elbow from sleep, she sleeping in planetary silence looking over her head at the clock. 12:17.

"What is it? she said.

"I have to go. The last train."

"Please stay."

"I can't, not tonight."

"I hate sleeping alone."

Dressing her smell into his clothes, shuffling into his shoes.

"I'll call you a cab," she said.

"How long will it take?"

"Half an hour at least."

"I'll never make it. This is the lousiest town for cabs, and at this hour out here. I'll have to run for it."

"I wish you wouldn't there are all kinds of creeps out there."

Holding her tawny once more at the door, kissing, the paste of both of them on their lips.

He heard the snaplock snap and two bolts and he was running like hell through the thug infested streets.

9

"You forgot this," Billie said putting his gold unicorn tie pin on his desk. Vera's gift birthdays ago.

"You made the train?"

"Just, by fifteen seconds."

She lit a cigarette. "Do you have a minute?"

He pointed to a chair. She sat statuesque, filling her clothes, every harpstring hair in place.

"I don't want to make waves, I've been here only a month, but do you think I can get another art director to work with?"

"Wanda Sload? I was afraid of that."

She nodded. "I've never worked with anybody like that before. I'm coming up with good stuff, but she won't do layouts to it. I thought we were supposed to work together. On we rap and she doodles around, then goes off and does her own thing – headlines, layouts and brings them to Tad after hours. Aren't you supposed to see them first?"

His turn to nod. "Welcome to the Army account." Only hours ago, heshe.

"Next morning she comes in and says with that freaky smile, 'Oh, I looked for you last night but you were gone. Tad happened to be around, asked what was cooking. I showed him. Tad liked this, Tad liked that' – never my stuff. She's driving me bananas."

"The new breed. If it's any consolation, no one can work with her. Wanda Sload's put it to every writer and creative director she's worked with. She's been thrown out of every group in the place."

"Then why do you – Tad – put up with her?"

"She's Tad's kind of people, and Frankie Pig's – they both operated the same way, over everyone's head to numero uno. Frankie's told her she can work for him in New York any time. Tad wouldn't like that, Frankie drafting one of his players. She knows how to touch that nerve. It's the Army, or else . . . all right . . . I'll talk to Tad, but I know how he works. He doesn't assign, he pits people against each other. He thinks that's the way to make ads. He likes to see blood flow in the gutters."

"Oh great . . . hassling isn't my bag. Look, I don't mean to dump on you, but . . ."

"It's part of my job." He fastened the tie pin. "I still owe you a dinner, and a bottle of Scotch."

"It's okay. It was fun."

"Tomorrow?"

She nodded.

"Whachya got, Ace?"

"An old scenario, Tad, with a new member of the cast. Wanda Sload's giving Billie Miller a hard time."

"I'd love to give Billie Miller a hard time." He put his hand in his pocket, jiggled his marbles, the father of five at thirty-two with a duck in Joan Houlighan's oven. The new breeders. "Wouldn't you?"

"Since you ask, I've neither the hard nor the time."

"Har."

"Thaddeus, it's not working out, the Billie-Wanda combination."

"It's got to work out."

"Can't we put Billie with another art director? Say, Joe, or Ottavio; get some of that boy-girl chemistry going. It usually works out well. All she wants to do is the best job she can, and she can't with Wanda. This can hardly be news. It's a rerun. Where will Wanda Sload Strike Next? This week on the Army account."

"Okay, so Wanda's tough, she has balls. And she's an art director who writes nifty headlines."

"Like? . . . 'The Army Will Cure You of Acne'?"

"Har. That's ballsy. She showed it to me."

"C'mon, Tad, it won't work, we can't make that claim. None of her headlines work, they're all nutty. Maybe for *Mad* magazine, not for LIFE or the *Reader's Digest*."

"Okay, I saw one last night, lessee now . . . okay, 'Girls in Today's Army Aren't Wacs.' Now that's tough."

"It's Billie's. The good ones are Billie's."

"What's the difference who writes them. We're here to make ads, and that takes ded-i-cation. And Wanda is ded-i-cated. She puts in at least a ten-hour day, she stays late like all the good kids . . ." Like you, Tadpole, with your four-mart three-hour lunches. You only get started at four.

". . . Look, Jud, let them fight it out by themselves, winner takes all. Billie will just have to hack it. Wanda stays on Army."

He would be going home soon, through Tad's court of good kids waiting around pointing to watches, "Half a day, Jud?" . . . "Banker's hours?" Idiots' delight.

"Some of us are on top of our jobs," he would say, smiling. "Goodnight" (ladies), and leave them waiting.

Leslie Madonna waiting to chauffeur Tad home.

Leeta Krantz and Wanda Sload waiting to show their balls.

Joe Concerto and adenoidal Kip Money just waiting.

Waiting for Houlighan.

Today is Wednesday, November 10th, the 314th day of the year.

54

The moon is between its last quarter and new phase.

The morning star is Saturn.
The evening stars are Mercury, Venus, Mars and Jupiter.

Those born this day are under the sign of Scorpio.

Martin Luther, founder of Protestantism, was born November 10, 1493.

On this day in history:
In 1871 journalist Henry Stanley found missing Scottish missionary David Livingstone in a small African village, saying, "Dr. Livingstone, I presume?"

10

Pyjamas, toothbrush, razor, new blade, shaving cream, after shave lotion, fresh shirt, socks, and a secret packed in his attaché casé, swinging along in his hand in the afterwork evening to Reading Terminal Market.

In the dark cavern butchers wearing straw skimmers from carriage trade days. Aproned greengrocers polishing fruit into jewels. He picked up a T-bone steak, two great garnet apples, a wedge of crumbly old cheddar, crusty sticks of French bread, let's keep it simple. A half gallon of Dewar's and a fair Beaujolais at the State Store.

"Hi," she said at the door, happy. "You must have bought out the place."

Lamp over the café corner, candles somewhere in the room. Somebody French on the stereo haunted by Cherbourg rain.

Unbelievably, she.

The phone rang the room into a room.

"Fix us a drink," she said, taking the receiver into her phone booth of hair. Whisperings. A giggle. "Sorry, I can't, not tonight. Rain check . . . I'd love to . . . Some other time . . ."

"An old friend," she said, sitting down. "Just got into town." Wet her lips, a deep breath . . . "Dom diLucca." . . . Looked in some rear view mirror, sipped her drink, came up smiling an I'm sorry smile. "He's a creative director in New York, small agency. I took his script writing course at NYU. Real good. He used to come into Philly a few times a month when they had an account here. It was always 'Hi, guess who, I'll pick you up later.' Just like that," a bubble of laughter. "They're trying to get the account back is why he's here. They're pitching tomorrow. He was high school Tri-County in basketball, a real macho guy, Lucky. Happily married, wouldn't you know, crazy about his two kids, lives in Long Island."

"The man in your poems."

"How did you know?"

> Lucky me, Lucky You
> I wear your name
> like a good luck charm.

". . . and the other poems."

"Oh right."

He took a long swig.

"Hey gang," she said, "this is now" and got up to refill their drinks.
"Not too much ice."

From the kitchenette: "You really put it away."

"It takes will power, girl. Ded-i-cation."

"Funny mans."

"Some day I'll write a book, Good Ol' Jud's Hangover Handbook.
Or What To Do Till The St. Bernard Comes."

"You're feeling no pain."

"I kid you not. I'll get a Guggenheim, or a National Endowment
for the Arts."

"Have you ever tried? I mean, for your real stuff."

"Thirteen times." She put the drinks on the table, his nut brown,
one cube floating alone.

Chug-a-lug.

"Now listen, girl. Jud's Handbook will offer salubrious advice.
Take ice. Ice is frozen water. Ice sinks ships. You know, the Titanic.
Before your time. Liquor is good for you, made of whole grain. As
bread used to be. Staff of Life." Chug-a-lug. "Uisge beatha, the water of
life. The good creative, the Puritans called it."

"You should have been a professor."

"I profess. *Mea culpa*. Now listen." Chug-a-lug. "You've been
drinking, right? You feel fine. Then you go to sleep. In the morning you
wake up with a hangover. You think it's the booze. Well, it's not. It's
the *sleep*."

"Are you hungry? Maybe I should put the steak on. You have
trains, all that jazz."

"No hurry," he said. "I'm staying . . . That is, last time you said
. . ."

"Oh beautiful. All night? Great."

She glowed out of her chair to the desk, took a sheet from it,
handed it to him.

> I love you
> because you were my friend
> before you knew
> if I'd be yours.

He got up from the table, paper in hand and sat down in the chair by
the desk, the red candle behind him. She took a deep drag on her
Parliament, her face watching him.

His eyes still on the paper, he said "All my life there have been
three words I've been very careful about, tried not to misuse – love,
genius, beauty. I have never used them unless I meant them."

"I love you," she said.

"You overwhelm me."

"Isn't that what love's all about?"

Across the room, her face in a drizzle of light, she said "I knew it

57

when I came to that part in your book where Ben fights to get his girl back after she's left him. I thought here is a man who can love all the way, no cop-outs, no ifs, ands or buts. I wanted to make it with him."

"I'm not Ben."

"You made him."

"I'm more than thirty years older than you are. I have a daughter older than you." He doesn't mention the grandchildren.

"I'm older than you'll ever be. In some ways."

The room listened.

"And the girl, you made her too, made her say, 'Find me, find me, make wonderful love to me.'"

The room was still waiting.

"I love you," he said, and saying it it was so.

They swam to the bed together, clothes falling away like leaves, her body fog in the shortfall of light. She turned the clock's face to the wall.

> Rain your gold hair, girl on me
> and shine
> your body . . .

He took off his ring, the Bell family seal, and placed it on her third finger, left hand. Azure field with stag head crest on a silver bar, three bells pendant, the ribboned motto: *Fulget Virtus* – Virtue Shines Forth. "I do," she said and opened like a magician's bouquet. In the sea of her bed, touching him here and there light as a web, foam-born Aphrodite. Time went somewhere else. "Fuck me, Jud, fuck me," she said. "Give me your cock." He was thirty forever again.

In the alley a door creaked open. A dog's shrieking bark as if impaled.

The ceiling crashed into volcanic sound.

"The guy upstairs," she said.

The walls shuddered in a bedlam of drums against an amplified voodoo of fractured music.

"I love your cock in me."

"I love your –"

"Say it," she said. "Say it."

" – cunt."

"Ah good . . . Now give me your juice."

It is morning in Philadelphia, workday light poking the shutters. She lies golden on her side and he knows it is morning somewhere else, too. Suppose she called the hotel in Washington. *I don't understand, you weren't registered, Jud.* Oh, a last minute change. Don't think of her name. No names, please. Names become people. Don't think. For conscience doth . . . He touches the hill of her hip. She doesn't move. He leaves his hand there, warm on warm. She turns, galactic, serenely smiling, waking to him. "Please?" she says, tenting the sheet off with her long leg, hair waved back on the pillow.

"Now?" he whispers through gluey lips, seeing only the back of the clock.

"Please."

He covers her with himself, she still burbling with last night's him, their mouths a mingled impasto of both, the cattle prod day at his back, she open eyed in a timeless ocean.

"I'll shower first," she says. "Then you while I do my hair." She turns out of bed, laughing, "Wha? Watch out where you step." On the floor by the bed plates with steak bones, bread crusts, a half bitten apple rusting, two fallen wine goblets, the near empty Beaujolais bottle. "We had us a party, I'll bet you don't even remember."

"I do now."

"It was between the first and . . . Say, there's instant coffee and French toast in the freezer, if you can get it out. I'll be out in a shake."

And breakfast somewhere else. Scrapple crisping and eggs once over lightly/bacon and eggs with hash browns/deep brewed coffee and thick home-made toast/and the horses out in the fields/maybe a morning moon.

Instant coffee.

He puts on the kettle and his pyjama bottoms, goes to her desk, puts a sheet in her electric machine. The clack of the first letter jars him. He reaches for a pencil.

> Rain your gold hair, girl, on me
> And shine
> Your body on my battles, scars and wounds.

> Your palm is water to my roots
> And all the light I'll ever need
> Is in your sky . . .

And, and . . . The words sit there, only the journey's beginning. A poem has to take you somewhere. Where this one? The shadow knows, but not he yet. The rest waits for him to get there. He puts the sheet in his attaché case.

She comes out of the bathroom towel-turbaned, her haystack dewy where he had lived last night and this morning.

It is morning in Philadelphia, and in the morning you go to work with your girl on your arm. *Natürlich*. Somebody waves to them through a bus window.

"We've been seen," he says, almost with pride.

"Big deal," she says and squeezes his arm under the bubble umbrella keeping her hair from the drizzle.

11

"Two mugs of Rolling Rock and two tuna hoagies," Jud told the waitress at Watson's Pub. Jefferson Hospital hangout. Booths full of interns, lunching beards in white coats, stethoscopes spilling from pockets, talking money – "Two years on Park Avenue and I'll be making a hundred thou." Hypocritic oath. And white-shoed nurses, here and there a very nice antiseptic white calf. "I hope I never get sick," he said.

"Are you going to Les Madonna's Thanksgiving Eve bash?" Billie said, nibbling her hoagie.

"I'd rather not, those post-office standarounds. But Vera rsvp'd and said we were coming. I wish she hadn't."

"Why don't you go alone? Or take me. Then we could be together later."

"You know I can't do that, Billie. All those flocking suburban housewives. They know I'm married and to whom – the people we work with."

"Don't you think they know about us?" Nodding. "You and me lunching almost every day, leaving together nights, coming in in the morning. Wow," she laughed, "they would really freak out if we came into that party together."

He drank from the frosty mug. "Good beer, Rolling Rock, dry, has a bite."

"Well, I'm not going solo. The invite said, 'spouse, or bring a friend,'"

"Which one, Louie Bocca? He knows most of that crowd."

"I know, but not Louie. He'll hassle me when we get home, want to stay, stuff like that."

"Can't you make if plain he's just to escort you?"

"You don't know Luigi like I know Luigi. We get to the door, he'll start climbing all over me. He's a real friend, been real good to me, but he just never quits. I don't need that Italian opera. I hate putting him down. I don't want that garbage." She looked at him, put her hands over his. "I don't want it. You know that. I just wish we could go together, come home together."

"Who, then?"

"There's always Hal Carter. He's an account exec at Manson's. He moved in with me soon after I went to work there. Nothing heavy. It was nice knowing he'd be around, someone who wouldn't get up and leave after –"

"Someone with trains to catch."

She smiled in parenthesis, touched his fingers. "– Who'd be there in the morning. I needed that. It was – there's a word for that –"

"*Gemütlich*."

"Anyhow, he moved out when Dom came along. Whatever it was it's been over a long time ago. He is a nice guy, a good friend. I can handle him."

"Hi, Vera," Pat Mooney said, snaking through the crowd highball in hand. "Hi, Squire, you're late." He took a deep drag on something that looked like a run over cigarette. The sweet acrid smoke made Jud sneeze.

"You've got a lot of catching up," Pat said, eyes bloomy through his aviator's glasses. "The bar's over there, if you can see it. Hail, hail, the gang's all here." He smiled away.

"I don't think he's quite himself," Vera said.

"He's happy," Jud said.

"You should eat something before you start drinking," Vera said. "Just look at that table. All those goodies. Let me fix you a plate."

"What would you like, Vera?" Jud said. "Dubonnet?"

"If they have it, otherwise, well, any wine, so long as it's not sherry."

Turning from the bar a drink in each hand he saw her at the far end of the room in a group, a tall bland young man alongside, smiling mildly surprised as if he'd just gotten up, and would, when he opened his mouth, speak cockney. Yes, he looks like an old friend she can handle, old friend. At the other end of the room Vera sitting alone, platter on lap.

"What's that?" Vera said as he gave her her drink.

"Campari, m'dear, the in drink this year of the Beautiful People in the *New Yorker* ads."

"Do you think I'll like it?"

"It's really quite good, even though they serve it here." He was beginning to want to laugh. "Take a sip through the straw."

"Like a soda," she smiled. "I like it. I wouldn't mind that on occasion."

"I'm delighted, delighted it pleases madame. I'll stock if for you, m'dear."

"Now you're getting silly, Jud, you should have something to eat. Try this," she offered a chopped something canapé.

"Excellent, excellent," some of the laughter broke through. Chug-a-lug. Looking across the room he saw her waving a cigarette like a baton, her face happy loose. (Did Pat give her a joint?) The galoot at her side still with his Stan Laurel look.

"You're getting wound up, Jud," she said. "What's ailing you?" Oh what. "Simmer down."

"Yes'm, Miz Vera," and knew he shouldn't have said it.

61

She stopped in mid chew, a tomahawk look, the severe schoolmarm now. She carefully swallowed what was in her mouth.

"Don't you Miz Vera me," she warned. "You know I don't like it."

"Antebellum amenity," he said. "A form of courtly address in the Old South."

"I've heard that before and I've told you before, we're not the Old South. You patronise me when you say that."

"My mother was a Buchanan from Memphis." He tried to laugh.

A hand on his shoulder. "Hi, Ace," it was Leslie Madonna, spoiled baby face in a blazer.

"My wife, Vera, Les."

"I'm so glad you could come."

"Such a nice party, your wife must be a wonder."

"We had it catered. Of course, Janet made a lot of her specialties, stayed up for weeks. She majored in food preparation. Strawhecker State."

"I thought it was Oral Roberts U, Les," Jud said.

"Wha?"

Vera said, "I think that's a Bible school, Judson."

"Huh?"

"Not to worry, Les, it's all in the mind. A great party, Les."

"Why don't you folks join the rest of the gang? Circulate."

"We'll circulate, Les," Jud winked.

"What does Leslie do at Fairleigh?" said Vera. "I know so little about the people you work with."

"Count your blessings," Jud said. "He's an art director and not a good one. I will say his layouts are neat, like a laid out corpse without too much make-up, and he knows how to crop a photo."

"He seems very pleasant."

"He should wear a bra, A cups at least. Well, shall we circulate, Vera?"

"Hi, Ace," pop-eyed Leeta Krantz elbowed by running interference for her drink.

"You have just seen," Jud said, "the youngest putative female creative director in Philadelphia, maybe the world. She specialises in hyperthyroidism and" . . . You just didn't say "balls" to Miz Vera.

"You should be more tolerant of other people's disabilities," Vera said. Then, "What's that she called you, and Les? It sounded like Ace."

"They think I was in the Lafayette Escadrille."

"But wasn't that World War I? You were . . ."

"They don't know the difference between wars. They just know it was before their time, something on the late late show."

Tad and his kids around him, lots of yeah, yeah and right on Tad. And just behind him, Billie, her face showy, flushed, eclipsing.

"Who is that girl over there? She's very striking, like someone in the movies."

Catherine Deneuve, twenty years younger. I shouldn't have come. This is crazy, psychic Russian roulette.

"Judson?"

"Oh yes, she's new, a writer."

"I think she's looking at you. She made a gesture."

"Well hello there," Billie said carefully, as if speaking to them on the phone, her eyes bloomy as Pat's her smile tacked to her face. "This is Hal Carter."

"My wife, Vera," Jud said, shaking Hal's mackerel hand, knowing at once Hal knew.

"So good to meet you, Mrs Judson," Billie said, spending one word at a time.

"Mrs Bell – call me Vera."

"Oh right, ha ha."

Are you ever stoned my love, Lord God of hosts. Take her home, he wanted to say to Hal. Hal just smiled still looking pleasantly sleepy. Or better still, I wish I could take her. Wouldn't that freak them out. Oh Billie.

Suddenly there was music soaking through the din and the smoke and Pat Mooney taking Billie by the hand saying "Let's dance." He threaded her through backs and shoulders behind him into the foyer, put his arms around her, stood rocking there. They were both laughing stumbling in place, Oh wow. Pat tried to twirl her around. She kicked her shoes off. Jud saw Vera talking to Tad. When he looked back he saw Billie slowly pouring down to the floor, still ha ha – ing, pulling Pat down across her. "I fucked her," Pat yelled. "I fucked her."

Nobody seemed to hear or see them except for the two small pyjama'd Madonnas sitting at the head of the stair.

Smearily pregnant Joan Houlighan, her face a palette of make-up, was saying to Janet Madonna, "You must give me the recipe for your heavenly shrimp roll." Kip Money was saying, "I'll have to dip into capital to build a pool." Black Belt Joe Concerto was flexing his karate hands. Tad was saying to Vera, "We're more than an agency, we're a family." Marge Murphy Concerto was just lace-curtain proud to be at a Main Line party. Leeta Krantz was shouting in her usual tone of voice.

Hal, still smiling sleepily, began walking toward Pat and Billie in a giggling heap on the floor.

12

"Baby, it's sure cold outside," Louie Bocca said coming in with Billie, slapping his reddened hands, smoothing his spot bald head.

Coat off, jacket off, he walked into the kitchenette undoing his tie.

"Hey, hold on there, Louie, don't get too comfortable now, you're not staying, you know. I told you, I just wanted to give you your Christmas present. No hanky-panky, see? Now be a good buddy."

"Aw c'mon bambina, 'tis the season to be jolly. Do you have any grass? I'm in the Mood for Grass," he sang to the tune of I'm in the Mood for Love.

"I'm off that stuff – forever."

"So I hear."

"So what do you hear?"

"The Madonna party. Hal took you."

"I should have known."

"It's a small world, bambina."

"Luigi, the eyes and ears of the world. Good old Hal, he always was a yenta. I told him to keep his mouth shut. Lookit, Luigi, I have a date. I've got to wash, change." She looked at her watch.

"Who?"

She didn't answer.

"Someone I know?"

"You know everybody, Luigi."

He began scratching his palm. "Lessee . . . Gil-Hal-Harvey-JohnJohn-Pat?" – not that painter creep Aaron Mosque? – the great three-day shack-up when nobody knew where to find her. "I got it. From the love light in your eyes, Billie girl, I'd say Lucky's in town. Right?"

"Wrong. You just struck out."

"Who?"

"None of your business. For Chrissake, Louie, come off it."

"Okay, okay." Ease off, Luigi, don't get the bambina too mad. There's always next time. "At least let's have a drink, auld lang syne and all that." He sang "Should auld acquaintance be forgot."

"Okay, paisan, just one. You get the friggen cubes out." She went into the bathroom. He opened the refrigerator. Two splits of champagne, Piper-Heidsieck, yet. Caviar, the real thing, herring titbits in wine sauce, Camembert. Well, fan mah fanny. He did a little black boy shuffle, finger twirling above his head, fictive transistor to ear.

On her desk a small Christmas tree festooned with seashells, snail shells, winking globes. Under it presents wrapped in carpety patterned papers, beribboned with tags. Over her bed a mistletoe hung from the ceiling. Joy to the world, Luigi hummed to himself, the King has Come. Who the mother who? He scratched his crotch.

Checking the tags on the presents he picked up a small oblong box. To Jud, with *all* my love. Ever your Billie. Here we go again. She came out of the bathroom.

"Hey, that's not yours. Put it down, Louie." He still held it. she took it from him. "Wait'll you see what I got you, old buddy." She reached for a flat package. "I hope you like it." She pecked his cheek, raised her glass, "Merry Christmas." For Louie – Thanks for everything, it said on the tag. He took a drink.

"So you've been balling the old dude."

"It's my life, Luigi."

"I told you, Billie girl, when we planned the Fairleigh caper, it's a fresh start, the big time, don't screw up – pun intended. Don't ball the first guy you meet on the job. Don't ball any guy on the job. You agreed."

"Just you, Louie, right?"

"I've always been there when you needed me."

She flashed – "Which hasn't been often, has it? Not that way."

"No, just to pick up the pieces."

"I'm sorry. I don't like putting you down."

He was itching again. He raked his palm with his nails. "Is he *good?*" he asked through clenching teeth.

She didn't answer.

"As good as Harvey, champ of the bedsprings?"

Her eyes sparked. "Who introduced me to Harvey, Louie? Who said I'd go ape over this guy? Who always wants a blow-by-blow after my dates? This kinky thing. Turns you on, right?"

"You've told me before."

"Only because you bugged me out of my mind. Now lookit . . ."

"Maybe some of it's my fault. Waiting between the acts. A yo-yo. Goddammit, Billie, of all people, Pat, okay, he's young, he's a swinger. But the old dude."

He snickered. "Our very own English squire. All that Anglophile shtik – Anderson shirtings from England, my deah, Irish tweed elbow-patch jackets . . ."

"Rave on."

". . . And those brogues from Bond Street, bespoke, yet. Tallyho-ho."

"On him it looks good, gumbah."

"He's from another world, Billie. He's old enough to be your father."

"He's younger than we are, Luigi, we were born old."

"What a laugh. To think how I coached you."

65

"I'm grateful for that."

"Gave you stuff from my reel." He laughed harshly. "Ads from my book. Told you to put down two years of college."

"Now let's not do Pagliacci."

"I knew the poetry'd hook him. The old dude. I still can't believe it."

"He's very special Luigi."

"And very married."

"He doesn't do it with her."

"You've got to be kidding. That's every married man's line."

"Everybody's married to someone or something. You to your mother in Camden."

"That could change, if –"

"No ifs, please, Luigi, not tonight."

No, not tonight. She was somewhere else. Again. He knew the signs.

"You look different," he said, "really happy."

"I am, Luigi."

"When's he coming?"

She looked at her watch. "Any minute now. He's been in New York checking interlocks, some new Army commercials."

"Well, I guess I'd better be going."

"Hey, you haven't opened your present." He still held it in his hand.

"I didn't get you one," he said.

"That's okay. Buy me a lunch some time. You have never yet picked up the tab." She laughed generously.

He looked at her child happy face, her abounding smile. Golden generous Billie.

"What a shmuck I've been."

"Go on, open it."

He sat down at the café table, undid the ribbon and wrappings. In the whispery tissue a gold wristwatch, elegant, thin, from Caldwell's.

"You're too much," he said.

"To old friends," she finished her drink.

He put on his tie, his coat.

"Take care, bambina."

"I will, Luigi. "

At the door he turned.

"You can destroy that man," he said.

"I know," she answered.

Jud ruddy, Jud glowing, Jud in his Russian fur hat and British warm, travelling the day to this door, at last here. Jud laden with packages.

"Hello, sweetheart," she said, kissing him. "You must be Santa Claus. Here, let me take these."

"*Bitte*," he said, reaching into the Bloomingdale's shopping bag.

66

"These need chilling."

"Oh wow," she said from the kitchenette undoing the wrappings. "More champagne. Dom Perignon – I priced that at the store – out of sight. We'll be floating in bubbles," she laughed. "And caviar from Iran. You must be the last of the big time spenders."

"It's our Christmas," he said.

She brought their drinks to the table. "For starters," she said. "Champagne later and things. How did it go in New York?" A domestic note. How were things at the office today, dear?

"Pretty well, we had to re-mix one spot. You know the producers, they really lay on the effects. But New York at this time of the year, the whole city's charged up. Everything sparkles, everyone's high. Studio parties, office parties, the whole place is a party."

"Wouldn't it be great to spend a weekend in New York, take in a show, eat at the great places? Jud, will we some day?" He nodded. "The Plaza," he said, "or the Algonquin."

Her hair in a snoody bun, they sat sipping and smiling. The green little tree lit up, the Tiffany lamp, the fat candles. Their Christmas the night before family Christmas Eve for both. He put his hand over hers. "Purr, purr" she said.

"You look content as a cat."

"I am when you're here. Honey" she said getting up, "I can't wait to give you your presents. I hope you like them. It wasn't easy shopping for the man who has everything."

"This calls for champagne," he said. They finished their drinks. She brought in the splits and two glasses.

"Not in those," he said and went to the Bloomingdale's bag, shucking the wrappings from two long stemmed goblets. "These were made for champagne. Crystal," he flicked one, it rang, "from Sweden."

"They're beautiful, Jud. Just for us. No one else will ever drink from them. You pop the corks." She laughed like a child when they hit the ceiling. "Merry Christmas," they said together.

She put three boxes down on his side of the table, a large one, a smaller, a small, lit a Parliament, sipped her champagne. "Beautiful bubbly, I love it. Well, open them, Honey."

"I think I know what's in the small one," puffing his pipe. "I'll open the big one first." A blue velour robe with a monk's hood, scuffs to match.

"Now you won't have to wrap in a towel when we have morning coffee. Try it on."

"Héloïse and Abélard," he said, the robe around him, the hood over his head.

"Who?"

"Lovers, a long time ago,"

"Tell me about them."

"Some other time, not now. Not a good Christmas story."

"Sad?"

67

"Very. Thank you, it's lovely."

"It's partly a present for me. I want something of you here all the time, something you've worn, that's been close to your body, that's you when you're not here. You understand?"

He opened the robe and folded her in it. Frankincense, myrrh, thermal murmurs, blessing of lips, the epiphanies of her under the hood.

The second box, full of kanøn, his unguents – cologne, after shave lotion, soap-on-a-rope, talc. "I love that scent on you," she said. "It mixes with yours. Now you won't have to shlep. them from home."

"Indian giver," he said and opened the smallest package. "A Dunhill," fondling the briar, "my favourite pipe," Cornucopia Billie.

"At least I can take this with me," he said smiling.

"Something of mine in your mouth. I like that." She smiled, he thought, wistfully.

"I never said thanks for the glasses," she said, a child who's been given something to wear for Christmas. No toys?

Should he tease?

"I think you're fishing," he said on a note of promise.

She laughed, a child caught out in its thoughts.

"Only a stocking stuffer," he said, and went to the Bloomingdale's bag. He put two packages down before her and reached into his pocket, placing a tiny cube on top.

"Which one should I open first?" she asked.

"I'd start at the bottom."

She undid the wrappings. Two record albums – Mozart's nineteenth and twenty-first piano concertos played by Geza Andor. She tilted her head, her look accepting the accolade.

"It was the theme music for Elvira Madigan, the most poetic film I've ever seen."

"I missed it," she said, but I think I heard it on radio, the music, I mean. They played it a lot at the time. Thank you, Jud, for knowing I'd like it. Let's put it on."

"Later," he said, "when we can listen."

She opened the second package – the Collected Poems of Dylan Thomas.

"I think you'll get a lot out of him, the things he makes his words do."

She gave him that look again.

She picked up the cube. "I think I know what this is. Just as you knew."

She undid the gold cord, looked at the small box and at him, took a deep sighing breath, removed the lid. A drop of rain in her eyes.

"Take it out," he said.

"Oh Jud."

"It's an antique Victorian lover's ring. I looked for weeks, Billie, (my love) not a one in all Philadelphia. I knew I'd find it today in New York."

She looked at the two gold hands clasped like a crown, fingers entwined.

"I saw one in England once. A small shop in London. Here, let me show you," he said, taking the ring. He drew the hands apart gently, revealing a locket. He opened the silver cover – on the back their names engraved, laurelled, and the date she had told him she loved him. "Jud – Billie."

She took the ring from him, clasping, unclasping the hands. "I've never seen anything like it, it's like something alive."

She looked at him as if the world were only beginning. She handed the ring to him holding her left hand out. He slipped it on, third finger, left hand.

"It fits," she said, "perfectly. How did you know my size?"

"My pinkie ring fits you."

"Now I won't have to give your ring back in the morning."

"Billie, Billie," he said.

"My husband," she answered.

They took each other's hands and touched lips lightly. She pulled softly away. "Now let's feast," she said.

She took the gifts from the table, stroked the ring on her lips.

"Pop the cork," she said bringing in the Dom Perignon. "Stocking stuffer."

"Just call me Old Nick."

Caviar on the table, goodies in jars, their corner of Paris. "One more thing," he said going again to the Bloomingdale's bag, coming back with a tin of biscuits.

"From Jacob's Factory," he said, "in Dublin, where they caught De Valera on the roof."

"What was he doing, shoplifting?"

"Something like that," he laughed. "He led an uprising against the British in nineteen-sixteen."

"You're so smart," she said and kissed him.

He laughed again. "My great-grandmother on one of my sides was descended from Irish kings."

Pop. The cork hit the shutters.

"Isn't everybody?" she said.

A door creaked in the alley. The impaled dog screamed. They almost didn't hear it.

"I hope that guy with the drums . . ." He pointed upstairs.

"Who cares." She went to the stereo and Mozart came into the room with his piano.

"This is the best Christmas I've ever had," she said, out sparkling the wine.

They drank the last of the foamy. She turned all the lights out except those on the tree. She rolled the bedspread back. "Look," she said at the mistletoe over the bed.

"I don't need a reminder," he said.

They slipped into each other's tide, riding it into sleep.

13

"Just one," she was saying. "One drink, it's on your way home, Stauffer's, it's right at the station."

He could see Billy Penn through his office window on top of his yellow clock on City Hall in the January night. Friday, not one of their nights. Monday, Wednesday, Thursday he had not been home.

"I've got to get home tonight, Billie, and I've still some work to clean up." He shut his eyes.

"I know," she said, "but I want you to meet her. Karla's my best friend – after you. I don't see her much anymore – she's into this heavy thing with this girl – I told you."

He put down his pencil.

"Please."

"Just one," he said.

"Oh great. We'll be there." Her lips and tongue said I love you.

She was trim, a good restrained body, her face a mask a lewd blankness. Billie bubbled, "It's time you two met." She signalled an apron. "What are you having?"

"A Beefeater Gibson – very dry."

"So you're Jud," Karla said.

"Call me Ishmael." Here I go again. *Le roi s'amuse.*

"Wha?" Billie said.

A pause. Karla said, "You're not Jewish?"

"My great-grandfather was a Melville out of New Bedford."

Karla shrugged.

"Sorry about that," Jud said. "It's the first line of Moby Dick. I play private games with myself. A bad habit."

"That's not what Billie tells me."

They laughed, breaking the ice. Billie was smiling again.

"The ring you gave Billie," Karla said touching her hand, a gold chain ring on her own forefinger. "It's very unusual."

"For a very unusual girl," he said.

"She is. I hope you really believe that."

"I love it, I love it," Billie said. "Keep talking, gang. But excuse please, I've got to . . ."

"Take a leak," Karla said.

Billie smiled that's Karla for you, leaving the table, looking back once.

"Do us again," he said to the apron.

Karla shook out a slim brown cigarette from the pack. He lit her. Two jets of smoke from her nostrils swirling her lacquered face.

"I know Billie, we roomed together for a while, our first jobs, the first apartment for both of us."

"So?"

"So I'm saying, I've seen her hurt. There were those who didn't count – most of them. Then the one man she really flipped over before you."

"Lucky."

She nodded. "She was hurting until you came along. I wouldn't want that to happen again. He was married, too."

Something paternal in that, a father checking a suitor's intentions.

"I think this is different."

"I never met a man who was."

"Or a woman?" She looked at the chain ring on her finger and took a drink.

"You think men have cornered the market on hurt?"

Her eyes were suddenly real through the mask. "Billie – she would have this thing about men. She has so much to give," she went on, "and she's gotten so little back – from them."

"To love is the ability to return it. May I tell you a poem? It's by a Scandinavian poet, Norwegian I think, Gunner Ekelöf . . ."

> To suffer is difficult
> To suffer without loving is difficult
> To love without suffering is impossible
> To love is difficult.

"He's been there," she said, really looking at him now.

"I don't know that I should have to say it, to anyone but her, but I guess you want to hear it from me. I love Billie, Karla."

"You give me good vibes," she said. "She is happier than I've ever seen her."

And Billie was back and Jud was saying, "I've got to make tracks, ladies."

Halfway to the door he felt her behind him, turned and she seemed to be flying to him on scarves spun from her eyes.

"Oh Honey, I'm so glad you came. You've made me so happy. You know what Karla just said? If she'd met you first she might have gone straight."

"I guess she's given us her blessing."

She kissed him. " Monday?"

Leaving the coat room he looked back. Their faces were close, Karla's hand over Billie's, two girls at a school reunion, laughing talking away.

Karla/Billie.
City of Otherly Love.
Who knows?
The Shadow do.

14

The elevator doors on the copy floor slid open as the receptionist called out to his back – " Jud, there's a call for you. Your daughter, she's downstairs in the lobby."

"I'll take it," he said, raising eyebrows at Billie.

She heard him say, "I'd love to, Dulcie. Yes, it has been a while. I wish you'd called earlier. I understand, but I've got a lunch date – no not a client – someone I work with here." Billie was making motions – you go ahead, I'll eat by myself. He shook his head. Billie came closer. "Why don't we take her with us?" she whispered. His eyebrows went up again. "I'll be right down," he said.

"My spur of the moment kid. She's been shopping in town and thought she might catch me for lunch."

"I'd like to meet her," Billie said.

"She's very perceptive. Her antennae will crackle the minute she sees us."

"Like father, like daughter."

"Dulcie shopping is an awesome sight to behold. Blitz warfare," he said in the elevator. "She does have excellent taste, goes like a guided missile straight to the most expensive racks *before* seeing the price tags. Always did, since she was a teen. Used to drive Vera wild. Endless battles of the budget. She's probably overspent – again – and will put the touch on good old Dad, her personal branch of the World Bank."

"A little bit spoiled by her father?"

"It isn't as simple as that. Vera believed the answers to rearing a child were to be found on the back of a Kellogg's Corn Flakes box. That's cruel and unfair; I shouldn't have said that."

Chic, petite Dulcie said "Hi Dads" and kissed him.

"Meet Billie Miller," he said.

Dulcie wanted to say oh wow but didn't, glancing from Billie to him with a well well what do we have here? look. Jud wanted to say, I told you so. Dulcie said, "I just wanted to say hello, took a chance. Don't let me . . ."

Billie said, "Why don't you join us?"

"You can leave your packages here," Jud said, stacking them behind the receptionist's desk.

Outside a razor wind slicing through St James Alley, Dulcie huddled in fur on one arm, Billie processional on the other. "I love winter," he said, "keeps you inside yourself."

"California, here I come," Dulcie said. "What a town, I looked all morning for something to wear to a party Bob's boss is giving. Would you believe nothing, not a thing, until finally, finally something I wouldn't have to die to be seen in."

"It's not all that bad," Billie said sisterly, "you have to know where to look."

"Have you ever looked at the society columns?" Dulcie said, leaning across Jud to Billie. "They all look as if they came in drag. I mean the men and women."

"Off the face cement bags and open-toed army shoes." Jud said.

"Hey Dad, that's neat."

"Natch," Billie said.

"They ought to rename this town," Dulcie said, her breath frosting, "Dowdyville, U.S.A. Absolutely no style."

"That's my girl," Jud said. "She always knew class from classy."

Coming into Watson's noon gabble she said, "This is a real cool place. Do you come here often?"

"Just about every day. It's handy."

"Oh not every day, Jud. We go other places, too, Dulcie – South China, Luigi's, Spats." Her voice hummed with connections.

Dulcie registered that and Billie's arm still snugging his. "You're looking great, Dad," she said.

"I think there's a table way in the back," he said looking around for the hostess.

"Hey gang, let's have a drink," Billie said as they were seated. "This is an occasion."

"Greatsville," Dulcie said. "I'll have . . ."

"I didn't think you drank, Dulcie, except for wine at dinner. And" (don't be stuffy) "that isn't drinking."

"I don't *drink*, Dad, but I do have a cocktail once in a while. You know, entertaining Bob's friends – I mean the corporate types. They can drink all *they* want to, right? give you a little squeeze in the kitchen, 'Bob's really moving up, you must be a great help,' while their wives are checking their hairdos and Playtex girdles. If you don't drink at all they think you're in AA. So you drink one, no more than two – *ever*. I'll have a Pink Lady."

Cocking her head, turning with birdy looks, "This is very nice, Dad – just like General Hospital – all these young doctors – there's one who looks just like Ben Casey. If I weren't an old married woman –"

An old married woman, not yet six years, and already, even if jest, phantoms of otherwhere ticklings. The fairy tale dreams of forever – what happens to them? There was that letter from college. "I just met the most wonderful guy. I didn't think they made them like that any more. Bob's a fraternity man but not a fraternity animal like all the others. Our first date we just had a Coke and walked and talked. He's so gentle, he has such good *manners*. You'll like him. Oh Dad . . ." Her fastidiousness had always been more than cosmetic, a kind of morality. He had counted on that to get her through the beer-swilling bashes. Always on the phone, even now and she a mother, her voice had a far off tremolo of childhood, and always seeing her again he was surprised to find her grown up in a sudden zoom lens of time abridging the years. He remembered a poem he had written after the wedding, a Family Wedding Portrait. Through the chatty buzz of their voices, Billie's and her's – they could be sorority sisters – the lines came to him now like an old dog wagging its tail . . .

> Glaze this moment grinful
> With bride and groom, the flash
> Lighting old snapshots in a lost album.
> Having not had her much while growing
> In and out of a house not so much home
> As other places – schools –
> A place to dance in. Now there cannot be
> The catching up – all her tomorrows earmarked –
> That talk we were always going to have
> And didn't.

Turning back to their frequencies he heard Dulcie saying "– that is a super ring."

He and Billie spoke the same moment, he to head Billie off – for God's sake, don't open it – she saying, "It's a Victorian lover's ring – a friend –"

And he, jamming the air with historical static – "An old Gaelic tradition. Goes back to Ireland, Claddagh, a fishing village in Galway . . . Used as a marriage ring . . . Even older than that – Roman times – the Middle Ages."

And Dulcie was nodding, "Uhuh, uhuh," fixed like a child living a bedtime story, making it what she wished, what it was. "That's really neat. I love that kind of stuff," ardent for more, more of the story still there in Billie's eyes.

He sits in a thunder of time, his two worlds spinning close, coalescing, his life being lived outside him, in other hands, his secret breached yet somehow sweet in the sharing. Billie and Dulcie here and now at the same table in immediate alliance, like family, and co-conspiracy – Vera displaced, the mother adversary. This is Dulcie now but always the sum of Dulcies then . . . Dulcie vs Vera in the mother-daughter battle of the century. A mandatory eight count for the knockdowns and go to a neutral corner. Jud Bell, reluctant referee and unwilling judge, winner take nothing . . .

"Please don't be hurt." Dulcie wrote her first freshman semester at college, the letter addressed to his office, "but I'm happier here than I've ever been at home. I know how much you wanted me to go to Bryn Mawr, but that was too close to home . . . only twenty minutes away from her and her Rules!" Yes, daughter, I know Vera's Rules of

76

Order . . . "There are rules here and most of them make sense when you think about it. But she had a *Rule* for every second of the day. There was only one way – her way. When I was a little kid and wanted to help with the dishes it was always wipe this side first, then the other side and place it down here just so. What the hell difference did it make which side you wiped first?" . . . Maybe Vera needed her rules to keep from flying apart, this dailyness not what she'd dreamed, a novelist husband turned adman provider, a child with a clock of her own, thinking somehow it was her fault and this the only way she knew how to contain it . . . "The point was to get the damn dishes done. And when I did it *my* way, she told me to leave *her* kitchen. It was *my* kitchen, too. And when I refused to leave . . ." Yes, daughter, you stood there in the doorway like Horatius at the bridge, your face flaming . . ." she slapped me and pushed me out. and then you were there holding me . . ." I thought your sobs would break you in pieces and me as well . . ."And she was saying to you in that white calm way of hers – 'Are you going to side with her again?" . . . J. Bell, eternal domestic cop . . . "And that last night before I left for college and we were sitting down to dinner, she asked me if I had washed my hands! My God, I was seventeen years old and she was still asking me for the thousand-millionth time if I had washed my hands! And she'd ask *you* too if *you* had washed your hands. Dad, I just don't understand how you've stood for this craziness so long. Why you ever married her in the first place . . ." In the first place, daughter, in the first place she wasn't like that. In the beginning, between a man and a woman, you become for a while what the other one wants you to be, Plato's other self. That is love, being born again in the other. You start your journey together to some Promised Land not knowing you have just left it. And step by step away you become what you are, perhaps what you always were unrevealed, and not what someone else wanted you to be. Later you become each other's history. Just look in any family's medicine cabinet . . . "Daddy, I really hate to ask so soon but I am really short of money. I really need some new clothes, a new tennis sweater, at least, and a few other little things. If you could send me $50 I promise not to ask for more until next term. Daddy, I really hate to stick a request for money in this letter and I know it looks horrible, but I really love you and miss you . . ."

As from sleep he was hearing their voices again, Dulcie saying, "Are you doing much riding, Dad?"

"The usual, weekends. I think I'll hilltop the hunt tomorrow, they're meeting a short hack away. I'd love to ride with the field but Roman's not up to it. It takes daily work for that. You know. Weekends aren't enough. Now if I had me a groom to keep him up. Say," archly, "an Irish girl groom – she could sleep in the barn . . ."

"Is that what they call a roll in the hay in your set, Mr Bell?" Billie said.

"Mother wouldn't like it," trilled Dulcie.

"No, Mother wouldn't," said Billie.

". . . He has heart, but it wouldn't be fair. He could pull a tendon, come up lame, not time a fence just right."

"Isn't that dangerous?" Billie asked. "All that jumping high fences and things? I saw an English movie once."

"The height of some kinds of pleasure are in direct proportion to their risk. Like fox hunting."

"What are some of the other kinds?" Billie's tongue touched her lips.

"Ah, I'll tell you about them sometime."

"Be sure to do that."

"Dulcie hunted with Pony Club, mostly drag hunts."

"Regular hunts too, Dad."

He nodded. "We used to ride a lot together, Dulcie and I. She was becoming a very respectable horsewoman. Natural seat, good hands."

"Those were great times, Dad, just the two of us hacking around."

"Remember your strawberry roan?"

"Romeo," Dulcie said, "he was a doll."

"A great little jumper. He could take a four-railer. Went over a fence like a feather. You won your first blue on him. Dulcie loved him until she met Bob."

"My husband. Would you believe, he's allergic to horses?"

"Taradiddle, piffle and fol-de-rol, as W.C. Fields might say. First time out, you told me, you took him riding at college, the horse ran away with him."

Dulcie's laugh rang. "Poor Bob, he would get a barn rat. Galloped him back two miles to the stable, Bob bouncing all over the place, I thought he'd be thrown. He couldn't stand being put down by a horse – and in front of a girl. He's got to be tops whatever he does. He's a good golfer, won the club championship last year, and a really smooth skier. We're going to Vail next year." She crossed her fingers. "If he gets that big raise." A private smile. "He will."

A private glitter in Billie's eyes. "Hey gang, you know, I think I'm going to take up riding."

A cat's cradle of eyes looped with wishes, from Billie to Jud to Dulcie.

Jud sees her dream. She says, "Then maybe sometime we can . . ." Already she's riding with Jud on a woodland trail, along meadows and streams, side by side, they come home to a fire . . .

"Groovy," says Dulcie.

"Kaff, kaff, harrumph, as Major Hoople might say," says Jud. "Riding is a skill best learned like anything else when very young and the bones are formed to the game."

"I'm game," Billie says.

"You'll need a good teacher."

She looks at him, *Well?*

He shakes his head. "And stabilised horses. Not some guy with a string of overworked underfed nags who clucks you around the ring."

"What about Nancy Marshall, Dad?" She was my teacher. She's great and she's just down the road."

Billie just down the road. He's in a play that somebody else is directing.

"Nan doesn't give lessons at night – no indoor ring. It would have to be weekends."

"That's the idea," Billie says almost under her breath.

"And she may be booked up."

"How can I reach her? You have her number?"

"I'd better talk to her first. Maybe drop over after the hunt tomorrow or Sunday."

"Say, Dad, after the lesson, you can show Billie the farm."

When are you going to stop hating your mother, Dulcie?

Billie takes Dulcie into her smile.

Jud raises his hand. "Check, please."

15

"A very cosy little hunt," Jud said coming in from the barn with Blitz bumping him, clubbing his legs with his tail. "Stayed with it all of the way. Nothing spectacular. No really long points. One, oh, maybe five miles – about ten as hounds ran. A bit of moiling about the bog as it were, some sticky going there for a while, a trappy gully or two, the usual larking about in the back, some damn suburbanite woman plumping around on a red-ribbon-tailed mare kicking the sky – the Master should rule those kickers out of the field – but on the whole very cockles-of-the-heart-warming stuff. Sorry you weren't there." He put his crop and canteen on the mantel, the good feel of lived with leather. "These little hunting flasks don't hold enough brandy," he said to himself.

"You know I can't hear you from two rooms away," Vera called almost shouting, her voice bawling nearer as on a balloon. Caw, caw, crows in the corn. "You start talking the minute you come in, flooding the house with words, not bothering to find out if I'm there or what I'm doing. I'm not a servant, you know. All I know is you're sounding like Churchill again. You do every time you get near the hunt. Probably ran into Morey with his usual tailgate hamper of bottled goodies out there in Pimm's woods. Don't think I don't know. I can tell by your voice."

Very perceptive m'dear. But not W. Churchill. No, not the PM, though I most admired him. Yus. Blenheim Park, K.G., and all that. Parliamentary pomp and circumstance. That's when I'm in me oratorical mode. More like the Duke of Beaufort, this, I'd say, with a dash, possibly, of old Jorrocks. Or Sir Laurence O doing his thing from minus to Upper U.

She was at the door of the living room. "Of course I'd like to hear about the hunt – but everything in its time. You should have the courtesy to wait until I'm ready to sit down with you. You've disrupted my schedule. I thought you'd be home for lunch. I'm about to put the roast in the oven for *dinner*. A gentleman . . ."

"Sorry m'dear. Got carried away. Feeling my oats." Well a bit of the barleycorn.

She narrowed her eyes at "m'dear." Well, it isn't like saying Miz Vera. A borderline case at best. Very moot. How would the House of Lords rule on that, eh Blitzer?

"Just look at those muddy boots." He looked. Ah, yes, Trimble's swamp. She shook her head, folded her work strung hands (so toil worn for me, Mother Machree) containing her further reproval.

Weekends above all should be harmonious times, almost the only times she had with him anymore. She let go of a sigh. "Why don't you change your clothes, Jud, and . . ." Wash up? "I'll join you in twenty minutes or so." She looked at the bell jar clock on the mantel. "Let's say half an hour." On the stroke of, no more, no less. He looked at his watch. "In a bit," he said, a clench in his jaw. "At least one day in the week I will not be pushed." He still wanted the feel of the hunt and the horse and the hills on him, not drifting away, leather on calf, sweatshirts of his coat smelling, oh yes, of Roman's salt sweat.

"And you may pour me a glass of wine when you fix your drink," she said, proposing conciliation before it was needed too late. "Even though it's not evening yet." A large concession, he'd know, in the interest of peaceful companionship. She looked into the air as if trying to find someone.

He said, "Right."

"I'd like to hear about the hunt." Her hand spreading, then dropped. She was almost out of the room when she said, "An early fire would be nice." Then, with a mourning smile and slightest wave of her hand, "*A bientôt.*"

Always the Master of Arts. When he met her mother she'd said, "It's so nice you and Vera have so much in common – books, music. I understand you have your M.A. too." Poor, dear *belle-maman* Mrs Brooke, she thought marriages were made in a kind of graduate school heaven. But if Shakespeare were *her* son-in-law he'd have to help with the dishes. At least set the table.

At the sideboard he poured a rainsoft Madeira into one of the carved crystal goblets his great-grandmother had left him, and filled the wide bell of a snifter halfway to the top with an Armagnac for himself. Now that's a stirrup cup. He drank some of it off and retopped it. Ah, much better that, already checking the hounds and the hills, the corn stubble fields from moving away, now caught, held by this softly clanging bronzed liquor like the sound of a horn, held in an English meadow. He swirled his glass. Cosmic stuff, this, keeps time in its place.

He raised the damper, put a spill to the laid fire, touching the fat pine kindling to crackles. Half-humming, half-singing, he conducted with his pipe the cantering chorus of the old hunting song –

'Twas the sound of his horn brought me from my
bed,
And the cry of his hounds which he oftimes led,
For – Peel's "View halloo!" would awaken the dead,
Or the fox from his lair in the morning.

"Stirring good doggerel, dog," he said to Blitz at his feet by the fire. "The best of all it's art, like Kipling. Has its place. Damn the mortarboard Mafia, cultural commissars. What?" Blitz agreed with his ochre eyes. Anything you say, pal. With you to the end. And seconded the motion with a gavel thump of his tail. There's a friend. Now a horse – more a sporting associate.

"Too bad you can't join me in a drop of the good creative. That's what the Puritans called it, you know. That's right, the Puritans – Pilgrim Fathers. Not all that grim, eh? In the service of God, of course. Right there in the Scriptures. A little wine, etcetera. You read about all those fish heads shoved into the mounds to grow corn, three to a blister pack in the local super – 10¢ off with a coupon. And you read all about Miles Standish, who never read anything but the Racing Form. And that Priscilla, the pinup of Plymouth. And John Alden, Miles's pr man. But you've never read, now have you? anything about where the good creative came from. I'll tell you Blitzer, they weren't carrying seed and mattocks and adzes and Coleman lanterns. You know what, Blitz, they must've been carrying in that Mayflower? They were carrying hooch – the good creative. That's why they had nothing to eat that first winter. Would have starved if not for those Injuns from Vitagraph Studios in their Model Ts loaded with all those A & P self-basting turkeys with pop-up thermometers, and Pepperidge Farm stuffing – maybe a house brand – and stacks of Mrs Smith's frozen, home-made, beltline punkin' pies. But at least they wouldn't have frozen to death. Drink first, eat later, that was their motto. Yus."

"Oh the fire smells good," Vera said coming in, "like apple cider."

"There's some apple wood in with the oak. That old tree that came down in the storm three years ago."

Sitting down in the chair opposite his, "Well now," she said, raising her glass bravely, "tell me about the hunt."

"I thought you'd never ask," he said, getting up glass in hand. "May I tell it my way, please, without interruptions for commercials?" She looked into her fire-winking wine closing her eyes, then at the glass in his hand – it was going to be like that – and nodded. She also looked at the clock.

He took a sip of the old bronze music, moved to the sideboard. She put her Madeira down and clutched once the arms of her chair. He slid a dollop of the old Château Dauphin – just twenty thousand bell-bottomed green bottles a year, from father to son, from father to son, old spiny vineyards, he'd been there, special arrangement, shipped through Marseilles, an Adolphe Menjou type of a fella – into his thin shell of a bell. A small château, a circle just out of the cognac heart's bull's eye. Hawked.

Walked up and down.

Blitz, his paws twitching in dream.

The fire, now in full command, spearing the room.

"They found in Mallory's cornfield – three furlongs, I'd judge, six perches, two rods away from the willow, weeping indeed into the pond – Charles James, a red shaggy dog fox, looking for his lady to love and cherish. Mebbe a cottontail, but no, soft Decembers make for early vulpine romance.

"Hounds opened forthwith loud and merrily."

She sipped her Madeira. Oh God, he is off and running in the eighteenth century again. And looked at the fire thrusting its fingers up and around the logs in a red/blue embrace.

"Foive times," (Lord save us, now he's in County Cork with the Scarteen Hounds) he raised his glass bell, "that rascal Reynard circled the corn field as if he were leading a July 4 parade. Never seen anythin' loike it in all me born days" (pure Sean O'Casey this with a touch of John Masefield, foine poem, Reynard the Fox, Yus.). "Foive times, 'ounds boilin' behind, givin' tongue, the field flyin' around as if they were on a merry-go-round. Ah, now but where's the brass ring? Where bluidy indeed?"

In the Abbey Theatre, no doubt, Vera said to herself.

"I'll tell you, m'dear – he was gone away, across Pikeland Road, straight up Wilkins' hill where a great regal buck, an eight-pointer, and his starlet doe were auditing the sport, hounds and field clattering after. He slithered right past them into the thicket behind, hoping to fox the hounds onto their line, but they weren't foxed, not 'em, them Penn-Marydel Fox 'ounds, with their great nose and cry. (Hounds belling the valley, I think, W. Shakespeare said. What's the play?). They didn't babble or riot not once, good hounds, and kept to their business, passed the stag and his Lana Turner companion without turning a tail. But he knew his business too, Charles James . . ."

Vera lowered her head. Mother was right: "He's charming and very mannerly, almost courtly. But I wonder if he is quite stable. Not at all like your Father. Poetry's fine in its place, but it doesn't pay the gas bills, you know. Your Father read Tennyson to me when we were courting. He put on a clean white shirt every day with just the merest hint of starch. Kept the same job for thirty-seven years, never losing a day. As to your intended, one minute he's so serious, speaking like one of my professors at the State Normal School – or even a poet – and the next like someone in vaudeville. Your Father likes him, and dear, it's not that I *dis*like him, but his moods shift so suddenly. One moment he's reciting in ancient Greek the opening lines of the Iliad, and the very next he is Groucho Marx. He's so hard to keep up with. I do hope he has a practical streak. Your Father, I suspect is rather taken by him. Now I know you won't misunderstand me – your Father's a very fine man – but he always was drawn, how shall I say? to the raffish. That man who did something at the race track, something to do with betting, remember? Signalled someone in the stands, I believe. Quite a sporty fellow with some education. Two years at Yale, I believe, or so he said. Brought your Father those special cigars and something he called private stock during Prohibition. And flowers for me. He loved to hear me play the piano and sing. Listened for hours. I think he took a fancy . . . I was much younger then."

". . . that we'd have to check at that jungle of vines and bramble –

you know that place, we always go round – or be torn apart by thorns with nothing but bog on the other side. So huntsman lifted the hounds (yes, now, that's very Churchillian) and cast and it was down the hill again, across Pigeon Creek and we were in Trimble's swamp . . ."

"You sound as if you were right up with the field, not hill topping."

"Ah, well, yes, I wanted to get a bit closer than that would allow and not look the freeloader. So I paid the cap fee. Don't look at me like that. I didn't push Roman, you know I wouldn't do that. We stayed in the back, took it easy. Some runs and some rests. A few fairly long checks. I paced him. He had a good time. You should have seen him. All joggy and tippity toes. Well, well, I haven't done this for a while. He's fine. Oh, knows he's been out. But he's fine. I gave him a good rubdown. He's in his stall munching away and telling Casey all about it . . .

"Well, we lost fox number one, gone to ground, clever varmint, but it wasn't too long before another was drawn. There always are some in the swamp. Hounds took his line and we were off and away over Judge Tullidge's pastures, then across the Indian Camp and, wouldn't you know it, he doubled back to the swamp. But this time hounds worked him through those thick bogs and woods, over Doc Hoffacker's meadows, right through Nate Collum's place and the Wallraven farm. Hounds handily cleared the guard wires on the telephone swath. I took Roman around, just a hand gallop and caught up where they checked at the highway. Then they flew in the open again, and we with them, across Jake Stillwagon's farm, over the rails at Cornett's, across Tom Falkner's corn stubble, over Colonel Lightbody's fields past that damned new subdivision – they'll soon be all over the place – right up to the old railroad embankment where we checked. Hounds feathered toward Drummer's Hill but Charles James the Second was gone. Not a trace. Probably went to ground along the railroad bed or found an old earth somewhere on Drummer's Hill. So it was goodnight Charles James, sleep tight and we'll meet on another day. Then Roman and I hacked home, jogged some, but mostly I walked him to let him cool out." Still hearing houndsong, Ike's tenor, Rambo's baritone, Jug's contrabass.

"Through Pimm's woods, of course."

"It's the shortest way home."

"Morey was there."

"Isn't he always?"

"The hunt's good Samaritan. Hah."

"You know he was thrown and rolled on. Broke most of his bones. He can't hunt anymore."

"Except women."

"Still has that terrible limp."

"That doesn't stop him from going through you-know-who's-back window."

"All I know about Morey or care to know is that he still wants to feel part of it. Riding to hounds was his life. So he does the next best thing, dispenses good cheer to his friends while they tell him about the hunt and remember old days in the field. At least . . ."

"He's nothing but a . . ."

A clench in his jaw. "Look Vera . . ."

"All right, but it isn't all right."

Let go, Vera, can't you ever let go?

Winter's early graybacked dusk at the windows, now plainsong sad, the trees ice-charred sticks that were oceans of summer leaves. No whisper of dogwood light now. What happened to joy, pure ungnawed at joy? Monday far off and its evening corner. What's she doing now? Alone? Weekends just down the road.

Fire stabbed at the timbers.

"Thank you for sharing the hunt with me. I'm glad you enjoyed it, really I am. But . . ." Skirting the thin ice of danger, risking the rest of the weekend going up in smoke, not able to stop. Sometimes, when you behave like this I think that I'm not in love with you any more, or even like you. But I love you. I'm not just any old housewife. I am a person. I have a mind. I will have my say. You had your day and left me here alone – I know you need your diversion.

He said, "But?" the pipe clamped in his teeth.

She sighed. "Why must you describe the hunt in eighteenth century language? This is the twentieth century. Can't you just tell it in modern American English?"

"The hunt is an eighteenth century sport, yes, I know, a kind of charade, a suspension of time. But that is its language. Good hunt minutes are still written that way. It's a form, like tennis – indulge me, but R. Frost said that free verse was like playing tennis without a net – or like a sonnet. Now, hark, as little Orphan Annie used to say: Your favourite music, and mine, is eighteenth century music. You enjoy eighteenth century painting, eighteenth century books, say, T. Jones. They've carried their times to us, not the professors."

"You don't write that way, your books, your ads."

"That's because there are no eighteenth century customers left."

"And all those accents you slip in and out of. They bewilder me, shifting so quickly. One minute you're some doddering old earl and the next you're Barry Fitzgerald. Can't you just be you?"

"The writer is an emotional mime. And," he couldn't resist, "what's mime is yours."

"Always joking."

"Jokes are the epitaphs of our emotions. F.W. Nietzsche. Wish I'd said that."

He poked at the fire, put on another sweet apple log. "let's have dinner by the fire tonight."

"Well . . ."

"I'll set up the trays, help you carry it in."

85

"In that case . . . That would be nice. Yes, let's."

"Another Madeira?"

"You know one . . ."

"It's Saturday night."

"Just a drop, then, but later."

"And Vera, I like the eighteenth century because they always went for baroque."

Her forehead puckered as if she were doing a crossword puzzle.

"Judson, Judson," she said leaving the room.

He lit the candles in his great-grandmother's candlesticks.

"Lovely din-din. Excellent roast, excellent everything. Done to a turn. A touch of the old tawny?" He picked up the port.

She shook her head. Once wine would have meant . . . A touch, his arm around her – a kiss . . . More than a year, now . . .

Candle glow. The fire's lusty heat. He knocked out his pipe in the grate, packed it with fresh St. Bruno, put a match to the bowl. "There's a" . . . puff . . . "girl in the office" . . . puff, puff . . . "would like to take riding lessons." Puff. "Heard from someone we ride, asked me for advice, where to begin," puff, puff, "what to wear." He waved his pipe. "That sort of thing."

"A girl. Do I know her?"

"A young woman. She's fairly new, been with us, oh now, let's see" . . . Puff. "She's a writer in my group. As a matter of fact, yes, you met her at Leslie Madonna's party last fall. Her name's Billie Miller."

"Billie Miller. There were so many people there. Such a crush."

"She was there in the gang around Tad." Puff.

"Tall," puff, "long blonde hair."

"Big smile."

"Oh, yes, I remember her now. She seemed to have a kind of spotlight on her. A vivid face. Something theatrical. Yes, but very pleasant."

"Yes."

"And she wants to take riding lessons."

"Yes."

"I hope you told your young colleague to find a good instructor. That's the most important thing, particularly in the beginning, get a good solid foundation."

"Precisely. That's just what I told her."

"Some I've known can do more harm than good. All they want is your money."

"My point exactly."

"It's so hit and miss."

"That's why she asked me to recommend someone. I thought of Nan Marshall."

"Of course. Nan's very good. But Jud, she teaches advanced riders almost exclusively now, three-day eventers, medal class jumping."

"Well, I ran into Nan at the hunt and told her about Miss Miller. She said Mimsy would be glad to take her. She has almost as many pupils as Nan. Some of her kids have been winning in shows."

"Of course. Now why didn't I think of Mimsy? Like mother like daughter. Ah, that's so nice."

"She was an A Pony Clubber."

"And took her instructor's certificate, didn't she? at that school in England she went to instead of college."

"Porlock Vale, it's tops."

"Well, Miss Miller will be in good hands."

"Mimsy wants her to be there – I stopped by on the way home – a quarter of eight next Saturday morning if she's to work in a private lesson."

"Does she live far from here? Miss Miller."

"Somewhere in town."

"She'll just have to rise and shine early if she really wants to learn how to ride."

"Right. She said something about her car being fixed. An ancient MG, I think, it's more in the shop than out. They can't seem to get the right parts."

"There's always the train."

"Right. And she might be able to get a cab at the station. Although at that hour." Puff. "She'd have to get in by seven-fifteen. Let's see, get up about five-thirty."

"And the cost, plus the lesson." She rolled a bread crumb in her fingers.

"Perhaps –"

"Well, if you think Miss Miller wouldn't be bored to distraction by two middle-aged folks like us – we're surely old enough to be her parents, probably older. She seemed quite young – she could, I suppose come back with you after work Friday. I don't know what we would do to entertain her. Does she play Scrabble?"

"You mean for dinner?"

"You haven't answered my question."

"Question? Oh, Scrabble. Vera, how should I know? I've seen crossword puzzles on her desk – The *Sunday Times*, *Sat Review* double crostics."

"Oh well, then she has a mind. Double crostics. Has she ever done those in the *London Times?* Those terrible-pun things."

"Vera, she *is* a *writer* for Fairleigh. She's a bright – person." Stop, Mac.

"Now that you've answered my question, I'll answer yours. Of course for dinner, what else? What did you expect? That I would put her in the barn while we had our din-din? Sometimes you seem to have taken leave of your senses."

Her mother's expression. The State Normal School diplomat. Now, Judson, the hook's in the gill, you bastard. Vera's most honest eyes.

"You and I haven't played Scrabble for . . ."

"Well, then, may I extend your invitation?"

"By all means. I'll write her a note – it should come from me."

"Of course."

"Get the guest room ready. We haven't had anyone here since the children came for Thanksgiving."

To grandfather's farm we go.

"We rattle around so in this big house, just the two of us. I think it may be very cheery to have your Miss Miller here."

"I'll tell her Monday."

"Monday," she picked up a plate. "Oh Jud I forgot to tell you, there's a meeting on Monday night of the Historical Association. Caleb Millhouse is going to show some very rare slides of the township and the old houses, ours among them, as they were more than seventy years ago. I told him we'd go. I knew you'd be interested."

"I am, you know I am, very, but I'm going to be in Washington Monday night, probably Tuesday, too. The Pentagon – Army business."

"Oh Jud, you're traveling more and more lately. It didn't used to be that way – a few trips a year, conventions. Now it's two – no, more like three times a week. Can't they get someone else to go? You are a senior man."

"That's why I have to go."

"Last fall on your vacation you said you wanted to work on your book again. When, Jud? You're away so much of the time."

"I know, I know. It's a big account, our biggest – thirty-eight million dollars. It pays for the hay and grain."

"Will it ever let up? I was hoping . . ."

"Some day . . ."

"No titbits for you, Blitz," his cool nose in her palm, "you've had your din-din." She stroked his muzzle.

". . . I suppose."

"Jud, there are some things, one thing in particular we must talk about. Long overdue."

Talk.

Gold rain of hair.

Honey drip.

Paris on Walnut Street.

"When, Jud?"

"Soon."

Still holding the plate she looked into the fire. Washed denim blue eyes.

"I do hope she plays Scrabble," she said, a bird on a branch listening for another bird's call.

16

"You're putting me on," Billie said. "I don't believe it."

He handed her the small square envelope.

The coins of her hair brushed the note paper with its unicorn crest of the farm. Her lips moved slightly, reading.

"She's invited me for the *whole* weekend. You didn't tell me *that.*"

"Surprise."

"This a gag?"

"That's her handwriting, Billie. No gag. not Vera," he shook his head. The saint of the straight. *Honi soit qui mal y pense.*

She turned back to the note. "What's all this about a second lesson? Who's Mimsy?"

"That's why you've been asked for the weekend. Mimsy's your riding teacher. I'll tell you about her later. OK, I arranged for a Saturday lesson. It had to be early a.m. Then Mimsy called – spoke to Vera – thought while you were with us you might like a second lesson on Sunday. Get you off to a good start. Vera agreed – that is if you weren't otherwise engaged. Sound equestrian pedagogical practice, she called it. Dig?"

"I still can't believe you swung it."

He winced.

"Judson." The first time she'd said his full name. "We'll be together all weekend."

"I think you should send her a note."

"Will I ever."

His phone rang. Tad's backfiring voice. "Ace, we've got a problem. The Expel campaign bombed. Third time around. We've got three days to come up with a winner or it goes to BBDO."

He put his hand over the mouthpiece. "I've got some spot welding to do," he whispered, waved, "See you later."

She blew him a kiss. Lips, tongue shaped "I love you."

"Ace?"

"Yes, Tad, I'm here."

"I know you're up to your ass in Army, but can you put a couple hours against it?"

"Sure Tad, I'm here."

"Great. I've lined up some kids – Leeta, Joe, Les – for a gang bang. You guys ought to knock it in no time flat. C'mon over, I'll give you the poop."

Monday. Mōnandaeg. Knob-kneed Anglo Saxon word. Sacred to the moon. Billie Moon. Milk legs. Under Milk Legs. Meanwhile Expel, crisis in trivia.

Joe Concerto came into his office with his used car salesman's smile, *caveat emptor*, drawing pad under his arm, shirt pocket bulged with Magic Markers.

Turtlenecked Les Madonna, his hybrid face vacant except for a seething surliness in his eyes. Pad, the latest Annual of Advertising Art. You shouldn't wear sweaters, Les, not with your boobies.

Leeta Krantz bandied in last, he knew she would, a pencil stuck in her hair, a lined yellow pad in her hand.

"My, what a distinguished group," she klaxoned, "and all for a crummy trade campaign." She looked at her Rolex. "I'll give it half an hour. It isn't my account."

"Let us pray," Jud said.

"How much does it bill anyhow?" Les asked.

"Peanuts," Jud said. "That's not the point. It's an account. It should get our best shot like anything else in the house."

The other three looked at each other. The house. The Castle. Old Fairleigh school tie.

"Why don't we just resign the account?" Leeta said. "Who needs it?"

Les said, "Yeah, it won't win any awards. Nothing I'd put in my book. What a waste of our talents."

Talents. What would you do Les, without your security blanket, the Ad Art Annual to copy from?

Jud looked at his watch. There *is* life in outer space and it's come here by UFO. It's the Pepsi Degeneration. Babes in Adland.

"Let's get the show on the road," Joe said.

Jud held up a pasteboard tag. "This is all we have to work with – the Expel label, the name. It's on every garment, mostly raincoats, that's been treated with the product, a rain and stain repellent."

"So what else is new?" Les said.

"Nothing, Les, that's the problem. It's been around a while, now there's competition. New brands, pretty much the same stuff, but new. Expel wants to hold on to its market. That simple."

Joe slashed at his pad with a Magic Marker. "There's these two guys in raincoats somewhere. A city street. It's raining like hell, see, and little by little," he raised his head, squinted, resumed stroking, "the first guy's raincoat just melts away until he's standing there in his skivvies. That's the one with Brand X. The other guy's raincoat, the one treated with Expel, it's OK, and the guy walks off laughing on camera."

"I like it," Leeta said. "It has balls. We could get Peter Falk . . ."

"Dear friends and gentle hearts," Jud said, "this isn't TV. It's a trade *paper* campaign – *Women's Wear Daily* – addressed to manufacturers, not the general public. And besides, Joe you're implying Brand X disintegrates fabric. The broadcasting code . . ."

"That's what Mary Wells would do," Leeta said.

What would you do Leeta?

Joe ripped the sheet from his pad, balled it onto the floor.

"How can we be creative with all these cockamamie rules?" Les said.

"You can't play tennis without a net," Jud said.

Tad's kids looked at each other again. Rules. The House, Old Fairleigh.

Jud swivelled his chair to the window. Billy Penn on top of his City Hall clock. Unlit, later he and Billie walking up Walnut. Our Gang. The world's in the hands of Mack Sennett.

"We need some words," Les said.

"Rain . . . stain . . . plain – you have a rhyming dictionary?" Leeta asked.

"Never touch the stuff myself," Jud said.

"Why don't you writers get with it?" Les said.

Jud looked at the Expel tag, held it up by its string. "It's got to be this."

"That dumb thing? It's nothing but a piece of cardboard," Les said.

"Then we'll make it smart," Jud said.

Leeta began scribbling, Joe doodled, Les riffled through the Art Annual. Jud rolled a yellow sheet in his typewriter. He leaned toward it as if there were notes on it and he about to play a concert. He clicked out a line. Three words. Twelve little letters all in a row. How sweet it is. He pulled the sheet, Scotch-taped the tag, strings spread, at a slant under the line on the page, push-pinned it to the cork board on his wall. He read the line aloud –

"THE RAIN CHECK."

"Not bad, Ace," Leeta said.

Not bad – that's a double Immelmann roll. With a loop. *Nein*, Max?

"Yeah," Joe said, "yeah," and got up to read the line.

"There'll be a line, maybe two, of copy, no more. Maybe not even that, it's all there on the tag. It's the message, the logo."

"Don't need more," Joe said.

"How many ads in the campaign?" Les asked.

"I think Tad said four."

"Well get with it, get with it," Les said.

"OK gang . . ." a Billie echo? . . . "Let's go," Jud said. Les picked up his pad from the floor, put it down, picked up the Art Annual. Joe was stroking away at his pad. Leeta looked at her Rolex. The man's size.

The tingle there again running down through his fingers. A fresh yellow sheet in the machine. This old spider has a lot of silk left to spin. Fission-fusion. He hit the keys hard, four-finger typing. A five

91

word headline. The Seventh Calvary rode to the charge. Another headline, four words. Can't one word ever say it all? He swivelled round. Our Gang, munching their mediocrity. And, yes, the bugles, to wind up the campaign – he'd schedule it one a day and repeat. One more billboard headline. His fingers hovered over the keyboard. V. Horowitz, here I come. He typed out three words. He had it taped.

"OK," he said, leaning back, "what've we got?"

Les said, "This doesn't turn me on. You know, give me a food account, like you know, a McDonald's."

"Something you can get your teeth into, eh Les?" Something you can *arrange* not create, eh, Les? A homogenised rubbish of sound and light effects jingling around a non-idea, sung by a cast of teen-age thousands marching out of a blender.

Joe said, "In a mo."

Leeta read from her pad. "Who needs a pain in the rain?"

From a girl with balls?

Mary Wells had a little lamb. And everywhere that Mary went . . .

"Hey, Leeta, that's great," Les said.

Joe said, "Whatchya got, Jud?"

He took the three yellow sheets, each with one line on it, and tacked them to the board. "OK," he said. "Same illustration – the Expel tag." He read the lines:

"CALLED ON ACCOUNT OF RAIN.
"KEEPS YOUR REPUTATION SPOTLESS.
"And to wrap it up –
"THAT'S THE TICKET."

Joe went up to the board, copied the lines on his pad. Leeta said, "You'll show my thing to Tad?" Jud nodded. If I won't you will. She looked at her Rolex. "Good show," she said. "I've got heaps of stuff to do."

Les said, "Yeah, like a date with her hairdresser." They laughed togetherly.

Jud looked at Joe as a quarterback in the seconds left dusk looks for someone to catch his pass in the end zone. "Just roughs," he said, "Joe, for Tad to look at."

17

After the parenthetical cold, from cab to Suburban Station, the platform was hot and steamy, urgent with Friday squirming, scarcely contained Episcopal shoving, workweek Philadelphia going home for the weekend. Self-ordained gentry solemnised by the old station names on the Main Line. Our Father who art in Devon.

"No, that one," Jud said, "on Track 2, the Paoli skipstop." He gripped her valise and tote bag, close haunched by her in the crowd.

"A seat-getting manoeuvre," he said. "Try to squeeze in ahead of me. They'll stomp me to death if I try, but you, now. Just think of yourself as the Statue of Liberty. I know that's in New York, but . . ."

"No way, they're really shoving, you'd think . . ."

"This was the last train from Berlin. I know."

"Is this what you do every night?"

"Not every night, love – look what you've saved me from – just twice a week, remember?"

"Jud, the guy pushing up behind me," she whispered, "he's poking."

"It's only his *Wall Street Journal.*"

At the stuffed door of the train a man squeezed aside to let her pass. Jud said in her ear. "See, the superclerks are giving ground to beauty."

A young horn-rimmed over-achiever staking his claim to a seat saw her standing. He sickened but didn't complete sitting down. Touched his hat brim. The man by the window, ticket in hatband, unfolded his *Evening Bulletin.*

"Sir," Jud said, "I'm escorting this woman to the State Penitentiary. I have my credentials here, somewhere, my badge. I'd appreciate it if you'd cooperate with the law and permit me . . ." Drowning in jowls the man snapped his paper and squirmed into the aisle. Jud swung her luggage onto the rack.

"Your coat," he said, "it's taking up half a seat. They must have used a whole camel to make it. I might have to pay half-fare for it. And besides you're going to be awfully warm in this sauna."

She corkscrewed up, wriggling out of her polo coat. He folded it over her bags.

"Better?"

"Mucho gracias, senor."

"Nada y pues nada."

"You're really hyper," she said, "and without booze. That little number you just did – the *law*."

"Oh, he didn't buy it. He thought I'm some kind of nut. He didn't need that. There are occasional cuckoos riding the trains selling subscriptions for the end of the world."

The train jerked, began rolling out of the tunnel.

"I still can't believe it, *me* going to your place for the weekend. Wouldn't they freak out at the office if they knew?"

"They know." Everyone knows. Except Vera. Even Dulcie who'd called him at the office that morning. "She's gorgeous, Dad."

The conductor gargled the leafy Arcadian stations – Wynnewood and Ardmore, Bryn Mawr and Radnor, St Davids, Strafford and "Paoli, last stop, all changes here, Kansas City, Chicago, St Louis."

Up the clattering wood stairs to the parking lot. "Over there," he said, "the white wagon, well gray, it needs a wash." He unlocked the tailgate, dumped her bags. "Meet Winnie, the Pooh-jo."

In the bucket seat beside him, Billie sniffed. "What's that smell?"

"Ah," he said, toeing the clutch down, "that's the dog. Blitzer. Eau de Chien. Isn't it heaven? I know he drools a lot, rotting the leather." He laughed. "He's mad for going on drives. All I have to do is pick up the car keys and he's out the door thumping away at the car. He likes to snooze in it, too."

"Well, Chanel Number Five, it's not."

"All right," he said, "you know, an Oxford don once told me that gentlemen don't usually reside in the city, and that if they have a Rolls Royce, it should be very old and smell of dogs. Well, this isn't a Rolls, but it's reasonably old and it smells of dog. I know he'll like the way you smell."

"Oh great," she said, putting her thermal hand on his thigh. "I can't wait be smelled by a dog."

"If there was daylight, I'd take you the long way round, to a ridge you can't see now, a few miles to the south, a mountain by courtesy – it's all perspective – a hill, really, and you'd see my place across the valley carved out of my hill. It was Eden when I came here, before the developments, country all the way home."

"With Eve." Then, "I'm sorry," she said. "All I know is I'll be with you this weekend."

Headlights following tail lights along the back roads until they began climbing. Cars bleeding off to side roads, fewer houses and lights.

"Covered wagons came through here, the old Conestoga Road, on their way West . . .

"Underground Railroad country, secret cellars under secret cellars. There's one on my place." He sniffed. "That's where I keep my wine, a place where people sweated their lives."

The road rose sharply, the car stabbing the dark with its lamps.

"About here, I begin to feel I'm in the country." He lowered his window a crack. Night air slapped in astringent with cold.

94

"That's good," he said. She said, "Brrrrr." He shut the window.

At the crest of the climb he turned the car onto an unlit road in the woods. "Another mile and we're there."

He stopped at a lane so she could see the sign hanging from its yardarm in the car's lights, a golden horned horse rearing. Unicorn Farm.

"I knew it would be like this," she said.

He shifted to first, turned the car into the winding, steeply descending lane, all cliff on the right, her side, edging it down. She looked over the side. "That's quite a drop. Suppose you should skid or something?"

"Roadway roulette," he said.

"How do you get out of here when it snows?"

"Everyone asks that. Sometimes I don't. I've been marooned, three days in a storm, V in Ohio with her mother for Christmas. It was great. I felt like Melville when he was writing Moby Dick on a farm in New Hampshire. 'I go out at five a.m. and feed the critters first, then myself,' he wrote Hawthorne."

"I don't see the house."

"My drive is a quarter mile and my house is at the end of it."

Down, down, and the lane flattened into an archway bordered by ancient life, giant Himalayan soft hair needled pines, spruce and fir.

"I can't believe it," she said, "It's fantastic."

And there were the bride and groom oaks and the lights of the house, and in the valley opening to her eyes and across on the Malvern ridge. "This must be on the edge of the world. It's like you can fall off."

"This is it," he said.

"Jud, hold my hand for a sec."

They heard the dog barking inside, his basso profundo alarm.

"He's not going to bite, or anything?"

"No," he laughed, "Blitzer's a fraud, as gentle on the inside – to friends – as he's ferocious on the outside."

"You'd better tell him I'm a friend."

"He'll know."

Getting out of the car she said, "Wow, looked at those stars." Looped overhead, bubbling, tangled in trees.

"Take a deep breath," he said, getting her bags. Wood smoke ribboned the air. "Out of this world," she said. "And that" – the coach lantern with its gas flame at the door.

"It's almost as old as the house. Seventeen thirty-five."

Vera stood framed in the doorway a few steps inside the room, a surprise of ringlets across her forehead. The fire lashed at the flue, oil lamps glowed. "Come in, come in; shut the door, Jud you're letting in all the cold." Yes 'm. A commotion of dog, bounding in greeting him, introducing himself to her. "Quiet, Blitz, down; don't be frightened, Miss Miller. Once you're in the house he knows you belong. He's just so big he gets in the way of himself. See, he's taken to you already."

"Billie, please, Mrs Bell."

"Then you must call me Vera; of course, we met at the Madonnas'. I'm so glad you could come. Jud, help Miss – help Billie out of her coat and hang it up in the closet." Yes 'm.

"Don't I get my kiss?"

Yes 'm.

"He hasn't been home since Wednesday. All that travel, I don't know how he gets his work done."

Jud picked up her bags. "One sec," Billie said, reaching into the tote bag. "For you," she offered a ribboned package. "I mean, it's not for the house." She laughed. "He's not to use it."

"Oh," Vera smiled. "You shouldn't have, Billie; but thank you, that's very thoughtful."

"Just some soap, from England, the ladies there use it. I thought you'd like it. Oh – and –" she reached in the bag again – "this."

"Now Billie, really. Let me see, that looks like something to drink."

"Champagne."

Vera shook her head, but her blue floret eyes were pleased. "You're too generous, Billie; after all, you work for a living. I know how that is. You should be saving your money. When I was a girl – a hope chest . . . Well, I must go back to the kitchen."

"Is there anything I can do to help? Mrs – Vera."

"No dear, thank you for asking, but the kitchen is my domain. I have my way of doing things; I'm sure you do, too. Wouldn't you like to freshen up? Jud, why don't you show Billie up to her room" She looked at the fire. "You know, it's like having Dulcie home from college again. She's our daughter. Married, two children, girls. They call me Grams, and they call him Pops."

"Hi, Pops," Billie said.

"She said that just like Kimberly – she's the elder. Yes, well, I'll join you two," she looked at the clock on the mantel, "in – oh – a while. And, Jud, I will have a glass of wine before dinner tonight."

At the door she turned. "Haven't you noticed anything different about me?" She touched her hair, the bangs. He thought Mamie Eisenhower. "My new hairdo; I did it myself."

"Oh, very fetching," he said. "Sort of the Fifi D'Orsay look."

Billie said, "Very cute, very becoming."

"This used to be Dulcie's room."

"I love that wallpaper – so sunny – those flowers."

"The pattern came from the lining of an old sea captain's chest. China trade in the eighteen-hundreds."

"And the canopy over the bed. I've never slept in a four-poster."

"It's an original, quite old, hand-carved right here in the county. Of native walnut."

"I'm here, I'm here," she said, sitting down in the creweled rocker. She rocked up and back, stopped, stretched out her hand drawing him down to her lips-parted mouth. He glanced back at the open door, bent stiffly down to the heart of her face. "Maybe later," she breathed – "tonight"

He straightened. "Billie, not here, not in this house."

"Why not in this house? Then it will be like mine. Ours."

He shut his eyes. "You have a riding lesson tomorrow, remember? at quarter of eight. You'll have to be up early."

She laughed, "I almost forgot."

"Billie –"

"Okay," she said, "I just love you so much."

"The bath's on your left down the hall," he said at the door. "I'm going to make us some drinks. See you downstairs."

"You play very well," Vera said, putting the Scrabble set back in the box. She looked at the score sheet. "You had more triples, and that marvellous triple-triple – eighty-six points. You're very clever. You must play often."

"I don't actually. It's a knack, like doing crosswords or crostics. It has nothing to do with brains."

"I wouldn't say that, one has to be literate."

"I've known some pretty dumb people who were real whizzes at crosswords. They didn't even know what the words meant, just so long as they fit."

"This has been very enjoyable. I don't get to play a three-handed game, except when Mother, my mother, visits. It's so much more interesting when more than two play . . . I don't know what got into you tonight, Jud, you were throwing your tiles away – nines and tens."

Vera stifled a yawn. "Wine makes me drowsy, I must have had . . .Well, now, no wonder, it's really quite late – for us – we're early risers. And you have your first riding lesson tomorrow, Billie. I think we should all go to bed, get a good fresh start in the morning."

"Right," Billie said. "I'll have one more cigarette."

Vera shook her head at the butt-filled ash tray on the table. "You young people have no regard for your lungs . . . Don't be too long, Jud." And to Billie, "Sleep well, my dear."

She scraped for a cigarette in the crumpled pack. "Would you bring me my bag, please, it's over there." He lit her.

"Let's have a nightcap," she said, "this is so great."

He poured two small brandies and sat opposite her by the still living fire, coals clinking.

"At last," she said, raising her glass to him, leaning back in her chair. "I could sit here all night."

Upstairs water running in the bathroom.

"Put another log on the fire," she said.

"We're going up in a few minutes."

"Just that small one. Please."

She looked at the fresh log's light flicking the ceiling timbers. At the oil lamps' misty globes.

A door opened upstairs, feet padding along the boards. A door closed.

"I understand now why you live here," she said. "What this place means to you. It is very special."

"Wait till you see it tomorrow, the woods all around, the fields, the horses. Every season here its own world. You can feel it moving around the sun. This is its hidden time, snow time, but every season . . ."

She took a deep drag. "And the hidden road."

He looked at her as if someone had told him the truth. He got up, poured more brandy into their snifters. Fire splinters on timbers, lamps guttering out. Blitz like a felled tree sleeping.

"What about the road?"

"It's like something I read somewhere. *Alice in Wonderland – Through the Looking Glass* – a book when I was a kid."

"You amaze me, Billie – always . . . The road –"

"Well, it's like you go through a door and you're somewhere else, like coming out of a long dark tunnel into another world. A hideaway. This is your hideaway. And it's like you go down that road every day and you . . ."

"Yes?"

"Disappear."

He poked at the fire, put on another log.

"Like you're hiding out."

He nodding. "Something like that."

"What are you hiding from, Jud?"

"From the books I didn't write, and the forgotten ones that I did."

"You can't hide from that."

"I know. I used to think this was my desert, a place of withdrawal before the return with a message, a gospel, a book. Like St John the Baptist, St Anthony, Moses, Christ."

"That first lunch we had, you said you lacked an essential ingredient. I think I knew then. I felt it. It started me thinking for the first time about going to bed, that maybe there was more to it than, well, fun. I don't knock that, the jollies. But if . . ."

" . . . *If I could touch you and daisies sprang up at your feet.*"

"Yeah, who wrote that?"

"I was sixteen, a poem to a high school baton twirler. She preferred the captain of the football team."

"I love you."

"I love you, Billie."

"Then why? You have me. You said there's a book in your closet half-finished."

"It all has to be part of a natural day, its rhythms a cycle. Good sleeping together, good waking, good working, good eating, good drinking. The mind blown free, not having to think about it . . . There all the time."

"You're saying I'm in the way, the nights at my place."

"I'm saying those nights should be . . ."

"Heavy, heavy – hey, we're going to work things out. You'll see. My horoscope says . . ." He smiled Billie Billie.

She toed off her shoes, slipped from her chair to the floor, drew her knees to her chin. In the cave of her skirt, her white valley.

A stifled bark from the corner, the dog's legs running in sleep, nose twitching, a smothered yelp.

"He has his nightmares, too," he said.

"I've never done it in front of a fire," she said. "I want to do it with you." She reached a lyric hand to him.

As he unfolded down to the floor he could feel the thick sleep of the just upstairs, the religion of innocence.

"Let's try it one more time," Mimsy called from the center of the ring. "And this time remember, you're posting not flying. Rise from the knees, not your feet, just enough to get your backside off the saddle. Just brush it."

Short, stocky Mimsy, her boots and britches crammed with equine authority.

"That girl is half horse," Jud said to Vera, both perched at the rail. "She knows a lot about horses but not about people."

"I don't believe she's eighteen."

"That's what I mean."

". . . OK, now snug your thighs into your horse. Get your heels down. Pick up your reins. Straighten up. Walk him around the ring once, then at the turn – trot."

"He won't walk," Billie said, her hair coiled in twists under Vera's hard hat.

"He's waiting for you to tell him. He doesn't know what you want. Squeeze with your legs."

"I'm squeezing."

The little gray horse stood there, planted.

"C'mon Wilbur, be a good guy," Billie said.

"Squeeze and give him the stick."

Wilbur's ears flickered. His tail swished at no fly. He picked up one foot then another.

"Good," Mimsy called. Now, keep him moving. Lean forward a bit. That's it – now, at the turn, shorten your reins, lean forward another notch – back straight . . . and *squeeze*."

Wilbur ambled into a soft little trot.

"You're bouncing – not posting. Come down from the clouds . . . From the knees – up-and, up-and. Good, good, keep him going. Take him around twice more – let him know who's boss, then ease him down to a walk and stop at the gate."

"She's too large for that horse; he's not much more than a pony," Vera said. "Makes her look gawky."

Vulnerable, he thought, when we're out of our modes, doing badly what others do easily well. Imagine Einstein on skis.

He helped her dismount, full in his arms.

"I love it," she said. "I know I was awful. But I'm going to learn how to ride. I love Wilbur, I wish I could buy him, keep him at your place. Oh, and I'm going to get an outfit – boots, breeches, hat . . . the works."

"Whoa, thar, it's only your second lesson."

"I'm sticking with it."

"I admire your determination," Vera said, "but perhaps you should wait a while. A good outfit's expensive, and if you should give it up you'll get less than half at the Thrift Shop, if you're lucky."

"I won't give it up, and besides, that stuff is so neat, it makes you look, well, so special."

"She'll be riding to hounds before we know it," Jud said.

"Don't laugh. You better believe it," Billie said. "Tally-ho." And driving back to the farm in the car – "This is the life. I never knew what I was missing."

Vera said, "Well, dear, get yourself a nice young man; that shouldn't be at all difficult for you; get married and settle down in the country. Occasionally a small place comes up for sale. Or you could rent in the beginning, say a tenant house on a farm. They're scarce, but they do come up once in a while. Wouldn't that be nice, Jud, if the future Mr and Mrs Billie lived near us? Now let's see, a nice young man." Billie said, "Come out, come out wherever you are."

"Jud, don't we know *any* eligible young bachelors in the neighbourhood? The Wallraven boy" – to Billie – "he's wickedly handsome. Do you remember Errol Flynn?"

"He's still at college," Jud said.

"The Collums' son, the one who's in business with Nate?"

"Look," Jud said, "it's beginning to snow."

Overnight – two inches of secret snow loading armpits of trees, dusting the druid pines, making the world a secret. City days before he'd be back. He put Billie's bags in the wagon.

"See you next weekend," Vera called from the front porch to Billie. "And maybe we'll do one of those *London Times* puzzles together; we've stacks of them in the attic."

"Thanks for everything," Billie waved.

He reversed the car out of the Quaker shed.

"Are you sure you're going to make it?" Billie said. "It feels slippy."

"Like you," he said, and drove off into the office week.

From ashes of the office week
The commuter shall not rise
Into something brightly new:
In the end
We are
What we do.

18

"Tally-ho –

"How do I look?" Billie said in the dining room doorway, an accoutred Godiva: legs lathed into shining black boots; thighs poured into skinfitting breeches; the short-skirted hacking coat nicely globed where it should be; crowned with a velvet hunt cap, a crop in her hand. "I feel ten feet tall."

"Isn't she stunning?" Vera said. "On a figure like hers everything looks tailor-made."

"Except over here," Billie laughed, tapping the crop on her haunch.

Her simmering hip. Jud politely applauded: "Straight out of *Country Life*. Or the winner's circle at Devon."

"I just about got into these and they're a whole size larger than I usually take. It's those great meals you feed me, Vee. I'll have to lose weight if I'm going to be seen in my bikini this summer."

That coming? still months away, Billie weekends away on her summer beaches? In her bikini.

"Have some breakfast," he said. "Eggs Benedict," lifting the chafing dish lid.

"Just coffee. Black. Okay, and one piece of toast. I don't want to keep Mimsy waiting."

"Your sixth lesson," he said, pouring. "Wait'll ol' Mimsy sees you. She'll ask you to give *her* a lesson."

"Har-de-har-har."

"Pass her the marmalade, Jud. And, oh, I'll have another half-cup. To be *gemütlich*. Thank you." A beamish smile at Billie. "The Saddler has such beautiful things. And the boots were a *buy*. Handmade by Vogel for someone who paid the deposit and then moved away. It's as if they were made for her."

"Thanks again, Vee," Billie said, "for taking me there, picking just the right things. He could have sold me the store. As it is, you'll have to get me a raise, Jud, if I'm going to pay for all this." Her hand went to her throat and the gold stock pin clasping the choker.

"I almost forgot to thank *you*, Mr Bell, for your present. Vee bought this for me yesterday, just before we left the store."

"A gift from you and me, Jud; I neglected to tell you. The finishing touch to her outfit. I knew you'd approve."

"Right," he said. "Very appropriate. Now you gals better be off. I'm going up to the study – stuffy word that – my workshop."

Something lit Billie's face, and Vera's – for her something from somewhere that was like an old tune.

"You haven't been up there for – I don't know how long –" Vera said. "But I always keep it dusted."

"I'm just going to look at something, get re-acquainted. You know, like meeting a mail-order bride. Someone whose picture you've kept in your wallet."

"I'll do the dishes when I get back," Vera said. "I don't like leaving things undone that should be done, but I simply have to see Billie mounted in all her splendour. And this time –" to Billie – "I may let you help me."

"Good luck," Billie said to Jud. "I'll see you later."

"Have a good lesson. Keep ol' Wilbur moving."

He took the manuscript out of the closet, put it on his desk and began reading in the skewbald February light. The people were there where he had left them, as if at a station, some sitting on their baggage, waiting for him to put them on the train. They had grown older, somehow, but they were the same, except for their left behind look. *Hope deferred maketh the heart sick.* He was not the same; he had been elsewhere, and they resented his long departure. They had been trusting travellers with him, their shadowless leader, and were now because of his defection – refugees. Their tickets were for trains that had gone by. They had gotten used to being nowhere. It had become a way of life. They had smiled and waved to him when he had told them not to worry, he had something to attend to. – "I'll be right back . . ." They had grown tired and ashy waiting while he was attending to something that had nothing to do with them. As if they had been wandering around a desert for forty years with no one to remind them of the promised land or come back from the mountain with an itinerary.

They were still there, the grownups, the children: Young Peter with his lollipop eyes still running away from his terrible news: *He ran, he ran in the dazed light of the woods. He had been running a long time it seemed – running, stumbling, running again. But the thing he was running from was no further behind than when he had started. So he had to go on although it was hard to breathe and there was no path any more. Just trees and rock and grabbing branches pushing him back because it was all uphill going now . . . He had begun running the moment his mother had said she was going to be married to Bruce. Bolted out the door across the clearing and into the waiting woods . . .*

I know, Peter. You lost your father twice. A two-time loser. And I sent Bruce to find you, while you tried with storybook magic to conjure the father who could not possibly come: *And still the face would not come, but now against the flickering red and black screen of his shut lids a man figure took form walking raggedly toward him. In the breathless quiet he heard the crack of a twig and again and footsteps. A*

103

shadow came between him and the sun, fell cool across his flushed face. *Against the awful pounding of his heart he opened his eyes. His wish had come true. It was his Father.*

Then his face crashed into tears.

It was Bruce.

And small Ann was there on an outing in the park with Bruce, her father: *They were following the path that led to the zoo, and every now and then she veered suddenly, tugging him toward the railing beyond which a pioneering yet mistrustful squirrel made tentative overtures to the human race. The sight of these smaller accessible creatures lighted a quick excitement in the child. The uncaged squirrels, the pigeons promenading with proprietorial step, the marauding sparrows and the uninvited robins were people more at home in her size of world. There was an understanding between them that there could never be between the little girl and the larger, always dangerous and therefore restrained inhabitants of the zoo. These, of course, were of immediate and transitory interest. The theatrical cavortings and snortings of the seals, the chimpanzees' meditative monkeyshines, the elephant turning his trunk into a hose and showering himself, never failed to ignite spontaneous laughter in her, shared by a quick upward glance at her father. Nor did she ever fail to feel with silent awe the lion's lazy smoulder, the useless violence of the black leopard's lethal pacing, or even the tiger's volcanic boredom. But, with the little creatures it was a more intimate affair. There were no bars between them, and among them all she was the strongest one, the peanut and popcorn giving benefactress – unafraid – come what may.* Little Annie, still in the bonnet and frock Bruce had brought her from Paris, *crouching with the mechanical abruptness of a toy and holding a peanut out to the squirrel.* And an IOU from the past she hadn't signed but would have to pay soon at *half-past four* years old.

And there, of course, was Fanny Murdock, Laura's mother: *Her short dumpling body seemed precariously balanced on two matchstick legs. Her face was weighted by a mass of rusty hair streaked with the many faded overlapping strata of old henna rinses. Its thick loose coils were wound into a cupola from which a dozen long black pins protruded like flying buttresses. In spite of her blue glasses and the frequent references to her blindness, she moved with ease and alacrity about the house and an air of seeing as well as listening. Her hands and feet were small and delicate. In her loose kind of toga she looked like something in a thrift shop window. No feature or part of her body seemed intimately related to any other. It was as though she had been put together with an odd assortment of anomalous items from the Flea Market in Paris* . . . Ah, Fanny you old troublemaker – *roosting in her rocking chair behind her blue lenses and stinging like a hornet every few minutes as she rocked* . . .

And Bruce and Laura that first time in Connecticut, in The Captain's House, on the Captain's bed, *the exact spinning center of the universe . . . The fog cast a pale snow of drifting light into the room. He heard the secret whisper of her clothes rustling to the floor, and she the buckle of his belt strike wood, each listening for the rushing life of the other and reaching. She stood shimmering, a small moon in the room, his shadow eclipsing her. The hollows of her face absorbed the dark . . .*

Below, the clock struck eight bells, summoning the watch.

Then she took his arm and stretched it and put her head on it and they slept. And he knew through the light gauze of sleep, still between sleep and waking, that she slept serenely unstirring like a child with her own good dreams, moving still in sleep when he moved, when his arm was cramped and he could no longer keep it under her head. Then he slipped it out and turned on his side and she turned too, fitting back to chest, curve to curve, the two good bodies folded.

He turned again, trying not to wake her and she turned with him; a dolphin turn, and they slept.

The fog peered in.

That's where he had left them, and the others, in the clothes of that time thinking the way people thought, speaking the way people spoke at that time. It was he, now from a different time, who had to go back and bring them through the rest of *their* time their emotional geography. To become one of them again – then. Or leave them in limbo, the things he had waiting to happen to them wouldn't happen, their lives forever on hold.

The phone rang.

And Vera was saying, "We're at Conestoga Hospital. Billie's had a slight accident. She's all right now. You're not to worry, but I think she'd feel better if you were here."

"What happened?"

"Wilbur threw her."

"How badly is she hurt?"

"A slight fracture in the ankle, Dr. Riccardi thinks. He was on duty in Emergency" . . . the red letters rang . . . "when we brought her in. An orthopaedist. They've taken X rays; she's in his office now. He made her laugh; a very nice man. A slight fracture; he thinks that's all it is."

"That's all it is."

"Actually Mimsy's the one's most upset. She drove us, but she should be getting back – a lesson."

"How did it happen?"

"Jud, can't that wait till you get here? . . . Are you coming?"

"Right away."

"Dr Riccardi's office is on the first floor, on the left of the parking lot."

"I'm on my way."

He put the manuscript back in its box, back in the closet.

The crutch and the cast had transformed her into a patient. She managed a post accident smile as they helped her into the car, Vera carrying her right boot.

"Don't you think Dr Riccardi is handsome?" Vera said. "And so young to be a surgeon. Anyone could see he was taken with you, the way his dark eyes sparkled."

On the rear seat, slumped in her polo coat, Billie – "Groovy. He's probably married with six kids. Keeps her barefoot and pregnant. I know the type."

"You two were getting along famously; joking, laughing."

"It wasn't his ankle."

"His eyes," Vera said, "so Mediterranean. He got the boot off without having to cut it, Jud. Sometimes they have to. That was very considerate."

"Neato," Billie said, the car filling with injured air.

"How did it happen?" Jud said.

"That dumb horse."

"I know how you feel, Billie believe me," said Vera, "but –"

"Yeah, but . . ."

"Billie had finished her lesson, Jud, and Mimsy was about to help her dismount when the phone rang in the barn."

"And she went to answer it," Jud said.

"Yes –"

"– And she dropped the reins."

"Not quite. She left Wilbur's reins high on his neck, just behind his ears."

"Oh God."

"He started moving and when Billie, quite properly, leaned over to get them –"

"He dropped his head and bucked."

"Did he ever."

"These kids," Jud said, "they don't think; they don't have to. They become so much part of the horse they forget what it takes to control him, even a good one. What it's like to be a beginner. She should never have left his head until Billie was off. She's a fool."

"She's not a bad kid," Billie said, "she was really very upset. She was crying when she went back. This never happened before. It's that Wilbur. I thought he was good – trained."

"He is so long as he sees her, feels her, hears the voice. He's Mimsy's horse; she rides him in shows. He's a champion jumper. He hunts."

"Now he tells me."

"He wouldn't have done it if she were there," he said to the windshield. "Or if she'd given you the reins. He expects to be

106

controlled. He was probably bored with a round-the-ring lesson –
horses get bored – and when he felt your dead weight on his neck and
his boss nowhere in sight to boss him, he figured who needs it. So he
dumped you. Like a kid who wants out from something he doesn't
want to do. All horses are perpetual four-year-old kids; they'll get away
with whatever they can. Mimsy should have known better."

"Yes," Vera said, "it was careless of her."

"Murphy's Law," Jud said. "If anything can go wrong it will.
Double that when it comes to horses."

"And Mimsy was telling me only minutes before," Vera said, "how
nicely Billie was coming along and that maybe next week we would go
on a trial ride together, the four of us."

"Yeah," Billie said, "Tally-ho."

19

"Playing with horsies, huh?" Tad said. How long did you say she'd be out?"

"Two weeks . . . till she can shed the crutches."

"Shit – just when we need her – a new women's campaign – the Big One is hotting up."

"She said she would work at home; she wants to; she feels pretty bad about this, Tad. I could take her the stuff, check it out, bring it in."

Tad leaned back in his swivelling throne, put his hand in his pocket, tugged at his crotch.

"Hey, good duty, I wouldn't mind checking that out myself."

Her public face. Her public hair. In the public domain.

"She's at our place."

Tad's eyebrows up. His gnostic smirk.

"It happened just down the road, the place she was taking her lessons."

"Just down the road? Oh."

"She can't get around very well, she needs someone to take care of her – meals – all that. I could have driven her home, but she'd be all alone hobbling around . . . Vera insisted."

"Vera?"

He nodded. "It was her idea. She's glad for the company. You know, way out there in the country."

Tad blew a smoke ring, looked through it at Jud.

"You have any kids?" he said.

"One – a daughter."

"Married?"

"Yup."

"And kids? – your daughter?"

"Two – girls."

"Hey, you're a grandpop."

His once private life a scribbled on billboard. Just call me Pops.

"Look Tad, you don't have to worry. The work will be done if I have to do it."

"It's her job."

"Of course. I was only saying we'll have the campaign."

"I guess we should send the flowers to your house, then."

"Flowers?"

"The old Fairleigh custom, Jud, when somebody's in the hospital – you get those right away – or been out sick for more than twenty-one working days and under the proven care of a physician – I think that's what it says in the Caring for Your People section of the department manager's book. Or had an accident, like this . . . Or died."

"Oh right. Yes – Flowers from Your Fairleigh Family. I saw the card once at a wake. Charlie Ballard's. He dropped dead three days after retiring. After thirty-five years. Never made it to Tucson. Hadn't thought of it, I guess, because I never got any."

"You're not dead, yet. Har."

Tad rocked up and back, blew smoke rings through smoke rings.

"Hey, that would make a great cigarette ad – the smoke rings coming in on a beauty shot of the pack. I wish we had a ciggy account."

It's been done, rustic Tadpole. Jud remembered a billboard, monster red lips blowing fat rings over Broadway. But, he said, getting up, "Ring in Some Real Pleasure."

"There you go."

Another smoke ring.

"You're somethin' else again, Ace. Say Hi to Billie for me."

Sire.

Walking up after work Walnut to Billie's, without Billie beside him, a look ahead smile on her face, the indentured day spun to an earned evening, the city centerless wandered. But not lost. She would be there, two women waiting for him on the night hill.

Walking alone, an odd spell of deliverance, freedom between the office behind his back and the web, the pendulum's independence as the clock ticks on to something. Fourteen long evening blocks to himself. The cold made the air seem clean.

He opened the door to Billie's apartment with his key, clicked on the light. The furniture looked at him: the stranger who comes in to a neighbourhood bar, the heads of the locals turning, eyes tangent to the intruder, all conversation suspended, the bartender leaning in mid wipe on the bar unsmiling at him. You're in the wrong place, buddy.

Billie sent me. To pick up some things.

He takes the small valise down from the top of the armoire, wipes the dust with a napkin he finds in the kitchenette. The room is something she's worn and shed like a skin. Their Friday morning coffee cups are still in the sink, the grounds still in the pot. A rag of nibbled French toast she didn't finish with the arc of her bite. He slides it into the garbage bag. A finger of Scotch in the bottle. The bed is as they left it.

The room echoes with her but will not respond to him alone. He takes out his list, pulls on objecting drawers that grunt finally open. The panties are where she said they would be, but the nightgown and bras are hiding under soft disarrays of silky things – it all feels like silk, like special skin – that coldly caress his hands. He feels the voyeur. He feels.

He snaps the valise shut. That's about it. An inspector's last look around. On her desk a typed sheet of paper.

Our Place

You didn't have to tell me
about the acres of trees,
or the house
standing in the middle
of the clearing,
or the dog
who chases the cats
around the barn,
or the horses
with their heads
held high.

I've known the trees
for years.
I've warmed my life
by the fireplace
in the house,
and stroked a beautiful
black dog
while he slept.
I've ridden the horses
with you, my head
held higher than theirs.

I dreamed the same dream
you dreamed, love,
and knew it was real.

Not one of your better ones, love, but I get the idea.

The room was still waiting for him to leave. He locked the door and walked briskly to the station.

The house, a soup pot of burbling voices, he hears as he opens the door. He is greeted by two wifely smiles. The place is full of female community. If only . . . why not two wives? – a bit Old Testament, that. They've been doing a patchwork quilt together. "For me," Billie says, "when it's finished . . ." He gives Vera her kiss, says "Hi, Hi" to Billie – "one of those Hi's is from Tad."

She, they, want a full report from Nimrod, the hunter come home to his hill. What did he say, Tad? Was he mad? What's going on in the office? Did that Wanda do the layouts *she* asked for? (No.) Did he bring any work home for her to do? (Yes.) Oh great.

"Ladies," he says "I'd like to get out of my work clothes, wash up and change."

He comes down penny loafered, sweatered and slacked. He goes to the sideboard. The two others smile in alliance on cue. Something has been rehearsed. Now it's opening night. The curtain is up. Billie speaks.

"We've decided," she says, "Vee and I," Vee nods, "we're all going to have just one beer before dinner, no hard stuff."

They've expected the look on his face.

"Yes, then, you'll be able to go to your study after dinner," Vera begins –

– "And work on your book," they finish together, beaming away.

Go into the garden, Alfred, and write a poem, as Lady Tennyson used to say to Lord T.

"I can get a better deal at the Goodwill Mission," he says.

"Let's try it, at least for a while," Billie says. He can hear Vera saying to Billie, I've tried, but maybe he'll listen to you. "We have been hitting it up."

Ah, *we*, hedging the corporate guilt and the committee consensus.

"Ain't democratic," he says. "I didn't get a chance to vote."

"It's still two to one," Billie says. Her lace panties in the valise. Herself in and out of her panties. Silkskin Billie. Laying legs up on the bed, saying, Slip 'em on me, Honey. What a way to start the work day.

"I have proxies from Blitz and Roman," he says lamely, stalling.

"Jud, please . . ." this from Vee. Billie nods.

Vee and Bee.

He shakes his head, not at what's being said but at this One Big Industrial Union. Harvey Finkel, the Jewish copywriter from New York, had a word for it. *Meshugah*.

"Dad always had just one drink before dinner," Vee says, "You remember?"

Do I remember.

One drink, eh. Old Jack?

An ill wind blows nobody.

He can play it two ways. Go along. Unthinkable. Lose all his perks that way. Or con 'em. Keep a supply in the closet as Vera's Dad did. Oh, Jack, you old salt of the earth, many's the time we visited, and you'd say, Come up to the den, son, there's a juicy passage in Gibbon I'd like to show you, making it kosher for us to exit from those two ex-schoolmarms, wife and daughter. So nice the two boys have so much in common.

You kidding?

And we'd have our belts, Jack, in the tobacco dusk of your den, shmoozing and sipping that molten thirty-six-year old Crown Royal you brought over the border before the stores had it here, you old Anglo Canadian, you. VSOP. Yes, you were a Very Special Old Product. With that slanting thatch of white hair, puffing a vintage ceegar and chuckling over some Englishman's barrel organ words. You loved words the way they should be loved, for their eternities, beyond time and fashion. Or a Ph.D's burp.

Or talking baseball. You lit up as if you were reading Homer. You knew all the RBIs by heart, hits, runs and errors. All the scores, inning by inning – before the computer – from the time Abner Doubleday invented the game. And the players: Honus Wagner, Ty Cobb, or some of those later kids like Gehrig and Ruth. "Who could pitch like an angel for the Baltimore Orioles and Boston Red Sox. People forget that. And then homer for the Yankees whenever he felt like." Well, not quite whenever, Jack. Not in the All-Star Game, July tenth, nineteen-thirty-four, when screwball pitcher Carl Hubbell of the N.Y. Giants, "standing like Achilles before the walls of Troy," you said, listing to South Paw, struck out Babe Ruth, Lou Gehrig, Jimmy Foxx, Al Simmons and Joe Cronin . . . in that order. Stanky, the Gas House Gang. Casey Stengel, that language assassin, malaprop field marshall, put you in stitches. Geniuses in baggy striped bloomers. Hee, hee, both of us sipping on old gold.

And after doing justice to a fifth, (what's 28½ ounces between friends. Share and triple alike). I mean *fini*, that's all folks, the end, your bride – as you always called her, you most kind and canny devil – Flora Brooke would contralto up the stairs, (she sang, and well, in the choir) – Time for the Happy Hour. Which meant *one* cocktail. We knew the drill. Spilled more than that, eh, Jack, in your study, you darlin' man. Then we'd walk tightrope down, steady there, mate, gassing about Gibbon or Dickens, both of whom you knew like the back of your hand, and you'd say, Oh, is it that time? Yes, a bit of the cheer would be welcome, my dear.

One drink.

I kept your secret, Jack. Scout's honour.

You and I hit it off from the start, when Flora sent you to check me out in my bachelor digs. You know, how many goats and pigs and sheep I could offer for her daughter's hand. You looked at the books on my walls, at the booze and the bucket of ice on the table, the Honduran mahogany box of cigars (I'd bought just for you. Yes, I'd cased you through Vera). And you said, and I quote: "I trust you will leave me your library in your will."

That, sir, is panache. Knowing that by the numbers you would destruct before I did. And also telling me, you're OK, kid. That was as good a thing said, as any of the great writers you not only admired but breathed by.

Jack.

John Jamieson Brooke.

Your middle name was whiskey. Not a boozer, just a rummy like me. White shirt with just a touch of starch and never missing a day because of hangover. You told me in your wry way, never have a hangover on your own time. Stop drinking on Friday, pick it up again Sunday night. We paid our dues, you and I, and didn't think we should get the Victoria Cross for it.

Jack.

Then we sat to.

Have a cigar, sir.

I can see you passing it under your Roman nose, in the connoisseur's ritual, fine-tuning it with a squeeze of your bump knuckled fingers, testing to hear if it was fresh, crackled. Wrapper, OK, filler, OK. Assaying the nascent ash. A gent if I ever saw one.

And a dram of the Old Parr, sir.

"Don't mind if I do. Neat, please, no ice."

I knew then.

That, and the way you looked at the books.

The flag never sets. We would have liked each other anyway, in spite of in-law. And to hell with the squaws.

Hey, Jack, remember the night we sat up after they'd gone to bed and I told you a Kipling poem even you didn't know? . . . *There's a widow in sleepy Chester, who mourns for her only son* . . .

We wound up on the floor.

Next morning, Flora said, "Birds of a feather."

Can't win 'em all.

Nobody bats a thousand, you said.

Do I remember.

Remember, Jack? Took you to the fights on my newspaper pass. Rocky Graziano and Tony Zale, the Rock vs the Wedge. Such elegant slaughter.

And later we moseyed down to Fox's corner, Rocky's father-in-law's bar. And we sat there listening to that Dixie combo, (remember that rained-on looking girl singer? She looked as if she were dying of TB), and kibitzed and that shmuck at the next table was drinking 7&7. Sugared piss, you said. Amen.

Well, Jack, I've got to go. They're ringing the bell. Put me mouthpiece in. The rounds get longer, the rests shorter.

Requiescat, old sod box, *in pace*. As long as it's ninety proof. Have a glass waiting for me. No ice . . .

Jud said, "All this is *ex post facto*. Unconstitutional. Tell you what. I'll keep the peace, Oh Great White Mothers, sign the treaty, effective tomorrow, and return to my wickiup peaceful. But tonight I mean to have a drink. One."

In memoriam.

A consultation of eyes, Vee and Bee.

"One," Billie said, "But beginning tomorrow . . ."

He raised his right hand, fingers crooked. "As long as the grass

113

shall grow." And poured him a brown one.

Score one for us, Jack.

"Bring your beers to the fire," he said. "I will tell you such tales
. . ."

Let the world wagge, and take mine ease at mine Inne.

20

The Blue Angel.

They're watching the late show. Fritz Lang's '29 morality flick from the forgotten novel by Heinrich, the forgotten Mann. Read it in college, Fritz, *Professor Unrat oder Das Ende eines Tyrannen*. Not on the class reading lists. Found it one day in the stacks. He was tougher than you on the old professor, a bit much on judgement and brimstone for off-limits tumescence. The black and white film brushes flickers of light and shadow into the room . . . You got to the pity without pitying. Marlene's ingenuous star-spangled strumpetry. Emil Jannings, the old crotch caught professor, flapping around in his rooster getup, crowing his cuckold cry, peddling his wife's porny postcards, her common denominator legs. What hath cock-a-doodle wrought?

Jud, leaning over the back of the armchair, is glued to the tube. He's inside it.

Every man's self-portrait.

Mine?

He's seen it with Vera at the Museum. So her head's appreciatively atilt with the flick-flack curator's imprimatur.

He looks at Billie who's yawning.

Here it comes. Marlene perched on a stool in net stockings up to her anvil, in that spumy café. The burghers go into a reverential hush, triangulating urges.

"Falling in love again," she sings, "Never wanted to . . . What's a girl to do? . . . Can't help it."

But she doesn't do it with Emil anymore.

And he's thrown it all away for those trademarked legs – his home, his position. His *Stellung*.

Jud slides some Armagnac into his shell. He feels like a cigarette, something.

And there is that famous fadeout. The apocalyptic Jannings back, more eloquent with doom than a face, turning from the Christmas lit windows of his once home, drifting off in his slippered walk in the implacably falling snow.

Alles kaput.

Tune in next Friday nite for another film classic.

"Well," Vera said, getting up from the couch, "One, I suppose, should be sorry for him. But I'm not. He broke his vows."

"But . . ." Jud began.

Billie thrust a finger into her pack.

Vera said "My, but it's late. You have a lesson tomorrow, Billie. Your first since . . ."

"One more cigarette," Billie said.

"You two," Vera said, "always sitting around in the dark when you should be in bed."

Billie coughs on her smoke.

"I'll be going up, Vee, after my cig."

"How can you see what you're doing?" Vera switched on a lamp. "Jud?"

"I'll be up in a few minutes."

Billie said: "I'm not taking the lesson."

"You're not?"

She shook her head.

"But you must, you have an appointment."

"I'll call it off first thing in the morning."

"That's too late. Mimsy won't have time to re-schedule."

"Big deal. I'll tell her I'm sick."

She lit another cigarette. "Maybe next week."

"If you don't get back up on a horse now you never will."

She shrugged. "Up on a horse."

"Billie, it's happened to others. I've bought some earth, had my falls. They say you're not a horseman until you belong to the Collarbone Club." He tapped his chest. "Cracked a few ribs in my time. So has Vera. She was even dumped once by Casey. Not his fault."

"Good old Casey. It's never the horse's fault − is it?"

"Some kid with a slingshot hiding in the brush let him have it, smack on the rump. He didn't know where it came from. He bucked."

"Like good old Wilbur."

"She had the wind knocked out of her. But she got back on right away as soon as she caught her breath, and we rode home."

"Goody for Vera."

Yes, goody indeed for Vera. From the memory bank: Her bruise blued cheek. Are you all right, darling? Trouble brings tenderness up out of the well. Of course, I'm all right. Stop fussing, Jud. But where are my glasses? I hope they're not broken. Bifocals are very expensive to replace. She squints at the ground. Stumbles. He catches her arm. Wants to . . . He finds them intact as they flew off her face on the grass a foot from her fall. Ah, now I can see where I'm at. I can't understand, she says, what happened. Casey's never . . . Was he stung by a bee? He tells her about somebody's darling monster, the kid with the slingshot he'd seen out of the corner of his eye. I wanted to go after him, nail him like a no trespassing sign to a tree. Just an affluent suburban kid killing people. *My* Johnny? He sings in the choir. But first I had to make sure you were all right. Of course I'm all right. Just look at Casey grazing. That's a Quarter Horse for you. Roman, I think, would have been halfway across the county by now. Brushing grass, earth and leaves from Vera. No, she will not ride Roman while he rides Casey

116

home. Help me mount, please. I am a bit shaky. But I will ride my own horse, thanks. Later, the X rays say, two ribs – hairline fractures. She doesn't count the lacerations. Poor Casey, she says. Your daughter, Jack, too.

"It's the only way," he said

Billie did something with her lips as if chewing

"OK, so I'm scared."

"This may sound corny," he said, "but it's true: the only thing you have to fear is fear itself. Everyone thinks F.D. Roosevelt said it. Before your time. He did. But it was H. Thoreau via A. MacLeish, FDR's elegant poet speech writer who wrote the script."

"Who needs it," she said. "Next time it could be my face. Stitches across it. Scars. Wouldn't that be just great." She crosses those legs.

The Blue Angel.

"No way."

From the head of the stair: "Jud, are you coming up?"

"Right away," he calls up. Then to Billie: "OK, you call off the lesson."

She gives him a shutter's half-second snapshot smile.

"But – tell you what," knowing she won't buy it, "I'll mount you on Roman tomorrow."

"Why don't you just mount me, who needs the horse?" she sort of laughs.

He lowers his head. "Billie . . ."

"Okay, okay. I don't like it already."

"I'll put a lead line on him and walk you around. He's a good boy. No tricks."

"So was Wilbur."

"Just walking, Billie, so you'll get the feel of it again. Nice and easy, just here on the place in the small field. It will be perfectly safe. I'll be there all the time, close, with the line."

"And I'll be way up there." She points to the ceiling.

"Let's try it. You can't let this beat you. You'll see, it will be all right."

"I don't know. We'll see in the morning."

From the head of the stair: "Why is the light off down there? Judson, are you coming up, or do I have to come down and drag you?"

"She's getting uptight about us," Billie says in the dark.

"Relax," he was saying to Billie rigid on Roman's back, going around the small field. "All we're doing is walking. There's nothing to be afraid of." Roman stepping sprightly along, his small Thoroughbred ears cocked forward.

"Walking. He feels he's full of running, like that's what he's going to do any second."

"Good action, that's all. He's just stepping out."

Roman snorted.

"Oh God," Billie gasped, yanking the reins. "What was that for?" Roman stopped, tossing his head up against the tight bit.

"He's just feeling good to be out."

"Well I'm not."

"Ease up on the reins. You're grabbing his mouth. Just bend your wrists in if you want him to stop. All he needs is a hint." Jud started him walking again on the line staying close to his head.

"Jud, I want to get down."

"You haven't been up five minutes."

"It feels like five years." She sat hunched in her defeated regalia: the shined elegant boots, the lemony yellow gloves, the drooping peak of her hunt cap.

"Lean back, take a breath. There's nothing to worry about. I'm right here."

They circled the field, Roman willing, not understanding. His gold Arab blood.

"My legs ache." He saw they were trembling.

"That's because you're too tense, gripping too hard. Relax, be a passenger. You're taking the scenic tour."

They walked a few steps. A pine branch brushed her cap. She ducked.

"Oh crap, why did I ever start this?"

He stopped walking, looked up at her disordered face.

"I mean, I guess this isn't my thing . . . The Collarbone Club."

He turned Roman's head, leading him back to the barn, obedient, wondering, stepping along.

"And I don't have one picture of me all dressed up on a horse," she said as he helped her dismount. The full and now sacklike weight of her.

Passing the covered pool on the way to the house, Billie said "I guess I'll never be swimming in that next summer, now there's no reason . . ."

Coming in through the French doors at the terrace they could hear a fracas of pots being banged in the kitchen, cabinets slammed, Vera exploding. "Damn . . . damn . . ."

They looked at each other, stepping back on the bricks.

"Even if –"Billie began. Her eyes flicked towards the house. She turned to the pasture, the barn, the still unleafed woods all around.

"Well, at least I won't have to play Scrabble anymore" she said, nodding as if she were reading her palm.

Spring
Summer

21

He was taking his coat from the hook on his office door when he felt the barometric pressure of her, mercury falling.

"It still feels funny," Billie said, "not going with you to the farm on Fridays."

Another Friday, another envelope in her hand.

"Don't read this," she said, "until you get on the train."

He knew what would be in it, Billie's hours away from him on slips of paper, prescriptions no druggist could fill, as in all the other Friday envelopes:

> Her time is kept
> by the shuttered room
> that clicks away her springtime.

> No sparrow sings.
> No spot of sun
> falls on her hair
> to keep its golden colour.

> Their loving
> owned the springtime hours
> when she was young
> and she was his.

And: Last night I dreamed
       on the violins of your voice
       that promised me the summer.
       Not long, you said.
       Summer will come.

And: Rainy day
       of missing love.
       the blue-gray
       music
       on the wall.

Another Friday. And this morning, after she'd shut off the police car howl of the clock, she'd said, "Let's not go in today. Please. Let's stay here all day. We've never had a full night and day together. Please. In bed. Wouldn't that be great. A whole night and day. Please. We'll have a ball. There's all kinds of stuff you like in the fridge. That's why I left the office yesterday early. To shop for us so we could stay in. Caviar, champagne. Your favourite kind. *Blanc des blancs.* Right? Please. We'll be so happy. Please. We'll eat, we'll drink, we'll have a party . . . float around until you have to go home. Jud, please."

The blind cupids plastered around the ceiling.

The impaled shriek of the dog in the alley.

"I've got a big day at the office," he said. "So have you, Billie."

"Yeah, fighting with dikey Wanda. What a drag."

"I'll get your layouts done. I promise."

You promised me the summer.

Billie said: "I've got three ads to do. And all I can think of is I won't see you till Monday. A whole weekend. I feel so lost. All I want is to be with you."

"I'll work with you on the ads."

"Yeah, they're already saying you're writing my stuff. When I was hung up on crutches at the farm. And you brought the stuff in. The worst part is it's getting to be true. Only yesterday Wanda said, 'Who wrote that headline? Jud?'"

Cans skiffling in the alley. Another garbage collection day.

"Jud, please. I just can't go in. Not today."

Her hand slid under the sheet, websoft on him.

He hiked up on his elbows.

"I've signed the articles," he said. "I have to go in."

She ripped the sheet off like a torn sail. "At least let me taste you." He cupped the gold bowl of her breast as she bent over him, its popped coral nipple. Morning love. Hatchets of light through the shutters, the day waiting to hack them down. He dropped back to the pillow, his pearls on her sunny mouth.

He took the envelope from her. "Monday," he said, filling the word with what he knew would be to her cold delayed promise. What else could he say here in the all ears office going home in the hall. He wanted to touch her, at least take her hand, when Ottavio passed his door swirling his bing cherry eyes.

"One drink at the station? Just one?"

He shook his head. "I can't, not tonight, Billie. I haven't been home in two days."

She nodded "I know," her face trying to smile. "Hey, I'm sorry." She touched a button on his coat. "Don't look like that. I'll be OK. Give me a sec, I'll walk you to the station." He needed to walk alone, to separate this from that, catch up with himself, a pause between worlds.

At the elevator doors in the lobby, Les Madonna with a Strawbridge & Clothier shopping bag loaded with drawing pads, Magic Markers, supplies.

"Looks like you have half the stock room in there," Jud said

121

pleasantly. "Free-lance going that well?"

"Some of us work at home," Les said. "On office stuff."

"Yes," Jud said agreeably, "and some of us work in the office on office stuff."

Billie pinched his arm.

Les pushed into the next car coming down, room for one more.

"You shouldn't have said that," Billie whispered in his ear.

"Why not? He's ripping the company off," he louder than whispered back.

"He's one of Tad's kids."

"That doesn't make him – or the others – less of a crook. Besides, he has no talent."

Ella Pot, the cockney receptionist passed in the hall, her bacon slab backside swaying.

"The London derrière," Jud said.

"Wha?" Billie said.

"Not to worry," Jud said. "Just the name of an old song."

All the way up Walnut she held to his arm, through the funnelling crowds to the platform, standing with him in the crush until the conductor called "Board."

He opened the envelope. Two handwritten sheets of yellow copy paper in her flourishing script. No salutation, no signature. Circumspect omission. If found, a letter from no one to no one. Or everyone to everyone.

I don't think you realise what's happening to me. I can hardly believe it myself. But I'm beginning to feel totally unequipped for coping with life. Except when I'm with you.

My depression is worse than it's ever been. Even when I used to feel totally mixed up and did crazy things. And that was almost three years ago.

I'm starting to feel that way again, and I'm helpless to do anything about it.

I even hate myself for writing you this. But I don't know what else to do. I shut all doors when I met you. Please – that's just a statement of fact. I don't want to open them. It's just that I don't have anyone but you. Even Karla – she's into this thing with a new girl.

I'm so afraid.

I can't stand being without you.

There's nothing else in life for me. When you're with me everything is all right.

Oh, don't worry, I'm not going to do anything. I'm afraid of that too.

But I don't know how much longer I can take it. It's not just mental pain, anymore. My whole body feels wracked. I need you all the time. You feed me. Without you I starve.

Will we ever be together?

Please.

If you could tell me that, somehow I'll get through.

Please don't think this is an ultimatum. It's not.

But I just have to tell you how I feel. Nobody else could really understand.

I just hope you do.

And forgive me for writing this at all.

I'll try to forget to be miserable because I can't see you and remember to be happy because I have you.

I love all of you with all of me.

And even more.

A crazy little verselet comes into his head as if she had written it:

Three Times a Week in Her Cosy Little Flat

Tell me you'll marry me
even if you won't.
Tell me you love me
even if you don't.

But I do, Billie, I *do* . . .

"Excuse me, do you have a match?" the man in the next seat was saying, showing an unlit cigarette.

He reached in his pocket, gave him the packet.

"I've noticed pipe smokers always have plenty of matches," the man said. "Have to, I guess, to keep 'em going. I smoked a pipe once . . . always going out. A nuisance. Carrying pouches and cleaners. Now with cigarettes . . ." he lit up – "Thanks."

"Keep them," Jud said, cutting off commuter camaraderie.

April. Aries. Her birthday next week.

"Paoli, Paoli," the conductor bawled, "last stop, all changes here."

22

Friday night she used to be out partying. Big night, Friday night –
parties all over the place – Louie, Hal, Karla. Hi gang. The Billie Miller
Fan Club Louie once called it. Friends in the bars. A good night for
singles in crummy Philamadelky. Jud's word. She sipped her martini.
Jud's booze. Only Bombay will do. Natch. "And just *think* the
vermouth, but it should be a good one, say Noilly Prat, extra dry. One
should think only good thoughts when making a drink." Oh Jud. If
only he'd stayed. He could have this once. I practically begged him.
Not even a drink at the station. Never on Friday. That's reserved for the
farm. Horses and her. All alone by the telephone. Neato. Friday. The
name comes from the Anglo Saxon for the fuckin goddess called Frig.
He's a whole liberal arts education wrapped up in a Brooks Brothers
suit, excuse please – Savile Row ten years old. "Good stuff, that, stands
up." With cuffs, yet. Like the Duke of Windsor. Louie told me, put
down some college on your résumé. He'll go for that. Hooboy. Dint he
ever. Frig. Monday's a long way away. Another lost weekend. Even
there at the farm, waiting for Vera to go up at night. But at least . . .
That time he came back from his ride and said as we walked to the
barn, Roman's reins in his hand, walking behind him like a big puppy,
"Have you ever considered clichés? They're really moments of truth, the
old heart of the matter. For example, 'Feeling his oats' – you've heard
that expression. Well, give a horse more oats than he needs and it's like
putting more coal in a furnace. He'll be supercharged. Like Roman
today. He must have had more than his usual. I let him work it out on
the hills."

"Are you supercharged?" I asked him.

"Riding always does that to me. What must it do for a woman?
brushing into the saddle, practically making love to the horse."

"Tell me another cliché," I said.

He looked toward the house. "Let me unsaddle Roman first, rub
him down. Stick around." He was always high after a ride. But always
the horses first.

"Now," he said, looking around again, "we will have a roll in the
hay. On good timothy and sweet clover." It felt like pins in my back
even through the old blanket. He smelled like a horse, clumsy with
rolled down breeches and boots. Who cared. It was great. Up in the
loft, the cats sitting on bales of hay, watching. Then we brushed each
other off. "Now I'll tell you one," I said. "You've just put the boots to
me." It wasn't too bad at that, at the farm. Now I won't see him three

nights, two days, like it says in the hotel ads. So he'll sneak in a call on the weekend. Maybe. Big deal. Then the phone will bop in mid-sentence. Old Vera's walked in from the good old barn or some place. She was good to me, old Vee, really took care. But how can he stand that woman? Everything by the numbers. A grandmother for a wife. Scrabble, scrabble and crostics. A kook. Well, here I am his essential ingredient and nothing's cooking till Monday night. Shit.

She stopped her foot tapping the floor, lit another cigarette. A joint would be better. No pot since that Madonna party, but even if, so what, you can't fly alone unless you're crazy. Jump through a window or something. Rack up a car. No thanks. Maybe I am nuts shacked to a married man. With the other marrieds, like Harvey, it was just for the jollies, understood, nothing heavy. It didn't count. Karla warned me, Louie. Good old Luigi. "Why don't you ring, you bastard," she said to the dumb phone. Maybe I'll take in a show. That's no fun alone, either. Her foot was tapping again. May as well have another drink. Sleep. Can't sleep the weekend away. Three nights, two days. Went to the kitchenette, tugged at the glacial ice tray – where the hell is that screw driver – ow. Fuck. Sucking her bruised finger when

The phone rang.

"Hi there, Billie girl."

"Loooie!"

"What's cookin, bambina?"

"Just sitting around. Where are you?"

"At the office. Had to work late. A new business pitch on Monday. Thought I'd give you a tingle. Long time."

"Yeah."

"You OK?"

"I'm fine."

"You sound sorta down."

"No, just taking it easy. Had a big week."

"Your leg OK?"

She laughed. "Since when wasn't it OK?"

He cackled, "I mean your accident – on the horse."

"Oh that. All gone, like it says in the ads. Hey, Luigi, thanks for the card. That was sweet. It was very funny. I should have dropped you a line, but I didn't see it until I got home . . ."

"From the farm. You were there a couple of weeks."

"How did you know?"

"Bambina . . ."

She laughed again. "Oh Luigi, your round-the-clock-news radio station. I should have known. You know everything that goes on this town. You always did."

"Like you haven't been to the farm on weekends for, oh a while, say a month?"

"No. I don't go there anymore. Who told you that?"

"Let's just say you've been seen alone, here and there on a

125

Saturday, Sunday. Like at the Gilded Cage. In the park."

"What a yenta town. Yeah, the biggest small town in the U.S.A."

"You and Jud?"

"We're solid, Luigi, he's my man. It's just . . ."

"Hey, Billie girl, all I had was a sangwich sent in for lunch. Whadya say I buy you a dinner? A drink? Any place, you name it."

"I'm fainting, Luigi. You *buying* me dinner. You must have struck oil."

"Pay day. I'm loaded." A switch? Mama mia always got the paycheque. You get an allowance.

"Hmn. Let me think." They could be seen. Someone blab to Jud. "I'm sort of comfy. And I am a bit tired. I'd have to dress up to go out. All that jazz. Tell you what. Why don't you come over here. I've got a fridge full of great stuff. But Louie –"

"Yeah, Billie?"

"Don't get any ideas."

"Who me?"

"No hassle."

"OK, I'll be there in twenty minutes. Start counting."

"Louie . . .?" The phone dead but she still said, "I mean it."

"Hello beautiful," he said at the door, going with his lips for hers. She turned her cheek.

"Listen, paisan," she said.

"OK, OK," bouncing in. He did his soft-shoe shuffle, buck-and-wing, snapped his castanet fingers – "And a hi-de-ho."

Laughter had come back to her. "Oh gumbah, it's good to see you."

"Likewise," he said, loosening his tie from habit.

"Keep your shirt on."

"Just coming up for hair." A Groucho leer, the hinged-knee strut.

"Luigi . . ." Friday was becoming Friday again. "Hey, what would you like to drink?"

He looked at her glass and at her. The beginning of the old Billie smile loosening up.

"No marts for me. That's suicide sauce. I'm just a plain Italian boy. Not even Sicilian. I can't even handle hot peppers."

"A Scotch okay?"

"That's the spirit."

Pouring Jud's J. Walker Black in the kitchenette, she called, "How's your mother?"

"What can I tell you? Another day, another complaint. Arthritis, bursitis, colitis, hepatitis, you name-it-itis. She was used to old Doc Colarossi – he delivered me – made house calls, held her hand, called her signora, and when she was balky, cara Annunziata. Between him and the priest she did all right. Well, Father Gaetano is dead – a High Funeral Mass, the Archbishop came. And so is her old Doc. And the new Doc, a young smartass . . . he wants to plug her into a computer,

126

all those tests . . . a woman who picked olives when she was a girl and pressed grapes with her feet. And the new priest – he'd rather talk about ecumenism instead of the Blessed Mother and miracles, and read book reviews to old paisans instead of running the bingo games. I bought her a medal blessed by the Pope. And you know what? She no longer has shingles. She wasn't sick a day in her life until my father died."

He sat down at the café table. Billie slipped into the seat across.

He raised his glass. "To old times," he said.

"To old times," she answered, sipping the white stuff, smiling.

"These are very nice glasses," he said. "Crystal. I haven't seen them before."

"Jud," she said, her head coming down.

"Hey, bambina," he said, "it's Friday."

"Yeah, in Philamadelky."

"Wha?"

"Not to worry, as the man says," she got up with her empty glass. "I think I'll have another. You?" She lit a cigarette from the stub. "'Scuse."

She returned with the drinks and as she sat down, hiccupped. "Who needs that," she said hiccupping again.

"We can get rid of that," he said, going behind the chair.

"Yeah, I remember, that night at Karla's party. What do I do again?" she hiccuped.

"Doctor Bocca's Magic Hiccup Remedy." He put his hands on her shoulders.

"You're just nervous, bambina. Relax. Now, take a deep breath, as deep as you can, until you can't get any more in."

She breathed in. "More," he said, "more. Now hold it. Don't let it out. Keep it in as long as you can, till you think you will burst." He spread his fingers along either side of her neck. She began shaking her head. "Hold it, another sec – now let it out slowly." He pressed down at the base of her neck. "Slowly, s-l-o-w-l-y, without moving." She exhaled. "Now breathe in slowly, as if you're just sipping the air. The trick is not to gulp it." She sat statue still, breathing shallowly, waiting, his hand still on her.

"Presto chango," he said. "You see, they're gone."

"Svengali Luigi," she said.

Still standing behind her his hands began moving down.

"Don't," she said, her eyes wide, looking ahead. "Louie, please."

A slight grit to his jaw. "Okeydoke." He stepped back, his fingers brushing her hair, and sat down at the table.

"You're a good guy," she said, reaching for her drink.

"You don't need any more booze. Hey, look, I've got a lid of the best."

"Acapulco Gold."

"Not any more."

"Panama Red?"

"Ice Pack, great stuff from the coast. No garbage, terrific, clean. The real thing. I rolled it myself."

"In your little Bugler machine."

"Try it, you'll like it."

"I don't know, Louie. I don't think that's such a good idea."

"You deserve a break today," he sang from the jingle.

"Yeah, I guess I do at that."

"Right on, Billie girl."

She sat back in her chair. "Hokay, just a trial demonstration. Just a few drags."

"You got it." He took a stick from a Parliament box, lit it with her lighter, drew a deep breath down and handed it over. She sucked on it, popped her cheeks out filling her mouth and swallowed, holding the smoke. She handed the joint back. Her eyes shone watery but she smiled, nodding.

He went to the stereo, held up an album, vintage Sinatra. She nodded approval, letting her breath out. He gave her the stick again as the music came on.

"Isn't that stuff really something?" he said. "Ice Pack."

"Super –"

"– Dooper." He did a dance step and they were laughing. The room was no longer overcast, filling with soft gold sounds of sunlight.

"Hey, Luigi, what's new around town?"

He sat down, the stick going between them.

"Nothing much. Let's see. I had lunch with Harvey. He wanted to know about you – and Jud, if it still was a thing."

"And you said?"

"I told him, you're still off limits."

"*Still.* Some good buddy. With Jud and me it's *forever.*" Then why was she laughing, laughing.

"Yeah," he said, lighting another stick.

"What's that for? With this Ice Pick one is enough."

"Ice *Pick*," he said, "you know you said Ice Pick."

"Hahahaha. That's very funny. What else, paisan, is newd?"

"Newd. Hahaha. Lesee. Hal Carter called me."

"Nude," she said, "that's very funny, gumbah," handing over the stick.

"Yeah," he said, "you break me up," holding the stick, not smoking but swaying a little.

"So what did Hal say? ol' Hal, a nice mans, but no –"

"Oomph."

"Oomph. Hahaha. Very funny, paisan. So what did Hal say?"

"He said you'd be back."

"Yeah? not with him."

"With whom? bambina?"

"Jud-Jud – that's *whoomph.* Roll ina hay. Morning fuck. Sweet

128

timothy. Clover bells . . . balls . . . bales."

He handed her the stick.

"C'mon Louie, whom else ast for me?"

"Lesee, Lesee." Her face seemed to be his face. Big flower. With gold hairskin, blueblueblue eyes.

She took a deep drag, held it, closing her eyes. Bloomy, bloomy. Ol' Frankie coming out of a silver moon breathing that Old Black Magic all over her. Kiss. She handed the stick back. He kept it away from his mouth. Oh bambina. Your mouth.

"Oh yeah," Louie said, "Gil Kerr."

"My first bosso," she said dreamily. "Hahaha. Whas he doin'?"

He took a short drag. Through the laughing sunshine somebody on the other side of the confessional told him another drag and you're gone.

"Gil Kerr. He's still buildin houses. Society Hill. Lotsa commissions, but doesn't wanna get big."

"Hahaha. *Big*," she broke up, shaking with happy tears. Louie was laughing with her. "BIG – he'd throw his rocks the minute he touched me."

"You told me."

Together now: "Hahahahahahaha."

"Ol' Gilbert."

"The Erector Set," Louie said. When I was kid, my father gave me one for my birthday. You made things . . . Nuts, bolts."

"You're a funny mans, ol' Luigi. Rectum Set. Haha. Nuts, bolts. Haha. NUTS."

He reached for his tie, loosened it somewhere and the top buttons on his somewhere shirt.

"Ol' Blue Eyes," she said, parsing the beat.

He squinted.

She waved queenly at the stereo. "Him."

"Oh yeah," he said, "Frankie."

"Yeah, Jud say he a great artist. Has his own in . . . in-del-ible signature . . . Like Beatles. Say they invented something. Like Mozahr."

"The old dude, whayuknow."

Frankie was all over the room doing it his way. Coming out of the walls, birds skimming around their ears. They were swimming in him, in and out of his eyes.

"My way," she said.

"Hey bambina." His shirt fell to the floor. "Member Johnny J's bash? Gilkerr 'n I took you home. Stoned."

"Don't get stoned anymore."

"You bet, kiddo."

His hand Disney ballooned toward her. They were swaying around in some kind hahaha ocean. Oh, a bed. How'd that get here? Five feet off the floor, floatin, floatin around the . . . Up near the ceilin. Gotta climb onta the dream. How I do it? JUMP. GRAB. PUSH UP.

129

Roll over.

Who say that?

"No funny stuff, Louie."

"Cross my heart." Condor winged crucifixion gestures. Wide as the world falling off it. Elbow on jaw.

"Hey you hit."

"Scusa . . ."

"Bambina."

"Eyetalian boys good to their mamas. Know how to cook. Make linguini, Loogi. Clam sauce. Hahaha."

"Ice Prick," he said and they were rolling around, sheet/pillow/legs. LAUGHING.

Then she felt somebody thing on/in her.

Wallpaper BlueEyes ballooms.

"Hey Frankie . . . sing . . .

"My Way . . ."

Upstairs the drums walloped the room.

The impaled dog shrieked in the alley.

"It doesn't count, Jud," she said. "It's only Loogi."

23

Proof sheets of his Expel campaign were pinned to the cork board in Tad's office. His four ads: The Rain Check, Called on Account of Rain, Keeps Your Reputation Spotless, and That's the Ticket. But not bandy Leeta's also-ran. They looked good. The simple authority of type.

Tad winked: "So clients will think I wrote them."

Har.

The prerogatives of office. The team head. Rah.

Dissolve the I into we.

"Department head ruboff," Tad said. "It comes with the territory."

"It's all in the family."

"That's the ticket, Ace."

"A privilege, Sire."

"It saved the account, Ace. Not just Expel, but Global Chemicals, Ltd., the parent company. They creamed. If we hadn't come through with a new Expel campaign they'd have pulled the whole shmear – thirteen million bucks. Thanks."

Thanks for what? It's my job. I'm not your serf. I work for the agency.

"A great save. We had two strikes on us going in with two out in the bottom of the ninth." The Villanova varsity bat boy. Couldn't make Notre Dame.

Not the first time, Tadpole. Remember American Dairies? No, that was before your time. You were still in production department, the ex-Marine typist. Not just an ad. I invented a *product.* Patented by the client. It wasn't even my account, but I'd heard we're in trouble. Give us a great promo idea, they said. (Or else.) So at home on the weekend I came up with a new ice cream – Red, White & Blueberry – for patriotic occasions: Memorial Day, July 4, Labour Day, and Thanksgiving. I even worked out the formula: raspberry ice for the red; ground bean vanilla for white, and fresh blueberries for the blue. Wrote the marketing plan. And the campaign. It's in the all-time Hundred Greatest. Brought in four million bucks over budget. When I walked into the local supermarket six months later, there it was in three-foot high banners plastered across the store front: Red, White & Blueberry. The account executive was promoted to senior vp with a bonus. And a cruise to Bermuda with wifey. I got a note from somebody up there. Terrific, It said. You've done it again. Thanks. Smiling, the boy fell dead. And you sit there diddling your mind about taking on Bernbach/Wells/Ogilvy in the Villanova Field House. How come you left out Leo Burnett, you Jolly Green Midget? You're not even a dot on their i's.

"The subsidiary tail wags the conglomerate dog," Jud said. He must share the cliché with Billie. The barebones reality of it.

Tad tamped his Camel (non-filter) on his labourer's nail.

"There are going to be some changes in the department," he said.

Jud said: "Oh," sealed messages shot through his muscles. Blind blips on the radar screen.

Tad swivelled around on his leather throne raised up on a platform behind the desk to give him height. The potty Roman emperor, a.k.a. Mussolini, before he was hanged by the heels.

"Yeah, but you're coming up roses."

Here it comes. He's going to put me in charge of Army, the whole thing. Thirty-eight million dollars – the biggest account in the house. He's bowing out. Can't run the department and Army and do either job right.

"First the bad news," Tad said.

Jud felt the capillaries contract along his skin. The scrotum shrinking corporate sea.

"I'm terminating Billie."

And all he could say was "Oh," again as the wrecker's ball slammed into the wall. Terminating. He saw Tad in a newsreel frame standing at the Auschwitz siding as people blundered out of the cars. Thumb up, thumb down.

Tad dragged on his Camel as if it were pot.

"I'm telling you this first, because . . . well, she's in your group, for one thing."

What's the other thing, Tad?

"And man-to-man . . ."

Don't you mean man-to-woman?

"She's a good writer," Jud said.

Tad looked out the window over the still unleafed park. "She hasn't cut the mustard."

"You mean she can't work with Wanda."

Tad shrugged. "That – and you've got to admit her copy is somewhat less than sensational."

"She's done some very good things – the women's Army campaign she turned in last week, for instance. Really strong copy and headlines." And as he said, "They're right on. They ring the bell," he knew Tad would be coming up with –

"They sure ring the old Bell," showing terrier teeth. Har. "Yeah, they're tough, all right." He reached for the rustle pile of rough layouts on the side of the desk, reading the headlines aloud:

"Not for Men Only. Today's Army."

And –

"There Are No Wacs in Today's Army.
Just Women."

132

And –

"How to Tell Your Parents
You Want to Join the Army."

Tad nodded. "Tough, Ace, real grabbers."

"I thought so. Billie has what it takes, Tad."

"Wanda says you wrote them, that the tough ones are always yours."

"Oh come on, Thaddeus, she's never liked Billie. Of course I checked them out as creative director, but Billie wrote them. She's hardly had a fair chance to show what she can do. At least assign her another art director. Say Joe. I think they'd work well together, get some of that girl writer-boy art director chemistry going. Then if that doesn't work out –"

"Lookit, Ace, I might have kept her on; I like a good looking young head around the shop, kind of dresses it up. But I've been told to chop a writer. Every department is dropping a body – some more than one, so let's count our blessings. She's been here less than six months. Let's just say, last one hired, first one fired. Okay? You're not to tell her, right? I'll tell her myself. Lookit, I'm giving her two weeks severance pay although she's only entitled to one. That's about it, over and out."

Too much coming together. Lit fuses of words: bodies. Termination. He looks at the dark haired kid on his raised swivelling throne and sees the *man* who once sat there not needing a platform to raise him. Cobble jawed Owen Pilgrim, crew cut, with his, yes, manly dependable smile and crisp white shirt chest-filled like a following sail. His first head of department, the man who had hired him, long gone away, the last of Old Fairleigh's tithing Baptists, onetime intercollegiate tennis champ and a helluva (pardon me, Owen) writer yourself in your time. Old Fairleigh time, before the new cave men began coming in. Even then, some of the later hands called you (behind your back, of course) Frank Merriwell and Boy Scout – because you didn't cuss or smoke or drink, not even coffee – and Preacher – because you taught Sunday School. Like, hey man, get with it. With what? Pot? You never preached to us. You simply performed the good tidings. Godspell. And if you were square, as some said, okay, you were foursquare. Right on, humanwise, as they say. You didn't know about bodies. Just people. You remember Brandel DeWitt? Who could forget. Ex-Phillips Exeter English instructor. Ex-Social Register, ex-would-be poet. Ex. There he'd be, toward the end, shaking and tremoring over his desk like a minor earthquake – when he came in. His bony white knuckled fingers actually rattling over the typewriter keys. When he came in. "Look at that guy," you said one Monday morning. "He comes in even when he is so sick. *Sick?* Shrinks aside and all that psychosocio crap (excuse me, Owen), the guy had the DT's. A once and always rummy . . . "Get him home, Jud," you said, "out the back way and put him to bed. Hire a

133

nurse to get some food into him. He's exhausted. Call the Ben Franklin Clinic, they'll know where to get one. And have the bill sent to me . . . personally." You didn't say, Take him to a doctor, or the Salvation Army, so maybe you knew all the time (whether you did or not doesn't matter – you behaved as if you didn't – you non-drinking tither). "We'll cover his assignments until he's well," you said, probably knowing, too, he'd never be. We'd been doing just that, Owen, Charlie Ballard and I, but I guess you knew that too in your Merriwell way. He'd been canned any other place in the world, but you didn't can him, although he was coming in less and less until he didn't come in anymore. "The guy has a way with words," you said. (When he came in.) You saved his face and his job as long as you could. And you knew all about bottom lines. Now that's true Religion, Owen, the real Samaritan thing. But you never thought of it that way. You would have been Gary Cooper embarrassed, if any one'd brought it up. Bless you, Guv; I don't think we'll meet again. I'll be in a warmer place, unless you run a department up there. You have a lot of merit badges, Eagle Scout Owen. I always wanted to call you Mr Pilgrim, but you wouldn't have it. "Name's Owen," you said that first day; I suppose that's very Rotarian. The biggest square and best boss a man ever had. You knew how to run a department. You respected people the way I respect horses and dogs and cats and frogs and dragonflies and snakes and bats (nesting in my mud room; they have to have *their* space, too). And turtles, and that copperhead in the abandoned artesian well. (Just don't tread on me.) Even the yellow jackets who sting me, raise welts, poison pipelines on my flesh. They have to live somewhere. It's *their* ground nest I mowed over . . . Those notes of yours that would come like a smile on a real rotten day – you had such a sense of timing – too much to do by deadline – when I could use a smile . . . *You've done it again, Champ . . . Jud scores another touchdown . . . Congrats – you've won another CLIO. But even if you hadn't, you would have deserved it* . . . It wasn't the score that counted. It was the try. Maybe it was corny. Bodies don't need that stuff. Or accountants or MBA's who sit up there chopping away . . . We who live by the word will die by the numbers (J. Bell, *Circa* –) . . . I hope there's a tennis heaven, Mr Pilgrim, grass and clay courts – your two-handed backhand could be stunningly wild – and a chilled case or two of Hires Root Beer. "Hire's to you," you would say at the annual company picnic, as shameless a punster as I. (And you probably knew we nipped back to our cars for a nip to survive the Baptist hilarity.) Good clean fun. Oh yes, and I hope you have your old Smith-Corona they retired with you, like a football jersey, so you can keep on writing corny notes to the angels. Like, St Gabriel, sir, you've been doing a great job at the Gates, letting some of those borderline cases in. They could learn a thing or two from you up there. All I would have to do was sit down in this office, once yours, and ask for a reprieve for Billie, and in your *decent* way you'd know what was going on in my head, when you sat in that chair like a duffel bag too big for its locker . . . But then I wouldn't have had to ask. You'd know. To you I was Judson Bell, not Ace or Squire or a body . . . You just glanced at my ads when I applied, and nodded. "They march," you said. "But what I'm really interested in is your novels." Oh wow. Two agencies turned me down *because* I wrote novels. And I wouldn't have had to tell you I'd paid my dues and was still paying them and that Fairleigh owed me. You would have said, as you did once, with your Merriwell smile, "Life's too short, Jud, to waste people on it." Pilgrims of the world unite . . . He looks at the clone on his swivelling throne, stub-lighting another Camel (non-filter). I'm still paying more than my dues, and saved your ass more than once, Tadpole. You owe me . . .

"You mentioned department changes," Jud said.

Tad reached for his ringing phone. "That can wait. No sweat. We'll be talking." He flipped him a dead-lidded wink.

Walking up Walnut with Billie, she seems to be swimming in quiet, a private sea somewhere, yet sending him signals – scarcely lit smiles, brave little buoys bobbing in dark. Her hand in his, her fingers press his palm with intelligence, a recurrent uncoded message meant somehow to be reassuring. Touch for more than its own sake. Does she know? But she can't; she would be devastated. Will be devastated. That Tad hasn't told her yet, leaving that freight for him to carry alone until he does. But there's something awake in all that quiet. Something maybe she's sensed, a rumour? on her own distant early warning line.

"Is anything wrong?" he asks, as if anything isn't.

She shakes her head. "How can there be? It's my birthday and you're with me."

But there still is no birthday laughter; just the would-be brave little smiles in an ocean of quiet.

He squeezes her hand. "I've made reservations for dinner – *Le Bec Fin.*"

"Oh wow," she says wowlessly.

"Nine o'clock, a civilised hour."

"Good, then we can relax a while. I *am* bushed."

"Tough day with Wanda?"

A light now in her face for the first time. "As a matter of fact, no. Would you believe, she was nice to me today, but I mean very. I couldn't get over it, like she was someone else. Didn't screw up one headline – even took my ideas for pics. Like she finally got the word."

She got the word all right, right? Tad baby.

"Did you talk to her again? . . . to Tad?"

"I haven't, no, not since last week."

"Hey, maybe she finally made it with Joe. It's like she's a new woman. She's really gone ape over that ape. The way she sits at his feet, honest really *sits on the floor at his feet,* looking up at him with those wild cuckoo eyes while the Mahster gives her some pointers, like

135

she's saying, Here I am, Joe, I'm ready whenever you are. Something's different, that's for sure – who cares why. If this keeps up I'm in Fat City."

"Her husband might care." Saying it jangles: there is a wife would care, thirty miles west of this gritty pavement, alone with a black dog tonight.

Billie's fingers stiffen in his, slip out and she's swimming away again in her separate sea, with not even the small buoy smiles bobbing. *That Louie, if he talks, I'll kill him. Put out a contract on him.*

At Broad Street the Harry Krishnas are still jiggling in acned fervour. Shave-pated boy dropouts swaying in flapping dhotis ripe for the laundromat, street grimy feet slapping cement. Swinging their sikha locks renouncing the girlness of the nice looking American girls in gold-threaded saris, swaying alongside, chanting the homebound commuters to their suburban nirvanas with tambourine mantras: Hare Krishna, Hare Rama, Hare, Hare, Hare, and let's have a few OM-OM-OM's, cheerleaders for Harry.

Inside her door her arms clamp at once around him in fierce clutching surprise.

"Hold me," she says in a wet bubble breaking against his ear.

He says, "What's the matter?" (darling) over her shoulder to the blank room, spotting his birthday card on the mantel.

"I'm afraid."

He shifts a hand under her wheat fall of hair up to her moist botanical nape.

"Of what?"

The room isn't talking.

"I love you so much." In a splintery voice.

"That's good," he says, "that's very good."

She waits. She's sent him a message from somewhere – wish you were here. A return reply card enclosed. It's suddenly waxwork awkward, answering questions requiring answers. Check the appropriate box: Do you love me? If yes, go on to the next question. How much? He has questions, too, but he doesn't know what they are. As the silence stretches to where she is going to ask him to mail it today, he says.

"Because I love you, Billie."

Some of the fierceness goes out of her arms around him, almost like a sigh. They've been standing there waiting for someone to tell them when to move and where.

And then in a birthday child's voice – "What did you get me for my birthday?"

"Ah," he says, putting his hand in his jacket pocket and leading her to their ritual café table. He takes out a small box.

"All good things . . ." she says, untying the ribbon. It's a brooch in a scalloped gold frame with a finely carved cameo face in delicate profile.

"Aphrodite," he says. "She came from the sea; foam-born Aphrodite the Greeks called her."

"It's beautiful, Jud." Her lips summon his birthday kiss.

"What was her thing? I mean, you know, what was she known for?"

"The goddess of love."

"I thought that was Venus."

"That's what the Romans called her. She got around. Assyria, Babylonia," a pause – "Philadelphia." She smiles compliantly. "Different places, different names: Ishtar, Ashtoreth."

The brooch in her palm she says, "I think she looks like me," turning her profile to him.

"There is a resemblance."

"It's so right, like my ring, special . . . She came from the sea . . ." She's dreaming an ocean dream, looks up from a surfy beach. "I just got a great idea. This summer, Jud, let's take our vacation together at the shore. I know just the place." She's already there. "It would be so great, Jud, you and I at the shore, swimming together, walking the beach . . ."

Thirty miles to the west . . . "I'd like nothing better, Billie – you know that – but I can't do that."

"Why not, Jud why *not*?"

"How can I? What would I say? I'm going off to the shore with Billie – you remember Billie, she came out here to ride. See you in a month, I'll drop you a card."

"Just two weeks – I'm getting two weeks."

You're not getting anything, love. You'll be looking for another job. Damn Tad, he should have told you.

"Even so, I can't just go off like that without her – on a vacation? What excuse could I give? Of course she'd expect to go with me." Then gently, "Wouldn't you?"

She looks at the brooch for an answer. "Sweetheart, I've got it." He knows she is going to say: "You're going *alone* – to work on your *book* – get away from it all. She'll have to buy *that*." She leans back, a chess player who's just said, "Check."

Your move.

Take your time. But it's ticking.

He's face-to-face with Aphrodite alive and well and living in Philadelphia. Born in the blood-flecked foam from the hacked off cock and balls of the god Uranus, flung into the sea from heaven. Different places, different names. "I love you so much," she says . . .

"Do it for me . . .

"For us."

Suntime with Aphrodite, salt sea, sky and sand.

"Please . . ."

"We'll see. Maybe a week – this isn't a promise."

She doesn't have to say, "Mate." Instead, she looks at the clock. "Oh great, we have time," she says, "before dinner. You said, nine?"

What did the Phoenicians call her?

24

Tad looks damply up, "C'mon in, Ace," winks, "shut the door," then back to the sheet in his hand, nodding, lip-reading. Handing the memo to Jud, "This will go out first thing in the morning."

A glance gives him the message, his eye piecing the crazy quilt story, stumbling on names, titles in a new order. Somewhere in his head the Grenadier Guards strike up *The World Turned Upside Down*. Music to go with the script. Cornwallis at Yorktown.

"No calls for the next half-hour." Tad says into his phone, then to Jud – "sit, sit."

"I think I'll have one of those," Jud says, pointing to the pack of Camels on the desk.

"Cigarette? I've never seen you smoke anything but a pipe."

"To every thing there is a season and a time to every purpose."

"That sounds like an old Owen Pilgrim ad."

"It's from a book."

"I haven't read a book since I was out of college."

Neither has my dog, he's about to say at Tad's point-blank eyes. But he doesn't. He downshifts with honour to – "I know. It's in *The Guinness Book of Records.*"

"Har."

You don't pull the trigger on a joke. Not even Tad.

"You're a character, Ace," Tad says, shaking a cigarette half out of his pack toward Jud. "Be my guest." He snaps his lighter.

The flame lighting his cigarette is close to the papers in his moist fingers. Touch it and Unicorn Farm is up in flames.

"Read, read," Tad says.

TO ALL CREATIVE DEPARTMENT PERSONNEL
It is my pleasure to announce that the Board of Directors of our Company has elected the following Vice Presidents: Leeta Krantz, Leslie Madonna, Christopher Money and Joseph Concerto.

Leeta Krantz. A native of Duck Blind, Pa., Leeta was president of her senior class at Fasnacht High and editor of the yearbook, *The Shoo Fly*. A graduate of Schrecklich Community College, where she was business manager of the Johann Sebastian Bach Tap Dancers, Leeta won her Associate in Arts degree with honours in her major, Foundation Garment Selling, and minored in Draperies. A management trainee at Lit Brothers, she moved from salesclerk in budget basement notions to junior copywriter in the advertising department in seven months. Joining us less than three years ago, Leeta has shown her stuff as copywriter, supervisor and creative director. At twenty-six, she is probably the youngest female vice president/creative director of any major agency in the country. She will continue to be responsible for the accounts currently in her group and taking on new assignments to be announced by me in the near future.

Leslie Madonna. After one semester at General Anthony Wayne Junior Military College, Les enrolled in Mrs Flanagan's School for Exceptional Youth where he had his first encounter with art, winning the Driftwood Award for Found Art with an arrangement of discarded automobile tires, and the Self-Hardening Ceramic Prize for the most unusual ash tray. He left the Philadelphia College of Art after a year because, as he wrote in his application of Fairleigh, "There was nothing more they could teach me." Les then applied his talents to where it's at – a number of Philadelphia and suburban ad agencies before coming to us where he's been an art director and supervisor. In addition to his vice presidency, I am promoting Les to creative director. He and his lovely wife, Janet, live with their three children (soon to be four) in St Davids.

Christopher Money. A sixth-generation Philadelphian from Chestnut Hill, Kip attended Druid Academy, founded there by his family, and the Money Institute of Money. Starting as an assistant vice president in the mail room of the Money Bank & Trust Company, Kip soon found himself writing envelope stuffers and matchbook cover copy. Sent abroad for a year, he returned to a copywriter's job at Fairleigh shortly after we acquired the Money Bank & Trust Company account which he has served as copywriter, supervisor and creative director. Kip, his lovely wife, Bitsy, and their three sets of twins, live in the

Money family compound in Chestnut Hill.

Joseph Concerto. A graduate of South Philadelphia High where he was on the football and wrestling teams, Joe earned his way through the Philadelphia College of Art by working nights as an enforcer in several Locust Street bars and as a towel attendant in a judo parlour. Starting as a sketch man for Pell, Mell, Helter & Skelter, the hot boutique in Manayunk, Joe went on to the Big A as assistant layout resizer at Kenyon & Eckhardt on the Ford Motor account. (With a guy like this on our team we should be able to get an automobile account. Detroit, here we come.) Returning to Philadelphia, Joe became a senior art director at Beck & Call. Although within only eight months he was named director of the art department and a member of the management team, Joe walked out with the Brotherhood of Postage Stamp Appliers Local of the International Teamsters Union when they went on strike for professional status recognition and psychiatric benefits. I am proud to say that I hired Joe right off the picket line. Art director and supervisor, he now assumes the duties of group art director. A Sixth-Degree Black Belt in karate, Joe lives with his lovely wife, Marge, and their four daughters (maybe the next one will be a boy, Joe) in Cherry Hill, New Jersey, where he splits his own firewood with his bare hands and is Scoutmaster of Troop 308.

. . . He must look up sometime. Tad's swivelling around half the compass, stub-lighting another cigarette. When I came to Fairleigh twenty-now-plus-years ago, only department heads were vice presidents. It took me ten years to make creative director through seemly steps from senior copywriter to supervisor to group copy head – another two before I was named vice president. (MUSIC: Up.) Among the first of my peers. VP at Old Fairleigh, it once meant something – a battlefield commission, a business knighthood, the bijoux of achievement. My card, sir. Kids now graduating from kindergarten in baccalaureate gowns and gold doctoral tassels. Instant coffee, instant tit, instant vice presidents. Just shake and pour from the easy-to-open package . . . *And,* it's *convenient* . . .

"That's quite a batch of vice presidents at one time," Jud says. "The board of directors' cookie cutter must have run amok."

"What? What? – Oh, gotchya. The board acts on recommendations by the department head. Me. Read, read, you're coming to the interesting part – where *you* come in" – and shakes out a cigarette at him.

The top of the next page says:

NEW ASSIGNMENTS – THE ARMY ACCOUNT

A few facts:
Now that the Army Recruiting Account is billing over $40 million . . . Now that we expect to announce a major new piece of business coming in next month – *which we took away from a New York agency* . . .
Now that I'm up to my eyeballs in new business presentations . . . Even I cannot continue to be involved in the day-to-day production and administration of so large and important an account as the Army. I will still personally check all major campaigns, but the daily ongoing volume of work – print, broadcast, posters, leaflets, brochures – will be handled as follows:

Les Madonna and *Kip Money* have been appointed co-creative directors, reporting directly to me. They will be IN CHARGE of the Army account.
Joe Concerto will be group art supervisor with all art directors and supervisors reporting to him.
Jud Bell will be group copy supervisor with all copywriters and supervisors reporting to him. In order to free-up Jud for this important assignment, I am relieving him of his duties as a group creative director. His accounts will be reassigned shortly.
Both Joe and Jud will be responsible directly to Les and Kip.
These assignments are effective immediately.

T. Houlighan

Senior Vice President
Director of Creative Services
Fairleigh/Philadelphia

Responsible to Les and Kip.

After twenty years of being *responsible only to the assignment.* It somehow being understood from the beginning that Judson Bell did his own thing, showed his copy to his seniors as a courtesy, *noblesse*

142

oblige. The thing that had to be daily done by so many thousand implacable deadlines as well as it could be done and always better. And Houlighan said, Let there be a great campaign: and there was a great campaign. And Houlighan saw that *it was good*, but what have you done for me lately? And Houlighan said, Let us make the adman in our image, after our likeness. So Houlighan created the adman in his own image, in the image of Houlighan created he him; male and female created he them to have dominion over all the agency, and every creeping thing that creepeth upon the agency.

Responsible to the creeps, Les and Kip.

No way.

Not for Judson Buchanan Bell.

After Fairleigh, then, what?

Some shlock Philadelphia shop? your friendly fast ad truck stop with its once-over-lightly-and-coffee-to-go accounts and meatball account men.

Where to, then?

No way.

New York? Chicago?

Good-bye, Billie. And the rustle of morning sheets as she stretches filling the room with palms, smiles him aboard her for early matins to open the day. Billie, tooling around in her lime MG enjoying her unemployment, waiting for him tonight. How will he tell her they've torn off his buttons? You can't bring a woman defeat, it dries up the juices.

And good-bye, Unicorn Farm, his homestead hill. Roman and Casey in a greed of grazing the young spring grass in the pasture. The cats are dreaming their delicious dreams on the baled hay in the loft. Blitz is chasing a rabbit who will never be caught. He knows what Vera will say – *Whither thou goest . . .*

But even if you were to pack up your losses and go, who are you kidding, Judson? coming up fifty-six next month. A calendar date, only a number till now, now it's a brand. In this game if you're over forty and looking, you're dead. You don't even have a book of your ads like everyone else running down to the mount room to paste up the latest proof – sometimes not even their own – into a portfolio to show for the next job. Or a résumé. You never needed them. This was the place, the Paper Castle on Washington Square. And the fat offers in this anonymous underground business that came your way unasked for from some of the best and biggest – Y & R, J. Walter, DDB – and which you turned down, thank you but no thank you, that was the day before yesterday.

Kleiner Mann – was nun?

Tad's lighter snaps. He's saying, "Okay, talk at me."

"*Responsible to Les and Kip?*"

"It's a formality, Ace."

"That's not what it says here. It says I'm responsible directly

143

to them."

"It's only a piece of paper, to keep management happy, a table of organisation, a flow chart. So they know who's supposed to do what to whom." He taps his typewriter. "This is where it's at."

"Then why didn't you give it to me? Les and Kip – they're not ready, they're *babies*."

"They'll grow into it. Lookit, Ace, I know they're not the hotshots they think they are. But I've got to encourage the young. Clients want to see young people up front. It tells them we're with it, we're swingers. Clients see gray hairs and they think we're still Old Fairleigh back in those funny red carpet days."

. . . Red carpet days. The Pilgrim touch. Reporting that first day at Fairleigh he had walked out from the elevator onto a red carpet running all the way to his new office. There was a two-foot high banner across copy lobby: IT'S JUDSON BELL DAY. His books on display. Flowers in a vase on his desk . . .

"I can handle it, Tad."

"Sure you could. You've got a great record, Ace. Next to me you're the best writer in the agency, in the country, maybe. And I'll tell you what – you're a better *ad*-min-is-trator than I ever cared to be. I hate all that paper shit, the reports, the creative managements reviews, all that marketing bull."

"It goes with the territory."

"Yeah. You've always run a tight group."

"And a happy one."

"They're not here to be happy. We're not here to be loved."

"It helps get better work."

"They're here to put out and we're here to make 'em."

. . . He'd never asked for anything here, not even from Mr Pilgrim, but he had to ask now before that memo went out . . .

"Give me the account for a month, Tad, one *month*, then if you don't think it's the best run account in the house," he holds up the memo, "you can give it to them."

"They already have it – and management knows."

"They could wreck the account, Tad."

Leaning forward Tad says, "*You're* not going to let them. You're going to teach them. It's your job. Every piece of Army copy will have your initials on it before it goes in to them or out of the House."

"Suppose they don't buy it?"

"Then make 'em. Sell 'em. Fight 'em. *Stomp* 'em if you have to."

Waving the memo, "But they outrank me."

"Rank, shmank, you've got to show balls, Judson."

"You're saying that no matter what I've done, or do, or can and will do, this is it."

144

"You should've been president of this agency," smiles, "But you're not."

"I never wanted to be."

"Everyone wants to be."

"I was too busy making ads."

"They're only markers in a floating crap game, chips. The stakes," he stabs a finger up at the ceiling, the board room above, "are won up there."

"No, I just wanted to be what I did best, creative director, putting it all together, art, copy, the lot. I don't even want your job although you probably think I do."

"Everybody in this department wants my job. That's okay, it keeps 'em humpin'."

"By the way," Jud said, "who's getting my accounts?"

"Leeta."

"I'll call my group together and tell them." His farewell address to his troops.

"Right, it should first come from you. And, oh yes, Leeta will be moving into your office; you'll be in the one next to Les and Kip so you guys can work closely together. Small, but nice. I had it once."

From a corner command post with four windows to an office with two on the row.

Jud stands. Should he salute? He walked in a colonel and goes out master sergeant. "Group copy supervisor," he says.

"Of the biggest account in the house, Ace."

Take it or leave it.

"And lookit, you're still a VP."

Hand me my vice presidency, I'll wear it to the Mummers Parade.

"Only the board giveth vice presidencies and only the board can taketh them away," Jud says.

Tad grants him a waxwork wink, picks up his phone, "Any calls?" waving him out.

And he said I was coming up roses.

Aria da capo.

Please omit flowers.

145

25

His bing cherry eyes checking the hall left and right, Ottavio balloons through the door with the fat man's bouncy light step, talking as he comes in, "Now don't get me wrong, Jud," – glancing back at the hall. "You got a minute?"

"Take two, Tavio."

His face swamped with news – "I waited until you came out of Tad's office."

"Have a seat."

Still standing, Ottavio says, "I don't know," – someone who's forgotten his lines.

"Sit down, Ottavio."

Sighing fatly he sits, under sentence. "Now don't get me wrong, Jud."

"What is it I'm not to get wrong, Ottavio? You seem very unhappy, my son. Confess your shabby sins to the good Father and receive –"

"Jesus, Jud –"

"Ah, you recognised me without me whiskers."

"Holy Mother." Ottavio fingers a fictive rosary.

"You were saying, Ottavio –"

"Now that I'm not in your group –"

"How did you know?"

"Everybody knows. It's all over the shop. Tad's people, they had a party last night, sort of celebration. I was there. I was *invited*, Jud."

"Mooney?"

Ottavio nods. "Him and his guitar."

The wandering minstrel boy playing for his supper.

"Tad?"

"Like everybody, you know, who's *in*."

"So, Ottavio, now that you're not in my group, or to be more precise, now that I don't *have* a group –"

"Now don't get me wrong, Jud, but now that I'm sort of with them, I don't think you and me should be seen together too much. You know, like we used to hang in the old days."

"Ah yes, the old days. Old friends, old times, old manners, old books, old wines – they're the best, somebody said, Ottavio."

"I mean – don't get me wrong, Jud – we'll still be friends. I don't forget, pal, you got me a raise – two – my promotion."

"You deserved them, Ottavio. You're a good art director."

"Yeah, but *you* made it happen."

"It was my job . . . We did some good things together."

"Like now I'm in Leeta's group."

"Ah yes, the one with the balls."

"I don't call the shots." He's at his beads again. "You've got to see it from where I'm at. Like where I come from you don't fight the mob, you learn to live with them. Like they go to the same church. It has nothing to do with how I *feel*. You don't know, but I went to early Mass this morning to pray, so you'd understand, so you wouldn't get me wrong."

To the victors belong the spoiled. "Take it easy, Ottavio."

Ottavio stands as if a gantry had lifted him, offers his hand.

A non-person doesn't shake hands.

"See you around," Ottavio says.

Jud makes the sign of the cross at his departing back.

26

Outside, in the Maywine evening, parked at the curb, the veteran lime MG with the top down, and the spilling gold coins of her hair. Someone's unfolding in awkward clamber on the passenger side wearing a Tyrolean hat with a feather and a whitish colonel moustache. The tall man stoops to her forehead – is he kissing her? – straightens up laughing. What's the joke? Jud pokes through the human shrubbery in the lobby. By the time he's outside on the street, hat and moustache are gone.

"Hi, Honey," she says, someone's laughter still in her face. Some place else still in the car.

"Good evening," he says, slipping into the cracked leather seat.

"Hey," Billie says, grinding the car into gear, "aren't you glad to see me?"

They always put the ball in your court, don't they? But he says, "You know I am." Darling.

Wheeling round into Walnut she says, "This unemployment isn't half bad. I went for my first check today – what a freaky place, all those types, like a Salvation Army soup kitchen – a hundred and eighteen bucks a week for twenty-six weeks. Not bad. And with what you give me," she puts a promissory hand on his thigh, "I'm doing all right. You know I don't think I'll look for a job for a while – there's nothing around anyway. This town is *dead*. Oh, there's this sweatshop with one of those gal-Friday-to-an-executive jobs where you're supposed to do everything, but I mean *everything* for – would you believe – *ten thou* a year? And the way those head hunters *leer*. One guy asked me to have a drink with him . . ."

The Tyrolean hat?

". . . Maybe I'll do some writing. A book." She laughs, "why not?

The Tyrolean, tell me about him. But he says, "Ah," he's full of ahs today and ah yeses, "and just *what* will you write?"

"*Lover?*" She skims a look at him as her legs pump for a light, the car skittering on the old trolley tracks. Wherever she was she's still speaking from there. "What's up?"

The usual thing, he's about to say, his thing snaking toward anodyne, her skirt furled to her thighs, close to apocalypse. But someone else said that – the usual thing, Doc. Mooney and his whoremonging guitar. To see Miss Miller . . . The feathered Tyrolean hat, bending to her unbrooding brow . . .

He says, "*nada y pues nada . . .*"

She says, "Wha?"

He says, "Nothing. It's from a Hemingway story." J. Bell, the old pufessah.

The light blinks green and the doddering car rabbits across Broad Street. On the corner the Harry Krishnas sway to a metronome Voice they want so much to believe comes from someone in charge – God or the multi-armed Wrestler. Take over, *somebody*, please. Why cope when you can turn yourself in and eat Vedic eggplant parmigiana and never again have to think. Isn't nothing grand. It makes you Shiva, round-trip commuters to Karma.

The Duck Woman in holey sneakers and whiskery sprouts, passes schlepping a shopping cart full of garbage, quacking – quark quark, quark quark – not a comment on anybody in particular but on the general disrepair. Her letter to the Editor: Sir, is this It? Passers-by en route to asylum in Bryn Mawr, Haverford, Wayne, allow she is nuts. But is she? She knows that words aren't even markers in a floating crap game. They don't *mean* anything anymore. What's to say? What's to buy? What's the good? Quark quark.

"How was your day at the zoo?" Billie asks.

He'd almost forgotten that in her land of milk and honey thighs, emancipated for driving, where he would pitch his tent to assuage the again spreading bruise of this afternoon.

"The usual mayhem."

"Boy, am I glad I'm out of that creepy place."

"Who was the gent?"

Eyes ahead, insulating herself in the traffic, "The gent?"

"The one who was in the car."

"Oh *him*" – as if aloud to herself. "Honey, that was only Gil Kerr. The architect, my first boss, gave me my first job. I was going to tell you –"

"He's just an old friend."

"Hey gang, wait a minute."

"I meant nothing by that." He's losing them all today.

"Time-out, fella. I was going to tell you when we got home – if you'd only give me a chance – about *my* day, about where I've been for *us.*" And she turns into the parking lot on her corner, the black man in the booth grinning her in with a wave.

"I'm glad you're with me," she says, pulling into her slot. "I finally told him that you and I were engaged, so maybe he'd stop with the remarks."

"Has he?"

"He still says things like, 'Pretty ladies like you need a man around all the time to take care of them proper.' Stuff like that."

The jeopardies of pretty ladies and their men. "I think I'll have a talk with him," Jud says.

"Look, if he comes out, don't say anything. Don't tangle with him. He has a record. He killed a man in a bar – with a knife. He's into all kinds of things. Numbers, dope. Let it lay, it's only talk." Taking Jud's arm she smiles at the booth. "At least, since he's been running the lot, my top hasn't been slashed once or my battery lifted."

"Damn," she says at her door, the phone ringing inside, "these lousy locks," twisting the double keys. "I think they're jammed."

"Let me," he says. "No," springing the bolts, "your keys weren't in far enough."

"Fix us a drink," she says, going straight for the still ringing phone. "Hon."

She seems so complete. Free as a kite that once got away when he was a boy and the string broke, and lost itself in the sky. But he must attend the loo.

He slaps cold Philadelphia water stenched with chlorine into his face as if that will stop the day from coming apart. Eyes stinging, he gropes for a towel without looking up at the mirror and the impeached face there. And comes shoulders squared into the kitchenette to pry the glaciered ice cubes out. And sees *two* plates in the sink rimmed with the remnants of meat ball cruds and maggot spaghetti: *two* clotted wine goblets. Last night's party plasma. Over the bookcase divider he hears whispered purling responses, muffled, he knows in her phone booth of hair, a kind of turtledove crooning. He hears her say in a papery voice one thing: No, he didn't tell me. We just got in.

He's shooting the Dewar's into their glasses when he feels her come in behind him, full and by. The extreme unction of her lips on his neck.

"The bastards," she says. "Why didn't you tell me?"

Putting her arms lightly around him she sees what he's seeing or seen: the remains in the sink. "Oh, I was going to tell you, Sweetheart," she says in a voice that is piped in muzak. "Karla was here last night. You remember my friend, Karla? It go so late she stayed over. It was like old times, a regular *hen* party." Karla, a *hen?*

He unclasps her hands, turns, not knowing what to read first in her face, hands her her drink.

Her bed is unmade. "What a mess. I rushed out of here to get to the unemployment."

At the café table she says, "That was Louie on the phone, Louie Bocca." Please don't ask if I remember *him.* "He dropped into Watson's for a drink after work and ran into some of the Fairleigh bunch. They told him what's happened."

The memo's not out yet and everyone knows as if they had always been in that dream where you're walking around without clothes and wake to find you're not dreaming. Even she before he could tell her.

"So he called *you* with the good tidings."

"He knows about *us*, Jud. So he calls once in a while. After all –"

He's an old friend.

"– He's an old friend," she says.

"If he'd been an Indian his name would be Running Mouth."

"So Louie's a yenta." She spreads music hall hands, smirks. "So what?" And she's never heard of Al Jolson. "It's what they've done to *you*." Why does he feel the muzak is on again? "Does –

Vera know?

"– Vera know?" she says.

He shakes his Uncle Tom head and downs the rest of booze in his glass and makes for the kitchen. Spaghetti and meatball Louie . . . Tyrolean hats . . . He pours a brown one.

"Let's not get bombed tonight. Please."

"This isn't London in 1940," he says, "and I'm not Ed Murrow."

"Who?" she says.

Vera would know; curator of their mutual history; their world at the same time.

"A chain smoker." Knock it off. Judson. Don't take it out on her. She wasn't born yet. To her Blitz is the name of your dog, Ace.

"Sorry," he says.

The muzak is off as she looks at him as if for the first time today, come finally home from wherever she's been, done, says, "Oh Jud, what are you going to do?"

You mean am I going to take it.

"Do? There isn't much I can do." She smiles I'm with you. A smile he can believe in: at last he can sigh.

"Those rotten creeps," she says, "they're not even in your league."

"Yes, but they own the ball club."

"Don't they ever. I ought to know."

"There's only one choice: I stay or I leave. I mean, go someplace else. Is there life after Fairleigh in Philamadelky? Not here, no slopshops for me. Another city – New York, maybe."

She lights up like a bulb. "They'd grab you, Hon." Would they now, lass? "That's where you belong, Jud. And, wow, you would get me a job and I'd come out and join you and we'd still be together. New York – we'd have a ball." They're in an apartment high over a river spangled with lights. They're having cocktails and dinner at – well, Jud would know the right place. They're at the theatre on opening night.

"I'd be throwing away almost twenty-one years," Babe, "the goodies they dangle, the bundle of carrots you only get if you go the distance," a thirty-year man, a lifer. He's not saying retirement, pensions – old people's words. "I guess I'll be here till they carry me out, probably die with my desk on, or tell me to go."

"They wouldn't do that, they're not *that* dumb. They need you."

"They need me if I accept the way they need me."

"There's no one there better than you."

"Beyond a certain point you don't have to be better. It doesn't matter . . ."

The times he woke up in the middle of night, led out of sleep by a seemlier word, kept like a jewel in a box carried on the morning train

151

to the office to be set into an ad already approved. Why bother, it's *sold*. Why change it? *They* wouldn't know the difference. Who cares? He cared; Owen cared.

". . . And it probably wouldn't be different anywhere else. It's a Houlighan world."

"It matters to me," she says, "You," just touching her lips to his, "matter to me." She's undoing his knitted tie – "I was going to tell you, before all this –" she takes a cat sip from her drink – "I went to the shore today." And he sees what he only looked at when he got into her car – the tinge of sun on her skin.

"With Gil –"

"To find *us* a place for our week. And Jud –"

There doesn't seem to be air enough left to take a deep breath this day.

"With Gil –"

"Please don't get uptight, Hon. Don't spoil my surprise. Wait till you hear. You won't believe it." There is a surprise in her face, a sunny gift for him. Don't be a churl. Anglo Saxon 1, a surly fellow, a boor. Let her unwrap her gift.

"Okay, so you went to the shore with Gil."

"Okay." She nods to his offer of brittle covenant. "After I left the unemployment this morning, I thought what a great day for the shore, but it's such a drag going alone, so I dropped by Gil's office. He *is* a good friend, Jud. He knows about us, that you're my man."

The word warms him more than the booze. He raises his glass.

"He's always been a guy who stayed loose, taking off whenever he felt like. He could have been filthy rich – oh, he's doing all right, believe me – but on a day like this he'd say it's too nice to kill indoors. When I worked for him we used to tool around a lot. It was a fun job."

Gil's tool.

"Maybe I should have been an architect – or a veterinarian."

She touches his hand.

"I told him that you and I were going to have a week at the shore together, that I was going out to look for a place. And you know what –"

"Married?"

"Divorced. Years ago."

Jud says, "Would you like a dollop?"

She says, "Okay, Hon," keeping the peace.

He comes back from the kitchenette with glasses awash. "Hello, Dollop," he says.

"I love you," she says. A codicil to their treaty.

He can't remember when he didn't love her. "So you and the master builder took to the open road," he says with as little edge as he can.

She lets that one go into the stands.

"Before we left he told me about this place he'd built for a client

152

in Avalon."

*. . . and among them all was a queen, and they all had black
hoods, and they all wept and shrieked when they saw King Arthur. Now
put me into the barge, said the King . . . for I will into the vale of Avalon
to heal me of my grievous wound: and if thou hear never more of me
pray for my soul . . .*

"A beautiful beach," Jud says, "I've been there, miles of dunes. I
used to be a collector of beaches."

"This place," it's there again in her rearview mirror, "it's on a
lagoon, all by itself. It has its own dock and a deck that just flies over
the water. It looks like it's made of rough boards, you know, weathered
and salty. Very contemporary, with it, but it doesn't stick out like some
of those places that look like they fell off a truck. It just belongs where
it is, it *fits* as if it's always been there, so *fresh*, so *clean*, it even smells
like the sea. And Hon, the inside is as great as the outside, like one big
room with a gallery all around it. And one of those free-standing
fireplaces and sheepskin rugs all over the place you can sleep on. And
wait till you see the bathrooms, one of them has a tub big enough to
hold four."

"Sounds like a seaside Playboy Club." A gym for muscular
fantasies, mermaids instead of bunnies. "Who owns the place, Hugh
Hefner?"

"Lover," she says, stubbing her cigarette, "let's go to bed or out to
dinner or something."

"Sorry," he says, raising his hand. So it's been a rough shoot, what?
Stiff upper lip, there, colonel. Don't chivvy the gel. Charge the Light
Brigade to your Master Card, Visa also accepted. Let's have some of
that grace under pressure. "Please go on," he says to her sea-gray eyes.
"I was curious how you got inside."

How long will this truce last? But she says, "If you'd only let me,"
lighting a cigarette.

"Okay," she is going to try it one more time. "Gil got the key from
the realtor. The guy who owns the place, a Mike Lambert – he's a
lawyer, young, loaded –"

The stag at the shore.

"– rents it out, not just to anybody, he's very particular, before the
season starts when he moves in for the summer. It's booked except for
the first week in June." He sees what she's seeing, a weekful only of
them in that house. "We can have it Jud. Say yes."

Lovers shouldn't be thinking of lucre, man and wife talk, but he
says, "It sounds expensive – a whole house, a place like that."

"Gil thinks," she's got her voice on a leash, "that because it hasn't
been booked by now – people do months ahead – and because it's
only a week, that he can get it for us –" surprise, surprise "– for *free*."

We're not going to spoil it, are we Judson? "We'll take it," he says.

"Oh Jud," her eyes are a lake.

"But I'm going to pay."

"But *why*, Hon, if you don't *have* to?"

"I have to. I can't be beholden, not to someone I don't even know. I wouldn't feel right."

"It's only a favour."

Favours for favours. "To you. As you said, this is for us."

"It will be *ours*."

For this patch of time.

"What would he charge anyone else?"

"The realtor said at this time – two hundred bucks."

"Fine, I'll send him a check."

"We could have a ball on that dough – champagne."

"We'll have champagne."

"It's a lot of bucks, Hon, to be throwing away, you know what I mean, what with the help you –"

"That's not for you to worry about. I will provide. We won't stint. Thanks to a lady, I have a fair purse, of shall we say, quiet money."

"A lady?" Her eyes narrow, "What lady?"

Why darling, your green eyes are showing. He loves it.

"A gentleman never reveals the name of his –"

"Who gave you the money?"

He laughs and it feels so good, the shoe on the other foot. Selah.

"Judson?"

He swishes the last of the amber among the ice. "I need freshener – you-all?"

"Jud*son*."

He's bonging with laughter, good cleansing glee. "All right," he says, "all right . . . I sold my Buchanan grandmother's yellow diamond. You've seen her portrait, over the Queen Anne chair; that was hers too."

"When did you sell it?"

"Some time ago."

"When I was canned."

"About that time, yes."

"I love you."

Please, not for that. "She left it to me in her will to be used for something special. She'd understand; she was that kind of lady."

"This is something special, Jud. It's going to be so great. You'll love the place. Gil said it's one of his best, he loved doing it, bringing it out of the sand into the light of the sea. Gil said . . ." Her head tilts against something that is coming into her eyes like a change of weather, and she's saying, "I won't go if you don't want me to, Hon, but Gil's having some people over next Sunday and asked me to be his hostess."

"A party."

"It's for some of his clients he's doing houses for on Society Hill. Like a business affair. I've done that for him before. You know, make sure everyone has a fresh drink, knows where the john is, pass the hors d' oeuvres smile, stuff like that." Kid, laugh.

Don't go.

"You accepted."

"We were coming back from the shore when he asked me. It isn't as if I'd be seeing you Sunday night. Weekends without you are such a drag, Hon. You know I'd rather be with you. It's just something to do, to kill time between seeing you. I'll be home right after dinner."

Promise?

"A favour for a favour."

"It's nothing like that, he's just —"

"I know, an old friend."

"Lover, there's nothing to be uptight about."

"It's your call."

Don't go.

"You don't like the idea." She lights one of her Parliaments. He reaches over for the pack.

"I've never seen you smoke a cigarette before."

"Neither did Tad."

"What?"

"Nothing. It's just my cigarette day."

"I won't go if you tell me not to. Honest, Hon."

"I don't have the right to tell you to go or not to. I think of you all alone here on weekends."

"You have her."

"Do I?"

"At least someone to talk to."

"Yes, that."

"And your horses, the farm."

"I talk to them."

"You're crazy," she says.

She is getting up, saying, "You're the best thing that ever happened to me."

Don't go.

"I trust *you.* After all, you sleep in the same bed with her. Don't you trust me?"

He doesn't answer.

"Jud?"

"Of course I do."

Don't go.

"Don't move," she says, coming full sail to him, kneeling in the now almost deadlight, her ivory hands at his belt, cupping him out, a moon looking up, "I've been wanting to taste you all day," taking him into the waves of her hair, into her graceful sea mouth.

Don't . . .

27

. . . *Go.*

His first spring mowing of the west pasture. The tubercular tractor coughs over the rock croppings. Winter phlegm. Needs a new muffler. In the near woods the crows are holding assizes in the gibbet trees. A vixen sunning her cubs downwind by the briary copse, safely close to her earth she can slip back to in seconds, knows that an engine's racket isn't a pack of hounds. A mockingbird mocks. A cardinal ignites the oak. Blitz leaves off nosing for moles up on the hill and is trying to marry the girl cat who knows never the twain shall meet. He is at least a foot above her, pumping the air. You're barking up the wrong she, Old Sod. The immaculate sky is a billboard ad for Sunday. The place hangs in green balance.

That Roman, cropping grass just over there, he's sniffed this tractor a thousand times in the field, heard its noise since he was coming three, knows it's a piece of harmless iron. But he's going to show how full of himself he is, aren't you boy? when I get to within thirty feet, cut a dido, snort, wha, this monster, and kick up his heels galloping flat out around the fence line, tossing, his head, Casey taking contagion joining the game of fake fright. There he goes, they go. High on a spring grass cocktail. Blitz barks for the sheriff. He turns: vixen and cubs are gone.

A shadow etched in black silence skims along on the ground: overhead the resident hawk is slicing the sky in half. He looks at the watch on his wrist. She'll be at the party at 1700 hours, less than six hours from now, anointed for evening, shining her cosmic body through whatever she wears, passing her smile like canapés in Society Hill. Have one, they're simply deelish. Hi, gang. Every upwardly mobile stud there with a Geiger counter clicking away in his pants.

From the bottom of the pasture, looking across the long upward slope, up there by the back terrace of their hilltop house, Vera putting in the tomato plants, waves, testifying to partnership, shared place and duties. Coming down to breakfast this morning, he read on her keeping room kitchen blackboard the day's domestic agenda ordered in two columns. Chalked in under V: Plant tomatoes and marigolds. Weed veg garden. Trim forsythia, lilacs. Stuff roaster. Jell cranberries. And, under J: Bring hay down from loft. Mow pasture. Spray fruit trees. A line across the bottom reads: Maybe a movie tonight? But only if it's a *good* one. Otherwise, Scrabble?

He waves back. Her yellow beribboned garden hat makes her

look young from here, a distance measured in years and arthritis. The cod in his piece stirs toward a shuttered room.

She should, at least, have asked him to go to the party. The party. *Gil knows about us.* Left it for him to say whether he could or not. Maybe I'll just show up. Hey gang, I saw your light as I was passing by and thought I'd drop in. That would be *freaky*, what? He just might have arranged it, told Vera on Friday he had to be somewhere so early on Monday, a Pentagon meeting, you know those reveille rising generals, early enough for him to have to take off Sunday night to be sure to make it, or get up at four in the morning to catch some ungodly shuttle plane an hour's drive to the airport from here, Vera saying, Oh *no*, I looked for our whole weekend together, we've had at least that, but I guess you should go Sunday night, stamping his phony passport with the visa of her consent, get a good night's sleep you poor man so you'll be fresh in the morning. How you must hate those hotel rooms. But even ingenuous Vera wouldn't buy that, not at this hour – Why didn't you tell me sooner? What do you mean, you *forgot?* Too late now to blow the rise and shine bugle, more like taps now. He's strapped to Sunday. You knew, Miss Miller, never on Sunday, the one code left in the broken code, so you could have safely asked me to come. But you didn't. You just wouldn't take the chance. You didn't want me there. Why? What kind of a party is this? Who's going to be there? Clients. Yes, like Mike Lambert? the young loaded lawyer you said old friend Gil was restoring a house for in Society Hill. Loaded for what? Or, for whom. Har. Party, party, the word echoing laughter he is outside . . .

"Jud."

Vera is standing alongside the tractor. "I called but you didn't hear me." Dew beads her face from the walk down the slope and her morning's exertions. *Plant tomatoes and marigolds. Weed veg garden.* "To tell you it's time for lunch."

"Must have been the noise of the motor."

"But it stopped some time ago. I've been watching you –"

"Watching me?"

Her floret eyes are not trying to trap him. They're the same uncompromised blue they were when he met her. Hardy perennials.

"– Just sit here and look at your watch. Is there something you have to attend to?"

"Yes, yes. As a matter of fact –"

Her smile waits in the still bell of Sunday.

"– Something to do with the office."

"You're still upset over what happened."

"– An important meeting tomorrow."

She puts her hand on his hand on the iron wheel. "You needn't be. It's going to be all right, you'll see. Things will come around again. They always do." For *richer or poorer. In sickness and in health.* "It doesn't change anything here, for us. That's the important thing."

"I was thinking, I should go in, prepare . . ."

"Don't be silly. It's Sunday."

And you weren't invited, Judson. Lights in the small mullioned panes of an eighteenth century window, Billie aglow.

"Come," Vera says, "it's time for lunch."

"What are we having?" he says, climbing down from the tractor.

"Cold baked Virginia ham, that sharp cheddar you like and salad. The rosé should be chilled by now."

"Wine with lunch?"

"To take off the edge of your Black Friday."

From his eye's corner he sees her trim figure alongside walking with him against the hill. Her limbs are neat, her skin smooth, no wrinkles except for a few outdoorsy ones at the eyes and almost no gray in the hair. She walks like a young woman, springy, taking his hand again as the slope steepens toward the sunwashed fieldstone house on the hill.

"Maybe now," she says, "with the change at the office, you won't be travelling so much."

"Could be," he says, "yes, that could very well be."

"That would be good for both of us." She stoops to pull a weed. "The common foxglove," she says, "*Digitalis purpurea*, it could kill the horses if they ate it."

"But they don't."

"One shouldn't take chances."

"No."

"An ounce of prevention."

"Yes. It's worth a silver lining."

"What?"

"A rolling stone . . ."

"Jud . . ."

"Oh, Vera . . . I think I should tell you . . ."

"You've been working too hard, for so long."

Another man, now, not her husband, probably older – a widower, say, with decent enough dentures, like old Mr Higgins up the road, looking to warm him in a winter bed instead of a hot water bottle, or a heated brick, should-would-find her sturdily attractive with enough BTUs in a Bryn Mawr field hockey goal-keeper sort of way, scrubbed durable features and able. She should have better than that marital shroud. On the breeze that fools with her hat's yellow ribbon he catches a whiff of the scent she wears, something girls wore when there were girls and men courted (you kidding, Doc), ah, Sweet Pea, clean and fresh as the rain bringing wind from the west. But there are no drums in it, no rutting musk. Her mouth doesn't sting. There is no arson in her skin; no felony.

He checks his watch, the second hand trips on each second. Less than five hours to go, cha, cha, cha.

"There isn't a movie worth seeing tonight," she says, "I checked the paper. They're all rated X."

"Isn't everything?"

She squeezes his hand. "I know what you've been through. You haven't shaved in two days. It's so not like you. You've always been so meticulous. I've admired that in you – *mens sana –*"

"You took honours in Latin," he says.

The straw garden hat turns. "I really hadn't intended to mention it. After what's happened, you're entitled to grouse."

Burn, you bastard.

She has served you well, nothing less than that, even after the first years' ambrosia turned to dried fruit at the supermarket. She signed the articles. She'll go down with the ship.

Touch her. *It's what she wants.*

I can't.

Burn, you bastard, alone.

"Oh," she says as they clear the rise to the house, "all this – it's ours." He does squeeze her hand, a small enough dividend on a lifetime's investment.

He's been lying stone still for hours, laid out under the shroud of a sheet in the moony light, nowhere to plug into sleep. The log splitter booms in his chest, won't stop. How does she do it, Vera? bundled in sleep so serenely, a child on a storybook carpet. We're all children in sleep, lost and found in the first forests. Blitz, too, at the foot of the bed panting away in dream pursuit of a Disney rabbit or their pensioner woodchuck.

What is she wearing tonight? Her hair, how is it done? The flowered blue evening dress? – then her hair will be coiled into a coronal loaf with a bulb at the top like a mosque. Or is she wearing – no, not, my god – those silk harem pants she wears for me when she's feeling a little crazy, and those high, glass heeled gold sandals, her hair tumbled loose. and makes me put on the hooded monk's robe she bought me.

The clock on the nightstand says it is past one a.m. She should be home by now. She said she'd leave right after dinner. He edges out of the bed, slips into robe and slippers, shuts the bedroom door behind him. Downstairs, one ear tuned to the bedroom above, he dials. The phone at the other end rings, drilling the silence. What do you say if she answers? I just wanted to know you got home safely. Or hang up, like all her heavy breathers strangling the night. He knows, even before the fourth ring, there will be no answer, but he lets it ring, as if she were there in the silence between the ringing, a kind of breathing connection. He replaces the receiver after the eleventh ring. It is one:fourteen a.m. He will never sleep again.

There's enough moonlight to make out the brandy decanter, a small snifter. He carries them up to his workroom. Outside the window the moon is sketching the farm, blocking out buildings in black shadow and chalked in light. The impossibly walked on moon. The brandy goes down like a sigh.

Typing might wake Vera, though then, in that first apartment when he worked at night, she would sleep through it. He offers himself, this night, to the page. The pencil's a finger, part of his hand as he bends over the blank unblinking pad. It's as it was when he wrote and didn't know he was writing. When there was something more, when it was done, than had been written, something almost you could hear. Always there. When it was good.

He stands, stretches. Lines swim up from the rest on the page –

> But when she hears the sounds of carnival,
> she turns and rises and is gone.
> Her heart red with my blood,
> loud with a stranger's song.

Lucevan e stelle.

The frisbee moon has spun west. The closed black woods wait like a door for a knock. The daffodils drowse toward the tap of the wand of light to release their gold stars. Forsythia is ready to shoot its yellow bells at the sun.

Downstairs the clock tells him the truth: four:fifty-eight a.m. He waits until five:fifteen, dials. There's no point in counting the rings any more. It's tomorrow.

The words on the pad are paid for.

I'll tell Vera I'll be coming home this evening. And tomorrow and tomorrow. She will be glad.

V Dolorosa.

28

He isn't coming, she writes in the notebook that says on the label: Things I Only Say to Myself. *It is nine o'clock, Monday, and Monday has always been ours since I met him.* She takes out another Parliament from the pack and lights it from the stub in her fingers. Touches her chaste chignon looped in a snood on her nape. She's not wearing lipstick to telltale a collar. *But he isn't here.*

Ella's bebopping around on the stereo. The Great Ella. What's so great about her? It must be me. I just don't dig. What the noise is all about. If all it takes is to jelly shake and burp around the beat, bababee. And those old granny glasses. Honest, at least she ought to wear contacts. She puts a song to sleep. She stops the record between a be and a bop, puts on Carmen McRae. *My Dream of Life is Here to Stay.* Yeah. Now you're talkin'. Her song. When she moans she means it . . . You can feel it way down here. *Now that you're here with me, now that you've come back . . . Who do you think is coming to touch . . . My heaven is blue. ohoho . . .Yes ah know, ah know, ah know . . .*

He knows, but how?

Did he call when I was at Gil's? He sometimes sneaks in a call on *Sunday, and the phone drops dead when old Vee comes in.* But he couldn't have called me at night with her in the house. He'd be sleeping. With her. *And he didn't answer my call to the office this morning when I got in.* I hate calling that creepy place when he's not at his desk and the receptionist picks up the phone. Oh, how are you, Billie? How are you? Have you found a job, yet? Don't worry, you will. Oh yeah, sure. Good luck. Your Mr. Bell just stepped out of his office. I'll give him your message . . . he must have gotten it. They're good about that at Fairleigh. That little pink slip on his desk: Miss Miller called and asked that you call her back. But even if he hadn't he always calls me on Monday after the weekend. *He's probably mad about the party, but he would have called to say he's not coming. At least answered my message. Unless . . .* he knows. But how? Now if bigmouth Louie had been there – I wouldn't put it past him – he might have pulled one of his poison- pen opera shtik. A voice in the night bit. Never liked Jud, he'd love to break us up, give him the shaft. But he wasn't there, thank God.

That Mike Lambert is something else, comes on like gangbusters. Tall, good looking, really built, I'd say thirty-one-two. Was on the crew at Penn, stroke something, went to Yale Law School. Knows everybody, a friend of Jack Kelly's, sculls out of Vesper's. A full partner in his own law firm, loaded, into commodities – whatever that is, I just kept saying uhuh – says he never loses. You better believe it. He just wouldn't give up. First he said let's slip away so he could show me the townhouse Gil is restoring for him just down the block. I said I couldn't do that I was the hostess. Then he wanted to take me home in his Jag and I said I was Gil's date tonight. So he said he'd like to date me sometime and I said I was going with someone. Hope you enjoy my pad at the beach, he said, wish I was the lucky guy. Well, maybe next time. I throw great parties there. *He's Aquarius, they're good with Aries. I read his palm. Hope there's a Billie in my future, he said. That guy is a pistol. We had a lot of laughs. He thinks Rod McKuen is great, is going to send me a copy . . . It was a great party. It got pretty late and old Gil asked me to stay. I just couldn't put him down. It didn't mean anything. Jud. Just a little rub-rub then hop goes Gil like a rabbit, and he's off to dreamland. It's not as if I got anything out of it. This probably blows our week at the shore.*

I should have known.

But I never do, do I?

Carmen's back where she started. *Now that you're here with me, now that you've come back . . .*

Please, Jud.

. . .*Yes ah know, ah know, ah know.*

29

"Hi Dads."

"Dulcie – long time."

"Are you too busy to talk?"

"No, Baby, never to you. So good to hear your voice." Still the little girl trill.

"How's everything, Dad?"

"Apple pandandy." She laughs, his kid. Filial glow.

"How's Vera?"

"How's *Mother*."

"Oh Dad, you know I always call her Vera when she isn't around."

"She's your mother whether she's around or not."

"Okay, how's *Mother?*"

"That's better. Just fine."

"Do we have to go through that routine every time."

"You've got to stop hating her sometime."

"Why?"

"Because it's time the War Between the States was over. She loves you, always has. she misses you."

"I suppose, in her way."

"Grant let Lee keep his horses so we could plough our fields."

"Huh?"

"Beat Your Swords into ploughshares. Let the land heal."

"Daddy . . . She's . . ."

"Yes?"

"Strange."

"No. Not really strange. She lives by her own set of rules."

"They never were mine."

"No."

"Or yours."

Sigh. "Okay, Love, just remember we're *family*, and it's your only one. Let's take it from there."

Pause. "Um, how's Billie?"

"Fine.. as far as I know."

"As far as you know."

"Dulcie, what's this all about?"

"Well, Dad, I had a funny call this morning." Dulcie's voice is an unopened package. Guess what's inside.

A telephone strings its sound in an empty room, eleven rings and no answer as light slits through the shutters there. It is five:fifteen in the morning again and outside his all night workroom window eye the mourning doves mourn . . . The flowers appear on the earth; the time of the singing of birds is come and the voice of the turtle is heard in our land . . .

"How funny?" he says.

"Billie called."

Her name sparks over that severed connection as if he had let the phone ring until now and she had just answered it. Long distance, but still a connection alive now in Dulcie's voice.

"Very interesting. Why did she call *you*?"

"Oh she's called before, you know, to rap. We like each other." Billie, surrogate mother, or sister?

"And what did you rap about today?"

"She wanted to know how you were, if you were all right."

"I'm all right."

"What's going on, Dad?"

"What else did she say?"

"You were supposed to see her on Monday and didn't show up."

"Just like that. Did she wonder why?"

"And you didn't answer her message."

"She could have tried again."

"She hates calling the office, says that place gives her the creeps. She thought I might know something."

"Did she ask you to tell me to call?"

"No, not exactly. But she did seem to make the point that she wouldn't be in the rest of the day, that she was off to the shore right after she'd talked with me, walk on the beach . . ."

"Alone?"

"She didn't say. You don't think there is someone else?"

"There has been a happening."

"Dad, what *is* going on with you two? You're both acting like a couple of kids."

"What's going on is between Billie and me, daughter. And since you ask, it's not going on any more."

"She loves you, Dad."

"Does she now?"

"Of course she does, or why would she even bother to call me?"

"I'm sorry you're in the middle of this. She should not have involved you."

"Why not? She knows about us . . ."

He's part of so many us's. Vera and he are an us; Dulcie and he are an us; Billie and he . . . One piece for three jigsaw puzzles . . .

"That we always could talk – about anything – ever since I was little. You once told me, I think I was ten, 'don't bury a grievance in silence, it could become a grief.'"

"You were twelve, daughter."

"Oh right, that time Vera . . . I mean, *Mother* . . ."

164

"Dulcie, Dulcie," he says in cradled embrace.

"Don't let her go, Dad, because of some dumb misunderstanding."

"This is not a misunderstanding; she understands, all right."

"I think it cost her something to call me today."

What is the going price of being an us?

"I don't know except what I know in my bones." And if I don't know that then I never writ, nor no man ever loved.

"Dad?"

"I want you to be happy . . ."

It's Make Believe Ballroom time,
The hour of sweet romance.

"You really haven't been for so long. Don't think I don't know. All those years you were just putting up, going along."

We make our beds and we lie about them.

"I did what I had to do. Dealer's choice."

"It's time you did what you *wanted* to do. You only live once. Take what you can get. *Now* is what counts."

"My existentialist daughter."

Her little girl laugh. "You never called me names, before Dad." He knows she knows what he means. She says, "I did learn *something* at college."

"You were the one always said you majored in husbandry."

"Well, I did get a husband and my degree on the same day, didn't I?"

"It's what you wanted."

"Your turn, now, Dad . . . My, that was a heavy sigh."

"She . . ."

"Yes, Dad?"

This child of his . . . who else is there he can talk to about it?

"Dads?"

"She completes me." He's immediately sorry. "Kiddo, I have work to do."

"I know, I've got to run, too; Kendal's beginning to yowl. Just this, Dad, her calling me, in a way, was like calling you. Don't wait for her to do it, but I have a hunch she will probably call."

Probability. In mathematics, the assignment of a number as a measure of the chance that a given event will occur. In any experiment there are certain possible outcomes. The set of all possible outcomes is called the sample space of the experiment. To each element of the sample space (i.e., to each possible outcome) is assigned a probability measure between 0 and 1 inclusive (0 is sometimes described as corresponding to impossibility, 1 to certainty).

Between 0 and 1. In a sample space.

"Say hello for me to the kidlets and Bob. And come out to the farm soon."

"I will, maybe Memorial Day – and Dad, take care . . ."

How do you do that? said Ernie Pyle as he walked point into the jungle on Ie Shima and a sniper's bullet that had his name on it.

Walking up Walnut crowded with lunchers produced by a factory that supplies human seconds for mob scenes, the city is empty without her, a body drained of its blood. He is amputated, rolling along on a coasting wheel chair with a mind of its own. Good old Philamadelky, a thousand bars to a bookstore and nothing much there except a few browsing beards nibbling the more pungent pictorial sex manuals. We will overcome. A city without Rilke. Nobody reads here . . . *that was the time, when he burst out of the world of your body into the narrower world* . . . But not without old Ben's Almanac, Philadelphia's catechism . . . *Early to bed and early to rise, Makes a man* . . . A city of Poor Richard merchants some of whom foxhunt and wear straw skimmers to town the first day of spring. We do have Mr Ormandy and his group hanging grace notes in that lovely Academy. And Eakins was born here, painting alone and unhung while he lived. And William Claude Duckinfield, the artful joke juggler who knew the town was a joke: If I had to choose between dying or living in Philadelphia, waal . . .

   Oops.
   "Hey fella, watch where you're going."
   "Sorry." Pardon my wheel chair.
   . . . There are no beautiful women in Philamadelky, except one, and she's from out of town. Oh, here and there a slack-pretty face that washes away in the shower. Walk down a street in New York, now, Chicago, Dallas, Duluth, (Yes) the two Kansas Cities (yes, yes,) and you'll bump into more Miss Americas than ever strolled the Atlantic City boardwalk. A city that throws no shadow. More a memory than a city: a cracked bell and Admiral Dewey's flagship floating in turds. Be sure to take the kids. Go, Phillies, go.
   "Hey mister, you're crossing against the *light.*"
   Hop it.
   "Jesus, that guy's askin' to get hisself kilt."
   On the block before Billie's the graffiti begin. Kafka was here. While Billie walks on the beach. Who's with her? It's a drag going alone. Wish you were here.
   His two keys unclick the locks and the scarred oak door groans open.
   Madam is not at home. This room never liked him. It puts up with him when she is there, just. the cherubs complete with small sculptured cocks stare blindly down from their chipped plaster heaven, their rites of spring suspended. But this is her lair and while the lioness forages, it is still hers, waits for her return, like him. The furniture stops talking as he comes in. The shutters are closed holding the room dusky cool like the shade of a tree on this hot May day. His bottled unguents sit in a row on the toilet box lid. His razor leans against her douche in a corner of the medicine cabinet. He hasn't been here in five days, that last

166

Friday morning together, the longest he hasn't been here since they met. I won't go to the party, Honey, if you don't want me to. The party that never ends.

He pours the three fingers left in the J. Walker Black into a glass, no dishes for two today in the sink, everything tidy, and sits at the café table. Lights up a Player, firm packed honey tobacco, Virginia leaf coddled in England. Cancer is good for you. There's a slogan for you, Tad, gratis, when you pitch your next ciggy account. Har. Like it or not he thinks to the room, I'm here.

That's better, now. He leans back. That Dulcie child. Let me not to the marriage of true – what?

He spends more of his weekday nights here than he does at home. Some of his things are here, hang in the wardrobe: pyjamas, (Natch, let's hear it for Heengland, Squire), shirts, Abelard's robe (she gave him, I want something of you here when you're not). He never told Billie the canon of Notre Dame cut Abelard's stones from him for diddling Heloise, his niece, between reading Aristotle and the Fathers of the Church. Old uncle Fulbert probably had designs himself. It was cold in those stone buildings. You had to do something to keep warm. And she was a beautiful chick. (Don't say that, Jud, it's not you.) Who is? What am I doing here?

This waiting room. They've come here from work together, carrying evening laughter and bags of food when they thought of it and even the sidewalks felt good. They've gone out of here for late dinner, paella at the Gilded Cage; eggs scrambled with lox and onions at Day's-all-night-deli, after their vesper – say it, Jud –fuck, and come home together as if it was home. They've had breakfast here when they remembered that mere mortals did that, or didn't when there was no time left after their grave morning love. He's come here, instead of there, from other cities at all hours, she waiting here by the art deco lamp as if there were no other place to go. And yet, when she's not here, the room rejects his transplant heart. He's a stranger, checking in at a surly hotel in the dead of the night in the middle of nowhere, told what the checkout time is before he can put down his bag.

It's like waiting for Billie in the visitors' lounge of that fleabag hotel. The matador in the Spanish Tourist Bureau poster on the wall is also waiting for her or for Hemingway. Olé. Papa, have one on me. Life is real, Ernest. This J. Walker works fast on an empty stomach. Just coffee this morning. Flung out of the house to be in her city, her field of force. Hook up to the network that might flash a signal: a square gray envelope in his in-box, a pink slip on his desk, a call. *Don't let her go, Dad.* That Dulcie. More like her Savannah Buchanan cousins than the Tennessee Bells. "Would I be here if I could?" The room tells him to keep quiet. After all, you didn't tell her not to go to that party. (She wanted to.) *And her calling me, Dad in a way, was like calling you.* Smarty-pants kid o'mine.

Maybe I'll leave her a note, ask her to lunch tomorrow. Just one more, then. To us. There should be another J. Walker tipping his hat under the sink, good man, that, in hunt boots and top hat. A toff if I ever saw one. No JWB, but there's a Black & White. Opened but still in its gift wrapping. Now I love doggies, but I didn't buy it. Oh well, don't get hungup on details. This isn't a book or an ad. What's real is now, over there, a field for her sheaves.

He goes to the Salvation Army desk for paper.

Sip. Well, a bit light this B & W. But there's a pile of work at the office. Take it easy. Remember Brandel DeWitt. Should he say, Dear Billie, or Dearest Billie?

On top of the desk, at an angle, the notebook. A label: Things I Only Say to Myself.

What things? He's seen it once before.

Sip.

He lights another Player, sucks the smoke into his head.

So he has/had the keys to the kingdom. Does that give him the right? Not cricket, this. Stands there a moment, takes the diary to their (?) table. Opens it in a cloud of smoke. He can't bear to look at the last entry first. He flips pages back. Dates stick him like thorns.

The one for the day before that last Waterloo Thursday night he spent here. *Louie was here*, it says in her stilt high school ballpoint hand. *He made a great salad with real Romano and those spicy black olives from La Bella Napoli in South Philly and his special meatballs and spaghetti à la Camden, the way his Mom makes. He talked again about his Mom, says she'd like to meet me, she's heard so much about me. No grass this time. He brought a bottle of Scotch. Luigi! Put out. His mother thinks it's time he settled down, had bambini. She wants a grandchild, maybe he'll be a priest. She has it all figured out. She has this house in Camden with a separate top floor apartment. I'd have to convert from Lutheran. I guess I still am, even though I haven't been inside a church since I was twelve. Neato. That's all I need, shacked up with Louie. I told him not to take off his tie – once he does that – but he did. Thank God for IUD. That sonofabitch gave me the trich once, or maybe it was Harvey..*

Those dishes in the sink. You remember my friend, Karla. A hen party. My arse. Cockparty, more like. Meatball and spaghetti Louie, scusa, Luigi. Harvey, old friend.

No grass this time. When was the last romp in the pot garden?

He flips pages back, May, April, there – a Friday. Not even a month ago. *We really got stoned out of our minds. I can't even remember the rest. I was really surprised to find Louie there the next morning when I woke up., I checked, he'd been there, leave it to him. What a head. Never, never again. Louie made breakfast, a cheese omelette. We took a long walk along Boat House Row and sat by the river. The Penn crew was out rowing against the wind, a few single sculls and one spunky small sailboat. It made a beautiful picture. Eakins' river, Jud calls it. Because the scullers he painted a hundred*

168

years ago, Jud said, will scull on the Schuylkill forever in that changeless light. Louie never talks to me like that, or the others. Louie said, look at those jocks breaking their balls. He trips on his name, as if he'd been there and forgotten. Woven into her life with a Louie, a Harvey, a . . . Hi, gang. *Louie said, what about it, Bambina?* She *I love Jud.*

Dearest Billie.

He checks the date again. Understand now those strange Monday tears he couldn't read. *Hold me, Jud.* Her mourning embrace. On her birthday.

Must send for a bidet from the Bon Marché (that's in Paris, Luv, France. I was going to tell you in the sometime about Les Halles. Then). For a Christmas present. Done up in a tricolour. Fifty-million Frenchmen can't be wrong. If there will ever be another Xmas. For anybody again.

That Harvey hieroglyph.

Flip-flip. Grow old along with me, the best is yet to be. Ah, so.

Harvey was here last night. that guy sure has vibes. he really goes down and up. nibbles the clit till I'm up the wall. Then as soon as it's over I wish he'd fade out. Not exactly soul food. He's just a great mechanic. Jud now . . . Yes, what about Jud? *Jud now, he cares about all of me.*

All of me. You? A song. The thirties, the forties? You've been around old geez. Dorsey Bros., Bennie, the elegant Artie shaw? The Krupa? His Bolero at the Savoy with Anita O'Day. *It's the killer with the new kind of joy, All the jitterbugs are swinging it out.*

They had vibes, too. Talk about your mechanics.

It's Make Believe Ballroom Time.

Vera's and my time.

Fred Allen and Portland. A clean well-lighted girl.

Well, Black & White Scotties (He looks at his watch) I never lost a day because I was smashed the night before. Always performed. Came in, even though I was dying, Egypt. Kissing the old bluest veins to kiss. *Age cannot wither her, nor custom stale her infinite variety.* Or something. Dreaming of a floating bed to sleep in. Signed the articles, I did.

You gets what you pays for. Add that to your Almanac, B.Franklin.

Moving right along, gang, flip-flapping back, what's this stops him cold, stanzas alone on the blue-lined notebook page. Dated the week before he came back from his October vacation, last fall to find her installed at Fairleigh, Waiting for him in his office:

SUMMER MEMOIRS

Her autumn heart is still writing
summer's memoirs
Between the sunhaired boys
and winter men

169

she shuts her door
and rests
a quiet fool,
a dream waiting for someone to dream her.
her body thinks:
I will make a snowman.
then I can make him
any which way I like
keeping him ice to ice.

Then
when my spring heart melts him
I will go back to the sea.

You never showed me that one, Billie. A clean home run, that one Billie, smack into the stands of poetry's ball park. Take your time walking around the bases. Doff your cap, Babe. It breaks my heart more than your men. Trash prose and flower poem, Billie. Poetry is God's newspaper.

Well, well. One more peep. The last entry.

Flip to the end.

The last one is Monday, the night he didn't show up. She hasn't written past the one, voyeur.

Just a little rub-rub, then hop goes Gil like a rabbit.

It's three o'clock in the morning, We've danced the whole night through. Except it was after five.

He lights another Player.

You learn something new every day. Luigi takes off his tie. Harvey has vibes. Gil hops like a rabbit.

Is there a doctoral thesis in all of that?

Sure. You can get one by mail these days. Experience counts as credit.

Gilouieharv, et Al.

Welcome to the club, Jud.

So many men, with so many pieces of her in their pockets.

So many men snarled in her hair.

You don't know the half of it, Dulcie.

Whatever happened to Artie Shaw – "Mean to Me" – after Ava the jardiniere? or Mickey Rooney. Frankie was there, too, the Man With the Golden Arm, about the time the matadors got her.

"Goodnight, sweetheart, till we meet tomorrow."

"Goodnight, sweetheart, Love will banish sorrow . . ."

Rudy Vallee, 31'?

"You Always Hurt the One You Love." The Mills Bros. Circa, then.

Well, folks, you've seen it here on TV. In spite of them all, the men in her life, the vicissitudes, pot does not conquer all, not the finer feelings.

170

No. All that doesn't matter. She still loves Jud. Tune in tomorrow on your local station, we're having a national puke-in.

You asked for it, Judson. You came for a peep show and that's what you got. A fat notebook, that. To know Miss Miller . . .

That S. Kierkegaard knew: Life can only be understood backwards, but it must be lived forwards.

Neato.

Soft Shoulder Ahead it says on the swiped highway sign near the bed.

Dearest Billie.

Thank God for IUD.

Today is Thursday, May 11th, the 132nd day of the year.
The moon is between its last quarter and new phase.

The morning stars are Mercury and Jupiter.
The evening stars are Venus, Mars and Saturn.

Those born this day are under the sign of Taurus.

On this day in history:
In 1858 Minnesota entered the Union as the 32nd state.
in 1910 Glacier National Park in Montana was created by an act of Congress.
in 1928 station WGY in Schenectady, N.Y., began the first regularly scheduled television programs.
In 1963 a truce between whites and Negroes ended in Birmingham, Alabama, with the bombing of the home of the Rev. A.D. King, brother of Martin Luther King.

30

At least he can see Billy Penn from his shoebox office by slightly craning his head. Blind Billy, under a charred sky in the ashy light. There is no air in this office. It's like trying to catch your breath after a marathon race. He leans over his desk to tug the window up.

The phone rings.

It's lumpy Gloria from Production, her casual gum-chewing voice: "Have you read the repro proofs yet, sweetie?" I know – "The messenger's waiting."

The phone rings.

It's stuffy Sylvester from Traffic:

"We need copy OK for the Reader's Digest resizes –" he's going to say – "P.D.Q. If I bring them up right away –"

The phone rings.

It's snappy Cindy from Art Clearance:

"The photos are in from Fort Bragg, scads – will you be in your office?"

"One good picture, Cindy, is worth a thousand prints."

"How's that again? Oh, sure, but you know photogs, they love to shoot around. The more clicks the merrier."

"Papa said, Cindy, a professional is someone who gets the most with the least."

"Whatever you say, Papa."

"Not Papa me, Papa Hemingway."

"I'll be up."

The phone rings.

An insurance salesman: "My name is Fred Larkin. I represent –"

"I'm insured, Mr. Larkin."

"Ah, yes, of course, Mr. Bell, a responsible executive in your position. But would your family have sufficient coverage to maintain the lifestyle they're accustomed to in the event that you –"

"Die–"

"Predecease –"

"We lead simple lives, Mr. Larkin. My wife, six children and I live in an abandoned station wagon under the Walt Whitman Bridge. A 1936 Ford, you know, the one with the real wooden body. Quite snug, really."

"Ha, ha, very good, Mr Bell."

"Yes, they're quite self-sufficient, I've taught them to beg. They're really quite good at it. My next to youngest especially, a girl – you may have seen her on Market Street in front of Strawbridge's – the one with the crutch –"

"You do have a sense of humour, Mr. Bell."

"It's tough on a busy day, Mr. Larkin, but one must try, always. See the sunny side of the seam. Yes? Drop in on us some evening, we have our at-homes after eight, when the tide is out. The '36 Ford. You can't possibly miss it."

The phone rings

An account man calling from Washington: "Hey, Daddy-O, the client is having some trouble with one of your ads."

"Which ad, Larry?"

"The travel benefits ad. You know, join the Army and see the world bit."

"The First Time I Saw Paris."

"Right on."

"Which client?"

"Lt. Colonel John T. McGirl."

"The gray grammarian."

"That one."

"He approved that ad three months ago. Went over every comma with his trifocals. Initialled the manuscript. In my presence. And the proof."

"I know, I vas dere, Charlie."

"It's running in the mags, Larry."

"You telling me, that's where he saw it."

"As if for the first time."

"He's very unhappy, maestro."

"Doesn't he remember?" Always re-doing yesterday's work in advertising.

"Clients don't have to remember. That's why they're clients."

"Remind him. Draw pictures."

"You never remind a client, except when it's time for a drink."

Larry Footlick. He sees his pinwheel face. Not a bad guy, just dumb, trying to cover his ass.

"So what nit is he picking today?"

"He says your sentences aren't sentences. Something about participles and predicates, whatever they are."

"It's a colloquial ad, Larry."

"Colloquial – I like that."

"Conversational, Larry."

"Keep talkin'."

"It's the young soldier speaking, the whole thing is in quotes. That's the point of the ad. This kid is talking to kids – tell McGirl – to his *peers*. It's one of his favourite buzz words."

"Peers, yeah."

"And tell him this isn't an essay. Or close order drill. The boy is talking, not parsing sentences, he's –

173

"Hold it – he isn't what?"

"Parsing. P-a-r-s-i-n-g, describing the parts of speech grammatically. Syntax. By the way, there's nothing dirty about that."

"Hey, that's good, bwana. Let me get that down. How do you spell –"

"S-y-n-t-a-x."

"Got it. Thank you large, Jud. Right up his old bippee. That ought to snow the old paper pusher. You've earned you pay today, Pufessah."

"Listen, Larry, just for insurance throw in the phrase, 'demographical surveys and research show'"––

"Show what?"

"It doesn't matter. They just show. He'll hear that and fall off his perch. Believe me. And Lar, if you like I'll call him. We'll parse together."

"No, no, my job. Thanks again."

"See you on the barricades, Lar."

Account men are really cartoons.

> Somebody had to invent them
> Somebody write their balloons.

The phone rings.

"Hi, there."

His heart rears. He can just say, "Hello, Billie."

"How are you?"

"Just fine."

Dead air, then almost a shout – "Where the hell have you been?"

"Where I'm supposed to be."

"You didn't show up Monday. Why?"

"I think you know why."

"Did you get my message?"

"I got it."

"Then why didn't you call?"

"Because it's over between us."

"Just like that."

"Not quite."

"Because I went to the party."

"You didn't come home that night, not by morning."

"How do you know?"

"I know."

"The party broke up very late, so I stayed."

"Yes." The small change of truth from a lie.

"I didn't sleep with anybody."

"Oh . . . I didn't say you had."

"Gil put me up in the guest room, a whole floor above his. He was bombed out. Would you want me out on the streets at that hour?"

174

"No, It was wise that you weren't."

"Then why the hell didn't you show?"

"Let's just say I have my reasons."

"I'll bet. Like what?"

"You've been seeing other men."

"Where the hell did you get that shit?"

"I'm psychic. You know, ESP. I get it from my Kendal great-grandmother."

Dead air again. "Did that rat Louie call you with some of his dago garbage?"

"Louie Bocca? Why should he call me?"

"Because he's jealous of us – you. OK, so I used to see him once in a while *before* I started going with you. OK, so he's been bugging me to date him again. He's pissed that I won't. It's like him to pull one of those Black Hand shtik. He's done it before, peddling that kind of crap about me around town. I told you once, the guy never quits."

"No, he didn't call me."

Pause. A sound like a scratch – a match – she's lighting a cigarette. He sees the phone cradled between her neck and shoulder so she can use both hands. How is her hair done?

"He could have told someone at Fairleigh that bull who passed on the dreck on to you. Like Pat Mooney, he hangs out a lot with him."

"Pat doesn't talk to me much." Any more.

"Diarrhoea of the mouth, that's what he's got."

He gave you trich, more likely clap, or was it Harvey?

His office door is clotting with people. Gloria from Production come to pick up her proofs. Sylvester the bloodhound from Traffic. Art Clearance Cindy.

"One moment," he says to the phone, holds up a traffic cop hand to stop them from coming in. Shakes his head. "A client," he mouths at them, pointing at the phone. Even they would't profane that holy of holies, the ark of the client. They aren't leaving, wait to serve their subpoenas. But they do not advance. They shake their heads too, pointing at watches. Let's get on with it. We have work to do.

"Listen," he says, cupping the phone, "there are people all over the place."

She says: "I don't think a phone is where we should talk."

She's holding a hand out to him.

"No," he says, "it isn't."

Oh, so softly, as when she wakes in the morning, turning to him, she says, "Are you coming over tonight?"

A flower is in it.

Your chance, Judson to break it. Or forever hold your peace. All you have to do now is say no and put down the phone and it's over. Yes, Billie, just like that. His attaché case sits by the side of his desk packed with fresh changes: Undershirt, shorts, socks. Even fresh blades. That he took with him this morning. *I have a hunch she'll call Dad.*

"I'll see you later," he says and waves at the door. There's suddenly air in the room as the clerks come fanning in.

Walking up Walnut he slows, time needs a slack, to catch a week's breath, before the period in his pocket is put to end the chapter. The patchwork May evening has cleared, in-between month with remnants of April rain in the air sewn to rumours of coming summer. He turns south into side streets, alleys, Quince, Fawn, but always swinging west. Father-Son-Holy Ghost houses in cobbled mews. Gaslit Camac Street. Silver buckle Smedley. Startled geraniums in window boxes and gossip glasses, colonial fanlights and fire marks. The leftover city before there was a country. And early Victorian brick faces with white marble stoops. Not a bad city, really, with man high buildings and a choice of time zones to live or get lost in.

I knew it was too good to last, Vera said when he called, your being home. I wouldn't say that, he'd answered. I may even be back late tonight if the meeting doesn't drag on till all hours and there's a shuttle plane. Don't push it, Jud, she'd said. Get your rest. Stay over. But you'll be home tomorrow, won't you? You've always been on Friday. Good Friday. *Stay over.*

Cutting across Rittenhouse Square, too early for gay encounters wistful or tough, just regular dog walkers now – a retired pork pie hat, a Mother Hubbard gown – and a mounted cop on the corner. A scopey Thoroughbred, that, a heartwarming load of country manure on the city paving. I'd hoped we'd be riding evenings again, Vera'd said, now that the days are getting longer and you've been coming home. We used to do that, remember? I'd have the horses ready, groomed, saddled and cross-tied . . . Her autumn heart still writing past summers' memoirs.

Crisscrossing back to Delancey, Waverly Place, the lit evening apartments among walled, private espaliered gardens, delaying still the moment of that door opening. She there. Her lamp dappled head. World enough and time now as Blind Billy floats above his yellow clock.

Somehow he feels he should not use his keys, tacitly reinstating his tenancy, as if this week hadn't happened, their pattern crazed. He presses the bell button, his hand on the hall door knob. And presses again. Still no answering buzz. Peers through the grimy glass and webby curtains, down the long hall to the door. It fills with a telling silence. He stabs once more knowing there won't be an answer, holding the yellowed button down, a stained, broken tooth. Or the key of an old piano that will never be played again. He can't help thinking that. He can hear the faraway bell above her door ringing, as if taking up the unanswered rings of last Sunday morning's phone call, ringing in that dawn's sleepless anger. A fine how-do-you-do, this.

Are you coming over tonight?

Maybe it's better this way. But why did she bother to do it? Not her kind of game to make a fool of him, anyone, her kind of put-down

176

. . . Unless her anger at his not calling, not answering her message, *where the hell have you been*, required this vaginal vengeance: You can't do this to me.

Is she there behind the door? taking that leaned-back long drag on her cigarette, a drink in her hand, her face flaming or white. It was not in her voice when she said, Are you coming over tonight.

Maybe she just stepped out to buy something, cigarettes, she's run out before, and he slipped on his mocs and gone to fetch them. She'd be back by now, the store is just down the block. Or wants him to use his keys, making him come all the way.

If this was what she intended, though, this hell-hath-no-fury payoff . . . He picks up his attaché case – I should never have brought it. You can't stand here all day, Judson, with egg on your face, someone may come, other tenants. He presses the bell button again as if he'd just come in, preparing a pancake smile. The vestibule pushes him out.

Outside on the brownstone stoop he checks his watch, heads down the street to the corner drugstore. Call Vera. Meeting was scrubbed. Explanations, dear, later. The young leafhearts of his oaks. Blitz, his hysterical greeting. Nickers across the fence through the night thick pines on the coming down road.

The street is awash with evening, and there from the corner through its parting waves, walking toward him, Billie. In jersey and jeans and clogs. Hardly a smile, but, he thinks, something like that there. Her hair in a chaste bun, her face – chastened? He shuts his eyes against its dazzle. They walk towards each other in ceremony. Planets stand still.

"I thought I'd walk down to meet you," she says.

"I took another route tonight."

"I thought I'd lost you in the crowds," she says. "Or –"

They walk side by side. He sees she sees the attaché case.

"That I wasn't coming."

"Yes."

"I said I would."

"I know, but –" She's stating a fact, not making an issue.

He nods. His Monday no-show. Take off without me.

They fill the small vestibule as she digs for keys in her jeans pocket. A small rondure there. She's gained weight. What? in a week? A lifetime week without her. It's the jeans, close as paint, nothing on underneath or her nippled jersey. As she scratches in pockets he catches her scent, new circumspect, breezy and herbal; no barbs, just very springtime.

"I don't know what I'm doing these days, I forget things. But I must have had them to close the doors." She does a little girl crouch, smiles – this is so silly – reaches into a back pocket defining haunch with some bumper sticker couturier's label. Bill Blass on everyone's ass, makes you think you've got class, why advertise him? He should pay you to wear them.

"I have mine," he finally says as she fingers her key chain out. And her door is opened. She waits for him to pass, a formal invitation to *her* turf. She seems to have grown taller, not small in surrender now as when she came up the street.

"After you," he says. "Shall we dance?"

And now he knows it's a smile, a slant of light on her lips, preceding him with the hint of a nod, her hair in its cloister snood. For once the room seems to say Welcome. Long time no see. The blood has been drained from his legs.

She says, "Excuse me, all this coffee I've been drinking. Pots," and goes into the bathroom, he standing there with the attaché case in his hand, the Pandora's box of his life. She pokes her head out of the john. "Would you mind making us a drink?"

"No, of course not."

The screwdriver's been Scotchtaped to the old casket refrigerator. He stands there a moment, a first time and a last, and hacks away at the usual glacier frosting the ice cube tray.

"Hi," she says, her face mint penny new.

That end-of-chapter-period in his pocket. "Hi." Hands her her drink. The lamp is already on.

""Thank you," she says.

"You're welcome. *Santé.*"

"When I walked down to meet you," she says, "I had this queer feeling that you had disappeared, that I'd never see you again."

"Like a nightmare."

Her face says, Oh, Jud, but she says, "We've always come up that way."

The snowman who melts in the spring. But he can't tell her. You'll still have Gilouieharv. But he can't tell her that, either. He sees her diary on the desk, at the precise angle where he'd found and replaced it. Things I only say to Myself. Not any more, Babe.

"Well," she says, letting her breath out, as if something were settled, nods to the café table. "We're here."

They sip, looking down at their drinks for answers in ice cubes.

"I wanted to walk, think," he says.

"I've been thinking too."

Oh. Is *she* going to disappear? Louie's hedged offer – *What about it, bambina?*"

Outside in the alley, metal shouts, a clashing of garbage cans.

"Trash night," she shrugs. "The city."

"Valéry said," he starts saying and stops. The old circuit riding Pufessah. Summa cum garbage.

"What did Valéry say?" The nubile student in the front row, her miniskirt legs crossed. Her eyes a light to read by. And please give me a passing mark, Prof.

"He said the city is virtually all of civilization."

Her head cocks to that, nods. Then she says, "You don't believe that – the farm . . ."

"No, not any more. Someone once said to me that I was the most urban of men."

"A girl?"

"No, as a matter of fact, a Sorbonne type. A man."

"When you were in Paris?"

"Yes. I was probably the first American he'd met who didn't ask where he could get a hamburger as he got off the boat train. Well, whatever."

"But not any more?"

"No. Maybe once. What's left of cities is just barricaded buildings. Blinds being drawn against mayhem and copped pleas. The American lesion."

"People still live in them."

"Exist."

There's such a quiet in her. She takes a cigarette from the pack and hands him a box of matches. "My lighter is on the blink."

I'll get you another, he wants to say, a gold one. Strikes the match. She dips her head, so lovely, to the flare, almost a curtsy, music playing somewhere among the potted palms.

Now that he's here and the silence sufficient, he needs her anger, her shouts on the phone, a Billie aroused to clang his anger against.

"I see you're back to your pipe," she says, I like that. It goes with you."

"Everything has its cycles."

Her eyes narrow a bit at his heavy gambit to re-open the game. He looks at his watch, a stagy trick.

"I suppose we should talk," he says.

She looks down at his ring on her finger, the heart clasped by Victorian hands.

"Do we really have to?"

"I think we must."

"Isn't this enough for both of us, being back? Can't we just start over from here, like it's a first time? Like it didn't happen?"

"But it did happen."

She lets her breath out and swallows. "Oh Jud, who needs the ag?"

At the slight tilt of his head she says, "the *ag*ony. Haven't we had enough?"

That's called begging the question, Billie.

"If we don't talk it out it will just lie there, fester. Break open sometime. I have to know. From you."

Her lips knit, she nods unwilling assent. Takes a sip from her glass. "OK. I told you. I went to the party – you could have stopped me. It broke up late. OK, I got bombed, thinking all the time about you. Not with me. We never go anywhere together. I mean – out. In the world. I couldn't stand up, much less . . . Gil put me up in the guest room, then conked out himself. That's *all* there was to it." *It doesn't count, Jud.* "Now *you* tell *me* how you knew I wasn't home."

"I called you several times Sunday night – I couldn't sleep."

"I haven't much either."

"The last one at five:fifteen. A.M."

Lucevan e stelle. The night of the snowdrop stars.

"OK, what about that crack you made about me seeing other men?"

"You have been."

She gets up from the table now, chainlights another cigarette. "I thought we went through all that on the phone."

"It won't go away, Billie."

"Jud, don't give me this ESP crap."

"You once said you believed in it."

"It was Louie, wasn't it?"

"I haven't talked to Bocca." Louie, somebody's failed pun. "If he had called I would have hung up on him."

"Then who? You're not levelling with me, Jud."

"Are you?" He gets up to freshen their drinks. "A bit light this Black & White Scotch," he says coming back glasses in hand.

Her eyes slit again. "Moving right along," she says, "someone must have fed you whatever you know or think you know – that pile of crap."

"My bones, my blood."

"Come off it Jud." She's growing taller again.

"Sorry, a bit heavy, that. But you know what I mean. I assure you, as I am sitting here – I *know.*"

He's had the place bugged. She glances around: at the lamp, the phone, the empty vase on the bookcase, old wires along the baseboards. No, not Jud. That's crazy, Luigi stuff. Only in James Bond. But he knows something. Must have been someone saw me in a restaurant – Frankie Bradley's, that steak night with Harv – someone from Fairleigh who told him. I thought I saw Wanda. The bitch.

She clicks the stereo on/off, turns, her all seasons eyes on his . . . Cop a plea, Billie. "OK, I had a few dates. Old friends. A drink, dinner out. That's all. It helped pass the time when you weren't here. Is that such a crime?"

"That's not all, Wilhelmina."

"Oh God," a dry chuckle escapes her. "Don't ever tell anyone *that.* What a name to stick a kid with." A secret she giggled to him one bedded down midnight, her hair skeined on his face, her Nibelung hoard, she leaning over him. "I could never live that down."

> How beautiful are thy feet with wooden clogs
> O postman's daughter,
> Your joints clothed in denim,
> Your . . .

Her phone rings. She shrugs, let it. He looks at his watch again, a cheap shot. "No, take it," he says. "I probably should be getting along anyway."

A bit of grit there in her cheek, now, that, sculptured bone line.

"OK," she says, picking up the receiver, "Hi."

Gang.

Her hair waves over the phone then she flings it back. "No," she says, "no way, José. Don't think it hasn't been and all that. But," she looks ocean eyed at him as she says to the phone, "no more dates – I'm engaged. Yes, of course to him." laughs into the phone. "Oh it's for real, all right."

He shakes his head, mouths "you shouldn't have said that." She nods, Yes I should. "Thanks. You bet. Bye now."

He goes to the kitchenette, throws ice, Scotties, into the glasses. He comes back to her standing.

"See," she says.

"See what?"

"I've closed the door."

"On what?"

"On . . . dates, since that upsets you."

"Dates," he says, "we're back to ground zero."

"Wha?" she says, "tell me , I know I'm dumb."

He shakes his head, "No, you're not dumb, Billie. Ground zero – the point where the bomb goes off."

"What bomb, for crissakes?"

"Us. They. All those theys. You."

"I told you, you heard it. I just shut the door."

"On me."

"Jesus, Jud, what do you want, blood? So I had dinner with an old friend or two, when *you* couldn't be here. What's the big deal?"

"Dinner," he says.

"Yeah, *dinner.*" Her eyes – the Fourth of July.

Seeing her and the gentlemen callers returning here to this room. Kid, laughs. A nightcap? *It doesn't mean anything, Jud* . . . "What about the dessert?" and sorry he's said it.

She folds back a shutter, a silhouette framed by the bay window. Street light looks into the room trying to make conversation . . . How does he know? Wait till I get my hands on Luigi, I'm going to kill that Camden rat. She swirls her drink, turns . . . On her desk, the notebook: Things I Only Say . . .

"You've been reading this," she says.

"Reading what?"

She holds it up. "This, my – I suppose you'd call it a diary."

"How could I have read it? We've always been here together." You'd never make CIA, Jud.

Still holding it up. "You've read it."

"I've never seen it before." Scout's honour: trustworthy, loyal . . .

"I was out all of Wednesday. Yesterday . . . You have keys. I told Dulcie that I'd be out. Did she call?"

"We talked on the phone."

"It was right here," she waves it, a red flag. "You could have."

"Yesterday, Billie, was one of those days. You've been there. I was in the office all day, sent out for a sandwich. From Nick's. Sliced steak on an Italian roll. Got home after ten." Stop.

She takes a sip from her drink.

"What you're saying . . ." he says. the D.A. rests his case.

She smiles a surgical smile. *That's* how he knows. "ESP," she says, closing the shutter. "Your bones, your blood. Your Kendal great-grandmother." Sits down with her drink at the café table. "Where do we go from here?"

He goes to the kitchenette, brings back the bottle of Scotties, sits down across from her."

"We don't need that," she says.

"We need something."

"Like what?"

"Like the truth." All kinds of truth floating around. Vera's truth, Billie's. His?

"So," she says, "What then?"

This probably blows our week at the shore.

"So this. If I hear it from you, whatever there's been" – done – "it won't change anything between us. We'll start from here, as you said. We'll go to the shore as planned."

"I'm a fool," she says. A quiet fool, her poem said. A dream waiting for someone to dream her. I did, Billie. He can't tell her.

"OK," she says, "the gory details. So I –"

"Why, Billie? *that.*"

"I get bitchy sometimes. Mixed up."

"We've been together six months."

"I know. I had to find out."

"Find out what?"

"OK, whether I really loved you."

Don't snort, Jud – Squire, Ace. "You mean you didn't know? After six months together, the way it's been?"

"When you're not here, sometimes. I had to find out."

"Just testing – one, two, three . . ."

"I know now, I *know*. And it's forever. Whether we go to the shore or not. I've shut the door." She's rising, a moon. "I only want you."

"Don't," he says. "Please stay where you are," gets up.

Pandora's box by the armoire. To know Miss Miller.

"Find me, Jud, find me again."

The echo he floated on into her life. No ifs, ands or buts. I'm not Ben. But you made him.

They still belonged; no knife had cut that; it was not over yet. The green life of their time had still to run, was running through them, was not spent, the fruit still in the flower. She had not been out of sight, just gone a little away into her part of the forest, but not beyond looking back, returning, the needle on her compass still pointing to him. Still seen if he looked through the right window. Never really not his in her way, prose-and-poem Billie. They still rhymed. She had not outloved him. Better even than finding is finding again.

"I love you," he says.

The moon's coming to him. Unwalked on, unlittered.

Lucevan e stelle.

Who needs the ag?

31

"Looking for ad headlines, Ace, in the papers?" Big tit Les Madonna, his new now co-boss comes in on Jud scanning a newspaper, essaying a funny. "I thought you knew them all." A klutzy remark, as Billie might say. An oaf, better shorn of his tongue and ears, as Jud might say. Also hanged drawn and quartered. A kindness, considering. Gresham's law VP, the hybrid Italo-Penn Dutchman. You shouldn't wear sweaters, Les. Or go back on your genes. Desertion, that, in the face of. Go tell him. A partial. His father's a fine surgeon, but his name's Madonna. Never mind he's chief at Penn, he came out of South Philly. His mother, now, came out of the hex signs, a shoo-fly Daughter of the A. Revolution. She grows ladylike herbs. Her antiques in his split-level colonial. Neither-here-nor-there Les. His dirty brass hair is the worm in his heart. Its Dutch gold alloyed by the Neapolitan pushcarts south of Eighth and Catherine Streets.

Jud folds his New York *Times* onto his typewriter.

"Too many pages," Les says, "all that *print.*"

"This paper," Jud says, "has the greatest comic strips."

"Does it have Orphan Annie?"

"On alternate Thursdays," Jud says.

"Today's Friday," Les says.

"Sorry," Jud says, "but there's Barney Google."

"I remember him," Les says. "When I was a kid."

When you are a kid, Les

"I haven't been wasting management time," Jud says. "The new campaign's all wrapped up."

"Just kidding," Les says.

"My reports are all done," Jud says, checking his watch, "they should be up from typing."

Les sits on the other chair. "Going anywhere, you and the wife?"

"Maybe a day trip, here and there. Too much to do on the place."

"It's none of my business, Jud, but how come you're only taking a week?"

"Saving the rest for fall riding."

"Oh, right, you have horses."

"Well, the horses really have me, Les."

"Different strokes for different folks," Les says.

"In a manner of speaking," Jud says.

Les stands, "Say, Ace, I really appreciate your help."

"My job, Les."

"I mean, the way you've wrapped everything up in a week. Considering . . ."

That I should have had your job, Les.

"I mean, other guys . . ."

Would have dumped it on you, Les.

"All that copy . . . Not my thing. I hope nothing hits the fan while you're away."

"You have Kip, Les. He's a copy man."

Les looks to the door, sits down again.

"Cigarette, Les?"

"I don't smoke."

So you won't live to be eighty, Les; what's time to a hog?

"If Tad gets his ciggy account we'll all have to, at least when the client's around."

"I'll tell him I have TB."

"Very good, Les."

"Kip," Les says, looks to the door again, "is mostly talking to his stockbroker, or making an appointment to have his hair blown. And besides . . ."

"Yes, Les?"

"I don't think he knows his ass from third base when it comes to words."

"Very few do, Les."

"That's what I mean." A little boy brightness before he unwraps his birthday present. "His stuff just lays there."

"Are you religious, Les?"

"I dunno, we go to church every Sunday."

"Next Sunday, Les, pray to the god of things as they are."

"I think I dig, Ace."

Don't be ashamed of your roots, he wants to say.

Les hauls himself up again, showing his wife's cooking.

"Well, whatever you do, have yourself a good time."

"Thanks, Les, I will. And . . ."

An eager "Yeah?"

"Hold the fort, sport."

"You look very nice, summery," Vera says as they stand by the side of the car, Jud in white ducks, sneakers, the flowered birthday shirt Billie gave him as blue as the young June sky overhead. "In a way I can't believe it, now that it's come, your going off like this."

"You said I could go, Vera, you urged me, I wouldn't have otherwise."

"I know, and I meant it; I'd do anything to get you back to your book. Somehow I feel –"

"Yes?"

She shakes here head. Please, Vera, don't cry. The only time in all the years I saw her do that was when we buried old Jack. Not a sound,

185

just tears.

"What – do you feel?"

There's a mist in her floret eyes and her lips tighten. "Don't mind me," she says. "It just seems so suddenly here."

"Tell me."

"I don't want to spoil your week."

The place seems cut out of glass.

"If I thought you'd feel this way, I wouldn't go." A call – Vera's quite ill – sorry, Billie? Oh great. Oh *yeah*?

"No, you must go. It's very important to me, even selfish, that you get back to your writing. Somehow I feel when that stopped other things stopped between us, that somehow it was my fault."

"Nobody's fault, except mine."

"And that if you got back to the book, you'd also get back –" she looks up at him, a long ago smile on the trembling brink.

He thinks: we save the important things we have to say when it's too late to say them, for departure times, as the plane waits, the train or the hearse.

"A week alone may be just the thing you need; get away from it all; clear your mind of the office, the trips; just you and your book."

"It will take me at least that long to become reacquainted with it again, soak in it, tie back into it. Then take it from there. But I promise to do that."

"That would make me so happy. The week without you worth it . . . Well, enough now of that. You should be off."

"I hate to leave you alone."

"Don't be silly, I have company – our critters . . . You have everything you need? she looks into the back of the wagon "–the manuscript?"

"It's in my attaché case."

"I don't see it, Jud."

He looks now: His old hotel-stickered Gladstone travelling bag and duffel are there, the typewriter, his blazer on a coat hanger. "I must have left it in the house."

"Oh Judson, really," she waves him off, runs into the house, Blitz barking his head off inside. Sorry, old timer, you can't go with me this time. Take care of her, now.

She's out with the attaché case. "It was by the door of your study. The reason for all of this – and you forgot it. Honestly, Jusdon, I would have had to bring it to you." Neato.

She's suddenly there at the door of the house by a lagoon, attaché case in hand. What a *surprise*. Come in (dear) come in, we were just having a drink. You remember Billie. Guess what? I ran into her on the beach. Oh Hi, there . . .

He puts on his dark sunglasses.

"They always make you look so wicked," she says, "some kind of bandit, almost as if you were totally someone else. You looked like that when I first met you, an exciting stranger." The never dead, still quivering first times. And he looks at her through the dusk of his glasses, a first time look when the leaves of the summer tree hadn't fallen, revealing the winter tree.

The plane is ready to board, now, for another sky. They stand at the thin edge of some thirty years. She says: "Don't get so wrapped up in your work you forget to eat. Or sleep. I've known you to do that in those days. First thing, after you've settled in, go to the store and stock up. There was an Acme, wasn't there? When you and Dulcie and I –. But don't try to shave pennies. Go to that store on main street, whatever they call it. I know they charge more, but this is you week. Pretend you're at Yaddo again, or the MacDowell Colony."

"Yes, I'll probably mostly eat out."

"Oh now, what's the matter with *me*? I almost forgot – a minute –" and turns into the house. He looks at his urgent watch. She comes out with a brown paper bag. "Sandwiches, for your lunch, and Thermos of coffee, so you won't have to fuss the minute you get there. You need relaxation before you begin your work."

He takes her hand that clasps his to a beginning. And a smile that believes what she was taught in school by old schoolteachers. Bless'em. She used to read Shelley to me while I waited for her to undress. Old Shell. Sometimes it was Keats. On their honeymoon . . . It could have been worse, Jud. An M.A. major in English who bought it. The whole nineteenth century package . . . sweetness and light.

He holds her hand in his in a Victorian afterglow. He wants to be in two places at once.

She's saying, "And please, Jud, don't swim out too far alone. My heart use to stop when I'd see your head disappear in the sea. And later, when she came along, Dulcie would say, 'where's Dads.' You're not one-and-twenty you know." Housman, dear old AEH, nobody reads you, you know. Except she and I. The Greek economy.

He bends to kiss her back to a lost time.

"Yes," she breathes, "go back to your book and come back to me."

"Thank you," he says, "my dear-est."

She touches his cheek. "Take care of yourself."

"And you."

"Don't worry about me, anything – just your book."

"If you do need anything, call on the Lloyds. Good neighbours. They're there when we need them and we're here when they need us."

"We took their dog to the vet."

"They helped put out the fire in our woods."

He looks at his watch again. "I'll call."

"Yes, better than my calling you. I don't want to come between the Muse and you.

The Muse and me.

The car moves up the drive. Blitz in the house barks at the

187

outrage. In the sideview mirror he sees her waving, framed there in her garden hat with the yellow ribbon, waving and getting smaller.

He's parked in the no-parking zone in front of her house, the motor running. Hall door and her door are propped open. She's lugging out a valise. There are two more in the vestibule. Hangers of flapping clothes like sails in her upheld hand.

"Oh Hi, I thought you'd never come."

"Let me," he says. "All this for a week? You'd think we're going to be gone for a year."

"My trousseau,," she says, sunlighting a perspirant smile. "We're going to dress for dinner – for everything."

"The weather is with us," he says.

"I know," taking a breath, "I've had the radio on."

"Is this all?" He says stowing the luggage.

"I think so. I'll have one more look and lock up. I've been packing since midnight."

"Hurry," he says, "the last thing I need is a ticket."

"Wow," she says, getting in on the passenger side. "What's this?" raising the brown paper bag by its scruff.

"Sandwiches, coffee."

"Old Vee," she says and frowns.

"I just couldn't not take it."

She puts the bag down at her feet. "What the hell, " she says. "We're off. I still don't believe it," and puts a hand on his thigh.

32

By the semblance of the once clean sea, by the edge of the paved over world . . .

The caravan loaded car crunches to a stop on the white pebbled drive. She turns with a smile between here and eternity.

"Like it?" she says.

"It's alone," he says, killing the engine. "Yes." Gets out of the car looking around: At the house on its spit of land, its shag of beach heather, clumps of tufted sea oats, here and there bearberry. At the deck flying out of the upper story, the tarp-covered boat nodding at the end of the dock, a twenty-six foot ChrisCraft. And across the marsh bordered lagoon, a sea inlet nudging the sandy banks back to the sea.

"Look," he says.

"What?"

"I think that's a heron, over there in the cattails, the reeds. Across the water."

"I don't see anything."

"Just stand still for a minute. They probably know we're here."

She shades her eyes – "Oh, something white.?"

"I wish I'd taken my binoculars." He squints: "There, it's an egret. Beautiful." Pebbles crunch underfoot as the bird in a lumbering run flaps into hieroglyphic flight to a Nile dream.

"Well, we're here," he says, time now a matter of tides and the sun. There is just a sniff of the sea in the air, not the gritty sting of brine, the boyhood vacation smell, coarse salt like sand in the nose. Neptune's ropy net over his sea slicked body. Thinned now, as if forced out of a clogged salt shaker.

"I want you to like it," she says pulling down to unwrinkle her jeans. A Marilyn Monroe gesture.

"I do. I'm glad you found it."

"I knew you'd be, I really did, even though . . ."

"Even though what?"

"That," she says, pointing a crimson fingernail at a small sign over the door.

"It's campy, I know."

He reads the lettered board, the name of the place: Anything Goes. In ye olde English script, yet.

He smiles, "you forgot to mention that."

She smiles back – "I knew it would put the whammy on it if I told

189

you before you saw it, this, the whole thing. Don't mind it, please," she says. "The place is really great. Isn't it?"

He wants to say: Your friend Gil knows what to do with wood and sand and place, but naming invites ghosts. No other names here, their first garden, but their own. He says: "It's right for us." And she sighs.

He opens the door with the tagged key the realtor gave him. "Oh yes, I've met the young lady," he'd said, looking out of his storefront window at Billie in the parked Peugeot at the curb. "Very pretty, your wife?"– a bit-young-for-you-look, what? – "She came by with Mr Kerr to look at the place. The weatherman says it's going to be a good week. Maybe a smidgin of rain on Thursday. I'll have to have the key back next Saturday noon, for the next folks. Hope you enjoy your stay."

Not kitschy as he'd expected inside. Clean cedar planks, a large cask of a room, distilled lagoon light filling the open and airy space. Sheepskin throws, a free-standing fireplace, driftwood beside. A graceful helix of wrought iron stair spirals up to the gallery.

She waits his approval, a not like her shyness, now they're here signing the honeymoon register.

"It's everything you said."

She nods gravely – I told you. "Wait till you see our bedroom." He follows, winding up and around the spun iron web after her lovely haunch. "Promise, you won't laugh."

He looks in. "Nothing wrong with a *harīm*," he says. The room is almost all bed, a round cake of a bed set low on the floor. Nods, "Why not, after all, form follows function." His belly can't hold his laughter. "For the man who has everything," he manages through guffaw.

"I think it's great," she says.

"I don't know about George Washington, but King Farouk certainly slept here."

She laughs now, too.

"Or maybe King Solomon with his thousand wives – all at the same time."

She bounces down on it, stretches. "I'm afraid you'll have to put up with just little ol' me."

"At least we won't have far to fall."

She's up, "You haven't seen anything yet," and opens the bathroom door. Light pastel tiled walls under a domed skylight. A global Roman tub sunk into the floor. Gold dolphin faucets, fluted shell soap holders, and in the glassed shower. A mirrored wall from mosaic floor to ceiling surprises them there.

"In Xanadu did Kubla Khan

A stately pleasure-dome decree"' . . . he says to her in the mirror.

"Who was he?" she asks him in the mirror.

"A banker, probably." or a rich young lawyer?

"You're so smart."

"Yes," he says to the girl in the glass. "To be here with you."

190

"Oh Jud," she just brushes his lips with hers. Their mirrored images walk out hand in hand.

Winding down the spiral stair she says, "I'm starved. All I had was coffee this morning."

"The sandwiches – in the car."

"I'd rather not," she says.

"Sorry. Nor I. Just that they're there."

"You understand?"

"Of course. Shouldn't have brought it up." Niceties the other side of deception.

"There's a real neat place not far from here, near the beach, Reo's, great hoagy stuff, not junk, root beer on tap in frosted mugs, real yummy pizzas."

"I know it." Summers ago, Dulcie, and –. "I'll get the luggage in first."

"We'll both."

"Then lunch."

"Then back here for our suits."

"One stop on the way back – Gallagher's."

"Oh sure, the liquor place. OK," she says.

"And then – the beach."

"Can't wait."

Unpackings:

Toothbrush by toothbrush in the imperial bath, side by side domesticity. She reaches into a tote bag, holds up a box, his favourite soap – on a rope– hangs it over the shower head.

"I brought mine," he says, "it's in the duffel."

"I wanted everything new." Smiles, hangs towels on racks. Brought those, too," he says.

"Don't you love these?" she says. I've been shopping all week." Hope chest Billie. "They're lovely," he says as she holds up a giant bath towel figured with sea horses. "And this one" – a starfish design. "Yours is the horse."

"Natch." His and Hers.

"Feel it," she says. "They'll make great beach spreads. "And this," dips again into the tote bag: his favourite shave cream. He leans his old Rolls razor next to it in the dolphin fringed medicine cabinet. "And this," nodding, a sidling glance at him – a vial of Old Delhi Mantra Body & Soul Oil. Guaranteed. It doesn't say for what. Bottled in Brooklyn.

"Anything goes," he says.

The two people in the mirror crack up.

Towel-wrapped they plough through the sugary sand, clumped bayonets of poverty grass, thrusts of sea rockets.

And the full bell of the sea.

Two-three miles out the blue band of the Gulf Stream sparkles. "At last," she says, takes a breath. The beach is theirs. A half mile to the right a blue-green umbrella, two toylike people, a toy child. Far enough to the left another family encampment on blankets, a coloured beach ball. No one is in the water. The sea is theirs, too. "It must be cold," she says. "Let's just sit and look for a while."

A cool onshore breeze. Hands interlaced, sunglassed, they lie on terry sea horses and starfish in the sexual sun. From under his shades he can see a lip of breast pout from her bikini bra, a few curled gold wires escaping the triangle mound below. The sun begins to anoint them. They lie in a hope of forever gold sleep. Her fingers woven with his slacken. Her breath slows. Up all night packing. Shopping all week. For a week in brackets. He lifts slowly up on an elbow. The now and then breeze has put a coil of hair at her lips, now lightly dewed. God, give me this girl. The calendar melts in the sun.

Her eyes open, she says, "Huh?" blinks, "I must have conked off." Looks around, "Oh, we're really here." And puts her hand to his cheek. "I thought I was dreaming."

"Really here."

"Let's never leave."

"We never will," he says.

"Promise?"

He puts a hand to her hair, kisses her forehead.

He says: "Not too much sun for one time. Your skin is so fair. You don't want to burn. Let's take a walk." She reaches a hand to him and he pulls her up. "You look great," she says, and puts a hand in his hair, as if the little patches of cloth they're wearing has put them in another dimension, a rediscovery.

Exciting stranger . . .Sun-coined, brand new.

"It's the shades," he says. *They always make you look so wicked, a bandit* . . . He thinks: One day you'll forget. Or remember as a series of fading, quickcut snapshots. Memory's freeze frames. But I never will, not the full life of it.

They walk hand in hand along the edge of the surf, their toes in a wash of chill foam, toward the distant Stone Harbor water tower. Ahead, a klatch of spotted sandpipers skitters up to and back from the swash with the ebb and flow of the waves. She stoops to pick up something, a small fluted shell. Holds it out, a sea gift.

"Give me my scallop-shell of quiet," he says.

She tilts her head. "I like that." Waits for exegesis.

"Sir Walter Raleigh. The first line of a poem he wrote in the Tower, waiting to be executed – beheaded."

"Wasn't he the one who spread his cape for a queen to walk on so she wouldn't get her feet wet?"

"The same."

"But why did they kill him?" Daddy.

"Love and politics." Child.

Gulls hack the air with their battering wings over the breakwater, scream over something there on the rocks.

"Gulls," she says, "always yakking, making a scene."

"That's what they probably say about us. Anyway," a movieland foxy grandpa look over his shades, "some of those gulls are boys." She looks back at him over her sunglasses: Funny mans. Also, I love you.

"I think it's time we took the plunge, it's getting hot," he says. "I'm going in."

"Let's do it from *our* beach."

They jog down to meet the Atlantic, she alongside in an unexpectedly awkward girl's gait, fisted hands pumping; he breaks off into a sprint and through exploding splashes is headfirst inside the green groin of a cresting wave in the original ocean's cold hand, its tidal grip and pull. He belongs to its god. Frogkicking, stroking up through the ocean wall he breaks the heaving water line on a glassy swell, turns shoreward shaking salt from his eyes, to see her bobbing, watching for him. He waves from the absolution of water. "See you in London," he calls. Does she hear him? Doesn't matter. A little macho, that. So what. He's sluiced off the years. Turns and strokes to the blue water horizon, his dipping gull winged Australian crawl. A fish from a boyhood book swims into his head: Swinburne: Strike out for the shore as the heart in us bids and beseeches athirst for the foam. Probably Guinness, Algernon, what? And rolls and floats on his back on the lift and fall of the sea, the sun licking him. The sea is my horse too. And remembers she is alone there, starts swimming back to catch an about to be born wave to come in on to her, armpit high in the surf.

"Well, Hi," she says, but smiling. "Remember me?"

"I don't believe we've met," and kisses her salt lips.

"You really can swim, man. I thought my heart would stop until I saw your head come up again. You were under so long. It looks pretty rough out there."

"Never could swim fast, or fast enough to make the team, but once I get going I can go on forever – three-four miles anyway. More. I just stop because I get bored."

"Lover," she says coming close, arms around him, his around her, bobbing together, touching toes just above the sea sand. "Go on forever in me, Jud. It's where you –" her last word is a breath – "belong."

"I know." It's also a breath.

"I'll never bore you."

"I know that, too."

"Then why can't we –"

"Billie . . ."

"OK, I'll be good."

They swim side by side along the shore to the breakwater and back; heave in the surf together, waves slapping against them;

193

splashing each other as they come out; lie born again in the sun . . .
The June breeze has picked up a lost March wind somewhere in the
sea, blowing sand, stinging, gritting the towels.

"Let's go in," she says.

"Race you down," he says, getting up, shaking sand from his
trunks.

"I mean back to the house. This sand is getting too much."

"One more swim, a dip, just to get wet."

She gasps as they plunge in. "Oh wow, the water's much colder."

"Tide's coming in." He dives into a gray whale of a wave, comes
up swimming. "This is great. I love it."

"You and the polar bears."

Cowled, wrapped in their beach towels again, they go back
through the dunes. "We've had the best of it," he says. Behind them the
orchestral sea sounding eternal codas as if Mahler had written it.

Showered and terry-robed, mermaid hair dank and hanging, she
winds down the spiral stair to him, terry-robed, too, his feet on a
hassock. He holds out a tall one.

"What's that?" she says.

"Ol' Jud's original gin sling." A quartered lime floats on top, the
glass frosted.

"The champagne?"

"That's for the dinner you threatened to make."

"Oh right," she takes the glass. "Mmmnh, very good." Sits by the
hassock, knees up, facing him. "Hey, this is really good."

"It should have a sprig of mint. I should have brought some.
There's a bed of it down by the spring."

On your farm.

"Oh well," she says, "this is great."

"We've lucked in on weather."

She nods: "To us."

"Cheers."

She sips, says: "Where will we have dinner tonight?"

"Henny's, I guess, they used to be open year round."

"I've been there. Stone Harbor. Good. Great seafood."

"One more of these," he says, "and we'll go. They should have fresh
bluefish – they're running."

"I hope they have soft-shells. I love them."

"Good idea, that's what I'll have, too. And a nice chilled Moselle."

"And a salad."

"And strawberry shortcake. Fresh, fat Jersey strawberries and real
whipped cream. From cows, not out of a tube."

"Not if I'm to get back in my bikini. I just about made it."

"So I've noticed."

She shows him a rosebud of tongue.

"Your drink, love," he says coming back from the bar.

194

"Thank you, kind sir." She sips. "You make a wicked drink."

"I don't fool around."

"No." Her eyes come from somewhere. "You did bring the book?" He nods. "I want you to work on it here. I meant that when I said it. You can do that in the morning; we'll have the beach all afternoon."

"I'll have to read through it first. Get the feel of it again. It's been so long."

"Would you read it to me?"

"I've never done that before."

"You didn't have me before."

No . . . "Maybe. It might not be a bad idea, hear how it sounds, whether it still holds up, means what I once wanted it to mean. To someone . . . well, across time."

"Like someone from now. Like you mean, with it."

"Yes . . . As de Tocqueville said . . ." he shrugs.

"Who he?"

"I have a garbage can mind, all kinds of things in it."

"Tell me what he said. Don't you understand? When you talk to me like that, I cream."

"Remarkable fella, a French aristocrat —"

"Natch."

"A young lawyer, came to this country when it was young, maybe a hundred-forty or so years ago. Travelled everywhere. Saw it with clear, original eyes. Wrote a book. He knew what we were and what we were going to be. That's the amazing thing — what we would become."

"Like what?"

"He said, 'in America, every new generation is a new people.' And that was when we were still forests and farms, long before Henry Ford, Standard Oil, the highways and suburbs, movies, F. Scott Fitzgerald and TV."

"Right on."

"Yes, he was, Billie . . ."

"You will read your book to me?"

"Mebbe, pardner."

"Please."

"We'll see how I feel in the morning."

"How do you feel now? she says, putting her drink down, rising. "Stay where you are." She unties the sash of his robe where he sits, spreads it like wings, lowers herself onto him, guiding him into her sea washed flowers.

And the evening and the morning were the first day.

33

On the flying deck over the green lagoon, reeds on the other side, the teeming marsh, morning coffee cups by their chairs, she brings him his attaché case.

"I thought I'd read it through first myself."

"That's not what you said last night."

"No?"

"No."

"When was that?"

"Oh, after the Tom Collinses at Henny's and the Moselle – you ordered a second bottle, you were so happy they had it, what was it? oh yes – Schwarze Katz – I don't know how to say it."

"Black Cat."

"Yes, and you called me your golden cat. *Meow.*"

"I did?"

"Yes, and also your lioness. And after the brandy there we had cognac here. You even drew a map about where cognac becomes brandy."

"We did?"

"You did. It was more like a target. The bull's eye, you said – I forget – something about only grapes from a certain place – where the true cognac comes from."

"So, I was onto that?"

"Oh yes, that was when you said my breasts were like clusters of grapes and I was a palm tree."

"My great-uncle Zechariah Bell, a circuit-riding preacher, had that underlined in the Bible he left me. He rode a bay mare named Sheba."

"You told me. But that wasn't the only thing."

"What else?"

"You said Mohammed was a very civilized fella because–"

"Oh *that.*"

"–he allowed every man to have four wives. Right there in the Koran, you said, in black and white."

"Giants in the earth in those days."

"So you said. Then after the nightcaps and we went upstairs–"

"Yes?" Following your comely hind . . .

"You said you were King Solomon and I was your thousand wives and you were going to have us – me – one right after the other right then and there."

"I did, did I?"

"Oh yes. And you said the concubines come later."

"I did?"

"Oh yes."

"Well, sorry about that. The grape is mightier than the . . ."

"Oh, I wasn't counting." A smile edges her lips. "No complaints, Lover."

She pushes the attaché case close to his deck chair. "Read." she says. He unsnaps the brass locks on the scuffed leather box, takes out the canary pages.

"The working title of this book is, *Novel on Yellow Paper.*"

"Oh wow, I think that's great."

"Not really. It doesn't say anything. It's just that, a working title, a peg to hang pages on."

"OK, read."

"Chapter 1."

"He really should have known better than to have gone up to Green Meadows that day. Green Meadows, "just under an hour" from Grand Central. It's fifty-seven minutes on the express, and no one ever mentions the reluctant local. It's always "just under an hour," according to Green Meadowans, as if any station up the line in Cornucopia County, just one minute more than an hour away, is somewhere on another planet. Nor do they ever say right out it's fifty-seven minutes from the city. That sounds like a lot of time put that way, like fifty-seven hours, almost.

"But then again, the actual going there was not the first step, although the solid act of getting on the train seemed to make it so. Who can tell at any time which word, what gesture, is a first step on a road that finally crosses a strange frontier? In this case the first step, unrecognized as such by either of them, had been taken a long time before. Eighteen years. Not even her letter which was suddenly there after all that time was a first step. And that's what made the whole thing an enigma.

"Being a writer, he had a ready-to-wear excuse at hand, a made-to-measure alibi. If there were some perfectly logical reasons for not doing something he intended doing, he could face them down by arguing that it was in the nature of an exploratory adventure vital to the replenishing of his grab bag of experience. After all, what was there to learn by sitting at home? And what could he lose by going here, there or anywhere, just this once? And there we have it again – that first step that goes a long way back into the future . . ."

He looks up at her listening face. "It's very mysterious," she says, nodding. "Books should have mysteries in them. Secrets. Surprises." He closes the binder.

"Hey."

"I'd rather not." Go on.

"You promised."

Egrets across the water on their stilts in the cattails, sea rockets waiting for midsummer to fire their lavender flowers.

He opens the binder again, flips a frew pages and begins to read.

Billie says, "No fair, you're skipping."

"I already see where I have to cut; no point reading what won't be there when it's done. Please, I have to do this my way, Billie. Just so you get the gist, the flavor."

"OK, Hon."

He reads: "Looking at her fully now for the first time since she had come in, the blindness that always misted a new meeting clearing, he was not at all certain he would have recognized her in passing. But the woman in the chair opposite his did recall now completely the young teacher he had not thought of in all those years until her first letter arrived a week ago. He did not think of a specific age, looking at her, hearing her. It was the spirit of a generation which went beyond its chronological time, intact and hopeful, a kind of dream pennant, her essential quality. A belief in vocation. In spite of the light fleck of honest gray at the temple she was still youthful, something still surging, eager. She had crossed the room with the same athletic stride, an almost manly bounding walk. And yet again there were subtle changes he could not define. Her chestnut hair, once combed back severely in a bun was now cheek length, framing her face with a girlish look. The slightly oriental slant of her blue eyes seemed lost now, except when the light caught the taut cheekbones with an upward brush. The long ago girl was somehow still there in the woman. Was it the awkward way she blew the full breath of smoke out, as if cigarettes had never become a daily need, but something that went along with the rare glass of wine? A new glint in her eyes sparked by just a few sips of sherry? He felt strangely older, as if he had done all his living, three lifetimes to her one. There had been girls who could drink . . ."

He looks up at Billie in her deck chair looking at him as if his face was a page she had missed in a book she was reading.

He reads: "They were sitting on a slab of rock below the Cloisters. They had walked around Fort Tryon Park; they had stopped at the herb gardens; they had heard the Gregorian chants, lonely for God, throbbing through antiphonal stone corridors and arches. The wind brought sprays of river smell to them, the wet earth smell of an old river that's been around, trying to clean itself of people. Below them the sun showered the Hudson with its gold standard coins.

"She had brought sandwiches, fruit, cheese and a flask of Chianti. He watched her putting the remains of their luncheon back into the wicker basket, deft woman grace, and was glad to be here with her. For the first time glad for the other two times they had been together and a little regretful they had been so much her doing. They were part of a landscape with no shadow. He looked at her now, not really for

198

the first time, but for the first time seeing more than someone inhabiting clothes, a pleasure of sunlight on the body.

"Hello," he said.

"She looked up, her brows punctuating surprise. A mascara emphasis that wasn't put there by a brush, as if a student has answered a question she hadn't asked. A something scribbled there, a new thing, not entirely certain it was there, but accepting it just the same, she returned his smile.

"'Oh – hello.'"

"They were now involved in the aura and weather of a thing apart. A meeting, its moment. A sunshaft moment with no future in it but theirs. They knew, without bringing it up to the light that this was but the seed, and that a seed has reason, and the reason is the tree.

"The wind was brutal now, rushing with barbed charges from the high fire-born rocks across the river. Under the piling scud of clouds their rock was cold, but neither he nor she would give the word of departure to end their afternoon. Their interior time would not strike return and the signposts of their country pointed away from the horizonless city. Laura stood on the slab, gusts snatching at her roughspun heather skirt.

"'Friend,' she said, 'I've just had a wonderful idea.'"

"I'm all for it."

"'Now wait a minute,' the schoolmarm again, 'this depends on how much of an adventurer you are. It's too lovely a day to wind up in the city. Why don't we go up to Connecticut, to my wonderful country hill? I want you to see it.'"

"It's after three."

"'We're right on the highway. It goes straight up to Danbury – and then we're minutes from the place. We'll be there in an hour and a half. Two at the outside, taking it easy. We always have coffee in the larder and there are dozens of cans. Or we can pick up whatever we want on the way.' . . .

". . . They turned off the main highway and followed a tarred road for about ten miles. 'The next turn,' she said. 'It's just about here that I know I'm in home country, my own part of the world, my own piece of ground.'

"They rolled over a small steel bridge. 'That's the Housatonic below. Another mile and we're home.' He drove slowly along the snaking road, a green sun-clinked tunnel along a shallow stream. 'That's our brook. Slowly now, it's just around the next bend. See it – there – that's our bridge.'

"He got out of the car and unlooped the anchor chain across the roadway. 'We park on the bridge,' she said."

He closes the binder on his lap. "So endeth the first day's lesson.". And leans back to the overhead sun.

"So they parked on the bridge," Billie says.

"Yes," he says, "they parked on the bridge."

"And then?"

"They went into the house, not just any old house, a house built by a sea captain – that's why it was anchor chain on the bridge, not any old chain – he had a secret, too, a lost ship. That is part of that house."

"And then what, when they're in the house?"

"What do you think?"

"They make it."

"Ah yes, but *how*?"

"That's what I want to know. Read."

"You sure you want to hear that part?"

"Read."

"The little log bridge over the brook with its silver birch railings made the place private, guarded. It was solitary without being lonely. Upstream a waterfall running by an abandoned mill noised onto the rocks and put a whisper into the air which sharpened the silence. All around firs, pines, pin oaks and birches, a stand of maples, studded the rearing hillside.

"They started up a steep winding path breathing the rich smells of dank earth and leaf mold thickened with the fresh budding leafage of trees. As the road ran into a swell of grass he caught a flash of white higher on the hill. 'There it is,' she said. Another twenty paces and it sailed into full view, a small trim-gabled house anchored in its own moving meadow harbored by woods. From here you could see nothing but the small anchorage of long grass, the house, the well, the shed listing into the woods, all guarded by the green lances of the trees, and miles away another hill remote and friendly to the west. The air buzzed quietly in the sun. In this country quiet you could know the luxury of hearing one thing at a time . . .

"'You like?' she said.

"I like. *Mucho*. It's the kind of house you can take a voyage in."

"'A voyage?' she asked, 'that's uncanny.'

"Why?"

"'The house was built by a retired sea captain. He was skipper of a destroyer. Lost his ship, they say, around the time of the Spanish American War. He was cleared by the court martial. But I suppose there are some things you can never clear, at least to yourself. A lost ship is a lost ship. When they gave him a desk job, he left. His idea of being a sailor was to be one on blue water. He built most of it himself. See that round porch above the south room? We call it the Captain's deck. He used to sit there in the evening watching the sky. Most of the things in the house he made by hand. Come . . .'

" . . . They were listening to old records played on the ancient handcranked phonograph. Every now and then the motor suffered a heart attack and dropped with a sickened thud into the stomach of some song. But even through its regular jog-trot rhythm the battered records called with an insistent nostalgic appeal: the scratched and still magic Carusos hung their grapey tones in the room; the silver McCormacks, the velvety Elmans, Paderewski and Galli-Curci. Bruce found a Harry Lauder but stopped his caterwauling, restoring the room to them. Outside, the curious country dark squatted at the edge of light, the island house . . .

"She rose with one unfolding motion, took the wineglass from his hand, drank from it and slid into a ballet step. '*Pas de chat*,' she said, turning and swinging out, the flaring skirt clinging to her fine leg. '*Arabesque*.' She pivoted to a stop.

"'Let's dance,' she said.

"To Caruso – or John McCormack?"

"'Oh you.'

"'OK," he said, getting up from the floor. "I think there's a *Missouri Waltz* in there, or maybe it's the *Marseillaise*."

"'Never mind,' she said, kicking off her shoes, and putting her arm around an invisible partner waltzed slowly around the room. "'I don't need any music.'

"He came up to her. A slight bow. "May I have the next dance?"

"She stopped. 'Invitation's lapsed,' she said as he reached for her hand, sidestepping out of his way.

"He went over to the mantel, found his cigarettes, lit one. *Oh lady*, he thought, *but the gambit's got to be yours*.

"She was at the window. *Why did I do that, why do I always* . . . She pushed the curtains aside. 'Look,' she called, 'fog, oceans of it. We're marooned.'

"He came up behind her and looked out. From the thicket darkness of the woods the fog rolled in. Cloud upon cloud coiling onto their patch of lamp-thrown light. She stood still, inches shorter in her stocking feet. He close. Her cheek burned. Her pulse tossed in her throat. He heard her breathe with a catch and a stop. She wasn't seeing the fog now, just hearing her blood's drum. He put his hands on her shoulders, turned her and kissed her and she seemed to be drowning.

"She broke off, keeping a body's width between them, but still holding his hand. 'What kind of a kiss was that?'

"There's only one kind," he said.

"But a *first* –'

"One kind for men and women. For children –"

"'You must remember, I'm –'

"He kissed her again and before she could think *not down here, upstairs, in my room*, they were armlocked and moving up the stairs together.

"The fog cast a pale snow of drifting light into the room. He heard the secret whisper of her clothes rustling to the floor, and she the buckle of his belt strike wood, each listening for the rushing life of the other and reaching. She stood shimmering, a small moon in the room until his body's shadow eclipsed her.

"On the Captain's bed, the exact spinning center of the universe, it had come to this . . . The hollows of her face absorbed the dark . . .

" . . . Below, the clock struck eight bells, summoning the watch.

"Then she took his arm and stretched it and put her head on it and they slept. And he knew through the light gauze of sleep, still between sleeping and waking, that she slept serenely unstirring like a child with good dreams, moving still in sleep when he moved, when his arm was cramped and he could no longer keep it under her head. Then he slipped it out and turned on his side and she turned too, fitting back to chest, curve to curve, the two good bodies folded.

"He turned again, trying not to wake her and she turned with him, a dolphin turn, and they slept.

"The fog peered in."

He shuts the binder on his lap on the flying deck over the last lagoon, leans back in his deck chair, closes his eyes. Hears her lighting a cigarette. "I'll have one," he says. "There's a carton of Players in the attaché, case. Light one for me, please."

He takes a deep drag on the mind scratching grit.

"I thought you were back to your pipe."

"I always smoked cigarettes when I wrote. Books, that is. It was like a hand you reached for that was always there. Helped being alone. I guess I've become a coward."

"All that jazz about cancer."

"Yes. If it's true, I can't take a chance now. I have no markers left. I'll need some time at the wrong end, the downhill side. Or I'm done. Just trading for time. The last resort of a scoundrel isn't patriotism, it's the excuse of responsibilities. An alibi."

"You're too hard on yourself."

"Not hard enough. I was once up to three packs a day. But I finished a book – books. You know, Billie, when you're alone in the night, when I used to be someone else, and all you have is that."

"You're not someone else."

"And all you have is the yellow sheet in the machine . . . And that friendly glowing stick."

"Why yellow?"

"To keep me humble. If it's on white, it seems more permanent, as if it can't be touched. As if someone else wrote it, you know. Almost as final as print. But on yellow – that's why, Novel on Yellow Paper – you can put the scalpel to it."

"Jud?"

"Yeah, Babe?"

"It's fabulous."

"You don't have to say that, love."

"I mean it. I wouldn't say it otherwise."

"No, I don't think you would. But then, all right, I'm fishing, why?"

"Well, let me see . . ."

The world is the flying deck, she terry robed, one long delicious leg showing.

"OK . . . it's like looking at a painting – remember the Eakins show we went to? –"

"I never forget." A curse. "We all die of memory, not anything else, just too much to remember . . . Excuse, please. You were saying . . ."

"That's OK. It's like looking at a painting. With people in it. Whatever they're doing, OK? And it's like you walked into the frame and you hear what they're saying, the way they talked, the way they lived. They're different, from another time, but that's what they were. Real – sometime else."

"If I weren't so lazy I'd get up and kiss you."

"Promises, promises."

"Different – you said."

"Yes, that bit about their making it, like they had to play a game, go by some rules – that shit about her dancing, who's *she* kidding, she wanted your rod, man –"

"It's a book, Billie."

"Oh sure, I know. Futzing around until they finally did it."

"You said it, it's what they were, then – not all that long ago."

"That's what I mean."

The way we were.

"That's what makes it so good. For them that was the way. That's what comes out . . . Maybe it was more fun that way."

"Well, I'm glad, really." The novel as time machine.

"I want to hear more."

He looks at his watch. "Tomorrow. It's time for Reo's. The beach."

"So, she had a fine leg."

"Not half as fine as yours – or anything else."

"Kiss me, Bruce – not a kiss for children – your book's made me wet."

Egrets across the water on their stilts in the cattails, sea rockets waiting for midsummer to fire their lavender flowers.

34

"Read," she says.

"You asked for it."

"Read."

He lights a Player, that old flying carpet of cloud, opens the binder.

"From the moment they passed Barnstable Harbor on the cape their sabbath week in the sun was overcast by skies of shifting clouds. But they had brought their own climate with them as if in a Thermos, and would not let rain ruin their seven days by the sea. Yarmouth Port, Dennis, Orleans, Wellfleet, Truro, Provincetown – they drove right to the headland point crooked out into the ocean, a finger of land hooking the sea.

" . . . On the moors near North Truro they found a room in a Portuguese fisherman's house. Its windows looked out on the sea, and except for the old sailor-widower they were alone in the place."

Billie is lighting another cigarette, but he doesn't look up. Just hears the snap of the lighter. He thinks he hears her say, "Jesus."

"'You know,' Laura said as they put their bags down, looking at the wide brass bed, 'we're like an old married couple.'

"'Sounds sad,' he said.

"'Oh no,' Laura said, 'It's just as if I woke up and you're still here.'"

This time he hears Billie say, "I don't believe it," and looks up at the face of a child who walked into her parents' room and found them embraced, not sleeping.

"Billie," he says.

"Read," she says.

"You're sure?"

"Read . . ."

"They walked out along the moors in the last of the afternoon to the cliff's edge. The sun, breaking through scales in the fishbelly sky, touched heather and furze and the gray rolling sea before them. Her skin turned gold with it, her sandaled foot an ear of corn. They descended the steep, narrow path in the almost vertical side of the cliff to the always sudden world of sand, sea and cliff. Off there, the lighthouse, its blind unlit eye.

"She was first in the water, her white capped head bobbing up, gasping, 'It's cold,' flailing the powerful icy surf and calling between the whale roll of waves for him to come in. He backed off poised and slashed into the water from a flat running dive. He swam underwater trying to find her in the now sungreen sea. But the sucking undertow roiled sand into the surf so that he had to shut his salt-smarting eyes and flip up to the surface. 'Cold,' she called. 'Icy, but won-der-ful.'

"They kept within feet of the beach, the unleashed ocean running in with near hurricane force. Their voices were lone gulls above the waters where no one else was. 'Can't swim,' she called. 'Tide – too strong. Just dunk –' A wave rolled over her. 'Like a doughnut,' she spluttered, coming up in its ebb. Then another foam-crested locomotive wave knocked her down. He plowed over to her and they struggled up together, their lodestar bodies warm where they touched and rolled and tangled. Then the clouds shut the sky and chill shadow turned the sea gray again. They splashed out spewing water, laughing, stumbling, arms around each other, the sea streaming from them. 'Oh,' she said, 'Oh.' They raced down the beach then back and stood towelling each other with the large rough towels she had bought just for this time . . ."

He hears Billie say, "Oh no."

And goes on . . . "He kissed her seacold lips, feeling the warming blood under the chilled smooth skin.

"'Good,' she said. 'Salt water taffy.'

"They threw robes over their shoulders, climbed the cliff path and crossed the moors to their room . . .

"Their summer week was spinning itself out in gray. Although there was little actual rain, and then in short slashing gusts, it hung there in skies of solid cloud. But every day they went to the deserted beach off the headland light and gave themselves to the tonic sea.

"Lying on the body-warm sand, her head on his chest, Laura said, 'I've never been so happy. What have I done to deserve it?'

"'Don't say things like that; it makes beggars of us.' . . .

"They began gathering up their towels and robes, their feet sinking in rough-grained sand as they walked to the cliff. At the top they looked over the fireless sea of flint, then walked more quickly, hand in welcome hand to the house on the moors as the hunting arrows of rain began to fall . . ."

". . . That's as far as I got," he says, "on paper, the rest has been rattling around in my head," closing the binder, "every day, would you believe it? Every single day. Getting into the Pooh-Jo, taking the train, doing my thing in that place."

"It's weird. I mean, like a crystal ball – you then . . ."

"It's a book."

" . . .us, now."

"Oceans and people have been around a long time."

"Yes . . . Do you know how it's going to end?"

"I knew that before I began it. I could have written the last page first."

"How does it end?"

"It doesn't. The end is another beginning. A step."

"Why didn't you, I mean, put it down?"

"Because the characters may surprise me along with way – they already have, you let Jack out of the box and you find Jack has his own mind – not really changing where it will end, but in what state they arrive there."

"I love you."

"A book is written with two hands. The right one," he opens it, palm out, "is the one with the lifeline, a kind of map, the story. The left one with the people in it, the mysteries, the left hand is the dreamer."

"Why is that?"

"It's nearer the heart."

"Jud?"

"Love?"

"You must finish this book."

"It's back in both hands. But–"

"For us – please. Don't you see? If it goes – it's got to, it's *good* –"

"That doesn't mean it will fly."

"It must. It will, then you can –"

Pay Vera off.

"Time, " he says.

"I take that away from you."

"It would take you away from me."

She pushes her deck chair closer to his. "Sweetheart, I love you. We're going to work things out. You'll see. We're going to make it. It's all there in your right hand – our map – I read it. We're going to be together. We've got to."

To work at what you want to work at. Love whom you want to love. Live with whom you love.

"I want to be."

"I mean all the time. Like this week."

Out of time.

"Yes," he says.

"Our last swim," she says on the balmy night beach.

"It's going to be cold," he says. "I can take it. I'm used to springfed water."

"I know, your pool. But this is ours, not even in your book . . . This belongs only to us. Special. Like a . . ."

"Ritual."

"Yes."

On the quicksilver sand in front of the murk of water, phosphorescent arpeggios played by catspaw waves, she unties her bikini bra and flings it back, and her G string pennant. He throws his trunks onto the sand behind him, takes her hand and walks into the shock of moony ocean.

"Wow," she gasps, "it-is-cold."

"Stay close," he says, swimming side stroke with her along the shore through broken dishes of moon.

"Not too bad," she says, "once you're in."

The sea is a hive of icicle stings. They swim to the breakwater and back where they started, put their arms around their dolphin bodies, bobbing together in the sleep breathing surf, the night ocean's dark excitement, her sea slippery breasts warm on his chest, her mouth wet warm on his. Tingles that aren't the sea's. "Oh Hon," she says, reaching a hand between them. "It's so small and cold," she whispers wetly into his ear.

"A temporary situation. All it needs is a warm shelter."

Hand in seacold hand they jog stumbling back to their blanket spread on the dune. "That was fantastic," she says standing lit by the moon in a moonlight of her own as he towels her dry, her silver face to the sea. "Now you," she says, rubbing him down.

"It seems we only just got here."

"I know," she says, putting his robe around his shoulders, taking his hand, kneeling back on the blanker, tugging him down.

"Here?" he says.

"Here on our beach." and he sees that her face is the same as the one on the brooch he gave her.

"It's been the best week of my life," she says. "Thank you."

"Don't say that."

"I know, it makes beggars of us."

He holds her, the whole altogether weekful of her, the just-the-two-of-them week. A few yellow flowers of light sprinkle the dunes. "Out of this world," she says.

"Yes." Out of this world.

"Some day," she says, "we'll have a house on the dunes and live in it all year round. Swim in the summer, walk on the winter beach . . .

"Jud?"

"Love?"

"Tell me we will."

"Some day."

He hears a small throttled noise. He tastes the warm salt of a divorced tear as he kisses her, finds her among gold harpsichord strings.

"Don't cry, Billie. Don't cry my love. "We're going to be all right."

"I know."

Below them the ocean is playing a thousand cellos.

35

I didn't need the cellos of your voice
to make me sad.
As if my sadness could be made
by cellos.

As if my sadness could be made at all
Or unmade by the tears that fell
into our well of days, our week that couldn't end
but did.

Days that laughed and cried at once
nights that rivalled days for sun,
dreams that wouldn't sleep.

I didn't need the cellos
of your goodbye to make me sad
as if we hadn't filled the day with them.

Each long look only waiting for the last.
Our eyes no longer eyes
but clouds.

As if it needed to be said at all.

As if you weren't gone before you came.

As if my sadness could be made by cellos.
As if my sadness could be made at all
I filled the air with my own violins
and let the rain fall.

Hysterias of rain lash the shuttered room. Air bucks in a lunatic wind drumrolling the garbage cans in the alley, an unseen mob let loose. A gunpowder reek in the room as if a pistol had been fired close to their heads. Their bed wallows in waves of sound, the sheets wet as sprayed sails. She wakes saying, "What? What's happening?"

"It's that hurricane up from the Gulf. It's finally reached us."

"What time is it?"

"6:22."

"It's so dark." She flips the radio on to a crackling voice . . . "the worst storm ever to hit the state . . . fifty-mile per hour winds . . . flooding everywhere . . . the Schuylkill over its banks at . . . forty known dead . . . damage in hundreds of millions. The governor has declared a state of emergency . . . Red Cross and National Guard troops . . ."

"Hey, what are you doing?"

"Getting dressed."

"What for? The office is not even open yet, probably won't be."

"I've got to get home."

"You crazy? It's raining rivers out there. You'll get blown away in that wind."

"Trees may be down on the barn, on the fence – horses all over the place – maybe the house."

"Come back to bed, Jud, you're not going anywhere."

"I've got to try, she may be in trouble, even hurt."

"What about me?"

"You'll be all right here."

"All alone – in this? Please Jud, stay with me this once."

"Billie, my place may be wrecked up there on that hill. You heard the man – fifty-mile winds – that roof is old wooden shakes – forty already dead, fires . . . I've seen what a twister can do when I was a boy."

"Why don't you try calling?"

Where are you supposed to be Judson, tonight, today? Washington? The Big Apple? "OK."

He picks up the phone, shakes his head. "Dead. No dial tone . . . I've got to go."

"How are you going to get there?"

"Walk to the station."

"In this pouring mess?" He's putting his shoes on. "Then you're really going?"

She arches those cathedral legs out of bed, her whisky hair pouring over her breasts, her knees. "Let me get something on, I'll drive you . . ."

> In the great rain of our separation
> my heart swelled with your blood.
> Your tides rose high against my loneliness
> until its banks were overflowed.
> Your waters kissed my earthen breast,
> washing away time in your current,
> swallowing miles in your flood.
> Despair left homeless, no tears for drinking,
> I drowned in your rushing river.

Fall

36

"To your new job," he says, raising his glass.

"I still can't believe it," she says. "A bank, me in a *bank*."

"It may be Dullsville for you, Billie, all those leaflets and flyers, rack stuffers to write. You know, Christmas Club stuff. It's not like an ad agency – any ad agency, even the shlocks. More like the civil service."

"That's hokay by me. So I won't be writing great ads. At lease I won't have a Wanda Sload on my back."

"The Wandas are everywhere, Billie. It's their world."

She shrugs, stirring the ice with a swivel stick finger. "Not in this place. You know where you stand. Your job is *your* job. I report to *one* man, the marketing VP, no one else. He's *boss*. He made that loud and clear. I get my assignments from *him* and *he* checks them out." A smile and a sip, "And it's three thou more than I got at Fairleigh. Three *thou*. And all those great fringe benefits. See-cur-ity."

"Yes, banks are safe places."

She glances up. "Hey, yeah, that's neat. Say, I might use that some day."

"Could make a throwaway line in a safety deposit box flyer."

"At least I got one thing out of Fairleigh. That name is still magic in this town."

"Your résumé did say you were there for more than a year, really implied you were still there."

"Hey, didn't you want me to get the job? How would a crummy six months sound? A dead giveaway. And you said you'd cover for me."

And Louie and Gill, et Al . . . the whole Billie Miller Fan Club. Besides, you helped her write it, Pufessah, in bed. Pencils and pads in the sheets. Much laughter and fun in the hay hay.

"Of course I wanted you to get the job."

Did he? Does he? He had been all her summer, a country of two. No one else in her landscape. She turning only to him with the sun. Walking down Walnut to meet him, her smile a separate light when she saw him swim out of the noonday or evening crowd. Idylls of lunch in the park by the river, sails and sculls dreaming by on the Schuylkill. "And I'll see you this evening, Hon." Waiting sometimes rain-shower fresh in the lime MG across from the office to be with him a half hour sooner. A job now, another country with its corporate boundaries, a closed nation of other people, a line drawn, he on the other side. Other people, you mean other men, Judson. Dazzling Billie, the new headspinning girl on campus. He hears the wolf whistles. *Laugh, kid,* the welcome aboard bit. *Don't you trust me Jud? I trust you. I love you.* Will you love me in December as you did in May? Equinox come again.

"What's he like?"

"What's who like? Oh, you mean my new boss?"

He nods yes, your new Boss.

"Oh him . . ."

Him . . .(he) . . .

"Oh you mean Ed Loach . . . Well-let's-uh-see-now. He's about your height, maybe half-inch taller . . . Um . . . abour thirty eight – doesn't look it – you know, the blown hair bit, two-tone shirts, gold cuff links . . .

To be thirty eight and not look it . . . O wow.

" . . .groovy clothes, St. Laurent suits, Gucci shoes."

How do you know? Did you see the labels? Make it light, Judson, let's not play the heavy, what? With a sewn smile he says, "Hey Babe, did you see the labels?"

She laughs, O, that-when-I-first-met-you-Billie-laugh. "He told me. He's that kind of guy. Not at all what I thought a banker would be like."

You can bank on that. (Har.)

"Oh yes, and he plays squash twice a week at the Racquet Club."

Two-tone shirts in the Racquet Club? Is nothing sacred any more?

"Well," Jud says, rising to freshen their drinks, "I think this calls for a celebration. Where would the new promotion manager of the Quaker City Bank & Trust Company like to dine?"

Has she heard him?

She orbits away. "And my office, I wish you could see it. Not like that cubbyhole they put me in at Fairleigh. Wall-to-wall carpet, two windows, the works. And I'm going to have my own secretary."

Miss Miller is not in her office at the moment. Who did you say? Is there a message? No, just tell her Mr Bell called. Yes, she has my number. No message.

"I can't wait till Monday," she says.

> Today is Monday, September 18, the 262nd day
> of the year with 104 to follow.
>
> The morning stars are Mercury, Venus, Mars and
> Saturn.
> The evening star is Jupiter.
>
> Those born this day are under the sign of Virgo.
>
> On this day in history:
> In 1950 the Fugitive Slave Act was passed by
> Congress, allowing a slave-owner with a

certificate to reclaim any slave who escaped into another state.

In 1857 the New York Times was published for the first time.

In 1928 it was estimated that 4,000 persons had been killed and property damage amounting to more than $30 million had been caused by a devastating hurricane which lashed Florida and the West Indies for five days starting September 12.

37

"C'mon in, Keed," Tad says through a non-filter Camel smoke ring.
So now I'm Kid.
What happened to Ace?
Kid who?

. . . Well, as you said, Jack, there was George Kid Lavigne, the all time great lightweight champ. And there was the Dixie Kid, born Aaron L. Brown, welterweight; 77 wins, 63 by KO; 6 draws, 23 no decisions, 1 no contest. Won the title on April 30, 1904 when he was fouled by Joe Walcott in the 20th round. (Not our Jersey Joe). You rattled it off like a Gatling gun. Almost no great fighters sobriqueted Kid, you said, ever fought over welter. Of course, how could a heavy be called a Kid? Very astute observation, that, Jack. And speaking of welters, there was Clarence Kid Ferns, no wonder he had to be good with a front moniker like that. Kids calling him sissy. With a *praenomen* like that, you actually said – good Canada dominie school you went to – chuckling into the glass of Old Parr neat I'd poured you. Oh, Jack. Latin words you said, were built like a brick shithouse, solid, foursquare. Hey, and Jack, remember that classy featherweight, Louis Kid Kaplan you told me about? 1925-6. I was a kid myself then, the one with what you called his snapping hook. There before you could see where it came from. I could smell the blood and sweat on those eight-ounce leather gloves. You were full of that people history. And you had to show me, old Toronto Kid newspaper boy, just how a hook was not a jab. You demonstrated the difference in angle and knocked over the lamp. Which you then counted out. Belle-Maman Flora and Vera coming in and frowning in 3/4 time . . . And there was Kid Chocolate and Jackie Kid Berg and Kid Gavilan, the one with the bolo punch. And the bantamweight Kid Williams with his flurring fists who lost on a foul to Johnny Ertle in the fifth round on September 12th, 1915 . . . And of course, the original Kid McCoy, that turn-of-the-century highly respected and durable middleweight. In this corner wearing purple trunks . . .

"What gives?" Tad says.
"This memo," he waves it, "you've put out on the Best Trade Ad Awards."
"Oh reet, that was great, the BTAAS, your Expel campaign took the gold."

"That's not what it says here."

"I know what it says. I wrote it."

"It says Leeta *and* I wrote the campaign."

A "So" through a smoke ring.

"You know I wrote them, Tad, all of them. When I showed them to you, you said . . ."

"Lookit, Keed, it was a gang bang, a group thing, you were all in it together. Who knows where the *i*dea comes from. Everybody contributed – you, Les, Joe and Leeta. That's why I put all the names in."

"Oh, Leeta was in the room all right, but the only thing Leeta contributed was one, *one* zero line that never got off the ground. You saw it and you agreed. I wrote them and Joe did the layouts."

"What's the diff, Ace?"

Ah, at least I am Ace again, right, Red Baron?

"You've got to have a closetful of awards - BTAAS, CLIOS, ANDYS . . ."

"That's not the point, the point is . . ."

"The point is the team score – not *who* makes the TD."

Except when it's you Tadpole.

"Anyhow, it's the kids who need encouragement, keeps 'em humpin."

Tad's kids, you wouldn't find them in your record books, Jack. Below the belt hitters, thumb in the eye scrappers, Fritzie Zivics, you'd call them. The Zivic brothers, you said, were known for shooting their glove laces into the worthy opponent's eye. Not your kind of kid. Or Owen Pilgrim's.

"Awards," Tad is saying, "makes us look good in the trade mags, gives the clients a cheap thrill. Kid stuff."

In this corner, Kid Bell.

The pink message slip on his desk says he's to call Miss Miller. Her new office number looks somehow clinical; almost all clean white zeros, very businesslike. Easy to memorialize. He's seen, no, heard it somewhere before, of course, the radio jingle, a jangle of shrieking harpies: "YEAH, the most *Interesting* Bank in Town, YEAH." Flatulent pun. Get it? Cymbals crash on the YEAH, yet. The vocal equivalent of a starburst. Now what dropout genius wrote that? Sounds like a bandy Leeta line. Says nothing, but manages to say it badly. Like YEAH. Team.

Pink slip in hand, tipping his head, he can just about see from his two-window shoebox office (she has two windows too, now) a jut of the corner tower of the building she's in and the QCB sign just this side behind Billy Penn on his yet-to-be-lit yellow clock. One of the town's oldest banks in the town's newest building. She should be able to see the Fairleigh Castle if she faces east. Can she see his window from her towered office? Another hour and forty-six minutes and he'll be walking up Walnut to meet her.

Could it be already a year since she flashed into his office? a whole patchwork year, in that wet-look getup, showy and fragrant, "because Fairleigh is number one and I'm ready for that . . ."

He dials – it feels like he's calling long distance, a different time zone – and asks for her extension.

"Hi, Love, how's it going?"

"Oh hi, just great," she bubbles. "This is a mar-vel-ous place. Everyone's being so super. You know, real helpful and friendly, they can't do enough for me. Let's see, I've had the grand tour, and, oh yes, met the *president*, a really neat guy, so natural. And I thought all bankers had to be over eighty and had gray hair. And listen to this – he said he hoped *I* would like *them*."

Ah yes, the first day of the corporate honeymoon. "That's wonderful, Billie, I'm so glad you like it. It makes all the difference. I'm sure you'll have lots more to tell me later. I've got a few things to –"

"Um . . . Jud . . . You were planning to come over tonight?"

"Planning?"

Always on Monday, it was taken for granted, after the weekend gulf. After their first week it needed no saying. The attaché case waits in the corner behind his office door.

"What I mean is, and please understand, Lover, there's this farewell dinner tonight they're giving this girl who's leaving . . ."

"Jud?"

"Yes?"

"And I've been invited. The whole department is going."

"Your first day on the job and you've been invited?"

"I told you, they're super people, really friendly. I even said I don't even know her."

"She's leaving today, on a Monday?"

"Oh, she already left – last week, but this was the *only* night she could make it. I really don't *want* to go."

"You could have said you had a prior engagement – a date."

"I suppose I should have, but it was so sudden and they were so great about it, including me in, you know, like one of the family."

"Where is this dinner?"

"Oh, where is this dinner? They didn't say. We're all going together as a group, right after work. Some restaurant somewhere . . ."

"Jud?"

"Yes, Billie . . ."

"You're not going to get uptight about this, are you?"

"I'll try not to."

"And Hon, I'll see you tomorrow. You *can* make it tomorrow?"

"Yes."

"I love you – you know *that* . . ."

"Jud?"

"Yes"

"You OK?"

216

"I'm fine, Billie."

"See you tomorrow."

He hangs up, the city between them.

38

"Of course I'm glad to have you home," Vera says from the dining room. "Glad, it's hardly the word, and on a Monday. I was just saying, Jud, I thought it unwise to bring office troubles home to the dinner table. I was reading only the other day in the local paper, in the Family Section, that dinner time should be pleasant, relaxing, a time for –"

Monday is time for Billie.

"A time for *what?*"

"What is the matter with you, Jud?" Vera says in the door of the living room. "You seem so angry, from the moment you came through the door. It's as if you're sorry the meeting was cancelled and you could come home."

A deep breath now and "I'm sorry, Vera." Smile at her willing blue eyes, her welcome home face. You've made this Monday a national holiday for her. I'm really sorry," he says again. A small enough coin in a cup. Cheap charity. "I'll tell you about it some time."

"Yes if you like, after dinner. The article said – it was by a doctor – that something occurs in one's system that could lead to a stroke if one were excited, emotional while having dinner."

If one were excited. "I'm not excited."

"Then why are you pacing like someone locked up in a cage?"

Stop pacing, lower your head, say, "I'm sorry."

"May we sit down to dinner? I was going to have some cold leftover chicken myself and a salad, but when you called to say you were coming home, I thought I'd dress it up in a pot pie for you, the crust the way you like it, crisp on the outside, fluffy on the inside."

Fluffy on the inside Billie.

"What did you say? It sounded like puffy."

"One more wee dram and we'll eat."

"You've already had –"

"You've been counting."

"Jud, dear, please . . ."

"Why are you sitting here alone in the dark?" Vera is saying. "You know I don't like it. It's as if . . ."

Yes, as if there were someone else in the room, someone you remember but never mention who used to sit in that chair alone with me in the dark, a night-blooming plant breathing the dark, filling the house, when you went up to bed.

" . . . you were cutting me out. I was so happy when you called to say the Washington meeting was cancelled —"

"Postponed."

"– that you would be home tonight, on a *Monday* – I ran out of the house to tell Blitz his Daddy was coming home. You haven't been home on a Monday in I don't know how long. And then you come home, your face full of thunder, and the first thing you do is pour yourself a drink, a large one, and take it upstairs before you've even washed and changed. You've never done that before. Such an uncivilized thing, to say the least."

"I'm not cutting you out, V."

"Well what would you call it, sitting alone in the dark when you could be keeping me company in the kitchen? I am alone so much."

Her voice stings as if he had stepped into a ground nest of yellow jackets. "I know, V, I know."

"But *I* don't know, I mean I don't know *why*."

She turns the table light on, sits in the chair across his, a dish towel still in her hand, sees the drink by his side, shakes her head.

"I didn't know you were still drinking. You never used to drink after dinner – you hardly touched yours tonight – said it sponged up the glow. And it used to be one, at most two, before we sat down to dinner, and so many times, years ago, not even that."

She leans over suddenly, covers his hand with hers. "Jud?"

"Yes, Vera" (my dear).

"Was it that bad in the office today, whatever it was?"

Bad enough, V. She said there was this girl who's leaving. I wish I could tell you, V. He shuts his eyes.

"I thought so," she says getting up. "You shouldn't let these things get to you so." She touches his hand again with her wedding band hand, the arthritic knuckle. "Let me get the dishes out of the way. Meanwhile," she picks up *The County Chronicle*, the hundred-and-fifty-year-old local daily from the coffee table, hands it to him, "I know you will enjoy the obits. You always read them. There are three over ninety today."

"And I'll bet" (I should have said, *wager,* Miz Vera) "they were all farmers and not one of them ever left the county from the day they were born."

"How did you know, Jud?"

"I know a lot of things that don't count."

"I'll be back," she says, doing a dance step, "as soon as I've done the dishes."

Oh no, not that, old flesh.

He tops off his drink, flaps the paper open to the column culled from the past, old, dry flowers of time, a nostalgic bouquet:

Fifty Years Ago Today in the County

. . . At the First Presbyterian Church cabin yesterday afternoon, the executive committee of the Chester County Christian Endeavor Union held a conference enjoying a picnic luncheon on the grounds.

219

All the plans for the coming year were reviewed and in the early evening the officers visited the Christian Endeavor Societies of Coatesville and Modena. Later all heard an excellent sermon by the Rev. George E. Gillespie in the Coatesville Presbyterian Church. Those in the conference were . . .

. . . Horace A. Beale, Jr. has been informed that a radiophone message from his station has been picked up at a point 500 miles north of the inhabited region of Canada, in the wilds of Ottawa. Mr. Beale has just returned from New York and on Friday evening he met a friend there who had received the word in a letter from Hartford, Conn., from the man who is engaged in exploration work and had taken his receiving set with him into the north . . .

. . . Over 200 employees of the Bell Telephone Co., from Pennsylvania, Delaware, Maryland and New Jersey, held a reunion at the Bellevue-Strafford hotel in Philadelphia on Saturday. They were members of the Liberty Bell of Pioneers and all had been in the service of the company for 21 years or more. Present from this section were . . .

. . . The Downington Friends School, located on the Lincoln Highway, will re-open this coming week for its fourth term. The School is one of a group under the general care of the committee on education of Philadelphia Yearly Meeting, whose visiting Superintendent, Olive R. Haviland, will have oversight of it.

No wonder they lived to ninety.

I wish I could tell you, V, there's no one else I can tell, old friend, and I can't hold it inside any more. You'll understand, old yokemate, won't you? Somebody has to. You see, V, she said there was this girl who was leaving – had left – and they were giving her a farewell dinner and she (Billie, that is) was invited. And it had to be tonight (our Monday) because it was the only night this girl could make it. Friday was always farewell dinner time any place I've worked. Invited, she said, to this send-off for a girl she didn't even know. Get that? And on the first day of her new job. You wouldn't believe that, now would you, V? you who believe. Well I don't believe it either, V. The whole thing is a crock . . . At some restaurant, somewhere, somewhere she said. Har, har. Hey gang. Some restaurant somewhere my ass (sorry, V). I'll tell you where, all right – in her apartment, that's where . . . WHAT TIME IS IT?

"What?" Vera calls from the kitchen. "Did you say something? You know I can't hear you from two rooms away. Wait till I'm through."

"Nothing," he says.

. . . In her cosy little flat, that's where. Can't you see it, V, the scenario? They've moseyed down from the office ha-ha-ha-ing away and just walked into her apartment. She's lighting the fat candles. Fix us a drink, she's saying to the grinning guy. There's stuff under the sink. (That's her booze cupboard, V.) There's some Scotch (mine), and vodka (mine), and I think there's a smidgin of gin. (Mine). And why don't you put on some music, she says, while I freshen up. There's all kinds of stuff. Opera, Mozart (mine), Carmen McRae. (Her favourite, V.) I'll be out in a sec, and pops into the john. She's forgotten to tell him about the ice cubes, V, they're always frozen solid. He'll need that screwdriver – it's on top of the sink – to pry those trays out of the freezer. Who? The grinning gent she came home with, that's who. My hunch it's the squash playing, groovy St. Laurent dresser, her new boss. *Droit du seigneur.* Executive fringe benefit. It goes with the territory. Or the neat guy new president. To know Miss Miller . . . Then she comes out of the john and says, Oh that's great, as he hands her a drink, Just what I needed, and laughs. I can hear her, V. Laughing. She goes into mezzo. Now they're sitting down at the café table (ours, ours) under the Tiffany lamp and the Paris poster. Kid, laugh. That's class, V. And all the time the bastard is thinking, O wow, what a setup I fell into. A really beautiful head like that (she's gorgeous, Dad – striking, you once said, V) complete with this great hideaway. (How is she wearing her hair – up like a Turkish mosque, breadloaf or straight down? Probably down.) And he's thinking he's in town two nights a week (you know, with the boys – that old story) anyway, playing squash at the Racquet Club less than ten minutes strolling away, a built-in alibi. I've got it custom-made, man. Then she says let's have one more drink before we go out to dinner and he says groovy idea. Now don't ask me how I know, V – I know. Now she's putting another record on, probably Frankie, and turns, and he sees that her mouth is an O and she has that smoky look on her face, and now he's getting up kind of slow and coming towards her, now his hand is touching her nape and she is saying Fuck me (what's his name) Ed, that's it, FUCK ME, ED.

"Why are you shouting?" Vera calls from the kitchen.

What time is it? He is standing alone in the blotted-out room, black blind. OK, yes, this time I will catch her out – my Kendal great-grandmother, ha – in *flagrante delicto*, the blazing fuck. Thank God for IUD, eh. I have keys (what time is it?). I will let myself in while they're locked on the bed conjugating the copulative verb, she one-hand candling his eggs as she breathes in her heat-husky voice, her hair raining all over her cloudy face, her legs in that lazy arch around his neck, her other hand combing his flesh, I love your cock in me, Ed. I'll say, oh, beg pardon, didn't mean to interrupt *juste au bon moment.* But I thought we had a date. This is Monday, isn't it? MY MONDAY.

"You're shouting again," he hears from a drowned somewhere . . . "From two rooms away . . ." Something about a dishwasher . . . "Can't hear." Her voice seems to be skidding in from the next room. "You'll have to come into the kitchen if you want to talk to me."

He can't see, tries to shake memory's ink from his eyes. But he hears from a long away boyhood the Sunday voice of the Preacher, his great-uncle Zechariah's Jew's-harp twanging voice – *And his concubine played the WHORE against him.* "For God's sake stop shouting."

Who? Where? Somewhere underwater. He's where there's light and a face he knows on a bobbing balloon. A voice he knows, too. Vera's. Yes. "Where do you think you're going?"

"There."

"You're drunk, Jud, you can hardly stand. I've never seen you this way."

Somebody else, that other one who's been shouting, not 'im, that jerk. The face he knows pops in and out of focus. He's got to catch it by the string when it floats in again. Now. "I've got to tell you, V."

"Tell me what?"

He waits for her face to come in again, her echoing eyes. Now. Hold it. "Wish I could, V."

"What?" She steps toward him, her hand outstretched. "Give me the keys."

"What keys?" It's a trick.

"The car keys you have in your hand."

"Not car keys."

"Of course they're your car keys. What do you think they are?"

(It's a trick. Sure.) "Keys . . . keys of the kingdom."

"Keys to what?"

"Yes."

"Give them to me, please, you're in no condition to drive. Please, Jud."

The balloon bumps his face. OUT OF THE WAY.

He's out of the house in a bottomless black lake, that other one she says is drunk, damn fool, he'll drown if he doesn't come up for air . . . Great-Uncle, that saddlebag Bible you left me, why did you underline only those passages, the ones you made me memorize, that hammered at WHOREDOMS and FORNICATIONS or singsonged of WOMAN FLESH – *breasts that are like two young roes which feed among the lilies, lips that drop as the honeycomb, navels like round goblets, bellies like heaps of wheat . . . Return, return, O Shulamite; return, return . . .* Who the hell was she, Great-Uncle? Who was *your* WHORE?

He's knocked something aside, a rag doll? and is in the car's cockpit and sees in his headlights' tunnel Vera's loud face, a crucifixion of arms outstretched blocking the road. "No, Jud, NO."

The car bucks as he jams the gas pedal down, skids, hurtles forward. OUT OF THE WAY. OUT OF THE WAY. YOU'RE GOING TO BE HIT. The frozen-faced lit-up doll is jerked off into blackness.

The car bolts up the hill in a scream of tires. Damn slithering dumb machine won't stay straight. Must be the leaves, the wet leaves, last night's rain. Its veering lights scissor the curving hill road, zig at the cliff, that's an eighty-foot drop, man, zag at the ditch, don't get into that, you'll never get out. Just missed it. No, that thumping sick sound,

222

shit, a wheel's spinning in it, must be the right rear. Come on, come on baby, give me all you've got, that ditch shallows out about here. Foot to the floor he turns the wheel full left and the car slipping forward suddenly springs at the giant oak coming at him.

39

CONESTOGA COMMUNITY HOSPITAL
Admission Summary

BELL, Judson B.

9/18

This patient is a well developed, well nourished 56 year old Caucasian male who arrived at the Emergency Room at 10.15 P.M. The patient is in moderate to acute distress because of pain about the facial area and in the chest and legs.

CHIEF COMPLAINT: It was reported that he was injured in a vehicle accident.

HISTORY OF PRESENT ILLNESS: This patient remembers little of the accident and feels he may have been unconscious for a period of time after the accident. His wife reports him leaving the scene of the accident and trying to walk down the road to his home.

PAST MEDICAL HISTORY: Operations – none. Patient's wife reports fractured collarbone and ribs in horseback riding many years ago. No history of tuberculosis, diabetes, heart disease.

FAMILY HISTORY: Generally healthy.

SOCIAL HISTORY: Patient is an advertising executive and is married.

Allergies – none.

Habits – smokes a pipe, an occasional cigarette.

Present medication – none.

SYSTEMIC REVIEW:

Head	–	No headache, fits, faints, convulsions.
Eyes	–	No symptoms of eye disorders.
Ears	–	No ache or discharge.
Nose and Throat	–	Infrequent upper respiratory infections (common colds).

Cardiorespiratory – No cough, hemoptysis, dyspnea, chest pain, ankle edema.

Gastrointestinal – No nausea, vomiting, diarrhea, hematemesis, melena, jaundice.

Genitourinary – No history.

Musculoskeletal – No injuries or disease of significance other than reported collarbone and rib fractures.

ADMISSION EVALUATION.

HEAD: No deformity.

Eyes – Pupils round, equal. React to light. Extraocular movements normal.

Nose – Dry blood in the nostrils. Tenderness on palpation of the nose at the junction of the nasal bone and the cartilage.

Mouth – Thru-and thru laceration to the lower lip.

Ears – Blood in the external auditory canal on the right which when removed from the ear exposes the tympanic membrane which is discoloured in appearance to indicate blood in the middle ear.

Face – Large irregular laceration over the mandible exposing mandible.

NECK: Normal range of motion. No tenderness. Trachea in midline.

CHEST: Tenderness to palpation over the sternum and ribs bilaterally.

Heart – Normal sinus rhythm. No enlargement, thrills, murmurs.

Lungs – Clear to percussion and auscultation.

ABDOMEN: Liver, kidney, spleen not enlarged. No masses. No tenderness.

GENITALIA: Normal, male.

EXTREMITIES: Moderate to severe lacerations over both legs.

IMPRESSION:

1. Cerebral concussion.

2. Possible skull fracture.

3. Possible comminuted fracture of nose.

4. Contusions of the chest.

5. Possible rib fracture.

6. Lacerations of the lower lip, thru-and-thru.

7. Lacerations of the chin.

8. Moderate to severe lacerations and abrasions of the legs.

PROCEDURES:

1. Repair thru-and-thru lacerations of lower lip.

2. Repair lacerations in the region of the chin.

3. Repair lacerations of the legs.

Following these, patient is to be admitted to hospital for observation for possibility of intracranial bleeding, vital signs, blood pressure. X-rays taken to clarify impression-diagnosed fracture, EKG to determine possibility of myocardial injury.

(Signed) Marvin L. Haupt, M.D.

Note to Head Nurse Ames: We better get a radiologist on the night trick. Even a Hindu is better than none. Love and kiss, MLH.

There are inkblot spots on the Green Man's gown. Dried blood Rorschachs. A fluorescent overhead moon.

Somewhere inside pain prowls, looking for exits. Some heavy beast has clawed him, its paw still on his mouth, other places, a snow numbness beginning to thaw into hurt. Pain's bottom line.

"Do you know where you are?" Green Man says.

Dumb question. Medschoolbull. But he says, playing the game – "Horsepital". That's the way Canadian Jack said it. Dad-in-law-out-law.

"Do you know what happened to you?"

You must be kidding.

"Mr Bell?" . . .

"Accident. Car."

"Very good."

What's good about that?

"Do you know who I am?"

"Doctor – Surgeon." You're going to do a number on me. Hey, let

226

me go home. Yokemate V, come take me home V, to the horses, old dog . . . the trees . . .

Now I'll ask one. "Do you know what Rasputin said to the Czarina?"

"What?" Green Man goes along with it. He has a truckstop tired seen-it-all smile. Teenagers splashed on telephone poles . . .

"Take me to your bleeder."

"You'll live," Green Man says. "Did you make that up?"

"Alla time. My job." Can't stop. Got a million of 'em.

There's a halo, some kind of moon ring over his head. Shine on Harvest Moon. Green Man turns, holds up a small machine, pushes a drop from its stickpin tip.

"Saw the movie," Green Man says, "*Nicholas and Alexandra.* Quite good. From a historical point of view. The cinematography. Excellent colour . . . Hemophilia . . ." He raises his starburst lance . . . "That's what the young prince had."

"The Czarevitch."

"This is going to sting a little."

"Yellow jackets." Jud says.

"What was that?"

"Don't fire–" the claws are tearing at him again–– "until you see the whites of their lies."

Green Man is poking his blockhead of ice . . . Cubes. Screw Driver.

"Do you feel this?"

"No."

"And this? Here?"

"No."

"And this? Here?"

"No."

"Good. I'm going to do some facial repair," Green Man says, "and on your legs. You're a lucky man, Mr Bell. I understand the car was totalled."

Goodbye, Winnie the Pooh-Jo.

He's in a white space, a cube of neutral light, away from them, slipped his leash, out of her city, free in a cruel white time. At a price. Worth it. Temporary leave with Purple Heart. You get what you pay for. It hurts to breathe deeply but he can breathe if he sips air. As a horse drinks. Roman . . .

"Comfy?"

A hominy down-country voice full of the clucking farm. From the southern end of the county, probably, (Bible Belt, KuKlux potato chip country. Rebel flag bumper stickers. Billboards – Jesus Saves. Ox roasts at the volunteer fire company, suckling pigs barbecued, turkey shoots, a killing a week by handgun or knife, yahoo motorcycle killers turfing

227

retirees' lawns) where it touches on Maryland, My Maryland, the Mason-Dixon line, after all where the South is supposed to begin and never ends. We forget, we forget our hates still are so simmering close. He sets something in motion to open his lips and a harrow disks over his face.

The White Lady says, "You've taken a lot of stitches."

Nice rural pie girl face. But he must tell her to put out that white scalpel light, give him back to his dark, bought and paid for but not by credit card, cold cash, so he can sleep. What time is it? In Philadelphia.

"Sleep," he says through clamped teeth. "Light. Out." Please.

"Oh, you want to sleep?"

He nods gratefully yes. Ask and it shall be given to you. Luke, 11.9 – right Great-Uncle? Now give me my sack of ball candy you have in your pocket.

"You mustn't do that, you have to stay awake. Doctor isn't sure if you have a skull fracture. And we can't take an X-ray till morning when we'll be able to tell. If it's a bad one – it probably isn't – but we have to be on the safe side, don't we – you could die in your sleep. Now you wouldn't want to do that to us, would you?"

Why can't I die for myself?

"That's why we're keeping the lights on. To keep you awake."

OK, I confess, I'll sign anything. I did it, whatever it is. Now let me sleep.

There's always a catch: you don't get what you pay for.

"How's your IV doing?" White Lady says.

Who's Ivy? Her name is Billie and she has murdered sleep.

"Everything's hunky-dory," White Lady says. "I'll be looking in on you – and the other nurses. If you need us just press this button here."

Good caring country girls, legs stuffed into virgin white sausage casings, sexy salami, heads decked by cute crisp little caps, breasts in white cupcake paper.

The light scorches his eyes.

"Stay comfy and awake," she says.

I thought you were my friend, White Lady.

Whooer you?

40

He sees the flowers first. Wild asters and lady's tresses, one goldenrod wand and the five-flowered gentian in a vase on the tray table at the foot of his bed. Sunlight, a good light, afternoon warm.

"You've been sleeping."

A voice good as this light.

Old V.

He turns on the pillow and sees her through rain.

A warm hand on his hand.

"Don't cry, Jud, I know it hurts. You're going to be all right."

You'll live.

Blindly he points to the flowers.

"From our place. I picked them before I came."

From our place.

"How . . ." and his stitched mouth is lashed . . ." long have you been here?" he says through shut teeth.

She bends to dab his eyes with a tissue. Her right hand is bandaged. His eyes tell her he's seen. Her eyes tell him we're not going to talk about this now.

Thank God you jumped, V, the second you did.

"Several hours. Don't try to talk, dear. I know it must be painful. But I've kept myself occupied." Oh, V . . . "I've spent the time reading." She holds up a book – C.P. Snow's *The Affair*, in the *Strangers and Brothers* series.

Oh, V, you've always preferred books in a series, trilogies, tetralogies, V, as long as I've known you. You were reading Balzac's *Comédie Humaine* when we met, for the second time round. All thirty-five novels (I bought you the complete edition on your first birthday with me. From some private library, fat pages still uncut.) And you know, V, you cried. As if I had given you the Taj Mahal and all the pearls of India. And what is that series that goes on forever. Yes, Anthony Powell's *A Dance to the Music of Time*. Books should go on forever, never end, you said. I guess you thought I was some kind of book you could read for a lifetime.

"I called your office this morning. They were very concerned. Said you were not to worry about anything. Just to get well. I promised to keep them informed."

My Fairleigh Family.

"And of course I called Dulcie, she was very upset. She'll come see you just as soon as she can. Maybe even today. She said to be sure to tell you she loves you."

Dulcie, daughter, you've got to call Billie. What's today? It must be Tuesday and she'll be expecting me over tonight. He shuts his eyes. Dulcie, child, come in, please, come in. Do you hear me? Now listen, you've got to call Billie. Over . . .. That's one thing you didn't repair, Doctor.

"I have to be going now, Jud," Vera is saying.

"Stay," he says, at a price.

"The horses," she says, "second feeding, you know. They expect their din-din on time and I don't like to disappoint them. But . . ."

She looketh well to the ways of her household, and eateth not the bread of idleness.

They'll be standing there at the barn gate, Casey and Roman, looking for her toward the house, nickering for their hay.

" . . .I'll be back this evening. Is there anything I can bring you – a book, magazines? *The Atlantic, Harper's*? So many back issues you haven't looked at. *The London Times Literary Supplement* came today."

He shakes his head no. Just bring back yourself.

"Oh, and I'll bring your pyjamas – you look so stark in this hospital gown – and your robe and slippers. How stupid of me. You know, Jud, I packed them but forgot to take them." Now there are stitches in her lips, too. "This . . ."

Yes, This, V. This This.

A cloud fogs her floret blue eyes and she turns, her back to him. He reaches and takes her unbandaged hand.

V – the eye of the storm.

And sees her in her old faded blue Valiant, the right car for you, V.

"Come back," he says, at a price, but it's worth it. She nods without turning around and walks out with a backward wave.

The sun slanting across his bed is a harvest of warm wheat, but somewhere inside him they've sewn up that cold yesterday moon.

I'm not going to think for a while, just be. Like Roman, Blitz, like a tree. Take a smiling snooze in the sun till V comes. BACK . . .

My first girl.

I was 12½ and she was an older woman of thirteen. She had long thick curls that bounced like springs when she walked. Her hair was the colour of orange blossom honey. She had damp violet eyes and her mysterious smile made me feel like a baby. She walked as if she was secretly married. When I first saw her my heart became a striped balloon and sailed away across the Atlantic. She left no room for anything else in the world. I just wanted to sit and look at her forever. Her name was Lily.

My first date.

They had allowed me to take her to the movies. The Saturday afternoon show, of course, at the Kismet. Janet Gaynor and Charles

Farrell in Seventh Heaven. It was a good movie – sad. And to buy her an ice cream soda afterwards at Conrad's and then walk her home. She liked black-and-whites. She never made that scratchy noise with the straw when you finish a soda but always left a little on the bottom. She also liked Rudy Vallee and listened to him on her Fada radio. I was invited to her thirteeth birthday party and bought her a ukulele with the money I'd saved for a first baseman's mitt. There were too many other people at her party, mostly old guys of fourteen. But at least I was in the same house with her.

Then one summer Sunday her parents drove off in their seven-passenger Willys Knight. She was sitting on her porch just down the street not doing anything, just being Lily. It was enough. Then she went inside and the world's sunshine with her. I walked down the block feeling cold, up the stairs to her door and rang the bell. She opened the door as if she had been expecting me.

My first kiss.

Inside. We didn't dare to sit down on the sofa. It would be the end. She took my hand and led me a few steps up the hall stairway. We sat on the same step looking into each other's eyes. I leaned over and touched my lips to hers. I know I couldn't have done it if her eyes had been open. Then she said, you'd better go now. I would never be the same. There was nothing left to live for. I had kissed Lily.

Someone must have seen me go into her house and told her parents. There are people like that. Because later that evening I saw her father talking to my father in our front yard. They were both nodding. They even shook hands. I was told I was not to bother Lily again. Me, *bother* Lily? Well, not see her, then. Not even a movie? No. Not even a soda? No. Not even anything.

They moved away not too long after that. It helped a little. There was no reason now for my heart to trip whenever I passed that house. But it did. It was all so leafy then.

Through green bubbles of dream he surfaces, a speckled trout rising, and smiles out of his doze.

"Well, you've been napping again, that's good."

Nurse – this one's a country looker, I'll bet she's raised a blue ribbon 4H heifer in her time – Nurse puts a large cellophaned cone (in a wicker basker) on the tray table. A tower of jumbo fruits from some King Kong orchard. "I've seen flowers and fruits," she says, "but I've never seen anything this big. You must be important. You'd need a knife and fork to get into those pears. This came with it, Luv." She hands him a foot-square card. No store-bought card, this. An original cartoon in dashing strokes: Man (he, Jud) in a head-to-toe cast on a hospital bed in traction. A pipe stuck in his plastered face, smoke billowing out of the bowl. But he's typing away anyway at the typewriter in his lap. Looks like Ottavio's style – good sketch man, that. The message says: If you keep at the job, the job will keep you. Old

Angus Fairleigh's motto, 1889. Har. Signed by Tad and the kids. Even Wanda. Mooney, I could do without you. It used to be Flowers From Your Fairleigh Family. I guess a VP rates fruit. Must look that up in Caring For Your Employees. It's all ye need to know on earth about truth and beauty and corporate caring . . .I'll be drinking my meals through a bent glass tube for a spell, but V, you will enjoy that fruit.

The phone rings. Dulcie says, in a hooded voice, "Mother told me it would be hard for you to speak. So please don't try to, don't answer, Dad. Oh, Daddy, what happened? I love you, Dad."

"Love you, Dulce."

"I'm sorry, I didn't mean to make you talk."

"That's ok, don't worry."

"You're going to be all right, aren't you, Dad?"

"You bet, baby."

"Listen, Dad, I called Billie."

Good old Dulcie, I knew you would. You're your great-grandmother Kendal's girl all right.

"She practically went into shock, said something about it being her fault. She wants to come and see you, but I told her I didn't think that was such a hot idea since, you know, someone might be there. I promised to keep her up-to-date."

"Good, Dulce. Thanks."

"I can't come today, Daddy, but Bob and I will be over tomorrow. Get well soon, Dads, please."

"Accident–tell her – skidded – wet leaves."

CONESTOGA COMMUNITY HOSPITAL
Discharge Summary

During the period of observation, the patient's vital signs were stable. Blood pressure was unchanged. Pupils remained equal and reacted to light. The patient's level of consciousness remained unchanged. X-rays on the day following admission demonstrated hairline fracture of skull, right, no intracranial bleeding. There was a moderately comminuted fracture of the nasal bones with the bones in good position. The chest X-rays demonstrated a fracture of the right rib, at the tenth rib, at the axillary line. There was no evidence of hemothorax or pneumothorax. EKG was done, which demonstrated no abnormality or evidence of myocardial injury.

On 22, September, the patient is being discharged. He is instructed to report to the office on Friday, 29 September, at 2:00 P.M. for follow up evaluation. He is instructed to use APC's with Codeine, 1.0 Grain every four hours, as needed for pain and to use Tuinal – 200 mg. h.s. for sleep.

232

41

Pills.

Never took 'em.

"Doctor's orders, Jud," Vera says.

"Don't need them."

"Yes you do, dear. Without them you're wincing all day and groaning all night."

"I manage."

"Last night you screamed. I thought it would wake the dead."

And never grutched the price I paid (R. Kipling).

"What are you trying to prove? That you can take pain?"

"I must have rolled over on that rib."

"You would have slept more quietly if you had taken your pill."

"I don't like the idea. The body takes care of itself."

"We all need some help sometimes. There's nothing shameful in that."

Whence cometh my help?

"Please take your sleeping pill tonight. I need my sleep, too, you know."

"We'll see."

"Otherwise you'll wake shouting again and prowl half the night, fall asleep when it's time to have breakfast.

"Here," she says, handing him a glass of water, the pill in her palm.

The pills they give you are liars, they lead you on into sleep then fracture, refract your dream.

They are three on that sugar sand beach. And there are palms. Selah. There is no horizon. No seasons. The sky and the sea are one, as they are. And they are wearing their silk. Sendal. The air is terraced, cool, warm and hot. Fruit falls at their sandalled feet.

The seabird says Peace.

The air sings it.

The moon gives its milk.

The sun its honey.

And they lie down together (one going apart for a while, the Old Wise One, so the two can commingle) against the night cold and the unsheathed moon.

One comes from the sea. O, that one. One is the wise blue flower from the forest. One has a lance by his side. He knows who waits in the hills. His, the blood, theirs the scarless wound.

They have found the magic the others are looking for.

We are kind to each other. Of water there is no lack.

The seabird says Love.

Let's get it on.

Who said that?

Give me your prick.

He crashes through the shattering window of dream. The patient's level of consciousness remains unchanged.

He's looking up at the ceiling, V in the guest room in respect of his gored tenth rib (the steering column) and his scabbing gashes. I don't think I screamed this time. I took the pill. Screaming can be endured as long as they can't hear you, or she.

God made one woman of Adam's rib, I have made two. No offense, Great-Uncle Zechariah, Preacher and God knows what else. Many's the time I sniffed that rawboned, sweetish pot likker, marrow of our Tennessee hills bearding your breath. But you never stumbled like me when you had a jug in you. And I mean, being respectful, sir, a jug, I saw you, Great-Uncle on our last great camping trip. You hunted with a flintlock Dechard rifle that was carried by one of your way back kin in the Revolutionary Battle of King's Mountain. Powder horn, ramrod, wadding and ball. If you can't do it the first (and only) shot, the first time you said, forget it. You have to give game a chance . . .

I want to stay in this smoke of October. As the maples and beeches burn their leaves first, then the chestnuts and oaks and the hickories go from yellow to brown. And to sleep without dreams.

Vera says –

He knows by the way her eyes flare like wicks in an oil lamp through her bifocals – she's going to say –

"Isn't it time you went back to the office? After all, you're all mended. I know you're still tender about the chest, but it's been a month since you've been home."

I'm beginning to get along with those pills. They make everything easy, cushioned, so soft.

He looks up from the *County Chronicle*. "It's going to be a cold winter."

"What makes you say that? It's been so warm. A beautiful Indian summer."

"Our local weather prophet, Milo Cornucopius, it says here in the paper, has been divining the signs. He says the woolly bears are sporting black coats. And the fur on the squirrels is thick. And, what's more, they're gathering acorns without their usual chatter."

"Sounds like Farmer's Almanac folklore."

A weather prophet is without honour in his own county.

"There has also been an abundance of crickets and the hawks are

234

flying low."

"Hawks fly high, hawks fly low all the time. I've seen them myself as you have, right here on our place."

"And here is the clincher. Listen to this. He says, and I quote, 'the deer are getting awfully sexy already. It's almost immoral. But it means a lot of snow for sure.'"

"Rubbish. Immoral deer. Really, how can they print such nonsense. Creatures are neither moral or immoral. They have no choice as we do. They just are what they are. Honestly, Jud."

We are what we are.

"V – is my face still awful?"

"Judson, you've been asking this for the last three days. Of course not. Just some pink lines around your mouth, like shaving scratches. But I don't have to tell you. I've seen you looking in the mirror."

"It's just that I don't want to go back like the walking wounded."

"What a ridiculous idea. They know you've been in an accident."

"OK then, V, I'll call the office tomorrow."

"That's good, I'm glad for your sake. You've been moping about. Not that I wasn't happy to have you home. It's been a strange *déjà vue* time. Like our first year, in some ways. When . . ."

When I was the one that I was and she was the she.

"And tell them I'll be aboard on Monday".

"I suppose you'll be taking those tiresome trips again."

"I would think so, it's part of the job."

And there's another call he must make.

42

More cars than ever it seems now on the road to the railroad station from the carpetbagger developments, sprouting like stinkweed unseen from his hidden hill but still there, Judson.

He waves a knightly gloved hand at the over-the-limit speeding citizen (where are the troopers?) coming down to the intersection. Courtesy, please. I've been here at least, let's see, three minutes. May I pass, sir? The clark in the Kmart suit gives him the finger and farts by in his VW camper. Tract house pioneer in a ten-gallon hat. Dan'l Boom mowing his handkerchief lawn with a sixteen-horsepower tractor. Suburban turd tooling to upward stupidity. Shot out on a wall and hatched by the sun.

It used to take all of ten minutes to get to the station. Mine were the first tire tracks in the snow. Except for a farmer hauling fresh milk to the rinky-dink depot. Now it's more like a half-hour.

Ah, maybe a little *noblesse oblige* coming down here, the bonused and stock-optioned Quality cresting the hill in a silver Mercedes 380SL, a true *nouveau* executive gent this, with two Alka Seltzers already pop-fizzing in him to settle his breakfast hash. The money has gone to his face and generations of barbecued prime steaks. Two snowmobiles used three days a year in the four-car garage. Probably lives in one of those genuine imitation colonials in Fox Chase Farms built on the old Havergill place by the Vandal Brothers who drove out the foxes and farms with laundered Mafia money. I say, m'lud, I've been here for almost four minutes. May I pass? The gentry burps by.

V's Valiant doesn't mind waiting. He finally takes his life in his hands and makes a left turn onto the roadway. Horns bray for manslaughter.

He surfaces up from the station to the city of streets, someone forgotten shipwrecked at sea who's reached a foreign country without a passport. She could be in the crowd going to work in the building behind him. He looks for gold among the morning heads and his legs turn to water.

He's at the door of his office, his old corner command post, when he remembers: It's been Leeta's now since last spring. Thank God she's not there – kid genius doesn't have to come in on time, it proves you're a genius – to honk him her megaphone greeting. Back to your size nine shoebox, Mac, and the old Fairleigh House Policy framed from a past beyond his over his desk:

Gong With the Wind.

His office feels tight as an outgrown suit. A paper avalanche covers his in-box, spills onto his desk. He takes a deep breath and his tenth rib's riposte tells him it isn't yet healed. Dr. Haupt said, You've got to breathe shallowly for a while. His window is blind with sun.

An acned voice at his back. "So you finally decided to join us."

"Hello, Les."

"Man, you were out a long time, it must have been bad."

Let's not talk about it please.

He says, "It could have been worse." I could have killed someone.

"So what else is new, Les?"

Les plumps on the edge of his desk. "Nothing much, Ace. I thought I'd come over to see you, but the wife is into yoga, three times a week, so I had to stay home with the kids."

Now he knows he's back. He hasn't been Ace for a month of a clean white room full of buzzing sun and stitches and a house on a hill drowning in autumn leaves.

Les looks to the door.

"Kip handled the copy while you were gone. He sure messed it up. It was so bad I had to get Tad into the act."

"Kip must have loved that."

Les shrugs, "Listen, that guy is retired before he has to retire. All that Chestnut Hill dough. He not only doesn't know shit about copy – he thinks he's typed some dumb words on a sheet of paper that it's got to be good – he's been trying to horn in on *my* end, on the *art*."

"Art is long, Les, and time is fleeting."

"Yeah, but he's making me look bad."

The neatest trick of the week, Les. The *New Yorker* will love it.

"Whose end is up, Les?"

"Huh? Well, you know what I did? If he's going to get into my end, I'll get into his. I got some extensions on copy due dates when we heard you were coming in."

"Thanks, Les, I'll do the same for you sometime."

Les looks to the door. "I told Tad, just between us, you should have Kip's job, you and me, you know, co-creative directors, running the whole account."

That's mighty nice of you, Les. I'm touched. Really. "And what did Tad say?"

"You know Tad – he said, 'Take Kip to the mat. Stick it to him. Show him your balls.'"

"A Great Idea of Western Man, Les."

"Wha? Oh Yeah, that ad campaign. Famous quotes from history and original art."

"That's the one, Les. Itty-bitty copy and lots of art. An art director's dream, a showcase."

"You've got it, Big J."

Les slips off the desk. Jud says, "By the way, Les, you still driving Tad to the office?"

"Most days. Unless he's out of town."

"Then you have the edge."

"You better believe it," Les says.

By craning his neck he can just about see Billy Penn sailing in the sky and behind him the tower of the Quaker City Bank & Trust Company, and turns to the paper mountain and the indentured day.

Walking up Walnut to Billie's in the suddenly here evening, the city's evensongheart pumping people into the streets, the attaché case in his hand, and he's in her small vestibule filling up with his month away, as if he has thought himself there. Or woke from a long sleep of better forgotten dreams. He doesn't remember walking or hearing the ghostly gong of release. Just leaving the vault of the Castle lobby. A first time in this funky hall that isn't a first time.

To use his key or to ring?

He rings and the hall door clicks before he has taken his finger away from the buzzer. He opens the door and at the end of the hall her door opens a wedge of light. The way it once did in an old November. A Billie stands there, but not that autumn Billie, or April Billie, or the beaches of June Billie.

At the door her lips touch his. She clangs with a new perfume, a vibration more than a scent.

"Wow," she says, " your beard scratches."

"I shaved," he says, "this morning."

"Come in," she says.

Were we ever we?

He doesn't know what to do with his attaché case. She takes it from him and places it by the armoire corner dislodging a man's umbrella which clatters across it. "Oh that," she says, "I borrowed it from one of the guys at the office when it was raining last week." And finger-end leads him to the café table, the Tiffany lamp lit, the fat votive candles burning, his drink at his (?) place. He sees Welcome Home scrawled large in lipstick on the mirror above the mantel as she says

"Welcome Home."

"You've cut your hair," he says.

She touches the manufactured waves. "Yes, that old ironed look is out. And this is so much more convenient. Besides, I'm an executive now." Laughs. She fingers the ice in her drink, sips.

"Do you like it?"

"Very becoming."

He sees himself coming to in a car upended against a tree, the ceiling light on. Hello Druid . . .

"I mean, do you really like it?"

"Yes, oh yes."

"I want you to."

. . . And Vera there pulling on the smashed door . . .

"I do, really."

. . . And stumbling down the road, spitting good blood, God Almighty free at last . . .

"I'm glad."

. . . And V there in the volunteer fire company ambulance beside him, those good local boys, siren hooting like the god of all owls, dome lights flashing and everything's fine . . .

There's a glitter about her. She's wearing earrings, glass chandeliers suggesting a ballroom filled with light and music and laughter.

He wants to say, You never wore so much makeup before, if any, I don't remember. But not like this. He says, "How have you been?"

"How could I be without you?" She stirs her ice with a flamingo fingernail.

"When I heard, when Dulcie called me, I felt it was the end of the world. That somehow it was my fault."

"Nobody's fault." We all carry our own moral no-fault insurance. "But my own. I should not have been driving." I could have killed someone.

Her eyes are more gray than blue. "Where were you going that night?"

"Somewhere east of Eden, the land of Nod."

"You wouldn't have found it."

"I had a key."

"I don't believe it, not you. You wouldn't have done that."

"I was on my way until the tree intervened."

She shakes a Parliament out of the pack, lights it, looks away over the smoke. "You could have called me more often. I couldn't call you. Every time I came back to my office I bugged the girl about messages. She thought I was out of my gourd."

"It was hard to talk the first week – I was all sewn up – until the stitches were out."

"Okay, but later. Three calls in the whole month. I felt so cut off. Like nowhere. I needed your voice to hang onto, Jud."

"She was in the house a good deal of the time."

Billie nods, this spangling Billie. "Faithful wifey taking care of her husband." Old Vee.

"Yes, she was very good to me."

"And now I suppose you're so grateful you're making it with her."

He shakes his head. "As a matter of fact she's been sleeping in the guest room."

The phone burglarizes the room. She says, "Excuse me." He takes their glasses into the kitchenette. Well, what have we here, Chivas Regal, not the usual house brand. Her voice is quilted behind the bookcase divider. She takes a few small bites of laughter no longer totally drowned in her once waterfall hair. Earrings and Chivas Regal. He opens the cabinet under the sink. A New Year's of booze. Quite a cellar, bottles stacked there like waiting suitors. The expensive labels. Cheap at the price. He chunkles the already screw-driver pried ice cubes into their glasses. Wait a mo, these are new, too, not-for-into-the-fireplace-tossing. Waterford cut crystal, this. These. And no one will drink from them but us. Famous last words. And over the bookcase divider hears her say moth softly, "I told you, he's coming back today. Yes, Ed, he's here."

Yes, Ed, I'm here.

"Right," she says, laughs once and hangs up.

"Ed who?" And sorry he's said it.

And star-spangled Billie answers. "My boss, Ed Loach. He plays squash twice a week at the club."

Who can forget.

"Just got through, thought he'd check up. See how I was. He's been real good to me. He knows about us. He wanted to come over and meet you. He's something else. I said, 'What's the point?'"

The point is the point.

She sits down across the time zone from him. Her eyes gone all ocean gray now.

"I went out a lot." Sip. "After it happened." Sip. "I just couldn't sit here night after creepy night alone. Not knowing what was going on. I don't think you know how awful it was. Not being able to see you. Or when, or even if I would see you again. Like you'd been swallowed up. I couldn't even send you a card. Just hanging."

He remembers a word he shouted that swampy night when he took out his keys to the car, a word he had no right to think. Not when it came to her.

"I understand." (Say her name.) "Billie."

The phone stings again.

She says, "Oh, no. What a drag. Let it ring. I'm not going to answer it."

He says, "Go ahead. After all . . ." She shrugs – if you say so . . . After all, what? Your month away coming home to roost. And goes up to the window, as if by unlatching the shutter and looking out at the alley he has removed himself, restoring her privacy. (She's doing those ghostly murmurs she breathes into the phone. He tries not to hear.) On the wide window ledge a slim book by Rod McKuen. Poetry-looking pages. Greeting card verse. The flyleaf inscription says, "I never take No for an answer." (Signed) "M".

"Oh that," he hears Billie saying, "it belongs to my secretary. She's into stuff like that. Got it from some guy who has the hots for her." And takes her place at the café table as if waiting to be served.

"People were really nice. I've made a lot of new friends." Sip. "Dates. I must have bored the living daylights out of them talking about *you*. Sips. "But that's all over now. You've come back."

Her incarnadined fingernails reach over and rest on his hand.

He says to his summer Billie, his surf-and-sand Billie, somewhere still inside, he hopes, this flashing Billie across the table from him. He says . . .And a strobe-light goes off in his head solarizing the September year-ago Billie coming into his old corner command post in that, well, yes, campy wet-look getup. He misses the long fall of that rain forest hair, she saying Fairleigh is number one and I'm ready for that. Or something like that. And all through that last year's October you rode a white horse in the dark woods of my mind, Godiva . . . And he says to that first-time November Billie, and to his Christmas Billie, and to birthday Billie, and to this supernova Billie fired from her job she couldn't hack last April's agony, and now I'm an executive . . .To all his Billies he says

"I love you."

"I still love you, Jud".

Still.

It turns his heart to a stone that is falling forever down the bottomless well of that room.

Walking barefoot on time's rubble, he says, "Tell me about your new job."

"I thought you'd never ask." She withdraws lobster nails to light a cigarette. "In a well-chosen word – Greatsville."

He says he's glad.

"I think I've found my own level. This promotion writing isn't so bad. Pretty straight stuff. Just tons and tons of it. So maybe I wasn't cut out to do a great ad a day. Big deal."

"Houlighan's law: A great ad a day keeps the pink slip away."

"Right. He may have done me the greatest favour by canning me. Here I am. Lot's more bucks, a secretary, a private office in the newest building in town. My name on the door. Lunch in the executive dining room. And guess what. They've upgraded my job. I'm looking to hire a writer, eventually two, who will report to yours truly. If you know anyone, I mean, you interview people."

"Not much any more."

"Well, if you hear . . .The pay's real good."

A Star Is Born. 1937. Frederic March, the fading screen idol, boosting Janet Gaynor to stardom and out of his pants forever. Or was it John Gilbert? No. He was the real soundtrack castrato.

A clatter of cans in the alley. A grind of voices. "Hey *mothfu.*"

"Garbage night," she says. "I'm thinking of getting a new apartment now I can afford it. I've just about had it with this dump. Who needs all that?" She waves at the shuttered off alley. "It doesn't even have air conditioning. Remember those nights?"

Do I ever, Luv, can I forget sliding and snaking with you in those swamp-awful August nights, greased slippery on each other in mutual greedy sweat, salt sea and saliva, me going to the fridge two A of the M to fetch frosty beers, *Rolling Rock* they were, brewed from pure mountain springs, the best extra pale in the world. And sitting up in the marshy bed we laughed at the campy but true copy stenciled on the staunch green bottles:

FROM THE GLASS LINED TANKS OF
OLD LATROBE
WE TENDER THIS PREMIUM BEER
FOR YOUR ENJOYMENT, AS A
TRIBUTE TO YOUR GOOD TASTE.
IT COMES
FROM THE MOUNTAIN SPRINGS
TO YOU
"33"

Amazing that "33". "33" what? we wondered. What could it mean? Some Latrobe cabalist's cipher? And you said, "Dummy, it means if you drink it you can make it thirty-three times." Natch. And to be dead honest, while we were runneling with each other's unctions, I thought, dreamed, yes, longed to lower my tropic blood in my cool well-water pool on that pine breathing hill of mine. It was that heat wave hot. We tried to sleep in the tub under the shower one night even though the drizzle of Philamadelky water felt like warm pee. So we poured the icy third beer over each other's heads and loved in the sweltering heat. And you call this a dump. It never had much use for me, true, and I never loved it until now. But it's ours. It belongs to us. I was born again here.

All this loveless office palaver. We're not our jobs, Billie. We're us.

O make an O with your mouth the way you did that nuptial November. And tell me you want to taste me. Take me into the hills of your palms. Take me into your city. Make me immortal again with your kiss.

He is bending over where she sits in the bell of her scent, her prismed earrings glinting, and touches her new mysterious lips with his. Her eyes are June water blue again. And she's rising, his New Jerusalem, all light into his arms. "In a mo, she says, moving away, "I'll hurry," and goes into the john.

Welcome home the lipstick says on the mirror.

She comes out unclothed as he's drawing a glass of water at the kitchenette sink.

"What's that you're popping?" she says at the tiny white tablet in his palm.

"Codeine. My rib isn't quite healed yet. I'd feel it otherwise."

He sees her seeing his naked scarred legs. His chest. Looks again at his face under the barebulb light. "Jesus," she says, "you klutz," taking his hand.

Tunnel of Love.

The city spreads its legs.

43

They're passing the piney barrens, the last stand of New Jersey woodland, skinny Watusi pines, warrior spears along the ocean drive they drove in that young June sun to Anything Goes, like the loblollies back home, I mean, back of my Daddy's place.

He fingers out the hammered silver Prohibition flask old Jack Brooke gave him from his jacket pocket. A little Wild Turkey never did nobody any harm. 101 proof. That sucker holds an encouraging twelve ounces.

She's driving the clunking MG.

"Jesus,"Billie says, keeping her eyes on the almost empty road, her skirt hiked well over those invitational knees. "Not this early, it's not even noon."

"No ma'am, just checking." He returns the slim flask to its warm nest.

"Learn to drink like a man," she says to the windshield.

Oh.

"This is supposed to be our anniversary celebration."

Our anniversary.

At least they know that together. Not the first November night a year ago – to see Miss Miller – but the night, two nights later, when she said, I love you because you were my friend, he put the ancestral Bell seal ring on her third finger, left hand. And she said, "I do."

Let's get away, she's been saying it since he came back. A weekend out of this town. Just us. We've got to. You can arrange it.

Like I mean . . .

(You better.)

Understood. I arranged it. Told V, I'm shooting an Army commercial at West Point. Near/far enough for a weekend away and back. V said, On a weekend? That's the first time you will ever have been away on a weekend. I have no control of the time, I said. Besides, it keeps the horses in hay.

She flips the screechy car radio on. "Swaheet Georgia Brown." A 78 shellac oldie but goodie. Lots of swirling brass in a knee-dipping and rising lilt, shiny together sound. Good heel-tapping stuff.

The pines march by in review.

"Hey, this is quite a spread," Billie says, "really lush," as he drops their bags in their suite at The Côte d'Or motel on the Avalon sands. "It must have cost you a bundle."

"Not too bad – off-season rates. It's practically empty this time of year. I was amazed they were open. This is one of their honeymoon suites, by the way."

"I wondered what it was like when we used to walk by it." In that sea-swallowed June. "Look at that ocean view," she says at the wraparound window.

"Would you like to have lunch? It's about that time. Or . . ." What?

"I'm not hungry. I was kind of up late last night. This girl from the office came over and we rapped till all hours. Drank too much vino."

You looked pale this morning, Billie, when I picked you up. I thought you were ill. I saw the two wine-clotted glasses. And you know I saw them.

"Let's walk on the beach," she says.

Two couples are separately drifting around the large raftered lounge. One very young glued duo with a stunned Just Married look and two elderly well-dressed grays.

"The newlywed and the almost dead," he says.

"Heavy," she says.

Outside a pale daffodil sun slits through clouds rolling in from the sea.

Which way? he looks. As if he didn't know.

"To our beach."

He takes her hand and they fall into step in the gritty wind toward a beach five miles away and a June that will not be there, Billie. But we're here in another November. Still. She gives her face to the gray running sea and her fingers hold his in an undertow grip.

Where have all the sandpipers gone?

"Did you bring a camera?" she asks.

"A *camera*? No."

"I meant to take mine."

"Not a good day for pictures. This light. Well, with a yellow filter.."

"We didn't take any last time. I don't have one snapshot of you."

Please give me something to remember you by . . .Pout-mouthed Libby Holman singing. 1930.

My head is an album of pictures of you, Billie. And not much else. Motion pictures and stills. Days and nights and all seasons. Indoors and out. By Boathouse Row on the summer river. At the snowed-in farm by the fire. In the shuttered room. On these dunes in the blessing sun and that fish-chill night when you threw your bikini away at the moon and we swam, warm-bodied demented seals mating on our beach. The film rewinds and runs all the time in the all-night movie house of my mind . . . I don't want to think or remember about those wine-clotted glasses or we'd have to turn back, Billie. Over and out. This isn't last April or May when I would have told you I saw them. Or tell you now what my great-grandmother Kendal knows from the grave through me. Venereal power politics. Love's game. This isn't last May. But I'm walking beside you by this scumbling surf and want to keep right on walking and never get there . . . *How are the mighty fallen.* II Samuel. 1,19., right Grand-Uncle Zech? . . .Wherever . . . as long as you're there. Here, now with your shorn and already sea-wet straightening hair and mascara melting.

They trek by the whale-backed waves, the lion-pawed surf.

"It's beginning to rain," he says.

Grapes of rain.

She says, "Shit, I wanted . . ."

(Hey, remember? This is our anniversary, Billie.)

"I know, " he says as lightning guts the mackerel sky and they turn heads down in the wind.

"I'm bushed," she says, peeling her woolly damp turtleneck off. "Light me a cig, Hon," and goes into the bath. "Hey," she calls, "I thought all honeymoon suites had heart-shaped tubs and mirrors all over the ceiling."

"Just in the Poconos."

Gurgles of steamy water, delicious sighs from the bath. "This is great, just what I needed," she calls. "Why don't you come in and scrub my back? or something."

She lies in a frothy meringue of bubbles, her hair heaped on her head, most of executive Billie swirled down the chromed drain: the neon daub of lipstick, the green eye liner, charred lashes, this one almost born again in the foam. A confection rising.

He towels her down as she steps to the bathmat beach, a willing Helot. Dewdrops webbed in her bunched hair, her body a cello. Dabs those defiant breasts and her creamy thighs. Puts cheek to a breast, a hand to her twin-dimpled back. *Shall I then go into my house, to eat and to drink, and to lie with my wife?* II Samuel, XI,11. Beat it Grand-Uncle Zech. Get lost.

"Hey, we have time," she says in a furry voice, "I feel so deliciously droopy."

And points an imperial finger, "Hand me my robe, Hon.".

That's twice.

Well, I'm still Hon.

In this paid for place, on this queen-sized bed she lies, her flung robe negligently open. " A nap," she says. "I haven't had one since . . ." and her eyes shutter down.

I could stand it better if you were totally naked, but this peek-a-boo view. A loop of terry cloth at the perky rosebud nipple. And the sash across the gold harpsichord strings.

Say it, Jud.

No, I won't.

Aw, C'mon.

But as you said, it isn't Jud.

Let it all hang out.

Cunt, then.

Peeled orange bomb.

Blow me up.

She breathes with a turning world in a cloud of her bubble bath herbals.

What am I supposed to do, read the room service menu? Or the local telephone book?

He shucks his belt buckle but he still has his shoes on. Pants won't go over. Unlace. And he's on the posh bed beside her. There's a metal box like a parking meter on the night table next to the bed. For a quarter, the label says, the bed will massage you. Two minutes' worth of mechanical masseuse. He swings his legs off the bed and fishes in his pants pocket. Two quarters. Four minutes of Disneyland roller coaster bliss. He chucks them in.

Oh wow.

"Wha?"

The bed is a bucking bronco.

He has to laugh or die, so he says, "It's a rerun of the San Francisco earthquake."

The berserk humping bed is tossing them up like pancakes.

"What the fuck," she says out of the last shred of her doze.

And he answers,"Exactly."

And now she begins to laugh as he tips over on her.

World without end she grabs his cock and slipstreams it into her land of milk and honey. And they rock, rock, rock to the metered clock.

Surprise: a new twist here: her toes crabclaw his sides. Usually over the shoulders, those legs, or arched. And a finger (hers) is on a lone safari probing a hitherto unexplored orifice (his).

My ass.

The thumping bed has gone out of shillings.

"Make me come," she says. "Now."

It was always I hope this goes on forever. Like I had the Distinguished Service Medal for perpetual motion.

So he begins to pump to some outside-of-him metronome beat and sees she is staring up, scanning some kind of news bulletin on the ceiling.

He knows he shouldn't ask what's wrong, so he says "What's wrong?"

"I'm beat. Not enough sleep. You'd better come."

"But what about you?" The conjugal desideratum, the tandem come.

"I don't think I'm going to fly. I just want to sleep for a while," and unhooks her legs from his ribs, drops her arms around his neck. "Just a time-out," she sighs. And then says, "Please. " Also, "Shit."

He unhouses his outraged tool.

247

"Do you want me to suck you off?" she says.

Driving back on the drizzled, go-to-church Sunday macadam, the field marshal urban Mau Mau with the shiv in the booth of her parking lot isn't there. A muddy, perhaps Zulu instead, tranced to the transistor before him . . . your people could run fifty miles on their warpath days and swing right into battle without losing stride – like looks up with a thirties movie watermelon smile, waving the roach in a hairpin so hopefully held in his graceful fingers. Hal-but-not-quite-lelujah.

Well, you won't die here tonight, Judson.

"Come in for a drink," she says.

"You were supposed to drop me off at the station. I promised I'd be home tonight."

"Later," she says, "Hon. I'll even drive you all the way. Please."

There seem to be several Billies walking around the room: the Billie who's calling him Hon again, a hook in his gills; a Billie who seems to be listening to something he cannot hear; the Billie who's floating almost to the ceiling who's watching them all. This room, he is sure, knows everything. But won't tell, loyal to her. OK. Now she's clinking about in the kitchenette, ice and glass. He puts an index finger to the ropy scar still on his chin, the cracked bump on the bridge of his nose. She comes out with a sort of smile carrying drinks.

"That was a great meal we had," she says, "in Cape May."

"Grand old place, all that authentic nineteenth century gingerbread. They've done a fine restoration job." End of tour, ladies.

"All that old silver and crystal, those great chandeliers, the *size* of that dining room." Sip. "A ballroom."

"That's what it was. President Grover Cleveland and Ulysses S. Grant stopped there." Or was it the furbelowed family of T.R. Roosevelt. Or all. Or none of the above.

"I know, it was all on the menu."

Bill of fare.

"I guess people lived like that all the time then."

"Some. I have an old steamer trunk in the attic my Buchanan Grandmother left me. All kinds of drawers and places for clothes and hats and shoes. The old labels are still on it: Southampton and Cherbourg, Milan, Rome and Paris and one from Madrid and Lisbon. And the ships: the old Berengaria, the Mauretania. A UDC lady she was."

"What's UDC?"

"United Daughters of the Confederacy."

"Sometimes I think you're still fighting that war."

"No, not that one."

Her eyes go behind her eyes. "Say," she says, "I've been thinking of taking up bowling." Sip.

Oh.

"Yes, the girls at the bank have a club. They've asked me to join."
He tips the Chivas down, the room waiting to hear what he's going to
say.

"How often?"

"One, two nights a week. I'm not sure."

"Which nights?" He touches his scar again.

"I haven't found out yet."

The phone lobotomizes the room.

She says, "Let it."

He counts the rings . . . One, two, three . . . twenty electroshock
lashes. The room is a cave again.

"Hey," (gang) she says, folding and sighing, "let me freshen your
drink."

"I have to go," he says, rising.

"There's time," she says. "Please."

Old Chivas, overrated but not unpalatable. This one she brings is a
real brown one, aha, so I'll dance to its loopy tune.

"Listen," she says, "Hon, I want you to stay over tonight."

"Billie, I promised."

"It's our anniversary," she says as the phone drills in. "You'd better
take it," he says. "This is getting to be like a dental session without
Novocain." He can drink all she wants, the phone is a chaser. He goes
for his anniversary weekend bag.

"OK, I'll take it," she says.

Yaas.

No phonebooth of hair to entirely muffler the message. Miss
Samson shorn. I'm getting to like you Chivas. And how about Mr.
Samson? Waal, he went down to Timnath and saw a woman in Timnath
of the daughters of the Philistines. And he went down (watch it, as that
Mooney would say) and talked with the woman; and she pleased
Samson well . . . Get out of my hair, Zech, Great and Grand Uncle
Preacher.

He listens into his glass. Semaphore monosyllables drop in like
stones. She is saying: "Yes . . .No . . . I don't know . . . NO." He listens
to her listening, an echo. "I told you," she says and hangs up sucking
breath, her face moony pale. Or is it because she has no make-up on?
"That was a wrong number," she says. "One of those heavy breathers.
Wanted to know what this address was, where he was calling. I didn't
tell him."

No of course not.

The phone has them cornered. They wait for something to leap
out of it at them.

"All this crap," she says, "who needs it?" Her eyes ticking – "Please
don't go home. I don't want to be alone tonight."

The room says Well?

"I'd better make a call, then." But not with you listening to me lie.
Like exposing myself on the street. An indictable offense.

Misdemeanour or felony?

"Would you mind?"

"No, of course not. I was going to tinkle anyway." And goes with a hungover smile into the john. Tricky johns.

Riddles.

And Samson's wife wept.

Well, regal Chivas, what now? Watercloset clunkings. Faucets stammering in there, spurting. Old brownstone plumbing gasping away. She comes out, except for the hair – Billie. Sees the drink he's built for her at their café table. "Oh great," she says, and all his life is an arrow. She looks at him out of another November. Sits. Smiles. Sips . . .His Billie smiles.

And her door buzzer buzzes, flaps, flops like a hit-but-not-yet dead bird.

And something in her is running. Up slopes.

The buzzer begins flapping again. Put it out of its misery, man.

He gets up glass in hand.

"Don't go out there," she says.

Chivas and I are going to find out.

"Please," she says.

"Somebody's out there ringing your bell."

"So what? This is the city." Her face has a kind of paste on it now. "Let it go."

He smiles to the Chivas and it, as expected, smiles back. Go ahead, don't be chicken.

He sits, but the flapping bird refuses to die.

"Hang on to your hat," he says, and goes to the door. Throws the bolts. And looks out. Peers.

Out there behind the grimed vestibule door a jogger's face. Much coiffed blown hair on the head. Open throat, tapered, designer western shirt. Pearly buttons. Peering. He too, through the fusty glass. Tall. Shoulders vitamins wide. Eyes by General Motors.

Jud's cock rises to his.

En garde!

And he walks down the hall. Gary Cooper. (Also Leander on his last swim.) "High Noon." 1952. You were four years old, Billie, not even jail bait then. The music: Dmitri Tiomkin.

He's never heard her scream, but she almost does now, a slice of her face at the door. "Come back. Don't open that door."

He turns with Coop's Academy Award-winning pain, his exterminated face.

"Jud, please, I beg you."

No one should ever beg.

The charge goes out of the hooch.

He has no long-barrelled six gun strapped to his thigh. Except for a blank-loaded dream. The Seventh Cavalry is on the late, late show.

The mod man peers through the window. Waves. Let me in. He is used to owning things. He speaks at him through the glass. He is the message.

"Don't let him in. Don't talk to him," he hears from behind him. "Come back here, Jud."

He turns from some brink of illumination, an ambush of blinding wisdom, to the crack-opened door that swings to accept him.

"Do you know him?" he asks as she clicks the bolts to. She shakes her head looking down.

"Have you seen him before?" Like I mean around the neighbourhood.

"I don't think so; I couldn't get a good look."

They wait for the world to come in through a wire; together in waiting. Her face is a drum.

"Not your run-of-the-mill thug," he says. "I'd guess he was expelled from at least three fourth-rate prep schools. Money there, in his nose. And he has red hair."

She looks at the floor as if she dropped something.

"Was he the man on the phone?"

She shrugs, How should I know?

Why are we whispering?

"Forget it," she says. "Life's too short."

She puts a record of the stereo sung by someone enjoying a bed of nails. But her eyes are still listening elsewhere. "Hey, I know," she says, "let's do crazy things."

Like what?

She's reaching into the bottom drawer of the carved armoire and comes up with a handful of black lacy silks slithering through her fingers. She makes ice cube laughter. "I'll be out in a mo," and swings hips into the john.

And what have we here?

Surprise: a porno mag pop-up Billie sashaying down the runway. Her face masked in Revlons. Her sabered mouth . . . I saw that Gypsy Rose, the longstemmed St. Cyr Lily and the Georgia Peach when I was a boy at the old Alhambra and it was no contest. The South won that on G-strings down . . . But here's Billie in fringed cutout bra with peek-a-boo holes for the areolas and cutout in the shape of a heart at her flaming heart of the matter. Say it, Jud.

"Happy St. Valentine's Day," he says, a boy at his first pleasure palace, Miz Lisa's place on Royale Avenoo, Freddie Fosdick throwing up all that beer and cray-fish in the parlour, after the junior prom and you'd taken the nice girls home. And that derbied black angel playing the piano as if his fingers were part of the keys. And, "What'll you have boys?" – that banana coloured Miz Lisa . . .

Billie sits on his lap and tongues his lashes.

"What's this all about?" he has to say.

"Let's just be happy," she says. "Have fun."

He reaches around for the snaps on her bra.

"Leave it on."

Take it off – that's what everyone yelled at the moment of spotlit truth just as the burleycue lights blacked out and the beaded rag was so lovelily tossed with a kick of the silver hip into the wings and a waiting king. And Freddie Fosdick croaked in his breaking choir boy voice in the smoky hush of that reverential moment, "Did you see *that?*" And the old hard-on house cracked up. And I wanted to crawl under the seat. *I'm* not with *him.*

Where am I? When?

Miz Lisa. You understood boys even when they filled out into men. One could do worse than knowing one of your girls. They were so *friendly.* When they laughed, they laughed. There was that Rosa. There are no substitutes, only replacements . . ..

He nips at her burleycue tits.

"Easy there, lover," she says, "you're hurting."

What do you think *you're* doing?"

"Just play."

He lips her legion of honour rosettes and puts hand through her cutout heart.

"Ah," says the Georgia Peach.

You should see me now, Dr. Freddie, Distinguished Dominion Professor of Psychology and Human Behavioral Modes at Sewanee.

Still fantasizing, Judson, I can hear you saying, you always were big on that. You can see them there on the runway but you can't touch them. That would destroy the illusion. The human psyche is too frail to posses a dream. It must either destroy or self-destruct. Or both. (You always covered your ass, Freddie. You'll be president, yet.) You can look at the tigers in the zoo. But don't get into the cage or open it. Those girls never come down from the runway. Except in your mind which has its own way of handling it. Or not handling it. (I read your book, Freddie; how come nobody ever called you Fred?)

Zats vhat you zink, Herr upchucking Doktor Fosdick.

"Let's take this show to the bed," Jud says.

"Can't we just fool around for a while like this."

Laugh, kid.

"We've been fooling around all weekend."

"Hokay, hokay."

I don't really want the Georgia Peach. "Aren't you going to take that rig off?" I want Billie.

"Don't be a kvetch." (You must have had a Jewish lover, Billie. The best way to learn a foreign language is in bed with a native teacher of the opposite sex.) "We're supposed to be having a ball."

She puts on another record, and the Trinidad Cavaliers Steel Drum Band struts bonging into the room. "Isn't that wild?" Georgia Billie says cake-walking right off the runway and onto the bed, presenting her portal of entry. (Did you see *that*, Freddie? Illusion? I've opened the cage and am going to bed with the tigers.)

Come and get it, that Georgia Peach used to yell up at the gallery as the spotlight tapped skipping among the bald heads in the crowd as if they were being knighted. *Or*, as she bumped, ground and spun her fringed tits like an electric fan, the ostrich plumes weaving over her tangerine head, dipping to holy crotch, *Are you-all too stiff to walk?* . . . Rebel yells. Yah-wah-hoos, stomping and finger whistles. "She's really red all over," Freddie, you said. Redneck cotton pickers waving Confederate flags, Freddie, as if we had won the War.

"Hey," she says, "take it easy."

"Sorry," he says, slowing his battering ram.

I can't seem to find Billie. So I'm fucking the Georgia Peach, Freddie. In her runway getup. Illusion? How do you like them apples? Caught her in a black fishnet as she stepped off the runway right onto my meat.

He's keeping drum time with the Trinidad Cavaliers, steely tympanists, clanging away. Ride that tiger. The mermaid body he's on is limp in its black fishnet, her eyes raining mascara.

"Billie," he says, coming home to her with all the love . . .

"You're wearing me out. GO."

He puts his body on automatic pilot, destination unknown, and his life at the cloud mountains of her face. He kisses her neck's hollow.

"For crissake, man," she says, "Throw your rocks."

Today is Friday, November 24th, the 329th day of the year with 37 to follow.
The moon is between its full stage and last quarter.

The morning stars are Venus, Saturn and Mars.
The evening stars are Mercury and Jupiter.

Those born this day are under the sign of Sagittarius.

President Zachary Taylor was born November 24, 1784.

On this day in history:
In 1869 women from 21 states met in Cleveland to draw up plans for the organization of the American Women Suffrage Association.
In 1944 Superfortresses of the American Air Force

253

took off from Saipan for the first World War II raids on Tokyo.

In 1961 the U.N. Security Council gave Secretary General Thant authorization to use force to settle the Belgian crisis.

In 1963 Lee Harvey Oswald, accused assassin of President Kennedy, was fatally shot by Jack Ruby in a Dallas jail.

A thought for the day: Scottish poet Robert Gilfillan said, "There's a hope for every woe and balm for every pain, but the first joys in our heart never come back again."

44

In the cave quiet room he can almost hear the pulse in her throat
beating. Flip-flop. His heart takes up, echoes the haywire drumming.
Chunks of time fall away. She sips her drink through a cloud, looking
at him, excluding him from her face. He dips in his head for words that
will not mean war. There aren't any. His smile, his frown - just being
Jud - could be a trigger: On September 1, 1939, Germany attacked
Poland because it was there. Ending the world. Across the table's
border under the Tiffany lamp he hopes for an ultimatum, something
negotiable – he has nothing to trade with, not even a white flag – an *or
else* would be a reprieve, a rope to latch on to. How can you be at the
end of your rope if there is no rope? Her bunned head replays an
earlier Billie who isn't there. The clock has run out of the room. The
bird flops in her throat. How does she love me? Let me count the ways:

> Your beard scratches.
> You're wearing me out.
> Do you want me to suck you off?
> Um, no, not tomorrow. I'm bowling.
> Learn to drink like a man.
> Let's just cuddle tonight, Okay?
> Man, take it easy, you're hurting.

> Gentle Jud, hurting
> Squire, Ace and onetime Hon.

She sips and calls a time out in a game you know, Judson, is over.
Fiddling with pawns after checkmate. Suppose I had made this move?
Or that?

"How was your Thanksgiving?" she says.

"Oh, the annual Currier & Ives greeting card thing. To
grandfather's" (he's said it) "farm we go." Hi, pops. "Dulcie, Bob, the
tots, locally raised fresh turkey, all the trimmings, our own homegrown
brandied peaches, and how have you been, Dad? Dad doesn't know
these days, but he says he's fine" (looking at her). "Bob falling asleep at
the televised Army & Navy game. One pre-din martini drops him like a
two-hundred-fifty-pound tackle." (I miss you Toronto Jack.) "You
know, a Bell Telephone Long Distance ad illustrated by Norman
Rockwell."

"You used to write that account."

Sweet Jesus, we're still talking.

"That's how I learned about life."

She sends him a flicker of smile from the auld lang syne. She's in love with him again for a sexless moment.

"And yours," he says, "Your Thanksgiving?"

"I went home," she sips, "stayed over." A message: You didn't sleep with someone last night? "Helped Mom in the kitchen," (a vision of aproned Billie) "she asked me if I had a boyfriend."

She laughs, not too bitterly, "*A* boyfriend."

And you said?

"I said, 'well, there is sort of someone.' To get her to come off it. She wanted to know his name. I said 'Pete.'"

"Pete who?"

"I said, 'Evans.' I don't know a Pete Evans. The name just popped into my head. Just something for her to chew on. This should keep her from bugging me at least until Christmas."

He calls a time out to breathe. "Excuse," he says and goes into the john. His unguents are gone, the myrrh and frankincense in the stocky kanøn bottles ranged on the toilet tank shelf, man signs of his co-tenancy here – shaving lotion, cologne, body rub, (you rubbed on me, Billie) talc, shave foam, shampoo. His brick-sized soap-on-a-rope that hung from the shower head. So many scented go-to-work together mornings, taking their open secret into the world. He opens the medicine cabinet. His spare razor is gone. And his Wilkinson blades.

He tries to put the toilet lid down without screech. Coughs loudly as it does. Sits, lights a cancerous Player . . . Not even an ultimatum. A come live with me *or else.* Beyond that.

Evicted.

Man.

Sheriff's sale.

He flushes, runs sound effect water from both taps.

He watches the dying bird flop in her throat.

"Where are you *supposed* to be tonight?"

Where am I supposed to have been for this more than a year? You never asked that before; just so I got here. I master forged the passports.

"I don't understand," he says, "the question." That's right, pull your galluses up, boy. Show some grit. Thank you, Great-and-Grand-Uncle Zech.

"I mean, what did you tell old Vee?"

"Does it matter?"

"Just asking." She sips.

The bird beats in her neck. *A quail once hit on the wing but not killed.*

He has one thing left. A gesture. *Le beau geste. Oui.* He can wave a white scarf flying, going down, right, Red Baron? in flames . . . His lungs fill with fierce free mountain air . . . I'm going to make it easy for you, babe.

"Do you want me to leave?"

Silence.

She sips. The bird is trying to break out of her throat.

"Do you want me not to see you again?"

Ever.

Silence.

The room (hers) closes in ringside. What now?

"Silence," he says – *Qui ne dit mot consent* – "gives consent." French, that, Billie. Fifty million Frenchmen can't be wrong. That's right, walk tall, Pufessah.

"I have my life to live," she says.

"You once wanted to live it with me. All right. Suppose you and I were to – "

"Look," she breaks in, face flashing, laying down words, a jackpot hand of cards on the table. "in ten years you'll be in your middle *sixties*, you'll be *retired*, and I'll be just beginning my prime."

The best was yet to be, Billie.

The bird has broken out of her throat and squats on his heart heavy with iron numbers.

I told you that in the beginning, Billie, we couldn't beat the difference in time. And you laughed and said you'd always be older than I. And I shed numbered time. And sees that the ring on her finger is not his, the Victorian lovers' ring, searched and found on jewellers' row that frostcake Christmas in New York, hands clasping a locket heart. Some kind of Zodiac ring instead, a blunt rams' head. Aries.

Easier always to tear someone out of your calendar when you've hedged your bet. If someone waits in the wings.

"Is there someone else?"

She shakes her head.

"I would have to accept that."

"No one special." Her eyes go into consultation. "No, not really. Just friends. Quite a few."

"And I'm in the way."

"I need my space . . . To move around in."

Not even alternate Thursdays?

Nod, nod. Nods fall from his head like leaves. He rises, takes out his key ring, removes two keys. "Yours," he says.

She shrugs. "I've changed the lock."

She stands in her private light, the full orchard year of her.

"Be well," he says.

Paris poster over the café table. The Hemingway bullfighter doing his chromo thing for tourista death in the afternoon. The Tiffany lamp staining the Salvation Army table. The swiped highway sign – Soft Shoulder Ahead. The room chorusing in her voice – You gave me my

257

best birthday, my best Christmas, the best week of my life.

Time Marches On. Also Movietone News.

"You're going?"

Nod, nod. Leaves, gray leaves.

"What will you tell Vee?" she says through Parliament smoke. "I mean, about coming home? You probably told her you'd be away overnight." As always.

"I'll think of something. I've become very good at that. She made it easy."

"It's late; you could miss that last train; you can stay here."

He looks, Do you want me to?

She nods.

Just   one   mo'   time.

45

The digital clock glows 8:31 when Vera picks up the phone on the third ring.

"Hi Mother," Dulcie says. "How are you?"

"I'm well, dear, and you and the children?"

"They're good."

You mean they are well, Vera thinks. Why must you use such sloppy locutions? I taught you better than that. Both good and well are adjectives, but good refers to behaviour and well refers to health which is what we are talking about.

"Oh, sometimes they drive me up the wall, but I guess that's what being a mother is all about."

"It seems we only get to see them on holidays. I miss them," Vera says.

"Well you would live way out in the sticks." Dulcie laughs to soften the charge.

"Your father won't live in the city; much less the suburbs."

"Yes I know, Mother, I know. How is Dad? I'd like to talk to him."

"I don't know."

"Isn't he there?"

"He's here, but he went upstairs right after dinner. He usually does lately. I think he went to bed. He's probably asleep."

"Asleep at this hour? It's early. Is he all right?"

"He's been working hard. Traveling. So many trips."

"And drinking."

"Well, yes."

"Wake him up, Mother, I've got to talk to him."

"I don't think I should do that. He needs his rest."

She hears Dulcie say "Damn." She wishes she wouldn't use such language. After all her upbringing. A pause, then, "I've got to talk to him, Mother."

"Why don't you call him tomorrow?"

"We're going to New York for the weekend tomorrow. Bob's parents are coming down from Rochester. We're leaving early. Bob wants to beat the traffic. And we have to get the kids ready. You know what that'll be like."

"Can't I give him a message?"

"Mother, please wake him up, it's important."

Important. Something's wrong. Why won't she tell *me*?

"Mother?"

"All right, Dulcie, but I don't know if he'll come to the phone. He never does when he's like this. He had quite a bit to drink."

"You just tell him I said it's important. He'll come to the phone."

"Hold on then, I'll go up and see."

Important. She's probably overspent again and needs money so Bob won't find out. A bauble, clothing most probably. something expensive she'll wear once and forget or maybe not wear at all. Like the clothing she'd bring back from college, boxes and boxes. A corduroy suit still wrapped in its tissue paper, never worn. Shoes. That lamb's wool sweater from England. "But Dulcie, why do you need more clothes when you have so many new things." "Oh Mother, that stuff isn't in this season." That stuff. Beautiful things. Dollars down the drain. And Jud never backing me up, putting his foot down. Secrets, those two.

Someone is cheating him out of the booze blackout he'd bought and paid for, his package of Lethe, shaking him out of the black hole he'd staked out as his, the only place he could go.

"Wake up, Jud."

"No, no." He keeps his eyes closed to hold in the darkness, the net of sleep, to keep himself in it, to keep himself from knowing what he knows. What he doesn't want to know. That it is over. Over, over, over. Finis, the end, curtains. That's all folks. Now the dark has been broken.

"Why are you waking me?"

"It's Dulcie, Jud, she's on the phone. She wants to talk to you."

Sleep is running away and he after it. "Tell her to go away. I don't want to talk to her. I don't want to talk to anybody. Tell her I'm sleeping."

"She says it's important, Jud." He unpastes an eye. Important.

"I didn't want to disturb you. I told her you're sleeping. That you need your rest. I asked her to give me the message. She told me to wake you."

The message. It had to be she. Now he knows as if he's known all that week it would come. Or did he? She had done it before, called Dulcie to get a message to him. But Vera . . .

"Tell her I'll call her tomorrow."

"She wants to speak to you now, Jud. They're going away tomorrow. New York, for the weekend; they're meeting Bob's parents."

He raises up on an elbow. The room throbs, dips in a rolling sea. "No, don't," he says as Vera reaches for the light switch. "No light, please." He has paid for his dark. Profanity of light. A blasphemy against the sacred and religious dark, the dark country of the bed.

"If you're going to speak to her, Jud, then do it now, she's been on the line quite a while. A toll call."

"All right, yes, I'll speak to her."

Vera holds out his robe. "Thank you," he says, shuffling his feet for his slippers. "You can't find things in the dark,"Vera says. "No light," he says.

"Here, sit down," Vera says. He sits on the edge of the bed, a patient in an escape-proof institution. She puts the slippers on his feet. Helps him into his robe. Conjugal kindness. For better or till death do us. "Thank you," he says. Vera stands there. He puts his hand on the bedstand phone. She stands there still. He nods. "Thank you." She shakes her head. "I better go down and finish the dishes," she says and goes out of the room. He picks up the receiver.

"Daddy, can you talk?"

"Yes."

"Where's Vera?"

"Downstairs."

"You sure? She can't listen in?"

"She can but she won't." Honest Vera. Truth above all. Even when it hurt. Truth the scalpel. Truth the light. Lying the mortal and ultimate sin. Deception equals betrayal. She won't listen in. Not Vera.

"Daddy, Billie called me half-hour ago. She was sobbing. She's shattered. She wants you back. She went out every night this week and says it was no good."

Went out, I know what that means. "She loves you, Daddy, she says she can't live without you. She says better the three nights a week than nothing at all, than not seeing you. She can't stand it without you."

"Take it easy," he says in a whisper, sensing a something. But never, not Vera. The phone flowers with Billie. The whole year of Billie. The year that had thirteen months. A phoneful of Billie. The big cat. The lioness. Her face leafed by yellow light in the carnal noon of the park under the heart-leafed lindens. In the everywhere snow. Her lamplight hair on the pillow. Her seawave body. Her tendril hands. Her petal fingers. Her blooming mound. The thermal springs of her mouth. "I love her so," he blurts.

"I think you're both crazy," Dulcie says. "I told her so. You love each other. I know she loves you. One week without you and she's smashed, a wreck. You should have heard her." Yes, but the others. "She couldn't stop crying. I think you two ought to stop the nonsense and get married."

"I wouldn't marry her if I could marry her tomorrow." His hand fists.

"Why not?"

"Because I don't trust her. She threw me away once before." Last Maytime's agony. "Kept me on hold while she *tested* our love with others. She had to find out, she said, if she really loved me. I never had to find out, not from the first. Then when I caught her out and cut it she said that the others meant nothing to her. Well, they meant something to *me*. Ah, but now she knew, really knew we were special and wanted me back."

"Look, Daddy, we all have our hangups."

That shadow of something again. He says "Hush," and listens. The room is an ear. The whole house. But not Vera. Never.

"Hangups. Sleeping around."

"It might have been different if you had married her. She said she thought you would."

"Dulcie, I told her I *wanted* to but not if the price was murder. Not if the price is another person's life. And that's what it would be. You can't throw thirty years out the window, not when it's another person's thirty years you're talking about. At least I can't. Just get up and say, I'm in love, I want out. See you around? Toodle-oo?"

"Oh come on now Daddy, let's stop kidding each other. We know what those thirty years have been like. What's Vera given you? All those rules and regulations."

"It was her way of putting some order in a disorderly world. A moral act."

"Thirty years of unhappiness, of pure misery."

No, daughter, it wasn't like that in the beginning, not in its springtime. What do you know about *our* moon-filled road in time's other country? A yellow ribbon tied, yes, to the fall of *her* young hair. Before love's arthritis set in.

"You were never right for each other, you know it. In all those years I never saw you happy, not once. As for Vera and me, well you know about that. She was never what I thought a mother should be. Not in my book. So you can't say you hung on for my sake. You should have gotten out a long time ago. Even before Billie."

"It may be too late. Billie's younger than you, my daughter."

"So what? You don't come on old. You're an attractive man. An accomplished man. You're interesting, fun. Lots of women, young women would think so. You've got something, Daddy, a lot of young guys don't have. Remember Denise, my sorority sister? She said I could go for him."

Again the ear on a stick. "We've been talking too long," he says. "Yes, I've got to go too. We're going away for the weekend. I guess Vera told you. Billie wants you to call. She made me promise to tell you. And I'd tell you what I'd do if I were you. I'd move in with Billie, or get a new place with her. Try living together. She wants to come home to you every evening. She wants you there in the morning. She wants to spend weekends with you, holidays. She wants the whole thing. I don't blame her. I'd take what I want and I'd take it now."

They're so much alike Billie and Dulcie, the same generation. Take what you want and the hell with who pays. "You'll call her now, won't you, the first chance you get?"

"I'll call her."

"I'll be talking to you Daddy."

"Yes, daughter, have a good trip."

"I love you Dads. Take care."

"I love you too, Dulcie."

He makes it to the window seat. Lights in the valley. There used to be so few, a handful in the hills when they came here.

She wants me back. He sits on the doorstep of the world again basking in the summer of her sunny flesh, her sheness. Outside in the valley the first December night, trees budding stars. To come again to the shore of her ocean eyes, sunbathe in each other's arms. Her voice, grave children singing. And the shadows, the others. The walked-on moon. The heaven and hell of her. She'll kill you, Judson, she almost did and maybe has already . . . Dead on the streets of his dream . . . She wants me back.

Now the lies would begin again. All this week he'd had only one thing to be grateful for. Somehow Vera hadn't found out. Had been spared. At least that. Now again the giddy and terrible tightrope he'd teetered on day and night for so many months. Every minute vulnerable to discovery, to ambush by time with the odds going up every second. It was only waiting to happen and someday it would. Caught on the barbed wire of his lies. Like this. Vera would call his office while he was away from his desk and be answered by the receptionist. And Vera would ask whether Mr. Bell had returned yet from Washington. And the receptionist would say Mr. Bell wasn't in Washington, that he'd been in the office all day. And Vera would say, feeling the years start to crack and now hearing herself as if she were listening in to somebody else's party line conversation, Vera would say, "But Mr. Bell left for Washington yesterday morning directly from home and said he'd be back in the office sometime this afternoon and I just called to have him pick up some things at the supermarket on the way home." And the receptionist would say, "Mr. Bell was in the office all day yesterday, too," and maybe his plans had changed and was there a message? And Vera would say, "I see. Thank you. No message. It isn't important."

That's how it would happen some day but it hadn't. Because she believed me. Unto the pure all things are pure. Just once, a close call. But she had been spared her portion of pain. Let that be mine. When I told her last week that the trips were over she was happy for *me*. "Now you'll come back to yourself, Jud. You haven't been well, you look like a ghost. Now you'll be home all the time I'll be able to take care of you. And maybe we'll get to know each other again."

Thirty miles to the east in her shuttered room she is waiting for his call. Enough to live on through the weekend between them. Cold by that window. He hitches his white terry robe closer around him, reties the sash. He listens for sounds downstairs. There are none, the house is thick with quiet. He goes down the stairs, through the dining room and stops at the kitchen. Vera is standing motionless at the sink staring ahead in a trance.

"Vera?"

She stands there unmoving.

"Anything the matter?"

263

She turns her head slow motion toward him, seeing not him but something, a film projected inside her, a smile that is not a smile on her lips. A web in which something is caught.

"Revelations," she says.

He knows but he asks her, "What revelations?"

"Your conversation with Dulcie. I overheard it. I didn't intend to, believe me. But when I came down I picked up the receiver and was about the replace it when I heard Dulcie say – I heard her clearly, she was speaking quite loudly – I heard Dulcie say, 'she was sobbing, she's shattered.' I couldn't imagine who, who would be sobbing and shattered that Dulcie should tell you. One of the children? So I listened."

He waits, offering himself up to rage, to tears, to the torrents of hate, to blows even. Only the smile that is not a smile and her eyes somewhere else.

Then she says, "Aren't you going to call her? Poor girl, she must be in a terrible state."

46

The blue loaded revolver catnaps on its side in the opened drawer of their bedside table, waiting to be commanded. By whoever will pick it up. Dumb neutral mercenary: a .38 Colt Trooper Special. Oiled. Cleaned. Efficient. No questions asked. Just waiting to do its job. Hefty. Professional.

You have committed pain, Judson.

YOU FUCKING CUNT.
YOU STUPID DULCIE.

At the window in the bedroom he sees again lights in the valley. First December night, still, a new solstice. Mad Anthony Wayne, over there on that ridge retreating from the bloody Brandywine. A Tory innkeeper whispers to a redcoat. Fifty-one dead and buried where they fell: the Paoli Massacre.

Vera ambushed. Like that, by a voice.

A knock at his bedroom door.

"Yes?"

"It's Vera." As if she has to say, as if it could be someone else.

Omigod.

"May I come in?"

May she come in. This is our house. Yours. And this room. Even though you've slept in this room only on and off since September, the totalled night of the crash. And your almost demise.

You have committed pain, Judson.

"Of course, yes, please." Pick up that thing in the drawer of our night table. Pick it up, please. I'll throw the safety catch off. And please
. . .

PULL THE TRIGGER.

"Jud," she says, "I'm trying to understand." She stands in the door in her practical, high-collared flannel nightgown. A modest fleur-de-lis pattern. She's done something to her hair. A touch of rouge at the cheeks. Lipstick. Sweet Pea cologne.

Oh, Vera.

He pads to the night table, takes the gun out. Throws the safety. Offers it to her, barrel toward him. "All you have to do," he says . . .

"What's that for?" she says. "That won't solve anything."

"Yes," he says, "it will. You'll be doing me a favour."

"You tried to teach me to shoot it once. You know how I feel about firearms."

"I bought it for your protection, for when I wasn't home."

"Sometimes I've been more afraid when you've been here. The way your face looked when you came back from those – trips. Who but you could hurt me?"

Oh, Vera.

"Everything's in our joint names."

"I didn't marry you for property. There wasn't any then. And I didn't care. And I still don't care about that. I thought I was marrying a poet. That's all that counted with me. I would have starved with you in a garret."

La Bohème.

She turns away a little. Her nostrils whiten. Jack's daughter, stiff upper, and Flora's too. School marm. The whole package.

Ask her, she'll tell you now in this born again moment.

"And you married? . . ."

"A Yale clubman . . . Skull and Bones," and she just about laughs. "An ad man . . . You betrayed more than me."

He throws the gun on her handworked bedspread.

"Please, not on that. Oil stains are hard to get out." She lifts the revolver as if it were a live lobster, puts it back in the drawer. Shuts it.

"You should have killed me," he says.

"I think it's *me* you want to kill."

"Never." Vera.

"Oh yes, then you'd be free."

"Free . . . for what?"

"For that . . . for that tootsie you love so much."

Toot-toot-tootsie, goodbye . . . Eddie Cantor, 1920-what? Toot-toot-tootsie, don't cry.

"I think we should talk," she says. "May I get into bed with you? It's cold standing around."

She pulls the bedspread down to the foot of their four-poster, folds it neatly, shucks sheepskin lined, pompommed slippers. Fluffs, props pillows against their backs.

"Now," she says, settling in beside him.

"What?"

"How it happened. I have to understand. Could it have been my fault?"

"No fault but mine."

"All right. You know. I had a feeling, back then, that last weekend she was here, before she stopped coming, that she had fallen in love with you – that's why she looked so unhappy – but that you were not responding. No, not *you* . . .Isn't that funny?"

"Vera, why must we talk? It won't repair anything."

"No, but it's all I have left. Talk. No husband, no daughter . . . I heard her, you know, on the phone, about *me*. I might have been able to take, well, you and she, those things, I understand happen – but what Dulcie said . . . Until the day I die I will not understand. To correct a child is not to stop loving it. The things I denied myself so she could have; she'll never know. I gave my best."

Punch and Judy propped on the marital pillows.

A scratch at the door.

"Blitz," he says. "He wants to come in."

"Poor dog. Creature of habit. He always slept at the foot of our bed since he was a pup. Until I moved into the guest room and he didn't know where he belonged, how to divide his loyalty. So he slept in the hall between."

"I'll let him in."

"Creatures," she says. "No wonder people get to prefer them to people. You can be sure of them. I used to think, like so many others, seeing old people cling to their pets – dogs, cats, canaries – even leaving their money to them in their wills and not to their kin – that age made them queer, that they had perversely abandoned their own. But it was they who were abandoned." She looks at the well-cold night beyond the windows . . . "I suppose we will have to sell the horses, but I would like to have the dog and the cats. It's a fair enough trade, don't you think?"

Two cats and a dog for Billie.

"We don't have to sell anything."

"I won't be able to care for them, the horses, wherever I'm going. And you have a job. And she . . ."

"You don't have to go anywhere."

"This isn't my place anymore. It's ruined. It's as if the world stopped and I've fallen off. Like the sudden end of that roller coaster ride we took in that stupid, stupid place the one time I went with you to a convention."

"Disneyland."

"Yes."

"Selling the horses means selling this place. Is that what you mean?"

"Well, you'll have to provide me with something to live on. It needn't be much. You can have most of it. Just so I can exist. I can always supplement that by finding something useful to do, teaching youngsters to read. I don't know."

"No. Whatever we have is yours, as much yours as mine – more. Don't think I don't know that. You made it possible, Vera."

"It's cost you thirty years in the pits, as you've said; more than half your life."

"*Our* life. But you're making decisions that are too soon to make. I know how you feel."

"*You know how I feel?*"

. . . You don't know how I've felt for years. Almost all we've had now together has been the riding. And a book you thought I should read. Not even that anymore. When have you last said "You've got to read this?" You haven't read a book in a year. Your own book unfinished, stuck away for years in the closet. I would have given everything . . . Where is the poet I married? the writer of novels, "throbbing with life, ardent, lyric, intense," it said in The *New York Times*. *That* man, where has he gone? the bright wit at parties, women touching his hand – as I so suddenly did – their hands on his arm, their eyes in his eyes. (I should have known then.) The once every night lover, afternoons, mornings too in the beginning, remember, Jud, when the curtains blew over the bed that first time and you said in my ear, "wheaten hair, creamy thighs"? Your once tender hands. What does Dulcie know?

. . . You stopped touching me even before – that girl. I wanted to be touched, to be reached out for. Not your cheek condescendingly turned to my kiss in the morning before you left for the office. I have lips. I have dreams, Jud. I dreamed the handsome young man from the mill who delivers the oats, it was he and it wasn't he, said he had fallen in love with me, with *me* old enough to be his mother, but he didn't care, I interested him, he really loved me, we made love. When I woke up I was relieved it was only a dream. I wanted it to be you, my husband. Other men come to the door when you're not at home, that intelligent tree man, the man who put up the gutters on the barn, the wandering carpenter from Paradise I told you about. Sometimes they get into my dreams. I don't want them there. I've been alone so long here day after day with only the creatures . . . I suppose you held it against me those nights I wouldn't have you, when you turned to me reeking of tobacco and liquor. The nights I slept in the guest room – you really stank. And when I came back you lay there like a warm stone. That was lust, not love.

. . . And I know as we lie here like Darby and Joan that you never forgave me that night in July two summers ago. It was heatwave hot, not a breeze, not even on our hill. We had been reading, the way we always did in the evenings, and before we went up to bed you said, "Let's take a dip in the pool. It will cool us for sleep." So we went out like Adam and Eve – "Being able to do this," you said, "makes everything worth it." It was a lovely swim, the moon almost full, some time after midnight. We let the air dry us. And as we walked to the house you touched me. In that way. (Was it the last time?) You wanted to have me right there, on the grass. And I know I said, "No not on the grass." It would scratch my back. I said, Let's go to our bed where we can be comfy. And you said, No-Now-Under-the-Moon. I just couldn't lie down on the grass with all the bugs and insects crawling about. We weren't sixteen, you know. You could have waited. There is a time and a place. Once in the house you scowled (have scowled ever since) and muttered something about "spontaneity" being dead. And that night you gave me back my borrowed body.

. . . Maybe we shouldn't have married. Maybe poets never should. We were so free in each other before, all that we were in our faces, like children, timeless. Then came Dulcie, the jobs and the mortgage – don't think I don't know – and we began seeing each other through bars. You were *responsible*, Jud, you made me feel safe. I respected you for it. Such a surprise, under that bandit look – I said to myself the first time I saw you at that New Hampshire art show, stay away from that man, he's dangerous – the man who said "I live off the land," when I asked what you did. The responsible-bandit-poet. How naive we both were to think there could be such a one.

. . . What do you know, Dulcie? . . . I used to come to his place on my lunch hour, he writing upstairs, and leave love notes in his mailbox although we'd be together that evening . . . I should have remained your mistress. Something seems to happen once things are signed. Papers. Something happens . . . What do you know about anything, Dulcie?

Beyond the bedroom windows first light is touching the valley fog like a wick lit by a match. Fog speared by bare trees and the horizon ridge a floating island. A Japanese scroll.

"It's morning," he says.

"We've talked the night away."

"Have we? What did we say?"

"There's nothing to say anymore. Why don't you get some sleep? I have to let out the horses, hay them; the other creatures to feed."

"Let me help. I always do on weekends."

"For me it's just another day. My job," she says. " Get some sleep."

"No. I'll make the coffee, then. Breakfast. Eggs over once, all right?"

"If you wish. Don't burn the toast as you always do."

Not *always*.

Silver fog turning gold in the valley. Billie's body like that in the morning. The arched hip of the world taunting the growing light. In my waking eyes. In that shuttered room.

You said, Vera, I should call her. You didn't have to tell me. She just had to whistle and I'd be there. Isn't *that* what it's all about? Farm, trees, critters – she is the turning globe.

The clock says it is 5:58, ante meridien.

Is she asleep? Has she been up all night, too?

You'll call her now, Dad?

Later, It's too early.

No, now.

He goes to his workroom window with its view of the barn. She's just going into the paddock, locking the gate.

269

He dials the number tattooed on his life. The first guilt-ridden ring . . .
two . . . three: "Hello?"

"How are you?" he says.

"Miserable."

Then: "Oh, Jud."

Then: "And you?"

"Miserable."

"Am I going to see you?"

"Yes."

"Monday?"

"Yes."

"The usual time?"

"Let's make it for lunch," he says.

"Oh." Silence. "Great."

"We'll talk when I see you."

"Where?"

"Wherever you say."

"You say."

"I can't think."

"Tarello's, how about that? It's near my office."

"Tarello's," he says. "Fine. I'll make the reservation. Twelve-thirty?"

"That's fine," she says. "Twelve-thirty."

"Twelve-thirty," he says.

Watching the coffee pot perking, the butter beginning its slide in the
pan, he sees something chalked on the keeping room blackboard:

How Vera Sees Judson Now
   *J*arring,
   *U*nloving,
   *D*emoralized,
   *S*avage,
   *O*bnoxious,
   *N*auseating,
   *B*etraying,
   *E*vil-tongued,
   *L*iquor-swilling,
   *L*iar.

The butter is sizzling, brown-edged. He breaks the eggs into the pan.
Takes out four slices of bread . . . Don't burn the toast.

"The dishes are washed," he says coming into the feed room (*Belle-
maman* Flora would have approved, eh, Jeck?) "Let me take over now.
I'll do the mucking out. Please."

She stands in the feed room, the fractured smile of the night
before back, eyes reading the screen of the whitewashed wall.

"Perhaps," . . .she says . . .

You've never said maybe, Vera, for as long as I've known you. Was that adverb not used at Bryn Mawr?

"What, Vera?"

"Oh, *you*. What are you doing here? This is my place."

"I came to take over the chores. You were saying, 'Perhaps,' Perhaps What?"

"Yes . . . I've been thinking. Perhaps you should go and live with her; try it."

"You can't mean that."

Her eyes are alone, nowhere. "I don't know what I mean. I suppose I'm trying to find out."

He reaches out a hand.

"No, please, no touch, not now, not yet, perhaps not ever again."

"Vera –"

"When I married you, I never thought I'd be where I am – or rather, am not. I don't know where I am. Everything seems so strange – the barn, the house, the things in them – the animals even. They all seem to have known, to have been in it with you, to have been a secret part of it, a secret shared against me. It's as if everything, everyone *knew* and didn't tell me."

She dips the scoop into the grain bin, not moving her head or her scalded eyes. "The horses have to be grained."

"Let me."

"It's always been my job. You had your job there and I had mine here, and together we made one thing, us. I thought that was fair. Everything belonged to us. Now I belong to nothing. Not even the animals, because they're not *us* any more."

"We can be again."

"Too much has happened."

"It won't happen again. It was an accident."

"It wasn't an accident. An accident happens once. You can mend from that, perhaps. This has been happening for a long time. A year, more, ever since those trips began, those *regular* trips. Every week. You used to be away once in a while, a night, two nights, a week at a convention. And you always called me, sent cards, from wherever you *really* were – San Francisco, Chicago – that time you did a commercial in Mexico. And you always brought me something from those places – that silver pin from Guadalajara, the turquoise bracelet from Taos. But these trips, this – oh my God – this accident – I've been in an accident for more than a year and didn't even know it was happening. Now it's happening all at once. It will be happening the rest of my life. I'm breaking all over."

The nickering in the stalls has grown louder. A shrill, demanding neigh.

"I'm sorry, darlings," she says, her hand still on the grain scoop. "I've never kept you waiting before. Go back to the house, Jud. I have

271

my work to do."

"Let me help, please."

The back of her parka to him, filling the grain cans, she says, "I've always prepared their morning feed the night before. This is the first time . . ."

A wisp of hay on her bifocals. He wants to brush it away. Doesn't dare. And on her hair.

The horses grunt at their hay, paw the ground snorting, the barn warm with their wintercoat bodies. The cats curled up in one ball on the window ledge. "You didn't know, did you?" she's saying to Roman swilling oats in his stall, rubbing his neck. "No. You are what you are, always predictable. You don't know what a lie is. You're always you."

Coming out with the empty grain cans, "Tell me," she says, "the truth, *if you can*, about those trips. I have a right to know. But it must be the truth; you can be honest with me now."

The gory details.

"What good will it do, Vera? More pain?"

"How much more is more pain? How much more can there be?"

He shakes his head.

"I must know. All I know now is that for a year, a whole year, my life wasn't really my life. Wasn't *life*. Some kind of charade. A coma. It's like waking up dead in the dark. I'm trying to understand what happened. Perhaps then – I have it coming, you know. You owe it to me."

Sighs are so stupid. Throwaway losses. "What do you want to know that you don't already?"

She opens the grain bin, puts in the cans. Turns, the hay wisps still in her hair, her eyes split by her glasses. "All those nights you were away, three times a week, once in a while, four, were you with her all of those times? Remember now, I want the truth."

He takes out a pack of Players. She points to the cardboard sign she lettered: No Smoking in This Barn.

"Most of them. There *were* trips – Washington, Newport News, New York – I usually arranged to complete them in a day."

"Ah, yes, all those times you got up at five a.m. to catch an early plane or a train. Checking tickets before you left - tickets to Graustark - so I could see . . . And then you came home to her."

"Yes."

"Three, sometimes four nights a week . . ."

"Yes."

Nickering in the stalls, velvet nostrils against the bars. "The horses want to be let out," he says, moving.

"My job," she says and slides the stall doors open. Honcho Casey lumbers out first in primordial pecking order as she pats his passing rump, then elegant Roman. Nodding heads. Hosses. It smells good here. Hay. straw. Cats curled at the December window in the daffodil winter sun.

272

"You know," she says, "I'm amazed she let you go off for a week by yourself. She must have wanted to go. A week at the shore, after all. With you. Such self-denial. I suppose that says something for her."

He doesn't know where to put his face, his hands. He knows he must look at her some time, at her eyes.

"Judson?"

"Yes?"

"How did you manage that?"

He knows he must say something: "Manage what?"

"A week at the shore without her, when you went off to work on your book."

Remember now I want the truth. You owe it to me.

"I didn't."

He shuts his eyes in the stillness; wants to be blind forever; deaf.

"You mean she went with you."

He nods.

"Look at me."

He opens his eyes to her icepick eyes.

A howl twists out of her mouth, an ambulance siren. "Oh my God." She leans against the grain bin. "Alone, you said you had to be *alone* with your *book.* And I let you go, *encouraged* you, so you could be with her. I was the one alone, day and night, thinking, even while mucking out, *mucking out,* you were finally getting back to the work you should do. I was *happy* for you. WHAT AM I GOING TO DO?" She is all shriek, banging her head on the stone feed room wall, tearing at her parka as if it were on fire.

"Vera." (Dear.)

She flails with her arm, her glasses flying off to the straw. "Liar Liar LIAR."

"Vera, please."

"I'm going crazy," she screams.

He bends to the straw for her glasses. She claws them out of his hand, flings them crashing against the wall.

"I don't want to see you anymore. I don't want to see anything. I WANT TO DIE."

"Don't Vera, please." Don't Vera, please.

"You should have killed me that night you almost ran me down with the car. You almost did, but I jumped. Well I wouldn't jump now. I thought you were blind drunk with the inhumanity of your job. But you were going to her, weren't you?

"WEREN'T YOU?

"ANSWER ME."

"Yes, but not for the reason you think."

"Hahaha. Not for the reason I think. Was there ever another reason? Did she ever read a book?"

He sees her cracked face and all he can say is, Please, Vera.

She looks into nowhere. "How stupid you both must have thought I was. You were right –I was. I treated her like a daughter, a younger sister, bathed her after her fall from the horse, when she stayed on with us. In *my* house. She said she liked being with me. I even went shopping with her for her riding gear. Bought her a present, a stock pin . . ."

He wishes she had the .38 in her hand now.

"Her riding gear . . ." Vera says dreamily. Running now to the paddock gate –letting it swing open – to the house.

He picks up her shattered glasses, picks through the straw for pieces of broken glass, and sees the raked gashes bleeding where she tore at his hand. That's all we need now, glass in a hoof. He locks the barn gate behind him. Or loose horses. Blitz comes with an offered stick in his mouth. "Not now, dog, not now."

She's in the living room, weaving, the long carving knife in her hand, breathing in gasps over a shambles of butchered clothes. A tweed coat sleeve ripped out of an armhole in two jagged pieces, legless breeches, the crotch hacked out. She's slashing away at a boot. – Billie's riding things she never took with her. He sees her modelling them, framed in the doorway the first day she wore them. Tally-ho. How do I look?

"The pin," Vera says, "I can't find the pin. She must have taken it with her. It was eighteen carats - gold."

How can he say: Please, Vera. And pulls himself up the stair, his legs clutched by unseen hands, to a dark, quiet place without pain that isn't there. Anywhere. Any more. Reaching the bedroom landing he hears the air hiss apart.

"You listen to me." And turns.

She stands at the bottom stair, her face full of her blood, the carving knife a sabre held up at the charge. She waves it at him.

"You," she breathes, "better listen to me. I've figured it out – three times a week, sometimes four, for a year, and the week at the shore – you . . ."

She shuts her eyes . . . "*screwed* her, at least one hundred and seventy-six times . . .

"Well . . .

You left out our anniversary weekend, Vera. Certain mornings. Nights in your house.

". . . you are going to screw *me* one hundred and seventy-six times, con*secutive*ly, night after night."

He measures her wound in the word she used and never heard her say. Even more in her not being able to bring herself to utter the standard four-letter word nothing could ever bring her to say.

"You hear me?"

You have committed pain, Judson.

274

Today is Monday, December 4th, the 339th day of
the year with 27 to follow.
The moon is approaching its new phase.

The morning stars are Mercury, Venus, Mars and
Saturn.
The evening star is Jupiter.

Those born this day are under the sign of
Sagittarius.

On this day in history:
In 1942 President Franklin D. Roosevelt
ordered liquidation of the Works Progress
Administration (WPA) created in 1935, in the
depths of the depression, to provide work for
the unemployed.

47

Pushing up noontime streets in a cast of thousands, already last year's Christmas plastic strung along lampposts, strewn in store windows, spastic mechanical Santas ho-hoing into the street. Peace on earth and the door of the Go-Man-Go Bar is wide open. I need a drink. (Learn to drink like a man.) A shrill of broads at the bar. Skip it.

The maitre d' at Tarello's controls him with funeral parlour courtesy.

"Name, plizz? Of curse. Your table, sair," and forefingers him to a corner. Stenographers from Catholic high schools and MBAs from Temple press against the ropes.

"How did he get in?"

"Wasn't he on the Mike Douglas show?"

Jud slips him the folded bills in his palm.

"Yesss," the maitre d' says like air going out of a tire and seats him, almost breaking his back.

"Would moosewar care for a drink, before thee ladee come?"

He wants to say, maybe hit is a boy. Also come off it you international Balkan. I thought Akim Tamiroff was dead.

"A double Gibson," Jud says.

"Commendatore," the maitre d' bows.

For another five he could be a papal count.

"*In mezzo del camino*," Jud says.

"Signore?"

"Oh, nothing. It's from a poem written by a kid from South Philadelphia High School, name of Dante."

"Dante? Lotsa Dantes in South Philadelphia."

"This one had to leave town in a hurry," Jud says. "A rival Mafia family, the Black Guelphs."

He is on his second vermouth oily drink when he sees her jigsaw face in the crowd at the rope. And rises, waving. And goes blind until she is growing there. Here:

"Hi."

"Billie," he says, as if to make sure.

He expected her smiling. Or crying. Or what? She seems to have run out of both.

"What will you have?"

"Whatever you're having." And sees. "Gibsons, why not. A good way to go."

"They don't know what dry is."

"Tarello's," she shrugs.

Her face is smeary as if she had put make-up on in the dark; her clothes out of a suitcase after a long trip; dressed in a taxi.

They sit at the table across from each other, agents for other people in other countries: a June beach Billie, a night-swimming Jud.

"Back on cigs," she says, as he lights her and himself. A long-fingered Parliament. A honeyed Player.

"Billie," he says the conjuring name again.

"I wasn't sure you'd come."

"You knew I would."

"Not this time."

"You should know by now I wouldn't let you down." You don't ever let anybody down, do, you, Judson?

"That was another time." An April. A May. "But it wasn't like this," she says, puffing, sipping.

Let us go then, you and I to the shuttered room.

"Not like this time."

A pad and a pencil appear at his ear.

"We'll order later," he says.

"Last week," she says, inhaling a headful of smoke, "I was the biggest whore in town."

Why are you telling me this?

"I fucked my head off –

"Did everything in the book."

Everything? How many variations are there? Orifices to fill? Combinations? À deux? À trois in the A & P Guide to the Kama Sutra. *Soixante enough.*

"Why are you telling me this?"

"Stuff like this gets around. I thought you'd better hear it from me. Also, if we're going to . . ."

He sees her phone number scrawled on men's room walls: Best blow job in town. She's chanting again –

"Every night –

"With another man . . . Well, twice with one –

"I went berserk –

"I cried on a lot of shoulders –

"Said your name – *in bed with them* –

"Over and over."

"Who were they?"

"Does it matter? The gory details? Men."

"You said you want me to know."

"What difference can it make? The names. I've shut the door."

That has no lock.

"Who? Louie?"

So many choicer catches swim in her voice.

She sucks a balloon of smoke into her stung, tired face. Fuck lag.

277

"Okay, there was Mike Lambert, and –"

"The man whose house we had at the shore."

"Yes. I met him at Gil Kerr's party last May. He kept bugging me. Calling. The guy never quit. Sent me a book. Presents." She looks at her ramshead zodiac ring. "Then in August –"

I thought you were mine, at least all of last summer, at least from May to the accident.

"August," he says.

"Yes. He called all the time. Asked me to go with him to the shore for the weekend. He was having a bash. I was going bananas without you on weekends. My place hot as hell, a heat wave."

"Tell me, *he* was the man in the hall that night. The man who rang your bell."

"Yes."

"You were expecting him."

"Yes." Your Honour.

"Then why did you ask me to stay?"

"I don't know. It was getting too much for me. He – you, it was all mixed up. Who liked what for breakfast. Eggs over or scrambled. I wanted to hold on to us . . . Then, after the accident, there were others."

"Your boss, the twice-a-week squash player. Ed Loach."

"Yes."

The pad and pencil are back at his ear. "The *scalloppine alla Marsala* is especially good today." She looks down at the menu, shakes her head.

"Two Gibsons," Jud says. "And keep the bartender away from the vermouth. Break his hand. Whatever it takes. I'll make it worth your while." And hitches a bill from his pocket. "Put your children through college."

Something sunny comes into her face: the birth of a smile: My old Jud, funny mans.

"You're coming over tonight?" she says.

"I can't."

"But you said you'd see me today."

"I said for lunch."

"I told you, I've shut the door on them. I need you. I'm all over the place. I never thought I'd ever have to say that to anyone. Even you. Please, make me feel good again. I want to be glad when I get up in the morning."

Navigator to pilot: We are now over the target:

"Vera knows about us."

She shakes out a cigarette, stublights it. "You *told* her?"

"As a matter of fact, Dulcie did - she didn't mean to. But when she called me on Friday, I was asleep. Vera woke me. I took the call upstairs. Vera went down to hang up. And listened in."

"Not Vera."

"Yes, Vera. She says she didn't intend to – and I must believe her – but heard something on the phone as she was hanging up – and listened."

"That's really funny," Billie says. "Before I called Dulcie, I was going to call Vera – tell her about us – that's how dragged out I was – that we love each other – to let you go. So we could be together without all this crap."

"Well, she knows now about my trips."

"You mean you spelled it out"

"I had no choice. Dulcie mentioned three nights a week with you. Quoted you. After that . . ."

She looks into her drink, divining, spears a pearl onion. "Hey," she says, (gang) blowing smoke, "That isn't all that bad. Now she knows, why don't you just tell her you want to be with me?" *Be with you. Vera aside, you've put so many horns on my head, I'd be the laughingstock of Philadelphia. There goes ol' Jud, the cuckold Pufessah. Billie's on-and-off prick. Cock-a-doodle-doo. Der Blaue Engel.*

"I couldn't do that."

"Why not? Why?"

"I don't think you quite understand. Vera's in shock, really. A walking wounded. To say she is hurt is like putting a bandaid on open heart surgery. Every second of every day she tries to stitch this whole thing together. Her Jud, not *her* Jud. She still doesn't want to believe I did this to her."

"I suppose she's had a lot of nice things to say about me."

"Not at first. No. Not even later. Not what you think. No name-calling, if that's what you mean. She thought you were her friend when you stayed with us. That you were falling in love with me, but that *I* walked away from it. She liked you, you know. For a while there you were her substitute daughter."

"Old Vee."

Yes, old V.

"So," she pokes in her empty Parliament pack. He offers a Player. "Those things are strong," she says, but accepts.

"Wait," he says, "I'll get you your brand." Goes to the vending machine by the bar. Fishes for coins.

"Always the perfect gentleman," she says.

"I once tried to be. There are lots of things one can be that are much worse than that."

"So where do we go from here?"

"Just lunch, at least for a while. There's no other way."

"Nooners," she says. "Oh great."

"I didn't mean that."

"Yeah." She sips.

"If I were to tell her that I'd be away overnight, I'd have to be where she can reach me."

"Okay, so you won't move in with me. Shack up in a new place. What I want. At least our good old three nights a week. She'll still have you. The way it was. She ought to buy that."

"Vera aside, that would not be enough for you. We'd be back where we are right now."

"I'd find something to do the other nights. Take courses – something. The main thing is she knows, okay? That can't be undone. I'm willing to give why can't she? I held off that Mike till he called me a weekend widow. That really got to me. So she'll be a widow three nights a week. And she'll still have her life, your name, her precious farm."

My precious farm.

"After all, she doesn't put out for you."

Is there marriage after the BTUs cool down?

Marriage is being able to say, "Do you remember?" *And the other replies,* "Of course I do." *And they walk hand-in-hand into one memory.*

The pad and pencil are at his ear again. "I'm going off now," the waiter says. "I've got to put in my tab."

Jud looks up – Tarello's is empty. Just the barkeep reading *Variety* at the bar. "Yes, of course," and hands the waiter some bills. "What time is it?" And looks at his watch.

"Quarter of four," the waiter says.

"Keep the change."

"*Grazie.*"

I've got to get back," Jud says, rising. There is no blue left in her eyes, just the gray sea. "Oh –" he reaches into his coat pocket, takes out a folded sheet. "– I started this the second time we were together, more than a year ago, but could never move it beyond the fifth line. It finished itself last week. Poems have to wait until they happen."

She unfolds the sheet.

> Rain your gold hair, girl, on me
> and shine
> your body on my battles, scars and wounds.
>
> Your palm is water to my roots,
> and all the light I'll ever need is in your sky.
>
> Once my sunlight hand
> looking for you in the dark
> found the sea,
> my mouth the nipples of your earth.

You left me without air,
water,
without earth,
seasons –
without eyes for my poems.

"It's good," she says.
    Outside Tarello's she says, "Then you're not coming over tonight?"
    "I can't do that."
    She turns west walking away.
    "I love you, Billie," he calls after her.
    "But not enough," she says over her shoulder.
    He turns east. The poem drops from her fingers as she crosses the
street.

    Today is Thursday, December 21st, the 355th day of
    the year with 10 to follow.
    The moon is approaching the last quarter.

    The morning stars are Mercury, Venus and Mars.
    The evening stars are Jupiter and Saturn.

    Those born this day are under the sign of
    Sagittarius.

    Soviet Premier Josef Stalin was born December
    21st, 1879.

    On this day in history:
    In 1620 the Pilgrims set foot for the first time
    on American soil at Plymouth, Mass.
    In 1942 the U.S. Supreme Court upheld the validity
    of six-week divorces granted in Nevada.
    In 1944 horse racing was suspended in the United
    States for the duration of World War II.
    In 1968 Apollo 8 blasted off for the moon orbit
    carrying astronauts Frank Borman, James Lovell
    and William Anders.

                            * * *

    A thought for the day: British poet Richard Trench
    said, "We kneel, how weak, we rise, how full of
    power."

48

Proof sheets piled on his desk, thumbnail commercials, memos, creative review board reports, glaciers of paper. He can see, by craning his neck, blind Billy Penn sailing his cupola, and a longitude shade to the left, the Quaker City Bank & Trust Company tower. Her sunglazed windows.

A knock at his open door and a "hem."

Ah yes, the Chestnut Hill scion of Union League interlocking directorates. (Family fortunes made selling rifles that didn't work to our troops. Other neat shystery things). His co-boss.

Christopher (Kip) Money, V.

Gold-plated schmuck.

As Billie would say. Said. On many an afterwork evening. And the shuttered room rang with 90 proof laughter.

"Kip?"

"I've been meaning to catch up with you sooner, Ace, but you know how busy we've been."

"Well, you've caught me."

A reedy "Ha," the goose honk sound of the local gentry. Or a Paris taxi . . . You should have had your adenoids removed when you were a kid, kipper . . . Maybe not. With them gone you'd have no persona at all. Like Les without his boobies.

"I know you're up to your eyeballs."

That's more than I can say for you.

"Sit," Jud says.

"Ace," Kip says, leaning confidentially adwise toward him, "are you happy in your job?"

"What brings that up, Kip?"

He frowns at a piece of print-out paper. A supermarket tape. Thank you for shopping us. "Ace," he says, "according to this you were out of the office from twelve to four-twenty a week ago Monday – without signing out."

"How does the computer know?"

"The receptionist clocked you. Look, it's none of my biz – I really couldn't care less. But Tad has been having everyone checked. You know – time in, time out."

Who checks Tad? In at ten:thirty, three hours for lunch.

"Did something slip through the slats while I was out?"

"No. But that's not the point. We've got to run the shop in a cost effective, businesslike manner."

"I couldn't agree with you more."

"Good. Good. A positive attitude. Is there anything we can do to help?"

"Help what?"

"With your problem."

"I wasn't aware that I had a problem."

Kip leans even closer on a correspondence school smile. "I don't mean to get personal, Ace, but when someone stays out four-and-a-half hours without signing out, there must be a problem."

"I went to a funeral."

"Oh, someone close?"

"Yes, very."

"I'm sorry." Kip rises, shutting his eyes in junior executive sympathy. "Still, you should have signed out. Or told us. We would have sent flowers."

"I will, the next time somebody dies, Kip."

"Oh, and you haven't been putting in the new time sheets – an ad number against every quarter-hour. At the rate we charge clients for a VP's time we could lose lots of money if it's not factored in. And remember, Ace, if you should have a problem, management's here to help."

It's always been there, framed above his desk:

> Rules for Work and Comportment
> at
> Angus Fairleigh & Company
> 1884
> Rule 4 - Employees who, from sickness or any other cause find it necessary to be absent from business even for part of the day, are expected to advise the Firm at the earliest opportunity of the occasion. Failure to do so will be accepted as indicating a lack of interest in performing one's duties, and therefore, in a continuing association with the Firm.

The old order changeth? Only the cast of characters: young fogies for old. Owen Pilgrim must have known those rules by heart, and when to walk between them. That most human factor.

And stop looking out the window, Jud. Rapunzel won't let down her hair anymore. And even if she did . . .

He mucks through the papers piled on his desk. A memo from management: A clutch of account executives have been anointed VP. Four at a smear.

283

It's gotten to be
If you're *not* a VP –
Then you must be the President.

He leans back in his oak swivel chair, once Owen Pilgrim's, lights a Player, and rolls a sheet of paper into his battered old Royal. He smiles for the first time in weeks and begins to type.

TO ALL ANGUS FAIRLEIGH PERSONNEL;

It is my great pressure to announce that Abernathy ("Abby") P. Crumfitz, Assistant Elevator Maintenance Apprentice, has been elected the 452nd Vice President of the agency.

Abby came to Fairleigh earlier this week from the Mrs. Grace L. Furguson Airline & Storm Door Company, where he was an Assistant Caulking Applier. Prior to assuming that position, he had spent almost 22 years on welfare.

A near graduate of Harold S. Shmidheiser School of Vinyl Upholstery, Abby was Dishonourably Discharged from the United States Army in 1939, after spending 3½ hours in Basic Combat Training. Prior to that, his name had been associated with a plot to assassinate the Postmaster of Topeka, Kansas.

A native of either Przlyrk, Poland or Atlantic City, New Jersey, Abby resides in the shaft of Elevator #3. He is married and the father of an undetermined number of children, ranging in age from 32 to three days.

I'm sure you all join me in wishing Abby a long and successful career at Fairleigh, once his prison term expires.

A. Blunderboss
Chairman of the Bored

He reads it over. Old five-martinis-for-lunch Charlie Ballard would have loved it (never missing a key on his personal Smith-Corona when he got back to the office, banging the work out as if it were water he'd drunk, except for his reddening neck). And tremulous Brandel DeWitt, ex-Exeter, schoolmaster, poet, noddling his head till you'd think his teeth would fall out. And the elegant, gone, gray Main Line remittance men serving their respectable time at Old Fairleigh. Even Mr. Owen Pilgrim, who would probably chuckle and say, Boys will be boys, and tuck it into his Fun File. Hires (root beer) to you, Marse Owen.

He goes down to Photocopy Department, taking the stairs, says to the cool Watusi maiden in charge, "Deeka, here's one for general distribution, to go out this afternoon to all the staff, please." He's given her hundreds of pieces of paper to Xerox. She never reads them; so much as looks at them. She'd never get anything done if she did. Besides, this is honky stuff. It's a job. Feeding chickenshit paper into machines. Besides, he's a VP, ain't he?

"Hey, J.B.," she says, "you gonna plant some more of them greens come next summa? And corn? Them luscious pole beans?" The way she sings summa brings it into the room.

"I suppose so, Deeka." If Winter comes, can Summa be far behind? "You bet, I'll bring you whatever we grow. As always." In bushel baskets, princess, for you and your Momma.

"It tastes like back home, when I was little."

"It tastes like that to me, too, Deeka."

"We dig, J.B." And turns her ebon queenly carved face to him.

"That blonde, leggy girl," she says, "worked here a while, you still goin' with her?"

He shakes his head.

"I thought she wasn't as took as you," Deeka says. "Like she was always somewhere else."

He puts out his palm. She slaps it. "You take care, now," she says.

There's more mail slopped over his in box, a robin's-egg blue envelope on top, greeting card square, marked Personal, underlined twice. The handwriting freezes his heart. He lights a Player, thank God, sucks the honey cloud in. Cigarette-writing nights return. Beaches. Turns, craning toward the QCB tower. Billy Penn floats in a sour December noon.

He slits the year's belly open. Unfolds the sheet:

Even though, Jud

I'm suddenly aware
of all kinds of things –
like how special we were,
and how unspecial,
how you were people other than
the one I knew –

285

and I,
I was other people too.
But what does it matter?
We loved each other,
though our other selves knew
there were easier ways
to live.
To live –
the wrong verb, maybe,
but the right adjective –
easier,
yes, this is easier.
Easier for surviving
in a world that knows
the other selves we didn't know
when all that mattered
was loving each other.
It matters still
to me,
in dark nights
with men who want to love me
and don't know how,
mainly because they don't know who
I am –
And I remember you –
not like I've remembered anyone
before
who cared like you
and didn't care
like you, in the end –
the end –
it had to come, I know,
it had to come, even though
there was not anyone before –
it had to come, even though
there won't be anyone again.

It wouldn't have worked, Billie, but that has nothing to do with it. What we had neither you nor I will ever have again. And what we had is like a child that grows up and lives it own life. That love is alive like light that goes on from an extinguished star.

Air leaks out of the punctured day. His watch has no hands. *It matters still to me, in dark nights with men . . .*
It matters still to me, Billie.

He cannot live in this airless cabin. Breathe. Or hear the pilot. Too much static, flak.

He's bailed out to the street, marshmallow parachute finally spreading over some foreign place. Sauerkraut Philamadelky. Air cold but footsock smelly. I've completed my missions. I-am-going-home.

He weaves through maggot lunchers in Kmart suits clogging the streets to see a gold fall of hair ahead . . .

"Hey, Mac, watchit."

. . . Steps off into the gutter, runs to catch up. Skips up onto the sidewalk behind her. "Billie," he says. The denimed boy turns around. "My name is Geraldine," he says. "I have a lunch date, but I'll be at the Gay Pay Oo Bar after seven. Bring cash, old boy, I don't take credit cards."

The city is still full of Billie. She is everywhere filling the city.

I know the pride and naughtiness of thine heart. I Samuel, 17,28.

Right? Great-Uncle Zechariah? You said I had a head as good as yours for remembering . . .

. . . I remember the best summa of my life, that horseback summa. Was I twelve, thirteen? A leaf on a tree. When you and I went horsebacking all over Tennessee. Momma said No. But Poppa said it would a make a man of me. Three months in the rough with Great-Uncle, and besides, Poppa said, he was your kin, Momma. So you had to say Yes. So we rambled all summa, the Preacher and me across once Choctaw country and Chickasaw. Whitetailed deer in the thickets, peckerwoods in the trees, bedding down bonebroke, you riding that Missouri Fox Trotter mare, Uncle, Jezebel now – Sheba long gone – and me on old pumpkin head Tom, the sweetest running walk Tennessee Walker that ever ate bluegrass . . . Woke by the Carolina wren at dawn, sung to sleep by her at twilight. You taught me all that, Great-Uncle. How to snag the meanmouthed blue catfish and goggle-eyed perch in the shallows. On a willow stick. No fancy five-dollar rods, you said. This is the Land of Peaceful Hunting you said the Choctaw called it. You must have had a Great-Uncle like you. And that blue-eyed pike you took most of an hour to land. Four feet long he was, well, almost. I've seen bigger you said. They ran six to seven feet long on the Buffalo River. Tougher to get, sweeter to eat, you said. And I thought I heard you say, "Like women." And we sizzled that sucker over the hickory coals, needle bony but sweet. And ate the wild hurtleberries we'd picked in your hat, big as your thumb. And as the stars looked down and loved us, you said –

"Boy," you said – and the way you said it, I could feel all your strong loving – "Boy," you said, "don't you ever forget any of this, it won't come your way again." My mind went a-rambling like wild geese in the West that summa. Camp meetings in fields, brush arbors, straw pens in the woods.

Ree-vi-val time in that chink cabin church. Calls and 'sponses:

Leader (he call): "Oh, where you runnin, sinnah?"

Congregation ('sponse):   "No hidin' place down heah."

And they all knew you. The black people and the white. Called you up
to preach, those hallelujah Christians. – "Give us the word, Brother."
And you picked up that defanged copperhead out of the box at your
feet, holy with moonshine and fixed them with your love crazy eyes,
your bony hand raised to a brimstone heaven, swaying: "I handle
snakes, I speak in tongues." And they fell down jerking on the floor.

"You gotta get their attention, boy," you said as we bedded down
in the barn. "The Lord has many ways."

The Word. That was your hold on them, Preacher. Not snakes.
Lots of Holy Rollers fooled with them things. But only one man in
those hills, in the state, in the wide brambly world, *you*, could tell the
whole Bible by heart, backwards or forwards, eyes closed. Someone
who could say – "Just put your finger anywhere in the Book, Sister, and
say me the verse" – and go on or back – *must* have got it direct from
God. Well, Great-Uncle, maybe you just did. A purgatorial gift from a
joking God.

You led them singing:

> My Bible leads to glory,
> My Bible leads to glory,
> My Bible leads to glory,
> Ye followers of the Lamb.

No you didn't need snakes to shiver and shake them to glory. I think
you just did it that once so I'd know everything you knew. Handing it
on. So I'd remember, so the old ways wouldn't die with you. You made
me your son, that summa. And they sang:

> Thar's a Baptist preacher, you can tell him by his
> coat,
> Don't you hear Jerusalem moan?
> Got a bottle in his pocket, 'n he cayn't hardly talk,
> Don't you hear Jerusalem moan?

I haven't forgotten anything in that boxful of summa you gave me,
Great-Uncle Zech, presents to last me a lifetime . . . That play party
with the girls all in ribbons and floor touching frocks, your brother
preacher invited us to. "Watch the dimples," you said. " dimple in a
girl's chin is a mighty bad sign, means the devil is in her. Beggar trash,"
you said. Beautiful crazy, the family's black sheep. Wore out plantation
people. You were smote as I am . . . What was her name, Preacher,
that gal you snorted about in your jugged half-sleep? I read your lips: "I
am not fitten, whatever she's done, to knock at her door." And before
your wide open eyes closed down, you smiled and I think you said,
"Took her to Chattanooga once, where the smoke runs up to the sky."

I have not forgotten.

Billie does not have a dimple in her chin.

And that harvest home square dance, the last night of our rambling. Families thick as cowbirds in a cornfield. Whitsun Bob, scrapin his fiddle, the last of the great callers, you said, "Remember him. There won't be another his like."

> Swing old Adam,
> Swing old Eve,
> S'lute your pardner,
> B'fore you leave.

"Turkey in the Straw." "Old Dan Tucker." "Chicken in the Bread Tray." We stomped to all of them.

I haven't forgotten. It's all there, or almost, as much as a book can hold, in that first novel of mine, *Blue Eyes of Spring*. Named after the flower you showed me that time. Published and dedicated and on it's way to you the day you decided to give up the dismal wearys. It reached you, standing on the drop-edge of Yonder and soon to be laid down in your silent grave.

You never stopped heartburning the worst kind over that little gal, whoever she was. A bur under your saddle, an itch you couldn't scratch. I know how that is, Preacher.

Well, sir, I've been a preacher too, preaching the good life on the layaway plan. Grace through goods:

> I pledge allegiance to the stock market
> and to the Gross National Product for which
> it stands, one conglomerate, irreversible,
> with cannabis and credit cards for all.

All done with that now. Who needs the mindsweat, the ag? I'm going home, getting out of her city. An ex-corporate con who's done his time. Tell V we're packing.

There's a place in Tennessee we camped on that summa, on the Buffalo River, a whole wilderness mile of your own on that white water river. And a still rock pool smack in the middle of it, so clear you can see thirty feet down to the sandy bottom, so hushed you can hear the fish thinking out loud. There's an old log house and a batten board barn, an orchard, some hurdle fence, stands of woods for the stove and some black bottom land. Not much of a farming farm, enough to raise for the table, bigmouth bass, wild turkey, but I'll tend to the crop I should have been tending, at last again. We'll sell our place, cash in the Fairleigh stock, the profit fund shares, have more than enough to live on the rest of our days out there. And Vera will heal there some, not ever really forget or forgive, but maybe not think of it all the time either. With just the two of us on the porch in the evening sipping our own peach brandy. We are each other's history and there is no divorce from that. Ace, Doc, Squire, Keed are signing out. Jud's going home. God Almighty, free at last . . .

Someone in blue with a badge in the middle of Broad Street is blowing a whistle.

Someone behind him is shouting "You jerk – you're crossing against the light."

Some poor bastard better hop it. God, some people are stupid. *He* doesn't see anyone crossing. What are they shouting about? And begins to sprint. He heard the thump whoosh squeal of brakes somewhere far off, in another street, another city. Someone else there being hit by a bus, No. 44 Ardmore, it says above the windshield. He can see it close as if he is there, a citizen thrown, lifted, sailing into the air in that city of sudden light.

An immediate slam of dark as his head hits the curb.

49

The phone is ringing in the shuttered room. The radio tuned low to WROK – "Your all-music-no-news-is-good-news-station" – is playing a Top Ten hit by the Pustules: "I Don't Need Draino to Blow Out My Pipes, As Long As I Have You." Billie says, "Shit," as she turns off the shower, grabs for a towel.

"Bambina?"

"For Christ's sake, Louie, you got me out of the shower. I'm dripping wet."

"Have you been listening to the radio?"

"What is this? Your All Request Program? I just told you I was in the shower. I'm soaking, messing the floor."

"Then you haven't heard, yet?"

"Heard what?"

"The six o'clock news."

"Listen, Louie, what's this with the news? I've got a date. Call me back in ten. No, maybe better tomorrow at the office. Okay?"

"I don't know how to say this . . . Bambina?"

"Flake off, Louie, I'm hanging up."

"Wait. Bambina. Judson is dead."

50

Today is . . .

To the Reader

Judson Bell's widow found the manuscript
of *The Lioness Poems* in his old saddlebag.
She added the following note: "My first
impulse was to destroy it, but I could
not murder poetry . . . Vera Bell."

The Lioness Poems
of Judson Bell

Le poème c'est une idée du coeur

The lioness awakens

The lioness awakens in her shuttered city room
spilling gold.
the lover at her side forgotten
by her dream wet thighs.

She floats into her mirror
rummaging in dreams

and sails into the street
and wears the city.

Summer the waves owned her

Summer the waves owned her
and the boys who rode them
filled her with surf.

Sea eyed she smiled
her body foam
humming with sun
through the basking season.

But when the gulls took back their autumn beaches
she came to me.
And through the winter night
I kissed a sea shell
and held the seas in my arms.

Autumn leaves

Summer was my gold
the sea
my glittering diamond treasure
Now I am love's weather poor
the bronzed boys scattered with the sand

Someone is writing my life
and I know nothing about her
A story waiting for words
or another summer

The city's trees
put on their evening coats of shade
going
Where?

And all around me rain
brings down the autumn leaves
the tattered treaties of the heart.

She lives in me herself

She opened me, took out the world
and lives in me herself.
Sleeping on the feathers of my voice,
bathing in my morning fountain.

She breathes gardens on the air,
birds leave her eyes singing her smile.

Secret with sun
the fruits she grows are days
and she returns the stolen stars.

My name is a brook in her mouth
and all the seas are cleansed.

She does not go to the window
nor answers knocks at the door.

But when she hears the sounds of carnival,
she turns and rises and is gone.
Her heart red with my blood,
loud with a stranger's song.

And my dead ones
with all that leftover love in their faces
step from the wings
to the stage
of my empty theater.

Once you flew to my mouth

I walked into the forests of your face.
Your birds were gone that sang your smile,
Your firefly woven eyes,
your tendril hands,
your petal fingers,
Gone.

Into the random night man
with no face of his own.
And the others gnawing a dark hour or two of your
flesh,
then gone into the alleys.

My stones grew leaves,
filled you with flowers
and fruit you would not eat
and stars you could not see.

Wrapped your soul in mine
to give your soul a shadow.

Gone, ghost again.

Once you flew to my mouth on scarves spun by
your eyes.

But it was he who drowned

Here by the semblance of the once clean sea
pride after pride of waves, combed lion manes
and surfy paws
roared rolling in.

On the white sand
in the young spring cold sun
the lioness let go his hand.
Love, she said, let me go first alone.
Her kiss a nail, nailing him to the ground.

And she
embraced the entering sea.

But it was he who drowned.

The city's evensong

The city's evensong heart is pumping
people into its vesper streets
and I go with its blood to your veins
waiting on Zion's hill where
your all seasons eyes
grow snow stars in summer
and when required
Calvary's bloodthirsty rose.

Let me in, my New Jerusalem.

To the heartline palm of your hands
your negligent breasts
to your scarless wound
and its trampled grapes.

Let me in.

Before those horsemen behind me,
my desert cousins with spears for teeth
put death's breath in my ear.

Let me in.

Seed that won't take in the desert
I carry with me
in my saddlebags
while the browsing camels along
chew their heads.

Let me in

to your well
to your dates
to your honey.

One night in your city is the price
I put on my life.

Instruct then the watchman at the gates.

Let me in.

The linkboy comes to the wall and
the city spreads its casual legs.

Matins, Lauds

And the rustle of morning sheets
as she stretches
filling the room with palms,
smiles him aboard her
for early matins
that will sing through the day:
Sounding prisms of joined lights
to the undersong bell
and the noon remembrance
of was
and is to be
through the otherwise cloven day
to evensong.

Women will not look at me again

Women will not look at me again
knowing you did
leaving only cinders for a heart
in your smoking rain.

Here
there
some may not know the signs
as we dance
in Acapulco
or Paris, France,

Until
somewhere
under bistro skies
she looks into
the dead volcanos of my eyes.

In the valley

In the valley
of your milk and honey thighs
Selah

Table set in the midst
of my enemies

I pitched my tent.

The search and destroy sun by day,
the ice dagger stars at night.

It didn't rain that year.

There was very little to want in that land
and what there was I had.

Fig
water
navel
mouth
your hand on me.

It was either die there
in the valley
in the shade of your palm
the well of your mouth,
or there in the sand
where their lances glittered
behind the rocks like eyes.

The lioness said:
I was here before
I will be here after.

What would you do?

Selah

That lioness

You say I want too much.
How too much
is too much
with your tabasco tongue
in my forever mouth.

Memo

Remind me
please
not to think of you
not to remember.

It doesn't matter
you said
throwing your prodigal hair
over the world.

When your clothes fell like songs
around your feet
we both looked into a mirror
that had only you in it.

That's funny
you said
I thought there was somebody here.

Her breadloaf hair

Under the voyeur sun
the chaperon rain

We planted forests
fields
coloratura lilies
in each other

Under the crazy sun
the serious rain

We drowned the clock
and lived where stars spend their holy days

Come then lightning twice
with your breadloaf head of hair
rusting the world's machineries
with a glance
yes
goddess

Come
with your breadloaf head of hair
and dress me once again in your gold skin.

Our island

Come back then to that hammock island swinging
between the blue eye sky
and roughneck sea
where air
is grape
skinned into wine by joking light
and the sea   THALASSA
horses
thrashed wild by winds   ANEMOS

Where night
tangents our torn sail dreams
into that port of morning sun
slitting our eyes
from flotsam sleep
as if they weren't made
for
turning all tides into one ocean

Us   EROS

I live here still
between our take it or leave it sea
its blue audacity of sky
that harpstring air
tending our goats and olives
ripe with your gold juice
and know that no one else's hand
can hold your prowling heart

Not even ever mine   THANATOS

Alert the stars

Alert the stars
first flower bugling sun through snow
melting winter people into spring
wind stage-whispering
you will return

blossoms for fingertips
mouths budding
promised fruit

that windfall rots
to feed next year's deceitful April

Our black goat eats another season

I burn my poems to heat the soup

Available light

Here on a god's bone rocking
on a mocking sea
scoured by still clean waves
the battering blue sky
air tinged by sun

Island
that is your song
waiting for you to sing it

In the insolent morning sun
its midday lash like love

In our wine cupped evenings
when the driftwood fire throws
tormented roses on the wall
and your becalmed hands
hope for something

And the wind is a man at the door

When your eyes are all that's left
of the available light of the world

When then

When then
you loosed the sunlight on your back
Your fireworks hair
kindling the sky

When then
your instep arched
its star
over the gunnels
of our where-are-we-going boat

Your bonfire smiles
lit someone somewhere elsewhere else

And made the sun-flogged sea
a desert

Set sail

What we thought we knew
and didn't know
we think we know now
and will not know again tomorrow

The sun has bleached my poems to the bone
I feed them to the birds who feed me song
finches, onfire cardinals
a vesper celebrating sparrow
and the ever mourning dove

As your breasts bud in my mouth
and our scorched helmsman
sets sail

My birds hail our boat dipping
toward our last again island
with their singing ring
our fingers always wore

As we return time-quieted
to the evening garden of your embering grace
in the ashes of your hunger

That sudden April

Returner always bringing
that sudden April of your thighs
Your comet breasts
and the love cloudy islands of your eyes.

I should have known
from our astronomy
when you come back
Your sailors sunken in your generous sea
you are the first snow falling on my heart
first apple flower on my face
your kiss a cry
and always first star in my evening sky.

True believer

You in the tawny olive
grape's explosion in the mouth
lovethorn's wine mound
and venereal hill
I climb to sanctuary
among your harlot evening flowers
and always vestal mornings
bathing your island temple with your sun
to take the last communion from your hands
is something only April understands

I called you goddess once
and half-believed it

Now I believe

In the cathedral

In the cathedral of our arms
we caught the sun
staining the windows
of our holy pleasures

(Popes and Bishops lay their mitres down
& kiss things other than their rings
Carouse in maytime meadows)

Treasures lay
in the wagons of your eyes

In your sea's wet

Your firecracker buds

The firecracker buds of our apple tree
wait all winter to explode in May

As your nipples berry our bed
sleeping beside me

A pasture
in its gown of snow

Waiting for the Fourth of July

Nails in my hands

I put up with the day knowing
you won't be there when the sun drops dead

Sweating my resurrection
(eyes sogged with dream
you standing in your separate light
when the sky was a pearl in your ear and
a sun that shone nowhere else was your heart)
your nails still in my hands
your mouth now vinegar
and the crossed wood my bed

And questions twist in the wind that aren't
questions

Why have you forsaken me

Reunion

It was supposed to be
the way it always was
or should I say, had been

But love's a grammar beyond government

I only know that your once mouth a verb
is now a proper noun

and that sleeping with someone
whose eyes
are waking somewhere else

that
having touched your sky
began
the free fall
of our long goodbye

You, Abishag

I would like now
(I find
the body wiser than the mind)
like my father the King David lie
with Abishag's young breast
to warm him/me
the battles done
a last command
that dying to be lipped to life
by you tomorrow's girl

The sword unbroken in my hand

Abishag

Mummers

Time as we know it, seasons that we wear
the sleeper by our sleep
the current air
were never ours to keep
only ours to bear
smiling on parade
as if they would be always there

And also stars

And also stars
their canticles
light years away

Still shed
upon our island
songlight

A phosphorescence
across galaxies of separation
the only death of light

So that my hand
touching your always witty breasts
derives from dream
a loving kingdom

Touring

"I love you"
she said

And he understood
that the central word

Ignited in a wick of wine

Was a tourist visa
to herself

For that evening

In some Montmarte

In some Montmarte
of our imagination

(A place is always imagined
even the place we are in)

Something occurred
along the Pont Dauphin

I was just a fare
in your taxi
taking me
no
where

Between

Between Vespers
Matins

Between the at last dusking
office bell
and morning's guillotine
we tell our night's short hours
hails and farewells conjoining
in such sweet nippled sweat
among our united and so loving nations

Living as we do on the heretic borders
of each other
requires visas
to countries we don't want to live in
anyhow

As

As the so long ago stars
hum light
you moon eclipsed
a lunar wanderer

Continue luminous
somewhere
your hair harping
wherever stars hang out

And galaxies attend your canticles

Au revoir

You will come chez moi
and fill my house with flowers
that always was à toi

And slow the speeding hours

À Bientôt

Le poème c'est une ideé du coeur

Tous le jour
ma fièvre et ta fièvre
brûlent les heures
jusqu'à nos ciel est rouge
delà le soir argent.

Et dans la nuit tu as m'amie
et quand encore le jour se leve
ma soeur

Le poème c'est une ideé du coeur

Gliding

There is this music in your flesh
where sun is spun into
arpeggios
of sculptured sound

We listen to
while in our hiding

Just gliding
gliding

From Eden on

In the garden of the lioness
there are flowers
and there is fruit

From Eden on
there's been no other truth

Through toothy winter
through bony drouth

There's honey
always
on her bee-stung mouth

Edelweiss

Her face a canvas on which summer sketches
the final mountain I ascend
to ice
and edelweiss
and her all seasons eyes.

And those who think that there is a betrayal
will never understand the truth in lies
or the white promise of the edelweiss.

Even bees

In that once arctic time
We caught the rooster sun
and made a summer in a winter room

When then
we opened night eyes on each other
the always morning sky was where we lived

In some place where there still are trees

And even bees
respect
our golden plunder

You naked, Aphrodite

You naked in that ice cold spring
's
rejuvenating waters
leafed above and branched
comb
&
mirror in your commanding hand

if Narkissos had happened
to be wandering by
he would not
fallen in love with his own face

but with the whole idea of love

so seen in your ordained grotto

& saved, embracing her,
Echo

Arches

Hadrian had his Arch
Tiberius
& Titus
and there is one called triumph
in Paris, France

Blind stone celebrating
death in epaulets
and sundry vanities
of war

But it is just right under
the arch of your foot
that life begins to dance

Suddenly arose

Suddenly arose
your petals on my mouth
in this north of snows
a kissing south

The milk and honey place
of your leafy mouth

Oasis
where no place is

Except
As if
As if

As if

Balance

A balance of leafed waters
halfhearted sun

November prestidigitates the seasons
out of its vaudeville hat

Pretends summer's orgasm
while delivering winter's calling card
overnight frost

A time of standing
in the belly of the compass

Looking to almanac answers
where love will come from

North
or south

And while I wonder
the sky invites me to your lightning

No, yes

The no of sleep
the yes of waking

among peninsulas of longing legs

your island

drifting on calendar seas

I swim to

to yes of sleep
to no of waking

There was a room

There was a room
where occasionally
poetry happened

The room
where your legs arched the world

Where your thickets
were overrun
by my antlered deer

November poem

And on this last November night
my flotsam fire
its seabird singing
to draw your landfall
footfall
is fevered more with memory
than what the sea cast up
to warm us once
ribs of drowned ships we gathered
as your sunset hair smoked over us
on our island evening

Waiting has made this beacon
the bone fire of a dream
so long delayed
by you in other harbors

I ague still
among your going
and whose improbable arriving

Hanging on

Hanging on to each other's heart
time lurches us
upon each other
going where

It doesn't matter
we have roundtrip tickets

Mine
is always to your always summer
where bluebells vein
your Alpine breast

Yours
to an island
not on any chart

Would you believe a poem in Philadelphia

When then I saw you
wearing the sun's plumed picture hat
astonished light
on your marmoreal mouth

When then
I saw the heartbeat in your eye

When then
you walked along a painter's river
in a dreamed city
as if the summering leaves and pleasant water
still lived in that dead painter's hand

You smiled

And all I wish is
that
Eakins could have
seen

You

Lip reading

as I
lipread
your pubic herbs

as I
astonish
even you
with pollen gold
no bee will have to airlift
among our flowers

our gardens hate the clock of morning
as the City weaves
its cerements upon us

and we drift away
to the embalming occupations

When I loved you in Philadelphia

When I loved you in Philadelphia
it was Philadelphia
with a silver buckle
on its shoe

We put there

And a candle
we invented with the honey bee
a small light for its own sake
we carried while we walked
a public shining of our privacies
coupling hand-in-hand
just (oh)
among the human shrubbery

We arched a rainbow over Philadelphia
as if the greatest string band
in the Mummers Parade
was strutting
across the racket ruined City Hall
in sleet and New Year's snow
they always made a summer

And as a dream remembered Paris
there is no Philadelphia any more
pillowed on your gold hair
or in this dark
your face
to flower in this last extreme

That

That last pawnbrokered autumn
the beach
finger-painted by a cloud-smeared moon
seals laving
in the winter-promising sea
we touching prayed
to forget forever land
and swim
without ever coming up for air
so necessary
to the internal combustion engine

Where are you driving to tonight?
Girl in blonde waterfall
the garden of a weekend in your eyes.

My wife sings up the mortuary stair well
caroling dinner

Yes, dear
I hear somebody say

And step by drowning step
enter
your blood moon
and
clanging sea.

As we pack

As we pack
our island summer into flight bags
the nets below on the sun blind beach
squirm
with red mullet, tuna, shark
caught now for food
and not for tourist cameras
of Germans always building forts
and Austrians topping them with whipped cream

(Killing, after all, can be gemütlich)

As we pack our seasonal nesting
astounded by the peacock sea
to return
to others waving
on less lucid shores

I swim the coral waters of your mind
composing you from alphabets of love

No matter

When we last glowed together
before the fireflies left
on Eakins Schuylkill waters

When last we glowed
on barges drifting down the Seine
past the gray eminence of Notre Dame
to the embracing Channel
and God's Atlantic Ocean

We shipwrecked on Atlantis
and lie there in the sea wrack
glowing

And it no longer matters
if it's snowing

Or whichever way
the wind is blowing

Downslope

The peak was never reached
although in dream he scaled it
himself the flag above the highest ice

Awake from snowed-in sleep
the way pulls downward
to camp in that near night with its last dream

Of love though lost alive as light
from an extinguished
star

And his dog finds him

Without eyes for my poems

Rain your gold hair, girl, on me
and shine
your body on my battles, scars and wounds.

Your palm is water to my roots,
and all the light I'll ever need is in your sky.

Once my sunlight hand
looking for you in the dark
found the sea,
my mouth the nipples of your earth.

You left me without air,
water,
without earth,
seasons –
without eyes for my poems.